Praise for Robert Lane

and the

Jake Travis Novels

The Second Letter

Gold Medal winner of the Independent Book Publishers Association's 2015 Benjamin Franklin Awards, Best New Voice: Fiction

"Lane has created a winning hero in Jake Travis, someone who is super-skilled, super-fit, glib, oddly bookish, funny as a stiletto..." — *Florida Weekly*

"A captivating book with lies and deceit as well as love and loss." —*Readers' Favorite*

"Fans of Michael Connelly, Ace Atkins, and Dennis Lehane will likely find Lane's book satisfying on how it hits all the right notes of a truly suspenseful story." —*SceneSarasota*

"There's a new kid on the block. Lane not only provides thrills, but does it while keeping a sense of humor. The reader could not ask for more." —*BookLoons*

Cooler Than Blood

"Lane delivers a confident, engaging Florida tale with a cast of intriguing characters. A solid, entertaining mystery." —*Kirkus Reviews*

"Gripping and highly enjoyable." —*Foreword Clarion Reviews*

"Entertaining and enjoyable." —*SceneSarasota*

"...an engaging page turner that leaves you guessing."
—*BittenByBooks.com*

The Cardinal's Sin

Finalist for the 2015 Foreword Reviews INDIES Book of the Year Award

"A cinematic tale...the prose is confident and clear, and the pacing smooth and compelling...readers will care about its characters. Another entertaining mystery from Lane—possibly his best yet."
—*Kirkus Reviews*

"It starts with a bang and never lets up...a sophisticated exploration of the relationship...in which the killing power of words vies with the powerful finality of the assassin's rifle. [An] exciting reading experience. Florida noir at its best." —*Florida Weekly*

"This brilliantly calibrated thriller bests the leading sellers in its genre. Lane's writing is sharp, evocative, and engaging... a novel that not only entertains but enriches its readership."
—*Foreword Clarion Reviews*, Five Stars

"Engaging thriller...a compelling, quick-read novel."
—*BlueInk Reviews*

The Gail Force

Finalist for the 2016 Foreword Reviews INDIES Book of the Year Award

Readers' Favorite 2016 Award Finalist for Best Mystery/General

"The plot crackles with energy and suspense. The pace is breakneck, the writing is crisp...clever. A consistently entertaining and self-assured crime thriller." —*Kirkus Reviews*

"Written with a razor-sharp wit and a keen sense of impending doom. *The Gail Force* is a page turner to the end." —*Midwest Book Review*

"A powerful rush of suspense. Jake Travis is one of the best leading men to take the thriller-fiction stage in recent years. Lane mixes confidence and doubt, steadiness and recklessness, and toughness and sensitivity in engaging proportions." —*Florida Weekly*

"Charm and humor permeate the pages of this surprising thriller. There's little chance anyone will turn the last page before developing a craving for the next installment." —*Foreword Clarion Reviews*, Five Stars

"Full of action, great characters, and tips on living the good life. This is one you don't want to miss." —*BookLoons*

NAKED
WE CAME

Also by Robert Lane

The Second Letter

Cooler Than Blood

The Cardinal's Sin

The Gail Force

NAKED WE CAME

ROBERT LANE

ISBN: 0692890955
ISBN-13: 9780692890950
Library of Congress Control Number: 2017908120
Mason Alley Publishing, Saint Pete Beach, FL

This is a work of fiction. Names, characters, places, and incidents either are the product of the author's imagination or are used fictitiously. Any resemblance to actual persons (living or dead), localities, companies, organizations, and events is entirely coincidental.

Cover design by James T. Egin, Bookfly Design.

In memory of my father

There are two parts of a man's life: when his father is alive and when his father is deceased. All men, whether they realize it or not, share this in common.

A man that studieth revenge keeps his own wounds green.

—Francis Bacon

The past is never dead. It's not even past.

—William Faulkner

NAKED
WE CAME

1

I was thirty-seven when the man suspected of abducting and killing my sister nearly thirty years before washed up on a beach less than a mile from my house.

"I told the police where I spotted the body," Danny Gilliam said to me. "His arm was lapping up on the sand, his wet shirt puffed up in the stiff breeze, and a couple of those dirty gulls were pecking away. They were more interested in his eyes and mouth than anything else. Damnedest thing is, his hair looked neat—greased—as if it'd been combed by the waves."

"They give you much problem?" I asked Danny.

"Naw. Detective Rambler—you know, like the car, the old Kenosha Cadillac? He stuck me a few questions about the location. They got there pretty fast, and it had bumped along...oh, I'd say a good ten feet from where I told 'em I first noticed it."

"Where was that?"

"Right off those busted piers at the end of Third Avenue."

We were sitting at Riptides, nursing a pair of cold beers. The bikini-top bartenders had just finished their charity chin-ups and were scooping up bills off the bar. The harsh afternoon heat radiated in from the beach, bringing

1

in the mildew smell of the Gulf of Mexico. In the summer, the beach is a desert with a mirage next to it.

The bartender who had done the most chin-ups flicked me a smile. I knew I looked good in that new shirt. I sat up straighter. Her smile widened. A man took the stool beside me. They greeted each other by name and started jabbering away like happy hens. So the world doesn't revolve around me—that's not my fault.

"You didn't call it in right away?" I asked as I involuntarily slouched back down.

"No reason to. There was nothing I could do for the man. Told 'em I parked my tan Boxster there every morning, put the roof down, and watched the sunrise to 'Hey Jude.' Song was only halfway through. I reminded them that it runs seven minutes and eleven seconds—easy to remember, you know, like Seven-Eleven stores. No way was I going to interrupt my morning routine for some wet stiff."

Danny and I knew each other from his daily ritual. I would often be running along the bay and pass him listening to "Hey Jude" just as the sun broke over Tierra Verde. I admire obsessions, as I am infected with the same disease. One day, startling both of us, I stopped and introduced myself. We drank breakfast that day and the next.

During the first breakfast, Danny had explained to me that his goal was to have Paul McCartney scream just as the sun crested the homes on the other side of Boca Ciega Bay. He'd started each day like that for the past two years since moving down from Rockford, Illinois, to escape his marriage. "It was fine for the first twenty-five years," he commented on his marriage. "Then we met each other."

He'd gone on to confess that he wasn't close to his two daughters but in the past year had started to enjoy time with his gay son and his partner, who lived on Treasure Island. He had pulled a picture from his wallet of the three of them at Epcot's Food and Wine Festival. "That's my boy, Austin, in the middle," Danny had told me. "His partner's name is Kenneth. They talked me into going over to Mickeyville. We blew through a three-hundred-dollar booze bill and walked it off in the process. I told Austin that evening that I had a good time. He just gave me a big ole hug—and why am I even telling you this? I barely know you."

I'd told him if he was buying, I was listening.

I centered my beer on the coaster and said, "The police give you a hard time?"

"Naw. I think they were just trying to get the timeline right, you know? They seemed curious that I didn't panic when I first saw it. I told 'em I did thirty as a cop up north. Turned it in when I hit the double nickel. Wasn't my first floater. When they make the connection and come by your place?"

"Two days later," I said.

"What led them to you? Rambler told me the body was clean. No wallet or anything."

I rubbed my stubbled chin. Might shave today. Probably not. "They traced him through his prints. That led to his house. In his house was a letter in his handwriting. There were two lines about my sister."

"Line one?" Danny asked as his eyes tracked the bartender with the pierced belly button.

"Admitted he abducted her. Mentioned the hotel we were at."

"And line two?"

3

"He killed her. No details."

Danny took a sip of his beer and said, "I don't think I want me any woman who can do twenty-six chin-ups. Homeless shelter or not."

I nodded in silent agreement. Kathleen would scoff at the suggestion of even attempting a chin-up.

I took a contemplative draw from my bottle, as if a little booze was a viable substitute for deep thought. I wasn't sure I wanted to dive into my past again. Previous attempts had left me feeling like water in a sink, swirling around with no control, down toward a black hole. I still had time to jump out. I'm a big fan of running from your past; it's an underrated, underused, and underappreciated method of coping.

Danny glanced at me and said, "You feel any closure or relief? I mean, you and me, we don't really know each other, but on the other hand, we know each other better…" He stopped, took a swig of beer, and suppressed a belch. "You know what I mean."

During the second breakfast, over bloody marys that were my treat, it was my turn to unload. I told Danny the story of my sister disappearing nearly thirty years before. It flew out of me like a queasy stomach finally erupting. Strange that I told him, for not even Kathleen or Morgan knew. Only Garrett. You realize you're done keeping things inside when you hear yourself talking. When it's your puke on the sidewalk. It's not a conscious decision. You hear your voice and think, *What the hell.*

And then this: *What else is coming undone?*

I hadn't told him that my deceased sister was like an open wound that festered and refused to scab. I wasn't sure I'd fully admitted that to myself yet.

"Someone buzzed me a year ago," I told Danny. "They let me know the case had been reopened. I've been making inquiries."

"So they know you're interested."

"They got the message."

"There's a lot of that going around—taking a peek at cold cases, on account of DNA," he said.

"I don't know how hard they peeked. They never found her body. No body, no murder. No murder, other cold cases get the dollars."

He nodded in agreement. "You buy that this guy—what was his name again?"

"Hawkins."

"Right—that he was good for it? After all, he confessed, right?"

"He did," I said. "Nice and neat, in a letter that served up a litany of sins."

"Then he surfaces, what, 'bout a mile from your house? Only thing he was missing was a red bow. He from around here?"

"Bradenton."

"Police have an issue with that—him floating in your pond?"

"They brought it up."

"Lemme guess," Danny said, "they suggested he was drowning in guilt and wanted to pen his memoir."

"They tried it on for size. I explained I hadn't seen the guy in years."

He arched his eyebrows. "You'd met him?"

"Questioned him one or two times."

Danny let out a low whistle. "I bet the detectives loved that. Boy, I would've been on you like a fly on shit."

I could feel his eyes on me but kept my face straight, staring at a neon beer sign behind the bar that the salt air had crusted and rendered dull.

"You really told them that?" he said, failing to hide his incredulous tone. "That you paid him a visit? More than once?"

"Better they found out from me than from someone else."

"You're right, there."

I faced him. "I informed the two detectives that I would have tied a block around his ankles and taken him out to Middle Grounds. Sixty feet of water and sharks."

He gave a ponderous nod of approval and said, "They buy that?"

"Rambler, your Cadillac buddy, told me that was a fine plan, but crimes of passion rarely have plans."

"No, sir, they do not. So Hawkins—he's your man?"

"He had run-ins with the law, but he was adamant that he was innocent. Said he wasn't that type of man anymore. Claimed he turned over a new leaf."

"I know those people," Danny said. "Used to rake them up every day and toss them in a pile behind bars. Shame I couldn't do the world a favor—pour a little gas on them and strike a match. You leave him conscious?"

"We did."

"We?"

I answered him by meeting his eyes with mine and then gazing away.

Danny drained his bottle and gave it a nudge toward the inside of the bar. "At Seabreeze," he said, "they told me you're ex-army. You recover stolen boats for insurance companies, but some think that's just a front. The rumor is you still do special-ops work for the government. You took out a couple of drug runners a few years back and were under the microscope for a short stack of hit men from Chicago found dead on Fort De Soto."

"They didn't tell you the hit men were from Chicago."

"I fished around for that tidbit myself."

"They tell you as long as my bacon's crispy, I control my temper?"

"A good maple glaze does the trick for me."

"Truth and beauty."

He gave me an acknowledging smile. "Listen up," he said. "Be careful when you talk to the cops. We're a fucked-up breed. The less you say, the better you are. Hell, unless you're the victim of a crime, you *never* talk to the police. And know this: they'll be back. You got a bull's-eye on your back, especially on account of you visiting the vic. What did they tell you the cause of death was?"

"Drowning with high alcohol content."

"Whatja think of that?"

"I asked Rambler why he was sucking up my time if it was a suicide or accidental death."

"His reply?"

"Slow day in traffic court."

"Hawkins had marks around his neck," Danny said. "Bruises. I could see them from the shore."

"I didn't get that version."

"Not surprising. They don't want you to know." He shifted his weight on the stool. "I'm not judgin' you, nor do I care. But lawyer up, my friend. You listening? Lawyer up hard. They got a circle around your name. They will remigrate to your front door. You can bank on that."

"Remigrate?"

"Yes, sir. Look it up."

"Appreciate the tip," I said with a courteous nod.

"They ask you point-blank if you killed him?"

"They did."

"And you said?"

"A thousand times. But not the last time."

2

They remigrated the next morning.

I'd just finished my predawn five-mile run, most of it on the low-tide sand of the beach. I was showering off outdoors at the side of my house that faced Morgan's. I kept begging for cold water, but in the summer, that was a wasted rub on the genie bottle. My hut is on an island that falls in the long southern shadow of Saint Petersburg, Florida, and fronts Boca Ciega Bay. That morning, the rising sun cast hues of yellow, salmon, and blue on the flat water. A woman in a kayak stroked confidently toward the gulf, which was less than a mile from the end of my dock. A wide-brimmed hat shadowed her face. Out on the sandbar, a fishing boat was collecting baitfish. The boat had no cover. The heartless sun already made the boat appear intolerable.

I entered the house, and Hadley III darted between two exposed studs. I'd decided to remodel my bayside bungalow, and cats don't handle change well. The plan was to open the interior by removing walls and installing a new floor. The floor was down to the concrete foundation, and the remaining walls and ceiling were studs and plywood. Above my head, pointed nails pierced the plywood where the roofers—right about the time Bill Haley was rocking around the clock—had missed the trusses.

My finished palace would boast a hand-scraped cherrywood floor and a vaulted white bead-board ceiling. Those boards were in my garage, along with my old oven. A convection oven had been installed two days ago. My albums and books were stashed away to protect them from the dust. Clear plastic, clouded with construction residue, shrouded my furniture, which was shoved together in the middle of the room. Two layers of plastic covered the 1962 floor-model Magnavox.

Winston Churchill said we shape our houses, and then our houses shape us. I wondered what the Last Lion would think of my current accommodations.

One of the few items left exposed was a five-by-seven photo of Kathleen on the kitchen counter. She was looking over her shoulder, the autumn sun glowing off the side of her face, her eyes soft and knowing. The wide frame was part of a window casing from a cottage that was torn down in Pass-a-Grille. Morgan and I had gone through the debris, salvaging pieces of wood. The front door, with glass covering it, now served as his desk.

I turned on the radio to an FM station. A classic rock song came on. I don't remember the last time I'd listened to the radio. I liked it.

Morgan burst through the garage door.

"Anything else?" he said.

"You get the two boxes and the lamp?"

"I did. You could enter a medieval jousting contest with the point on that lamp."

"Kathleen dubbed it my *pickelhaube*."

"Help me out there."

"The pointed helmets the Germans wore in the Great War."

"Right. Well, your German helmet floor lamp won't last until noon."

Morgan had recently taken over operating the local thrift store, which was open four days a week. Since assuming the responsibility, he'd aggressively canvassed the neighborhood for donations. Morgan was raised on a sailboat and, on numerous occasions, had smuggled families into the States. He'd found his stride helping people obtain clothing, furniture, and kitchen items. I'd oftentimes assist him. I thought it might make me a better person. That's what I tell myself, but my volunteer time is more of an insurance policy—in the event that a few good deeds can atone for past sins. It's my version of Pascal's wager.

"The police were by," Morgan said, his eyes holding mine. A moon talisman hung around his neck. A string from his father's navy bunk served as a tie to bundle his ponytail. "Twenty minutes ago. I was in your garage, loading up. They said to tell you—if I saw you—they'd circle back within the hour. You taking out those studs today?"

"Today is sledgehammer day."

I had previously told Morgan that I knew the deceased man at one time, but I let it go at that. I needed to tell Kathleen first. I didn't want her to be the last to know. Morgan would handle that position better than she would.

Morgan left, and a car ad blared over the radio. I shut it off. Who can listen to that crap? I brought up my song library on my phone, hit shuffle, and clicked up the volume on the Bose wireless. The heavyweight speakers were unplugged and buried in plastic.

The doorbell rang just as Judy Garland started crooning, "Have Yourself a Merry Little Christmas." Shuffle—

I knew better. But it was sacrilegious to turn her off. Besides, the hell with Saint Louis; I would have met her anywhere.

I opened the door. The same two detectives, Rambler and Yarborough, who had briefly questioned me the previous day, stood side by side. Behind them, across the street, Patsy was wheeling in her empty trash can. It was missing a wheel, and one corner dragged on her concrete driveway. Detective Rambler asked if they could come in.

"No."

"Any particular reason?" he asked.

"Just had the place cleaned."

"Really," he said, peering over my shoulder. "Looks worse than the last time we were here."

"I could observe the same about you."

Yarborough let out a harrumph as he brushed past me and into the house. "You hear him invite us in, Rambler?"

"I did," Rambler responded. He strode past me, but not before his eyes professionally scanned the room.

"Careful," I said. "My cat bites."

"You got a hamster too?" Yarborough quipped.

"Cat ate him. You got five minutes."

"Jesus!" Yarborough exclaimed. "You live in this squalor?" He paused before squeaking out, in a few notes higher than his usual voice, "Christmas music?" He swayed his head. "I'll be a squirrel's dick. The screwed-up people you meet on this job."

I picked up the phone, hit a button, and Judy dropped out of our lives. We'd have to muddle through without her. I went to the fridge, opened a beer, and took a swallow.

"Four and a half minutes," I said.

Rambler took a step toward me. He wore too much aftershave, and his left eyebrow needed trimming, as if he'd gotten distracted and forgot to finish the job.

"Relax, Mr. Travis," he said. "Your admitted association with the man who abducted your sister intrigues us."

I took another gulp of the breakfast of champions.

"You have nothing to say to that?"

"Four minutes."

"Screw this elf," Yarborough said. "Let's book him just to teach him a lesson. Dump him in the tank for a few hours."

I held up my phone. "Anything else you'd like to add?"

Yarborough clenched his jaw and scratched between his eyebrows with his middle finger. He struck me as a man who struggled to make an impression. The type of person who, having infinitely fallen short of others' expectations, no longer put forth the effort and was now desperate not to be relinquished to the shadows. I hid a deep breath and lectured myself not to play his game.

Rambler cut his partner a look and said, "We'd like you to cooperate in helping us. Be a good citizen. Think you can manage that?"

I turned my phone off and stuck it in my pocket. "Off the record?" I said to Rambler.

"Off the record."

"I killed him and made sure he'd surface a mile from my house so I'd be the prime suspect."

Yarborough clucked his tongue on the roof of his mouth. I kept my gaze on Rambler—he was the alpha dog.

"I doubt you'd repeat that to a prosecuting attorney. Why don't you give the truth a swat?"

"I never had compelling evidence that he abducted my sister. If I'd known for certain, I've already told you what I would have done."

He bobbed his head, as if each bob helped to solidify his opinion of me. "I believe you," he finally said, but I didn't believe him. "But here's where I get stuck. I think someone wanted you to know that Hawkins was dead. My theory? To keep you on a short leash. I've looked at your résumé. You've done a lot of damage." He held up his hand as if to ward off a protest, although none was coming. "No charges; you're clean. But you're not telling us the whole story. You don't strike me as a man who sticks to the periphery of the action."

"It's appearance only," I told him. "His death does not indicate any direct or peripheral involvement on my part."

Rambler gave that a second. "Maybe someone wanted the message overnighted. Any idea who that might be?"

"Accepting your thesis?"

He nodded.

"No," I said. "What was the cause of death? You're homicide detectives, not grief counselors."

I wanted to give them a chance to back off the alcohol-induced drowning and come clean with what Danny had told me—that Hawkins had been found with choke marks around his neck.

Rambler said, "He drowned. Lungs full of water."

"Word is he was already dead when he did his guppy act."

Rambler's somnolent eyes canvassed my house. "You doing this work yourself?"

"Most of it."

"Takes time."

"Keeps me off the street."

"That might be a good thing for you, Mr. Travis. Since our last meeting, we had time to go through Hawkins's house. You know he lived in Bradenton, don't you? 'Course you do. We found a horde of pedophile smut. This guy's been sick for years. The world won't miss him. We also found a picture."

"Who?" But I knew and was ticked at myself for instinctively taking his bait.

"Your sister. It was an old photograph. From around the time she was abducted. It pins him closer to her disappearance, adds a little weight to his confession."

"She died thirty years ago at the age of fourteen," I said, failing to control the anger in my voice. "Every photograph is old."

"Would you like to have that *old* picture?" Yarborough baited me, but I'd already been hooked once.

"You can keep it."

"Glad you feel that way." He clucked his tongue. "We may need to store it as a permanent item."

They headed for the door. Outside, Rambler turned and said, "Something else bothers me." He waited as if he expected me to respond. When I didn't, he continued. "The victim—maybe suicide, maybe not—was on his second set of a few fingernails. That's not including the two that never grew back. Not recent, but someone squeezed this guy hard."

"Interesting."

"That's one way to get—how did you phrase it—'compelling evidence,' isn't it?"

"Drive safely, gentlemen," I said. I shut the door.

I pivoted and faced my mess. My sliding doors to the screened porch were open. They were nearly always open, since I prefer fresh air, even hot air, to closed quarters. A five-foot buoy that I'd lugged back from the beach after it washed up in a storm stood in the corner of the porch. It read, "IDLE, NO WAKE." Sometimes that's good advice; other times it is not. Discerning the difference is the nasty trick. A great blue heron squawked from the edge of the seawall as it took flight. It was my world, but it felt alien to me, as if I no longer belonged in it. I needed to get my house back in order. I headed to the garage to get the sledgehammer.

Instead, I kicked out a two-by-four with a high right kick. Then another. And another. I took out a dozen more with a hammer and bare hands.

Soon I had destroyed all nonsupporting beams. I went to my study, ignoring the splintered lumber that needed to be collected and hauled from the house. I groped under the plastic that covered my file cabinet and extracted a worn cardboard file.

Out on the screened porch, I withdrew a newspaper article from the file and tossed it onto the dirty glass table. It slid next to the Tinker Bell alarm clock. I'd forgotten to set her today. Too late. I was already drinking before five. Pieces of splintered wood clung to my sweaty arms. It would be another two-shower day—maybe three. I gently placed the newspaper article on my lap. My eyes rested on the yellowed newsprint. It had come to symbolize my deceased sister and was one of a few tangible items left from my past. When I brought it out, it summoned powers and feelings I could neither control nor understand. At a young age, my world had failed me—delivered a knockout blow—and in many ways, I was still scrambling to get off the mat. Although I'd vowed in the past to find my sister's abductor, I'd failed. Time and time again.

A fishing boat skimmed the water a hundred feet off the dock. A dog in the bow was pointing the way, its ears flapping behind it. Such confidence. Anticipation. Eagerness. I wanted to be a dog in the bow of a boat, the rising sun behind me, the open waters before me—no clue where I was going, but not a note of hesitancy in my being.

Someone had surfaced. Taken a breath. Risked being discovered in his attempt to forever keep me off his trail. He'd taken a gamble. If it took my last dying breath, I would see the panic in his eyes as my hands tightened around his throat. I refuse to let my life be defined by that which I have failed to do.

First, though, I had a far tougher task.

I had to tell Kathleen that once, I had a sister.

3

"The Montelena chardonnay, please," Kathleen replied to the bartender in the bow tie.

"Sir?"

"Double Jameson on the rocks. Put wings on it, will you? And make that Montelena a bottle."

"Hmm, starting with a double," Kathleen said.

"And a bottle."

We were sitting at the bar in the lower-level steakhouse at the Vinoy Hotel in downtown Saint Pete. It was clubby. Dark wood. Stools you needed two hands to move. The low-trayed ceiling was crisscrossed with heavy beams, and the Chairman of the Board dropped out of nowhere and settled in as though he owned the place. It was his kind of joint. A joint that, when you walked in, made you feel a little taller and your problems a little smaller.

Kathleen's blond hair was tied back with a chocolate hair tie. Small silver seashell earrings dangled from her ears. I'd bought them for her in one of the shops on Beach Drive. I was impressed I remembered that. It was a big step for me.

The bartender deposited my whiskey in front of me. He uncorked the bottle and gave Kathleen a sip of the wine. She nodded in approval. I would have preferred him to serve her first, despite my plea for urgency.

"Let's see," she said, smoothing her cream dress. "The first time we were here, I believe I confessed to you that I'd started our relationship under a false pretense."

"You lied to me," I politely pointed out. "Besides, we never started our relationship."

"No?"

"We collided."

"Collided," she repeated. "I don't think so."

"No?"

"No. 'Collide' implies hardness. It belongs to things like wood and steel—dense molecules of substance. It's not celestial, like the heart or soul."

"All right, Lady Wordsmith, what do you suggest?"

"I'm not sure," Kathleen said with an air of indifference. "That can be your assignment." She took a sip of wine and then placed the long-stemmed glass on a napkin on the glossy bar. "The second time, you informed me that you'd killed a Catholic cardinal in London by accident. On our vacation. While I slept."

"You were steamed."

"You're being kind."

"Let bygones be bygones."

"Do you still have your dreams?"

"No," I lied.

"Yes, you do. You talk in your sleep."

"Then why ask?"

"To see if you still lie."

"How'd I do?"

"Straight As, baby."

"Practice makes perfect," I pointed out.

She tilted her head. "The world dodged a bullet when you wisely declined to go into education."

I put my drink down and cupped the back of her neck with my hand. What I really wanted to do was swipe the bar clean and lay her on it. I leaned in and traced my finger over the corner of her mouth, where age was just starting to manifest itself—bring that red-ass devil on. I hovered my lips over hers and lightly touched her lips with mine. She breathed into me, and I took her air in as my own. There is nothing in the world that gets me higher. Maybe bacon. But that's not an apple-to-apple comparison. It's a kiss-to-bacon comparison, and that's disturbingly wrong.

"We need to get through dinner," she whispered.

"As you once observed," I said, giving her a quick kiss and pulling away, "I'm a sucker for you. That's three levels above eternal love."

"One above Shakespearean love," she mused.

"Just below nonfunctioning sexual obsession."

"Something to aspire to," she said in a husky tease. "Maybe I will keep you around, stranger."

"That, and I cook."

"Simple needs."

Bow Tie interrupted us and asked if we were ready to order. I requested cold-water lobster for Kathleen and an eight-ounce filet for myself. He asked me how I wished my steak to be prepared. I replied that I wanted it to complain when I sliced a knife into it. I told him we'd split a wedge salad—and to plate it on two plates, with extra tomatoes and the dressing on the side for the lady—and to bring half a dozen oysters before the salad. I handed him back the unopened menus.

Kathleen took a patient sip of wine, letting the fermented grapes slowly trickle from the glass. She was never in a hurry with alcohol. It wasn't the main event for her but a faithful companion for the early evening's transitional hours. She never used it to enhance the midday hours or add rowdiness to poolside events. It was her evensong, a benediction to the day.

"I like that," she said.

"Like what?" I asked. "Having a man who's a sucker for you?"

That brought another smile. If there was a thingamajig that recorded smiles, Kathleen would clock in at over a thousand a day. Each one was a rising sun.

"Ordering without glancing at a menu," she said. "There's something definitive about it. It's comfortable knowing yourself—knowing ourselves—well enough that we don't require prompts from an outside source."

I took a manly sip of my whiskey and adjusted my weight on the stool. The envelope in my jacket's inside pocket rubbed against my chest. I withdrew the envelope, opened it, and placed the yellowed newspaper article on the bar between us.

"About that 'knowing ourselves' stuff," I said.

She spoke to the paper, not to me. "How bad is it?"

"We're fine. I've been remiss in not telling you something."

"You smoked the pope?"

"No. Nothing like—"

"God?"

"—that. Read it."

She picked up the newspaper article from thirty years ago and read it, while I fumbled with my whiskey. She considerately placed it back on the counter. She paused, as if she were collecting her thoughts—or tempering her anger—or thinking of ditching me—and said, "Why didn't you tell me?"

"I couldn't."

"That's not—we'll come back to that. You had a sister, Jake."

"Yes."

"You don't think that…that's something I should have known?"

I flipped up my left hand. That should pretty much explain things.

The bartender presented the oysters to us. What had sounded enticing a few minutes ago couldn't hold its appeal. Eager to maintain an element of normalcy, I dosed one with horseradish and gave it two chews before letting it funnel its way down my throat. I rinsed it with whiskey. Both the oyster and the whiskey deserved better.

"She was abducted thirty years ago," I said as a lame excuse as to why I'd never told her.

"You were a little boy," she said.

"I was."

"Tell me. Then, afterward, I'm going to be furious with you."

"You going to cut me off?"

"It's not funny."

"No, it's not. Either way."

"Maybe I'll skip ahead and be furious now."

"But you're not."

"No," she said, using the word in an affirmative sense. "Why is that? If you'd told me this a year ago, I would have exploded. Now I assume that I just get bits and pieces over time."

"I could say the same about you."

"How so?" she challenged me.

"That comment you made a few months ago, about believing in angels."

"Nice try, bucko—but not tonight. Besides, that's hardly on par with *this*."

She tilted her head toward the copy of the newspaper article resting between us. Her right earring swung forward just a tad, as if it too wanted to get a jab in at me. I wanted to remind the damn thing that if it weren't for me, it would still be suffocating under a glass display case.

"Speak," Kathleen demanded.

"There's not much color I can add. Her killer was never found. DNA testing has resurrected cold cases. I've been bugging law agencies the past year."

"This past year?" she said. It wasn't a question as much as a statement as she came to grips with my deceit. *Deceit— that doesn't sound so hot. How's this: my reluctance to share my past with her until I'd extracted revenge for my sister's death.*

The bartender swung around. "How about another four inches?" I said to him, nudging my tumbler in his direction.

He gave me a discerning look. "Are you driving tonight, sir?"

"Yeah. I got a tank out—"

"Jake," Kathleen said.

"No." I kept my challenging eyes on him. "We walked over from a condo. Make it a single, pal. Hate to get a scout in trouble."

He shuffled off. Kathleen allowed me to diffuse before I started in. We avoided making eye contact in the mirror behind the bar. I fortified myself with the last of my whiskey and took the dive.

"Family summer vacation," I said as I pivoted to her. Her hazel-green eyes were waiting for me. "We drove to Florida. Stayed in a motel. It happened on day four."

"The Vanderbilt Reef Motel, right?" Kathleen interjected, trying to slow me down.

"We'd been there before. Two other times. It made a difference. My sister and I knew the place. My parents felt comfortable. They'd thought about going someplace new but decided to stick with the familiar. They never got over that decision. That alone was enough to sink my father. That stuff never makes the papers."

The salads came, and I forced myself to nibble at it. I'd never thought what it would be like to tell Kathleen, and now that I was, my emotions were on spongy ground.

"It was two in the afternoon—that article said three, but they got that wrong. My sister wanted to go up to our room on the second floor and get a book. She was reading one a day. My parents were on lounge chairs under an umbrella. My mother was napping. We were never allowed to go to the room alone. But we were getting older. We'd been talking it up for weeks.

"My father told me to go with her. There was a game room on—"

I blew my breath out and reached for my new whiskey that Bow Tie had politely placed in front of me.

"Slow it down, babe," Kathleen said as her hand found my shoulder.

I took another swig of whiskey, as if the faster I drank, the quicker I would get it over with. "We were supposed to stay together. I stopped by the game room. I stood there playing mindless games while—"

"Stop it. You were, what, seven?"

"Nearly eight."

"How old was she?"

"Just turned fourteen. Our birthdays were a month apart."

"Seven, Jake."

"I know."

"You remember it as a man, but you were a child. There's nothing you could have done."

"No one knows that," I shot back with the conviction of someone who'd played alternative scenes in his head for thirty years.

"You must realize—"

"*Realize?* I let her down. She's dead. That's what I realize."

Our meals arrived, and we picked at them out of obligation. Tony Bennett took over from Frank Sinatra. Such a better voice, but he couldn't match Sinatra when it came to imparting upon the listener that his was a life aged in the finest of oak casks and perhaps, just by listening to him, so was yours.

I glanced over at Kathleen. Her eyes were moist and red. She was experiencing more pain than me. At that moment, like a crack of a baseball bat striking a ball, I realized I wanted to marry her. I *had* to marry that woman.

I forged ahead, strangely relieved, and exalted, that a big chunk of my life had suddenly and serendipitously come into focus.

"My father found me in the game room—asked me if I'd seen my sister. He woke my mother. Told her she was missing. She was confused, like you are when you wake up from a nap and you don't know where you are. Then his words sunk in. I didn't know a day could be so bad and last so long."

My body shuddered. I felt like a fool. Kathleen reached to me. "You don't—"

"They went to the room," I said, eager to get it over with. "Asked the hotel management. Questioned everyone in sight. 'Have you seen a girl in a green bathing suit?' Called the police. The book she went to get was Matilda. It still had the price tag on it. She was always afraid to take the tags off for fear that she'd rip the covers. It had been on the nightstand. It was gone. They figured she was abducted after she left the room."

"That's why the paper called it the Matilda case," Kathleen noted.

"Some reporter coined that. It came to symbolize my sister. You know, anyone see a man with a young girl carrying that book, give us a call. The National Center for Missing and Exploited Children, formed after the Adam Walsh case in '81, was still in its infancy. They did all they could do."

I pushed away the rest of my filet with a dismissive shrug. "At first, my father was livid with me—yelled at me that I was supposed to stay with her—but then he calmed down. I give the man credit for that. He realized that laying it at my feet wasn't going to help find her."

"Do you hold him accountable? He could have gotten off his duff and gone with her."

"I saw what the guilt did to him. The bad days, weeks, months, and years were still to come. Hope drifted out of my parents' lives like a leaf riding a tide."

"And you?"

I gave that a second before replying, "You know when you get into the car and start the engine, and your favorite song comes on, but it's near the end? And all you can do is imagine the part you missed—what you didn't hear? That was my childhood after my sister died. All I could think of was what I missed."

"I'm—"

"My parents went dark about six months later. That's when the probability of finding her alive hit zero. My father turned to the bottle, and my mother turned to God. Neither was worth their billing. His liver never stood a chance, and no God could be roused to bring her back."

"They both died not long after, right?"

"My father walked out of his own life. He lasted three years after his little girl went missing. I was too young at the time, but I know now that those three years weren't anything close to living. There's a lot of ways for your life to be over before you die. That's a hell of a thing to learn before your first kiss."

"You—"

"My father was a big man, bigger than I am."

Kathleen took a knife and lobster fork to her crustacean. She started to slice into it but put both utensils down. "Your mother died of breast cancer, right? And that's when your aunt Joelle stepped in?"

"Stepped in and moved us around. Aunt Joelle was in marketing and never gave up the search for greener pastures. We packed up again the summer I enrolled in college. You know the list of new students that referenced their hometowns? I was from a place I'd never lived at."

I didn't tell her that when I was in seventh grade, Aunt Joelle drove me to a shrink's office every Tuesday at four in a futile attempt to get me to deal with my sister's death. Dr. Honaker tried to get me to say the word, but I never did.

"You should have told me."

"I know. I—"

She half-shoved and half-punched me on the shoulder. "What were you thinking, you...pumpkin brain?"

"Hold on, now. I would never—"

"Save it. Why now? Did something come up with DNA testing, or did a gush of common sense overtake you, and you decided to come clean?"

I let my breath out in preparation for the second act.

"A body washed up less than a mile from my house. Man's name was Leonard Hawkins. He was under suspicion years ago for her abduction but was never charged. The police are being coy as to the cause of death, but he was likely murdered. He left a handwritten letter, confessing to abducting and killing my sister. A picture of her was found in his home."

"I see. You were forced to tell me before I read it in the papers. Impressive. Just bowling me over, here, buddy."

"I never thought of it like—"

"Skip it. We'll tackle the bigger issues later. Hawkins confessed, right? That's good, isn't it?" Hope was rising in her voice. "You have closure and—"

"I'm the prime suspect."

She punched out her breath. "Gotta hand it to you, trouble. You're a hit parade tonight. Do I want to know?"

"Your call."

"Did you?"

"No."

"OK."

"You believe a practiced liar like me?"

"When the chips are down, your honesty flares up. You said Hawkins had been under suspicion. Did you ever meet him?"

"Garrett and I paid him a visit."

"Ahh…I wondered when Captain America would come in. That's enough. You left knowing Hawkins wasn't the man?"

"We did."

"The police—did they connect you to this Hawkins chap?"

"They did."

"Do they know you paid him a visit?"

"Yup."

"And?"

"They'll rattle their swords, but nothing else."

"So certain."

"So foolish," I said, tagging on a commentary about myself.

We gave Bow Tie permission to clear the dishes. He asked if there was a problem with our dinners. I told him I had a K-ration in the tank before I came in, and I wasn't that hungry—a comment that I'm sure did nothing more than reinforce his opinion of me as a common jerk. I left a big tip and then was disappointed that I'd done so. After I signed the chit, I stood and started to pull back Kathleen's massive stool.

"Sit back down, slim," she commanded. "We're not done yet."

I did as I was instructed. That was a testament to the power of her voice over me.

"We're tackling the bigger issues already?" I said.

"We are."

"That's not my strong suit."

"It's a stacked deck."

"Won't make much difference."

"Her name."

"What about it?"

"Say her name, Jake."

I felt sorry for myself and wondered where the hell that came from. I should have stiffed Bow Tie. *The hell do I care?*

I shrugged. "It's how I deal with it."

"You're not dealing with it."

"Your thoughts, not mine."

"Say her name. It's good for you."

"I thought your PhD was in English literature," I said in a tone sharper than I intended.

"It's a pretty name."

I scanned the room to make sure Dr. Honaker wasn't lurking nearby. I knew I would beat four-eyes the moment I met him. Someone should have told that man to trim his nose hair. Sitting there asking me if I liked New Kids on the Block and Madonna. As if he and I had shit in common. I spent Tuesday afternoons fending off his overtures and staring at his tangled and wiry mess. Behind him, black mollies kept pressing against the glass of an aquarium. Above it was a sign: "When I let go of what I am, I become what I might be." Evidently some twit named Lao Tzu got the credit for that peach.

I'd missed a lot of hoops time with my buddies, including Garrett, although he knew where I really was. While they practiced layups, I counted black mollies and wondered how you could let go if you had nothing to hold on to in the first place.

I'd not said her name since the last day I'd seen her. *You lost, Dr. Smirk-Face Honaker.* Besides, I never called her by her real name. I called her Brit. She called me Jake-o. I never shared that with Honaker. That cat wasn't even in the game. Brit and Jake-o. There's no one left in this trashed world who knows that.

"Say her name," Kathleen said.

"No."

"Say it."

"Buzz off."

"She's listening."

I felt that in the gut.

"Brittany," I stammered out for the first time in thirty years.

And like Frank and Tony dropping down from the ceiling, it all rushed back into me, but it's nothing I can talk about or share, for the deepest parts of us are always alone.

4

We crossed Beach Drive, hand in hand, after a horse-drawn carriage carrying a family passed in front of us. The air smelled of water and was filled with the sounds of the city: the thrum of live music, the growl of engines, the occasional timid blare from a horn, and the chatter of people walking by, whose words represented fragments of lives we would never know.

Kathleen made some comments about the special folk-art exhibit at the Museum of Fine Arts, but I was fake-listening. We passed Second Avenue North, where the new pier was under construction, and continued to Central before turning back to her condo. We were filling our tanks before heading out again. I'd just as soon sputter on fumes to the finish line.

In her ninth-floor unit, I poured an inch of Graham's 20 Year Old into two port glasses. We settled into cushioned outdoor chairs on her balcony overlooking Tampa Bay. A waxing three-quarters moon brightened the water. The shadow of the balcony's railing lined the tile floor, making a crisscross pattern. Up high, the senses of the street were diminished, but the thick and sultry air remained. It seemed unnatural that something so heavy could float so high.

Kathleen's hair was down. Her feet rested on top of my legs, and she rubbed her big toe on my calf muscle.

She tussled her hair, sucked in her right cheek between her teeth—nothing humorous has ever come from that move—and said, "When you and Garrett left Hawkins, were you positive that he was innocent in Brittany's case?"

"I thought you didn't want to know."

"I changed my mind."

"Leonard Hawkins was a known pedophile," I explained. "His name surfaced quickly after her disappearance, but they could never pin it on him. Garrett and I introduced ourselves to him over five years ago."

"And?"

"He claimed he was straight. I believed him. There was a reason he was never charged: Hawkins didn't do it. He was on Vanderbilt Beach the day my sister went missing, but only during the morning. Garrett and I were suspicious that he manufactured his own alibi. We tried to break him so he'd admit as much. His insistence convinced us otherwise."

I threw back my port as if I was taking cough syrup.

Kathleen took a delicate sip of her port. "Does Morgan know any of this?"

"No. He's next. I thought it best if you weren't the last to know."

"You *are* afraid of me."

"You have no clue."

"What makes you say Hawkins was murdered?"

"Bruises were found on his neck. That indicates he was strangled and left to drown."

I glanced at her and was surprised to see she was staring into the night.

"Those detectives," she said, turning her head to me, "they think—what—all these years later, you got in the mood one night?"

"Some variation of that." I'd filled her in on the elevator about my conversation with Rambler and Yarborough.

"So…" She nestled her legs up underneath her. "What you're saying is that you believe he gave a false confession. But why would he have done so?"

"He was likely coerced. Maybe he had family who could be threatened—used as leverage against him. I don't know."

"But you're going to find out." She didn't wait for confirmation but continued. "His body brings it back to you, doesn't it? The person who took Brittany is still out there. Even worse, that person's trying to either put you away—for reasons that are perhaps totally unrelated to Brittany—or trying to stop any further investigation into the case."

"You'd make a great detective, but you'd rob the world of a sexy Eudora Welty scholar—and, sadly, there's so few of those left."

I tossed up the end of the port glass, but there was nothing there. I'd been doing that a lot lately—hitting the bottom of the glass before I realized it.

"When do you expect to hear from the DNA testing?" Kathleen asked.

"The sheriff's office in Collier County said any day. It's possible that the perpetrator followed her into the room. They found strands of hair on a pillowcase that they didn't think came from her. It was a hotel room—no telling how long it was there."

"They kept it?"

"They did."

"So if it comes back and doesn't match Hawkins'…?"

"Then it doesn't mean much, unless it matches a known criminal."

"But if it does—match him, I mean—then it *was* him despite what you previously said."

I took my time with that, as I'd been mulling that over ever since I learned that they were looking for a DNA match. I stood and stepped toward the rail. The moon gleamed at me. Silent lightning streaked the horizon as if someone were setting off flashbulbs. Each bolt illuminated dark thunderheads that hung in the heavens like invading spaceships from distant galaxies.

What would she look like today? Would she have kids? Would I? Would her living have materially affected my life? Am I nothing but the product of that random act—a by-product of her abductor?

Kathleen stepped beside me. "If it matches Hawkins'?" she said, seeking to clarify her earlier comment.

"Then someone planted the evidence," I said turning to her. "Someone who is capable of such things, who needs to protect himself, and who doesn't want me looking any further into her disappearance. If it matches Hawkins', then I've got a problem, because he didn't do it. Someone blackmailed him and then committed murder to seal the envelope. The blackmail was to get Hawkins to confess; the murder was to permanently silence him. His death meant nothing without a confession. His confession meant nothing if he could recant it. Throw in trying to pin his murder on me, and it's a neat little package."

"One more: why now?"

I shrugged. "The emergence of DNA testing poses a threat. The real perpetrator's DNA must have been in that room, or so he feared. He's a powerful figure to orchestrate such a cover-up. He can't risk it coming back to him, so he's trying to close it and pin it on me."

The next morning, the Collier County sheriff's office gave me a courtesy call to say that Hawkins's DNA was found on the pillowcase. The Matilda case was officially closed.

I blew it back open.

5

It was three in the morning, and I was camped outside Hawkins's house. It was a 1950s blockhouse that appeared, from my drive-by late in the afternoon, to have been recently painted. A stepladder and two five-gallon paint cans rested in the side yard up against the house. The yard was landscaped with colored gravel and flawlessly trimmed shrubs.

I don't think I'd paint my house if I were planning to confess to a crime that would put me in the slammer for the rest of my life.

PC and Boyd were in the back seat of my truck. They'd followed me in their own car, which was parked a block away. PC and Boyd were a pair of juvie offenders I was trying to rescue from the system. PC housed an oversized IQ, and Boyd—was just Boyd. I'd recently begun to wonder if my desire to help them was related to the loss of my sister and the subsequent disintegration of my family. I wasn't one to dwell on stuff, but sometimes stuff dwells on you.

"How long?" PC asked. He wore a Steelers 2011 Super Bowl Champion hat. The Steelers lost that game.

"Don't know," I said. "A few days. I need to know if anyone comes and goes."

"You know, Jake-o," Boyd cut in, "we were going to Key West for...what's his name?"

Boyd had always called me Jake-o. I'd never told him I once had a sister who called me that. I didn't mind. In some manner, it seemed a reincarnation, although, of what, I wasn't sure.

"Hemingway contest at Sloppy Joe's," PC said, coming to his buddy's rescue.

"Right," Boyd said and then smacked his gum. He had a full beard and wore a black T-shirt with the name "Daniel Simpson Day" on it in white. "All these beards who look alike. PC thinks I'd make a good one in thirty years. Thought I might get a little practice. Get in the groove of the man."

"You'll need to gain weight," I said as I glanced over my shoulder at Boyd. "Drink yourself to death, suffer from bipolar disorder, ignore your children, and put a slug in your brain. So don't groove too deep."

"Beards," Boyd wisely pointed out, "are only skin deep."

PC said, "Anyone in particular we looking for?"

"No," I said. "Anyone who has interest in the house."

"And now?"

"Move the truck and wait for my text. If someone approaches, give me a call."

"Rodger-dodger," PC said.

"What's with the hat?" I asked as I put on latex gloves. I didn't really want to take the time, but curiosity triumphed.

"You know they make up hats, T-shirts, all that stuff, for both teams before the championship games, right? Football, baseball, it doesn't matter. The team that loses? All that stuff gets destroyed or shipped to Timbuktu. It's like alternative history, and I'm a collector. If you come across any Indians 1997 World Series merchandise, grab it.

They had all the paraphernalia, along with the champagne, in the dugout in the ninth inning of game seven and had to yank it."

"I'll keep it in mind," I said, but my mind was no longer focused on anything he'd said.

One good pull and I was in through the sliding back door. I wasn't familiar with the house. When Garrett and I had confronted Hawkins, we'd snatched him from his car and taken him to Florida scrubland in the event it turned out to be a one-way trip for him.

I kept my flashlight low to the ground, even though the blinds were shut. The air was thick with stale tobacco, but the house was neat and clean. I assumed the police had confiscated all the electronics, and I was correct. There were also no checkbooks or address books. The wastebaskets were empty.

Nothing caught my attention other than Hawkins had a girlfriend. Women's clothing littered the closet, and make-up was in the cramped green-tiled bathroom. The grout was clean, and rubber gloves rested on the edge of the bathtub, along with a tube of grout cleaner. Cleaning the bathroom grout had to be the last thing anyone would do before taking the one-way elevator. Between the exterior paint job and the grout, Hawkins's house was screaming at me.

I cracked open the refrigerator door. The interior light revealed the usual hodgepodge of items, plus four containers from Jersey Sam's Deli. The containers had staggered expiration dates, indicating that Hawkins was a regular customer. I closed the door. The refrigerator door had a business card of the local UPS store stuck to it with a magnet from Harbor House Marina. They both went in my pocket. I started to leave but spun around and went to Hawkins's bathroom. A red toothbrush, a pink toothbrush, a comb, and a hairbrush were scattered on a beige Corian vanity. It was hard to tell in the low light, but the clean and stiff bristles indicated that the toothbrushes were relatively new. I placed them in separate zip-lock bags and texted PC.

A minute later, he pulled up in front of the house. He vaulted over the armrest dividing the two front seats as I climbed behind the wheel.

Boyd was in the back seat, his phone casting a soft glow over his face. "Says here," he said, "that there was another Sloppy Joe's in Papa's day—you like that? That's what they called him. He spent most his time at—"

"Turn that damn thing off," I said. He flicked it off.

"Sorry, Jake-o. I did have my hand over it."

"Anything?" PC asked.

"Nothing. You know the drill." I threw the truck into gear and took the corner to their car. "Anything and everything you see, you tell me."

"Boring work."

"How're your classes coming?"

PC and Boyd had been repeatedly expelled and readmitted to high school. I'd made a deal with them that I'd pay tuition at the downtown Saint Petersburg branch of USF. Their end of the bargain was to cease being repeat clients of the local law-enforcement agency and to cover the tab for room and board. Neither had a streak of violence in him, but white-collar crime was giggle and kicks for PC when he was bored, and bored was his natural state.

"They don't let up for the summer quarter," PC said with pride. "Especially if I'm going to skip a year and apply to the business school."

"Especially," Boyd chirped in, "if I'm to have any chance of finishing my four-year art degree in six years."

"You know I'm going to pay you back," PC said.

"And you know," Boyd said, "that the chances of me ever—"

"I told you, forget it." I pulled up by their car and turned to them. "No one's a hero here. Don't get caught. Need the lecture?"

"Naw," PC said. They both clambered out. PC turned back and held my eyes for a second. "Last time, that guy— Lambert—died on our watch. We'll do better."

He slammed the door before I had the chance to tell him not to worry about it—and to close the door quietly.

It was three forty-five. Too late to go back home—too early to make my stops. I drove to a beach parking lot, reclined the back of my seat, and attempted to sleep. I tossed and squirmed and tried to tame my mind, but it was not to be. Although I didn't know the story arc I was embarking upon, I knew the final scene. It played over and over in my head. I could taste it. See it. Smell it. Hear it. Feel it.

I kill the man who killed my sister.

6

"**C**an I help you?"

Jersey Sam's Deli was less than a mile from Hawkins's house, and it opened at 8:00 a.m. It was now 8:05. I was hoping to learn more about Hawkins's final days by talking to people he might have associated with recently. In front of me, according to his name tag, was Roderick. Roderick was a man clearly appreciative of food but less so of a hairbrush.

"Know this man?" I said. I brought up a picture of Hawkins on my cell phone.

I rubbed my neck with my other hand. I had a crick in my neck, courtesy of the front seat of my truck. Sleep had finally taken me, and I hadn't wakened until the sun brightened the sky with orange-ribbed clouds beneath an antiseptic blue sky. I race the sun every morning. On those catastrophic occasions when it wins, I'm in a foul mood all day.

Roderick hesitated and then said, "Never saw him before." He spoke as if his words were caught in his throat. His left ear appeared to be lower than his right ear, or perhaps it was because my head was slightly tilted to alleviate my neck pain.

"Yes, you have," I said, still massaging my neck. "He came in here several times a week."

"If you know, why ask me?"

"To know if I'm dealing with an honest deli man or a lying deli man."

"You want some food, pal? I'm Roderick the meat seller. If not, take your atti—"

I dropped my phone, reached over the counter, cupped my hand behind Roderick-the-Meat-Seller's neck, and slammed his face onto the countertop. I grabbed his collar and dragged his body over the counter, shoving him against the cold-cut display case. I stuck my hand under his chin, snapped his head back, and welted my eyes to his.

"Did you know him?" I said to his frightful eyes.

"*Gee*zus, man. What's with you?" His face was jigsawed with confusion and fear. "Yeah, yeah, I know him. Big deal. He's a regular, you know. Why'ja do that to me? The hell's your problem?"

I loosened my grip. *What the hell is my problem? I'm not going to learn anything by blowing my top.*

"He's a known pedophile, and I got skin in the game," I said. "What can you tell me about him?"

I released my grip and adjusted his dirty name tag. His nose was bleeding. I swiped a napkin from a dispenser and gave it to him. He blotted his nose, his nervous eyes never leaving mine.

"Sorry, man. Your sister? Daughter?" he said, trying to calm me down.

"My sister. I know he came here often. He's dead, in case you're holding a can of spam back for him. Washed up a few days ago."

He dabbed his nose again. "Sorry about your sister. Yeah, yeah. I knew him. As a customer, I mean," he spurted out. "Here couple times a week. Tuesdays and Fridays. He

43

and—but I got nothing to help you. I mean, don't shoot the messenger, right?"

"Who?"

"Who, what?"

"He and who? You were about to mention a name."

"Ahh," he said, hesitating again, but he likely still felt his recent encounter with the countertop. "I don't know. Some lithe redhead. Skinny thing with chicken legs. Don't know her name. Listen, they'd come in together—nice couple. I don't know what else to tell you. I'm a deli man. They were just customers."

"Lithe?"

"Yeah—ya know—willowy little number."

I asked for a more thorough description of Lithe the Red, but he was tapped out. I gave him my card and the usual line about letting me know if he recalled anything else.

On the way to the Harbor House Marina, I called PC and told him to be on the lookout for a redhead. She would likely return for her clothing. Someone forced Hawkins to pen his confession. Maybe he shared that with his woman.

Before entering the marina, I took a couple of deep breaths to compose myself. Roger Scurlock, the owner, had never seen or heard of Leonard Hawkins. He passed out over a thousand magnets a year.

"Second-best marketing tool I ever used," he informed me while stocking a lift-top freezer with frozen bait. "Numero uno time was when I had topless girls pumping gas. Ninety cents over Riverbend's price, but I had boats lined up to Pensacola. Pretty sure Ellefson—that's the Swede who owns Riverbend—was the one who gave me up. When the police came and cited me? They took their time. My attorney wanted me to sue, take it all the way up to Tallahassee. Said our higher prices could be construed to be a private-club entrance fee, and if those girls wanted to get a tan, then they had every right. What do you think?"

"Are you positive you never seen this guy?" I held up a picture of Hawkins on my phone.

"Pretty positive." He let the freezer lid slam shut.

"Look again."

"Sorry. What do you think, about the fuel dock being a private club?"

I stroked my neck, passed out another card, and thanked him. I headed to the marina's restaurant, Sad Annie's Fish and Drink. I had one more scheduled stop, but the coffee and bagel I'd had before introducing myself to Roderick was fading fast.

"What do you have that's fresh?" I asked the barmaid. Her thick brunette hair was braided and hung over her left shoulder like a rappelling rope. I placed my arms on the wood counter. It was sticky. I left them there.

"We got yellowtail snapper in yesterday," she said. Her voice was dull and listless.

"What did you get in this morning?"

"Tilefish."

"That, on a bun, unsweetened iced tea, and a draft."

"You're early. I don't know if Wolf's filleted it yet."

"I'm in no hurry."

"Sure you are. Wouldn't be eating lunch now if you weren't."

She reached into a freezer that was brittle with white frost and gave me a cold beer. The beer was halfway gone before she placed the iced tea on the counter. I took a sip. It was sweet.

I made a series of phone calls. I left messages with FBI Special Agent Natalie Binelli; Brian Applegate, an intelligence geek with SOCOM at MacDill Air Force base in Tampa; and Patrick McGlashan, a sheriff's detective in Lee County, Florida.

Binelli and I had recently worked together while I was undercover helping the FBI rope in a Miami art dealer whose true passion was murder.

I'd sat next to Applegate on the bus on our first day in the army. We'd kept in contact ever since. Garrett and I used MacDill on numerous occasions when we performed clandestine work for Colonel Janssen, our former commanding officer.

McGlashan was a long shot, but he held the most potential. Although he was Lee County, one north from Collier County, he might provide insight as to how Hawkins's DNA got mixed in with thirty-year-old evidence. We'd corroborated when a young woman, Jenny Spencer, went missing while on his turf.

My tilefish was lightly floured and pan-fried. I squeezed fresh lemon on it. It flaked off the fork before it got to my mouth. It was a great piece of fish despite the grungy counter. I told Rappelling Rope to switch out my iced tea but make it to go.

Binelli was first.

"Still mad at me?" I answered her ring.

"Shitbird," she spat out with such force that I jerked the phone away from my ear.

I neglected to mention that I'd left her out to dry while closing down the murderous art dealer. At the time of my betrayal, she'd accused me of being the aforementioned species, although I had specifically questioned her if the species even existed. Everything had worked out fine. So I thought.

"The two million," I started in on an explanation. "It wasn't for—"

"I already figured that out. Whatyawant? Forget it. You'll use me however you want, with blatant disregard for my career."

"Want to try this five minutes later?" I offered.

"Shitbirds don't get five minutes. Shoot."

"A man suspected of abducting my sister thirty years ago washed up near my house a few days ago," I rushed out. "Name of Leonard Hawkins. The local police don't buy the suicide or accidental-death angle. They're circling me like buzzards."

"She OK?"

"Dead. Missing for three decades."

"You never told me."

"Seven billion people in the world. You're the third person I've told."

"You're kidding?"

"I don't do that."

"You have issues," she said.

"I've been told."

"Now I feel like a shitbird."

"Imagine our nest."

"You serious? I'm the third?"

"Man's name was Leonard Hawkins."

I gave her the synopsis and a request for DNA lab work as my phone signaled another call. "It won't be that easy," she said. "It takes time, and I'll need to improvise a reason."

"Right up your alley. After all," I reminded her, "you were in theater once."

The call I'd missed was from Detective McGlashan. I hit McGlashan back but got his voice mail again. I gulped down the rest of my beer, picked up my new iced tea in a Styrofoam cup, and dropped a twenty on the counter. In the truck, I punched the address of the UPS store from Hawkins's refrigerator into my GPS. Fifteen minutes later, as the straw sucked up iced tea, I pulled into a characterless suburban strip mall.

In the UPS store, a Native American man stood behind the counter assisting a lady in plaid shorts, a checkered blouse, and a nasal voice. She could fix two out of three. She methodically filled out different address labels. She asked the man to explain her shipping options and then cross-examined him for his opinion of the best way to deliver her parcels. When it was time to pay, she spent two and a half days fidgeting in her purse for the exact change. There are three things in this world I cannot tolerate: red lights, crows, and slow people. There is no hope for any of those. In my world, jails would be crammed with red lights, crows, and slow people.

I selected a hefty padded envelope from a wall display. I placed the two toothbrushes, the comb, and the hairbrush—still in protective plastic bags—inside. Speedy left, and I positioned myself in front of the man behind the counter.

His black hair was tied in a ponytail, and his shirt was starched and smooth. His name tag, unlike Roderick's, was spotless. It read, "Harold." He didn't look like a Harold. He looked like Son of Buffalo Hunter. I held up the picture of Hawkins on my phone. I introduced myself and inquired if he recognized him.

"I can't really say. I get a great number of people in here every day."

"Look hard, Harold. It's important that I find him."

He gave it a serious study and then said, "I can't help you."

"If you change your mind," I said as I handed him my card.

I placed the padded envelope on the counter and instructed him to overnight the package to Binelli's address. I wanted to make sure it was Hawkins's DNA and see if I got a hit on any known criminals. It was worth a try but not much more than that. I thanked Harold and left.

McGlashan called back. We made plans to meet at the Fish Head restaurant at Fish Tale Marina on Fort Myers Beach. I knew the area well, since I spent my first year out of the army there before I'd relocated north to Pass-a-Grille in an attempt to clean up my life. I could have settled on a phone conversation, but when you want information and a favor from someone, your supplication is best done in person.

I got on I-75 south toward Fort Myers. The truck clocked along effortlessly at eighty. I put rock music on low. It was one of my favorite combinations for clearing my mind: going fast but sitting still, seeing the name and title of the song on the navigation screen but not hearing it.

Ninety minutes later, I turned off Cypress Lake Drive onto Summerlin Road and fueled up at a gas station. As the pump methodically clicked away the gallons, I thought of Kathleen and wondered if she would be interested in the stone from my mother's engagement ring.

I don't know about those things, and I have no one to ask.

7

"**G**ive me the name again?" Detective McGlashan asked.

"Hawkins. Leonard. Not sure what, if anything, is in the middle."

"You got a lawyer?" I'd given McGlashan the complete story, from my sister's disappearance to Rambler and Yarborough's twin visits.

"I do."

I didn't mention that I hadn't bothered to call my lawyer, Garrett. Garrett had been a sniper with the Rangers and now, in the afterlife, practiced corporate utility law in Cleveland. Nor did I divulge that my lawyer was the man who'd helped me extract a few of Hawkins's fingernails under a moonless sky before a drenching rain, and bolts of lightning, had sent us scurrying into a tin-roofed pole barn, where an obstinate family of raccoons were waiting for us.

"What are you proposing?" McGlashan said. "That Hawkins's DNA was planted after the fact in an attempt to frame him? Switched out in the last year or so before the cold-case detective took a look?"

"You tell me. Is that plausible?"

He ignored my question and asked, "You ever go back to the original detectives who handled the case—what— thirty years ago?"

"I did. Lead detective was a man named Daryl Chenoweth. Ever hear of him?"

"No."

"We talked. Decent enough guy. Said he never saw a case with so many people at the scene and so few clues."

"Think it's worth taking another swing at him?"

"He retired in '04, his ticker three years later."

McGlashan grunted. "Next to being on the end-of-watch board, that's every cop's worst fear. How about when they notified you it was reopened?"

"Detective Melissa Dendy gave me a ring. Strictly protocol. Her lack of enthusiasm was palpable. I don't hold it against her. With no body, I'm sure she had more relevant cases. What about it? Is it plausible that the evidence was switched out?"

McGlashan took a sip of his iced tea and gazed away from me and out over the stagnant water of the basin. The adjoining marina was summertime quiet. We were the only patrons sitting at the bar. The restaurant had no walls facing the water, only garage doors that I'd never seen down. The oscillating corner fans slugged through the thick air as though they were stirring pudding. A sign behind the bar noted that Key West was 200 miles south, and Put-In-Bay was 1,250 miles north.

We each had a package of crackers and a bowl of seafood chowder that could have passed as spackling compound. The crackers were stale. I'd asked the bartender for another pack, but she assured me it was a lost cause.

"Theoretically, it can't happen." McGlashan's tone indicated a reluctance to discuss the topic. He lifted his spoon to take a sip of the chowder but then reconsidered. He put the spoon back in the bowl. The heavy spoon did not dent the chowder.

"But," he added, "I'm not going to spin my wheels with you about the probability of crooked cops, let alone a simple favor or payoff."

"No need to waste rubber," I concurred. I took a drink of water and chased it with a long pull from a bottle of beer. My back was sweating through my T-shirt, fusing it to my skin.

"The evidence is catalogued," McGlashan continued. "It needs to be signed in and out."

"If you didn't want your name associated with that act, what would you do?"

"Some things never change—I'd slip the record keeper a doughnut and tell her to keep her trap shut. No record, no trace."

"How would I find out if that occurred?"

McGlashan cut me a look. "You hear what I just said? You can't."

He dipped a paper towel in his water glass and swiped his forehead with it. He was in short sleeves and long pants. Loops of sweat circled under his arms.

I said, "You know anyone in the Collier County office?"

"I do."

"Worth it to ask around?"

"You mean stroll in and idly accuse them of tampering with evidence?"

"Some people like doughnuts more than others."

That earned a guttural harrumph. I took a drink of water and let an ice cube slide into my mouth. I cracked it. "Go in the back door," I suggested to him.

"Meaning?"

"Request the evidence from my sister's case yourself."

McGlashan nodded patiently in approval. "And see who objects, who gets nervous?"

"What do you think?"

"Why would I do that?"

"You got any missing persons from around the same time?"

"That'll work, even standard procedure. What they have now clearly puts Hawkins in the area."

I wondered why, if it was standard procedure, I'd been the one to suggest it.

He blew his breath out. "My son and I are going to Colorado next month. Doing some fishing with a couple other guys a few miles out of Idaho Springs. I'm not going to miss this heat."

"He still with the SAS?"

He'd told me when we initially met years ago that his son was involved in a joint exercise with the British SAS.

"Finished eighteen months back. He's out now, like you."

"Doing OK?"

"Doing OK."

"Can you tell if the evidence has been tampered with?"

He leveled his eyes at me. "Maybe, maybe not. I'll let you know whose curiosity I arouse. What's your plan, if and when that person steps forward?"

I drained my bottle and placed it on the narrow rubber mat that ran along the inside of the bar on a lower level. A pelican plummeted from the sky and smacked the water. Tough way to make a living. God was wise not to give them big brains; they'd have migraines all the time.

"If I did have a plan," I said, "do you really want to know?"

"Keep me out of it." His cell rang, and he gave it a quick look. "I've got to scoot. Do *not* squeeze some lady's tits just because she accepted a chocolate glaze to hand over an evidence bag. You got that?"

"Loud and clear."

He held my gaze and then stood, and we shook hands. He darted out. Either he was late for a meeting or he couldn't wait to get into his air-conditioned car. Probably both.

I reclaimed my seat and ordered another beer. A cloud ruptured, and a downpour pelted the roof like a machine gun. Five minutes later, it ceased, as if it were embarrassed by its eruption. It did not alter the temperature or humidity.

PC called.

"We got Red," he said. "She just pulled up in a chick-yellow SUV and went into the house."

"Don't lose her," I said and dashed to my truck. Halfway there, I spun around and hustled back to the bar. I left a pair of tens on the counter next to the half-eaten package of stale crackers and two bowls of concrete chowder with spoons embedded in the surface like a piece of abstract art.

8

PC, Boyd, and I were in my truck parked outside a double-wide. Red and green light bulbs dipped like fingernail moons under the eave of the roof. An empty boat trailer was tucked off to one side.

"She was in Hawkins's house for about half an hour," PC said. "She lugged out a couple of suitcases and landed here." He wore a 2014 "Stanford Rose Bowl Champion" T-shirt.

"She was dragging those suitcases like dead dogs. We helped her put them in her car," Boyd said with a note of pride.

I wish they hadn't made themselves known—they should have known better—but I didn't want to scold them.

"See anything unusual in her car?" I said to whoever wanted the question.

"Naw, a few Beanie Babies," PC said. "I thought we buried those with pet rocks. She also had a twelve-string guitar. What's the action, Jackson?"

"Ring the doorbell and see what happens," I responded as I got out of the truck.

I took a breath, rang the doorbell, and folded my hands in front of me.

The door opened. "My name is Jake Travis—"

She cut me off with a stinging slap across the cheek.

"I know who you are, you son of a bitch. That's for what you did to my Lenny." She went for another strike, but I caught her wrist with enough force to convey that slapping time was over.

"I'd like to have a few words with you," I said, completing my introduction.

"I don't ever need to hear your name," she barked out at me. I freed her wrist. "He was clean. He didn't deserve what you and your friend from hell did. He told me you'd be comin' back if anythin' happened to him. Said I had to be nice. But I don't want to be nice. I want to tear out *your* fingernails, Mr. Jake—" I pushed past her and into her house. "Hey, I didn't invite you in."

"Why did Hawkins tell you I'd be back?"

She paused and exhaled sharply. She was noodle thin and coiled with energy. Her legs took forever to reach the floor. Despite her hair being tied behind her neck, the frizzy red mess sprayed out like a fishnet frozen in midthrow. She wore cut-off jeans and a white shirt with a pink seashell on the front. Her arms and cheekbones were powdered with freckles. Multiple loose bracelets were on each wrist, as if she'd raided a pharaoh's tomb. I'd put her a decade on either side of fifty. I liked her, but I didn't know why.

"I told Lenny I couldn't talk to you," she said. "You understand that? Two of his nails never grew back. They said they would, but it never happened. I'd rather see you dead. Can I make that any clearer?"

"No, ma'am."

"Don't you get all polite on me. I know who you are."

"Why did Lenny tell you I'd be back?" I repeated in my most amicable tone. Her home smelled like one of those stores Kathleen would drag me into, and I knew by the scent there would be nothing in it for me.

"Don't talk like that—saying his name like you were his friend."

I held up my hands, palms out to her. "You want to do a couple laps around your house to burn off your hate, go right ahead. You want to do what Lenny wanted you to do and help me find who really killed him? Then grow up and calm down."

She considered that and said, "I'm gettin' myself a beer. You want one?"

"Sure." I was surprised how fast she came around. There are advantages to having a naturally charming and warm personality.

"Then go down to the corner, muffin-brain."

"You don't have a gun in that fridge, do you?"

She waved her hand as she brushed past me on her way to the corner kitchen. "I can tell you took the short bus to school. If I was going to pop you, I would have done the happy deed when I opened the door. Would have dragged you in and told the cops that you rang, stepped in to me, and grabbed my titties." She spun her head around to me. Her hair followed in an angry mass. "Self-defense, Officer. 'Stand my ground'—you know, Florida's legalized-murder law. What's a poor girl to do?"

"You've given this thought."

"Bet your scrawny ass I did. My mother always told me to be polite in my own house. I got Miller and Miller. What's your pleasure?"

"I don't have to go to the corner?"

"I just told you what my mother told me."

"Miller."

"Men are so predictable."

We relocated to chairs on a screened back porch that had been added on to the house. It looked over a lush backyard with a white plastic fence that afforded privacy from her neighbors. Black pots were mounted on the fence, their green vines thick with grape-size flowers trailing from them. A fountain in the middle emitted the spa-soothing sound of trickling water as a concrete angel gargled bubbles from its greenish-yellow algae mouth.

For the third time, I asked her, "Why did Hawkins tell you I'd be back?"

"Lordy, you're hitched to that question."

"You have no idea."

"Listen, I'm stone-sorry about your sister. But Lenny had nothin' to do with that, and you know it. He was in a bad crowd when he was younger—you lay down with dogs, you stand up with fleas—but no more. He was a good man."

Rambler had told me they'd found incriminating evidence that indicated Hawkins was an active pedophile. I wondered if that had been planted as well.

"I believe you," I said. "I am sorry for your loss. It's a shame what—"

"Oh no, don't you go butterin' me up. I ain't no piece of toast. You and I? The only reason we're cooperatin' is because we have a common enemy. You ridin' with me on that?"

I took a sip of cold beer. On the floor next to her was a potted plant with a sign stuck in the soil. It said, "Grow, damn it."

"Understood," I said. "What's your name?"

"I don't want you and me bein' friends."

"I'll find out, so why not tell—"

"'Cause I don't want to."

"Fair enough, Red," I said. "My question stands."

She slumped in her chair and gazed away from me, out toward the fountain. She started to reach for her beer but withdrew her hand and folded her arms. She brought her legs up underneath her and then brushed back an acre of hair before again folding her arms. She fought to control her breathing.

I took a sip of beer and kept my eyes on her.

"A few weeks ago, Lenny took me out to dinner." Her voice was calm. I wasn't expecting that after her opening number. "It was our date night. Usually on them nights, Lenny was the king of hearts, but on that night, he was out of sorts. I was all dressed up. One of life's big sucks is when you get dressed up just to get let down.

"He took me to the Blue Marlin. Think we ever had the money to be goin' there? No way. They say money talks— ours just said good-bye. I thought I might even get him out dancin'. Lenny preferred to sit, but once on the floor, he could tear a rug.

"I was sippin' my tomato bisque soup. It was so light it tasted like a cloud. I remember thinkin', if a tomato and a cloud had a child, it would be that soup. He told me a couple of men approached him when he left the barbershop. Gave him a choice: either confess to abductin' and killin' your sister or they would do terrible things to me. Said if he or I ever went to the police, those terrible things would be waitin' around a dark corner."

That explained what someone held over Hawkins to gain his written confession. It also explained the type of people I was dealing with.

"Did he—"

"I sat there," she interrupted, "starin' at that soup and thinkin' what a dummy I was for thinkin' my life would ever be worth shit. I remember my mom gettin' all pretty one night to go out with my daddy. She was so happy skirtin' out the door, and I was so happy seein' her like that. But when she came home, she'd been cryin', and they weren't talkin'. I never felt so bad for her. No one told me my time would come."

The concrete angel got a few gurgles in before I asked, "Did he tell you what these men looked like?"

"He always likes goin' to the barber. After I was done feelin' bad for me, I felt worse for him. He was just tryin' to get a haircut."

"Any description?"

"I heard you the first time. I didn't need him for that. We came home one day from Publix, and they was sittin' right here, all calm like. Asked Lenny if he was ready to confess. Raped me with their eyes and told Lenny what a fine woman I was. A real pair of creepballs. Men like that steal the smell off shit.

"One of them took Lenny to the kitchen, where they had him write that bullshit letter. Said they needed it for protection and wouldn't use it. Said if Lenny or I ever squawked, they'd be back for me. Know the dumbest thing?"

"What's that?"

"All the time they was here? I was worried about the salted caramel ice cream meltin' before I could get it in the freezer. I knew it was stupid, but I couldn't stop the damn thought."

"It's natural to—"

"That night, when we were gettin' ready for bed, we noticed our toothbrushes and combs were gone. Lenny, when we realized they must have taken them, looked real sad and said, 'Ah shit.' And then he said, 'I'm sorry, baby.'"

"You saw the letter?"

"No. They took it with them. Lenny wouldn't talk about it none—trying to protect me, you know?"

"The men?"

"You're a damn bloodhound with your questions. Already told you: creepballs. Buzzed hair. Shit smell. One had a red arrow tattoo on his upper right arm. Started at his elbow."

She took a sip of her canned beer. "Lenny told me that night that you'd be back. That if anythin' happened to him, you'd be the only person in the world—on account of what you and your bastard friend did to him—who would know he was framed. Like I said, he had problems back then, did some stuff he wasn't too proud off. But he never touched your sister. He was movin' on. Makin' a new past every day—to hell with the old one. Know what Lenny called the past?"

"What?"

"A dead day."

"The police found underage porn on—"

"They told me that. Looked at me like you might stare at a bottom of a trash can covered with maggots. I told them, 'No way—someone put that there.'"

"Did you have anyone working in the house when you weren't here?"

"No. I assume the creepball boys broke in, wouldn't you?"

I nodded as my mind explored the possibilities. It was likely someone planted evidence on Hawkins's computer

61

as well as tainted the evidence in Collier County. Someone who could slide in and out of local jurisdiction. Someone with connections. *A powerful figure.*

Or was I mistaken about Hawkins? Was I searching for a ghost because I refused to believe I'd read him wrong and hadn't taken the opportunity to kill him myself? I didn't think so. The men who killed him weren't the law. They were men who wanted the Matilda case forever closed. Hawkins's insistence to Red that I'd come around only fortified my belief that he was not the man who abducted my sister. He likely knew he was a dead man walking but tried to keep that from Red.

Red said, "Did the police come to see you?"

"They did. Insisted that he drowned. But he was likely dead before he hit the water."

She bobbed her head in agreement. "The police never tried that drowning shit on me."

"You inform them of your visitors?"

"No way."

"But you told me."

"Followin' Lenny's instructions."

"What else did the police tell you?"

"Not much. I blabbered over and over that he was innocent. One of them just stared at me and kept clucking his tongue like he was an autistic cow. I know I sounded like some…"

She stopped talking as her eyes wandered out to her garden. A teak table with two chairs was off to a side. Different levels of potted plants, on wrought-iron tables, circled the small backyard. It was rain-forest green and lush. It was a corner of her life she could control.

She puffed her breath out. "I just want to be left alone. Play my guitar, and tend my garden. Lenny wasn't goin' to take it lyin' down. Hell, he even thought of goin' to you to help him get out of the jam. You believe that, after what you did?"

"That tells me—"

"He said I had to forget that—that you had the motive to find who really took your sister, and that was the only way his name would be cleared. Said you would follow the men who came after him, knowin' they would lead to the truth. Told me if he died, that you were his only hope of revenge from the grave."

She straightened up and gave me a hard look. "What do you think of that, Mr. Jake Travis?"

"I—"

"He wanted so much to leave this earth as a good man and not the man people thought he was." She balled up her fist and brought it up to her mouth. "Then, on account of his past, he died for me."

I stood and walked over to a bookcase with a steel frame and wood shelves. It held potted plants, three Beanie Babies, and stacks of worn songbooks for guitar. Small yellow sticky notes protruded from the sides of the songbooks. They were dirty, as if they'd been thumbed through for decades. I wondered what songs they marked, which ones she would never play again.

Hawkins had been in the area the week my family and I were at Vanderbilt Beach. He had a history. The police had put a target on his back, but they never had enough evidence to convict him. He was innocent. Now, on account of his proximity three decades ago, he'd been framed and murdered.

I picked up a book titled *Kittens on Christmas Morning: Purrfect Ways of Overcoming Grief.*

"I just bought that," Red explained. "It looked inter-esting. I'm not one for that 'seven steps to happiness' shit."

"Any good?"

She snorted. "Too damn mushy for me."

I placed it back and absentmindedly picked up a Beanie Baby. I was buying time, hoping something would surface.

"That's my mom," she said. "They both died too young. I don't have nobody anymore."

I turned to her. "Come again?"

"The two Beanies Babies. The one in your hand and the one that was next to it. They're stuffed with my mother's and father's ashes. I miss them powerfully."

Maybe that red hair of hers had fried her brain. The stuffed animal in my hand was a brownish bird with a long beak, and the other was an orange-striped tiger.

"I always thought my mom was like Beak the Kiwi Bird—a little odd lookin' but just as cuddly and sweet as you'd want. My daddy was a lot like Zodiac Tiger— 'aggressive and courageous, candid and sensitive.' That's what the tag says on Zodiac. That was my dad, all right.

"I know what you're thinkin', but it beats puttin' them in some old cigar box or feedin' them to the fish. Besides, I'm still mad at my mom—I ain't done talkin' to her yet, you know? On account of her flirtin' with my boyfriends when I started bringin' them home in high school. Makin' fun of my red hair and stringy legs—all in front of me. I know that don't sound like much to you, but to me, at that age, it was a ball-buster. A young woman's confidence is a fragile thing."

I turned to her and said, "I like your hair."

"Thank you."

"You can't be too mad at your mother—you said you missed her."

"I see you have a novice degree in relationships."

I nodded, unwilling to contend the point. I jutted my chin at the third Beanie Baby. "What's its story?"

"That's Tuffy. He was supposed to be for my dog, Butler. Lost him 'bout a year ago. But don't worry, he ain't in there. My neighbor to my right, facing the house, Miss Asshole? She just hated Butler. Always said he was pissin' in her yard—she had a point, but never mind that. After I had him cremated, I spread him one night over her front bushes and yard. You cannot imagine the deep and profound sense of pleasure I get knowin' that he is forever messin' in her yard."

"And Lenny?" I carefully placed Beak the Kiwi Bird back on the shelf next to her husband, Zodiac Tiger.

She let that sit between us for a few beats and then said, "We're not married. He's got a sister up north. It's up to her."

"But if you could?"

She teared up and said, "It ain't none of your business. I don't know you that well. I don't ever want to know you that well."

I went to her and bent down, elbows on my knees, my hands clasped in front of me. Our faces were at the same level, no more than two feet apart. She had hazel eyes and freckles on her cheeks that looked like they'd been penciled on that morning. Silver anchor earrings dangled from her ears. I wondered how much thought she'd given in what earrings to wear. Despite her bravado, up close, she was small and vulnerable. Her hair was half her mass, her attitude the other half. She smelled good—sweet, like for-sythia.

"Tell me, Red. Something to help me find the men who murdered Lenny. Think. Remember."

She gave an embarrassed shrug. "They drove some bland four-door when they left. Lenny said it was likely a rental."

"Keep digging."

Her eyes roved over her garden and then came back to me. "I told you about the arrow, right? The buzzed hair?"

"Accents?"

"Had 'em all right. But I couldn't place 'em. Nothin' I ever heard. One of them European countries maybe? I ain't no good at that. I can count the zip codes I've been in on both hands."

"Height, weight?"

"One like you. The other a little shorter but thick—like a pine tree you snip off at the top, and it grows outward."

"Limp or scars?"

"I'm sorry."

I stood and got a card from my wallet. "Call me," I said as I handed it to her. "Anytime."

She took the card and then reached for my right index finger. She held it in her hand as she tilted her head up, her eyes searching mine. "He had a nail like that—like yours. Split at the end of it."

My fingernail, courtesy of a car door, had split when I was a child. It remained split.

"A split nail," I said.

"The one who was notably taller," Red said. "He picked up my guitar, and I noticed his fingernail was split. I noticed it 'cause it's hard to play guitar with a split nail. I told him that too."

"Told him what?"

"That it's a little hard to play a guitar with a split nail. I was tryin' to be nice, thinkin' I could win them over."

"Anything else?"

"No." Her eyes dulled. "You ever play guitar?"

"No."

"Neither did Lenny. He wanted to learn, but you took care of that, didn't you?"

9

McGlashan called as I drove back home. He'd requested the evidence kit from my sister's case. The case log indicated that several strands of hair had been pulled from the bag, and as we previously knew, the DNA matched Hawkins's. Detective Melissa Dendy had requested Hawkins submit to testing when she was handed the assignment. McGlashan indicated there was nothing in the evidence kit to arouse suspicion. He said they planned to open other cold cases and see if Hawkins was a match for those. He vowed to keep me apprised if any of those cases in any manner related back to my sister. As far as he could tell, the evidence had not been tampered with. Not including Dendy, he was the first person to sign it out in over twenty-five years. He had no comment on my question regarding his progress in discovering who had unofficially signed it out before Dendy grabbed it.

When I entered my construction zone, I made a beeline to the refrigerator and dropped several ice cubes into a tumbler. The sound of the ice tinkling in the glass gave me a momentary sense of normalcy. I poured whiskey over the ice, bathing the cubes in the caramel-colored liquid. I added a splash of water—my version of drinking less—and collapsed in a cushioned chair on the screened porch.

"Tomorrow's another day," I said to Tinker Bell. Tinker Bell gave me the unwavering look of support I'd grown to expect from her. There's a real advantage to having a plastic alarm clock be your sponsor. Her support is unfaltering, her objections muted, her judgment reserved.

Binelli rang.

"What do you got?" I said.

"Struck out. Nothing on Hawkins that you can't Google."

"That's what I get for my tax dollars?"

"It's eight o'clock in the evening, and I'm still in my office."

"It's thirty years, and my sister's still dead."

"Wow-zee. You'll die young with that attitude."

I took a healthy dose of liquid smoke and said, "It's important to have goals."

"It's too late for this. Anything comes up, I'll let you know. Kathleen knows, right?"

That was the first time Natalie Binelli had mentioned Kathleen by name. She was always, "Your woman."

"She does," I replied.

"Good."

"Giving me tips on my love life?"

"Just making sure you haven't gone totally off-road."

"You'll get the package in the morning."

"Bathroom items, right?"

"Correct," I said. "You should find Hawkins's and one more, likely that of his girlfriend. I just visited her. I doubt she's in your system. Let me know if anyone known shows up."

"You know, I can't just—"

"I appreciate it."

She paused and then said, "The girlfriend's name?"

"I don't know."

"Thought you said you just visited her?"

"Didn't catch a name."

"You're one of a kind."

She disconnected before I could waste my breath defending myself.

The osprey that craps on my boat landed on one of the lift pilings. The top of the piling looked as if someone had dumped a can of white paint on it. I strolled out to the end of the dock, and the hawk took flight with a protesting screech. The tide was out, and the water had receded to the fourth piling. The exposed wet sand, coupled with the sea grass that lay flat like wet linguini, created a dank afterbirth smell. The sinking sun behind me illuminated the evening thunderheads like a floodlight, highlighting their pregnant dark underbellies in white and yellow while rendering the water gunmetal gray.

I took a seat on the bench, surrounded by calm water and evening solitude.

Not a damn thing popped into my head.

I like being alone, even seek solitude. But when I arrive, I rediscover that solitude's a bad date, for stay with her too long, and her corrosive character wears on me. Nor do I expect prescient thoughts to emerge from such rituals. I'd lumbered back to the house too many times hauling the same empty truths that I'd gone out to the dock with. But that doesn't keep me from habitually seeking the end of the dock, where I half-expect to meet the proverbial mountaintop wise man or discover a dormant part of my brain suddenly willing to dial in answers and calm my existential angst.

Applegate, my intelligence buddy from SOCOM, called.

"First of all," he said, "this is your sister we're talking about, right?"

"That's correct." When I'd called him, I'd given him her name and the details of the case.

"I'm sorry, bro. They never found her?"

"No."

"There was nothing I could find. Hey, you still go to that bar—Tides, or something like that?"

"Riptides."

"Yeah, yeah, that's it. That was a cool place. I don't get there much. I'm driving home now. Maybe I'll see you around sometime."

"Thanks for checking. Have a good night."

"Later, bro."

BRIAN APPLEGATE WANDERED INTO Riptides fifteen minutes later. His jittery and wandering eyes spotted me, but then finished drinking in the room. We shook hands before taking seats at the outdoor bar. To our left, over the Gulf of Mexico, the day surrendered with beauty. A psychotically wild orange-and-red sunset blossomed in the sky, reaching toward the heavens like a spreading wildfire. Every day the dark and the light change places. The light starts its presence with soft, electric yellows and blues and then, in the evening, dies with patient brilliance.

I turned my back to God's calling card, took a trickle of whiskey, promised myself to drink less tomorrow, and said, "What have you got?"

"Not much, but this for sure—someone doesn't want you stoking the fire. I ran a search on our system. Nothing came up. Zippo. But this is your sister we're talking about, right? I got two of them—geez, I can't even imagine. So I kept digging, not deep but wide."

He bobbed his head as though he was still talking to himself. His untamed eyebrows, mustache, and thick brown hair displayed no evidence of attention—as if he'd been drawn on an Etch A Sketch. His cheeks were naturally red. He was more teddy bear than man. He was a long shot to have any information on her case. But after 9/11, the government had mutated into a genetically engineered information- and data-gathering virus. Applegate was part of that strain.

"I cross-checked everything," he continued. "Someone snuck a peek at you when your sister's case was reopened last year. Oftentimes, those files get checked for compliance purposes, other times it's someone wanting background info."

"Who requested it?"

He motioned for a bartender. A woman in a black bikini top and a silver cross that rested low in the valley of Eden came over. He allowed his eyes to dream for a moment, ordered a Yuengling, and then said, "Listen, bro, anything bad there, I mean detrimental to you, I would have let you know, right?"

"We're good. Who looked into my file?"

"I don't know. I have access to who requests information—I was granted that about a year ago. But there's a level that can block what even I can see—the Holy Ghost."

Silver Cross plopped a mug, already losing itself to condensation in front of him. He took an eager sip, plastering the tip of his mustache with white foam.

"The Holy Ghost?"

He nodded and took a drink at the same time. It was not a feat without consequences. He licked his mustache.

"Spell it out for me," I prodded him.

"That's what we—the squad I work with—call him, or her. You ever go to church? You know, 'the Father, the Son, and the Holy Ghost?' And you're like, who's this ghost guy, right?"

"It's the Christian doctrine of the Trinity. They split their god into three parts."

"Yeah, yeah. But in our world, no one knows who he or she is. There's no trace. Total block. Questions are met with stares warning you to return to your pew. All I know is that your file was opened. You can assume that someone knows everything about you, and that person does not wish to be identified."

"My sister's case?"

"It's all there."

"I appreciate you telling me this," I said. "Anything else you can add?"

"Zilcho. Ask you a favor? Lay low—you and me. I don't want to be poking around the Holy Ghost."

"You got a burner?"

"Shittin' me?" A piece of foam flew off his upper lip, like a white dandelion. "I get caught with one of those and they'd pack my ass on the Guantanamo expressway."

"What's our channel?"

"I'm tapped out here, bro."

He was telling me he didn't want to be involved any further; whether he was really tapped out was another matter. He took a nervous sip of his beer, his eyes staring straight ahead at nothing.

I gave him a moment and then said, "She's been gone thirty years. I'm the only one left from the family. The only one who thinks of her. Every day. I owe it to her."

It came out like a sob song laced with teary-eyed sentiment, but I wasn't there for style points.

He blew his breath out and raked his hand through his shaggy hair. "Not a word. And I was never here." He cut me a look. "We cool on that?"

"Nothing will come back to you."

He gave that a second to make his point. We both realized that information and events were often beyond our control.

"The State Department," he said.

"The request for my file?" I said, seeking clarification.

He gave an affirmative nod.

"You broke the ghost?"

He cocked his shoulder and smirked. "You tell my cube mates and me that there's someone who doesn't want to be known, who thinks they're better than us? That just jazzes us up—it's game on, big guy. But if the ghost finds out? That door will slam shut, and we'd be back to square one. It's like the British in the Second World War—at Bletchley Park. They broke the German code but still had to allow some ships to sink and people to die. Otherwise, the Germans would've known their code was busted. You with me? Same with us. We have to be...selective about what we react to."

"Don't let me be the sacrificial lamb."

"I don't know any—"

"Tell me what you're afraid to tell me for fear of revealing your position."

"I didn't say we knew—"

"This is a one and done." I cut him off and then realized I should have acknowledged his sacrifice. "Listen, Brian. I appreciate what you're doing for me. I need a name."

He cast his eyes down to the bar and then quickly up to me. "Carlsberg," he said. "Bernard Carlsberg. While the request came from the State Department in DC—and I do *not* know who requested it—your encrypted file was sent to this Carlsberg stiff. That's where State wanted it to go. That's all I got, bro."

"That name means nothing to me."

"Carlsberg's an attorney, but he's not your man. He's fifteen years older than you and was studying economics in London when your sister went AWOL. He's blue-blood East Coast. Law from Princeton, like his father before him. His firm walks the line between being lobbyists and attorneys."

"Any dirt on him?"

"Naw, he's clean. His firm, though—you can find this on your own—represents some nasty people."

"Nasty they're murderers, or nasty they don't put the toilet seat down?"

The right side of his woolly-worm mustache curled up. "Bit of both. He defends the piss on the toilet seat, but that doesn't yank our cord. He has connections to arms dealers—that's a big nasty, and it's why we, and State, keep tabs on him. His clients need to wash money and skirt tax laws. Bernard Carlsberg is particularly deft in those maneuvers. You know that's how they got Capone, right? Guy wasted dozens of people, but they put him away on tax evasion. Not much has changed, except now, moving the dough is a more challenging game. It's always the money, bro. There is no battling evil. There is no victory bell. Just money."

He chased his words with a long drink of cold beer. "Johnny come marching home, my ass."

"Carlsberg," I said.

He ignored me. "One million dollars in hundreds only weighs twenty-two pounds. Fits into a shopping bag and is untraceable. That's what we're up against every day. We've got to stop printing Franklins, man. Our own currency is our greatest enemy in our battle to fight terrorism."

"Carlsberg."

"Right."

"He's in DC?"

"You're gonna love this." He cast his eyes around, as if to make certain no one was listening, and then landed back on me. "He's got three homes, but his favorite is on Tierra Verde. A good swim from you. He's camped out there now. Check out 'Citizens for a Floral Florida.' Carlsberg's holding a fundraiser at his castle for it. It's an itty-bitty feel-good nonprofit, but you can imagine the company."

"I owe you."

"Find the sicko who took your sister." He stood. "Then we'll be even."

I stood, and we exchanged a wordless handshake. He sauntered a few yards toward the parking lot but then turned back.

"That part when you laid out that you're the only one left who thinks of her every day. Would you have said that if I hadn't told you I had two sisters?"

He waved me off with a smile that told me he knew I'd hit below the belt, but he was fine with it. The night took him. I sat back down.

Silver Cross dropped by and said, "Another one, hon?"

"Pardon me?"

She looked puzzled. "Whiskey. Can I get you another?" I pushed my tumbler toward her. My promise was to drink less tomorrow, not today.

10

I often seek to emulate Donald Duck. It seems like a low bar, perhaps even a childish endeavor. It is neither. It is an elusive and worthy goal.

My five-mile run had nearly done me in. I was doubled over, hands on my knees, fighting for my breath. My heart was drumming like syncopated timpani drums.

Maybe the booze doesn't flush out every night, but a little carries over to the next day. Maybe age was pinning me like a voodoo doll. It didn't help that the air was so thick you could cut it with a chainsaw and stack it like cords of wood. I thought about lowering the punching bag in the garage but, instead, rinsed off under the outdoor shower as I rehydrated with two bottles of water.

Then I lowered the bag and pummeled the snot out of it.

I showered, again, but this time I rehydrated with a bottle of Corona. Halfway through it, I grew weary of it all. I dumped the rest of the beer on my head, still foaming with shampoo.

I dried off, got dressed, and went into the kitchen. I fried my last four strips of bacon, flattened a leftover stuffed potato, and then fried it in the bacon grease. Three eggs over easy, toast, and coffee completed the ensemble. I hauled it, along with my favorite coffee mug, to the screen porch. The mug has a silhouette of Goofy, Mickey, and

Donald on it. Donald is last in line. Although the smallest of the three, he holds himself with dignity, purpose, and confidence. That's not easy—for duck or man.

Hadley III came in through the cat door and dropped a dead gecko at my feet. If she wanted to trade bacon for gecko, that cat was out of luck. I went back to the kitchen and retrieved a piece of two-day-old trout from the refrigerator. I placed it on a plate in front of her. She settled down with her front paws scrunched under her and ate patiently. For a carnivorous hunter who drew blood every day, she was a proper lady around food.

Morgan came through the screen door—he didn't drop a gecko at my feet. He glanced into the house and flopped on the cushioned chair next to me. He held a can of beer in his hand. He took a sip of it, placed the can on the table, and shoved it away with his foot. He was done. One taste in the morning kept him away from it until the evening. Alcohol had taken his father, and he treated it with great respect. That both our fathers had succumbed to booze and that he had learned from that, and I had not, was something we had never discussed.

He leaned over, scratched Hadley III behind her ears—which sent her rear up in the air—and said, "Want help?"

My house was littered with the splintered two-by-fours I'd torn down the previous day. I hadn't felt like cleaning up. Didn't much now, either.

"I'll get it later. You hungry?"

"Already ate."

I gave him two slices of bacon and said, "Got a minute?"

He took a bite of bacon and said, "You own me."

I told him everything. He listened patiently, while his eyes slipped smoothly between the bay and me whenever a boat passed by. Neither of us are capable of ignoring boats when they cross the water in front of our homes.

"Garrett and Kathleen?" he asked when I finished.

"Garrett's known. I just told Kathleen."

"Just?"

"Probably should have clued her in earlier."

Morgan nodded in agreement and said, "It's a big thing, and a long time, to keep to yourself."

"Don't make me regret sharing my bacon."

"Her name?"

"Her name was Brittany." I said it for the second time in thirty years.

"That *is* her name," Morgan said.

He often referred to his deceased father in the present tense and frequently told me about conversations he had with his father in his dreams. I'd noticed that Red also referred to Hawkins in both tenses.

He added, "You think Carlsberg has a client who requested the information?"

"That would be my guess."

I'd stayed up on the screen porch until one in the morning gathering information on Carlsberg and his firm. The single notebook I'd doodled notes on was still on the glass table, next to the Copacabana and monkey-palm ashtrays. The monkey-palm ashtray was new. I'd swiped it off the *Gail Force*, a yacht I'd been on while engaged in the undercover assignment for the FBI.

I reached over and set Tinker Bell. Let's see if I can make it to five before drinking. The beer at the outside shower didn't count. There's a little-known law in Florida: if you live on an island, you can drink booze before ten, and it doesn't count toward your daily quota. It's terrific for resale value.

Morgan said, "So the real abductor is still at large and either has friends in high places or occupies such a perch himself." He eyed a catamaran that was sliding past the end of my dock. On the stern was its name, *Lost Cat.*

"Appears that way," I said.

"And there must be some evidence that connects that person's DNA to your sister, since he's gone to considerable lengths, including murder, to close the case."

I tilted my head in agreement.

"But doesn't he create more risk by tainting evidence, and killing Hawkins, than he eliminates?"

"It's a gamble he's willing to take," I admitted, for the thought had occurred to me as well. "Once the police close my sister's case, the real killer will get the best shut-eye he's gotten in thirty years."

"Carlsberg's role?"

"He's likely a conduit to obtain my file. He can hide behind client privilege."

"What's the group he's involved with—Citizens for a Floral Florida?"

"They parcel out funds for parks and occasionally take a mild, politically correct stance against development. Other than that, their major functions are to hold fundraisers where politicians and corporate chieftains rub shoulders. Next pow-wow is Saturday night. Cabbage Key."

"What did that cost you?"

"Two K."

"Not going solo, are you?"

"The other K's accompanying me."

"You didn't need to do that," he said.

"Do what?"

"Give me two pieces of bacon to atone for not telling me earlier about Brittany."

"Is that what I did?"

"You've never spoken much about your past," he observed, "but I knew it would surface on its own."

"Up periscope."

"My father insists the past is like a rudder on a boat: it's always behind you, but it determines where you go."

"A reef took mine out years ago."

"He says the best sailors always keep a steady hand on the rudder."

It was an unusual tone from him, and I caught myself sitting a little straighter and feeling a tad embarrassed about my witless retorts. Morgan wasn't one to lecture, although he had every right to. I took a sip of lukewarm coffee and wondered if Donald Duck held a steady hand on his rudder. Perhaps that is a key to dignity, purpose, and confidence.

If so, what chance did I have?

11

"What is it we hope to achieve?" Kathleen asked as we waited for the Tierra Verde drawbridge to lower.

"Mingle. Shake the tree."

"He's already aware of you. You don't think something from that tree won't bonk you on the head?" She pulled down the visor and checked herself in the mirror. "You know, like those coconuts I'm always worried about?"

"It's a possibility, but if you're going to stir the waters, you're bound to make a wake and get a few coconuts on the head."

"Here's to a night of mingling." She ran a finger over her right cheek and then flipped up the visor. It snapped back into place. "And mixed metaphors."

We pulled up on the circular paved-brick drive of Carlsberg's Mediterranean-style gulf-front house. For a thousand dollars a plate, we were supporting the Floral Florida's Beaches for Kids program. The program provided funding for classroom education and field trips to educate children on Florida's beaches and the sea and land life that depended on those beaches. According to their website, People for a Floral Florida was a nonprofit 503c headquartered in Tallahassee, the muckraking capital of the Sunshine State.

I dropped the key fob into the valet's hands just as PC and Boyd whirled by on the street on their skateboards.

They would note the license of every car that arrived. I would forward that information to Binelli. I tried to make out what losing team PC was honoring, but he turned away from me. Morgan had my boat, *Impulse*, anchored off the mangroves two houses east of Carlsberg's place. If anybody came or went by water, I would know that as well.

Kathleen wore a yellow dress with a high front. The back of the dress was closed across her shoulders, and then it spread open midway down and dove deep into the gentle inward curve of her spine. I was dressed in linen slacks, a white silk shirt, a blue blazer, and leather shoes with no socks. People talk to you and treat you at the value you assign to yourself. I was in the mood to be valuable.

We walked under a trellised archway and entered through double wood doors that had a concrete lion on each side. A couple of tree trunks in suits stood inside the front doors. One of them checked my name off a list he had on a tablet, while the other one visually frisked Kathleen. We entered a foyer with white marble floors that shone like a skating rink. A curved staircase was to the left. Ahead of us, the rear doors were open. Outside, a three-man combo played under a sensuously curved coconut palm at the corner of an infinity pool.

Kathleen spotted her friend Sophia Escobar, who used to reside in the neighborhood. We weren't aware she was attending. Kathleen scuttled off to greet her. I scuttled off to greet the bar.

"Whiskey," I instructed the woman behind the bar.

"What kind?"

"Quickest one you can grab. Now. Time is fleeting."

"Hmm…a discerning drinker. I'm a fast draw; help me out."

"Jameson on the rocks. Make it a single rock."

"Like you?"

"Sadly, no woman will have me."

"Why is that? You hardly seem picky."

"Beats me. I cook, clean, and make passionate love in the moonlight, but I've been told that's old-fashioned."

She suppressed a smile. "Totally out of style. I can see why you're such a desperado."

She had an alto voice and just creamed "desperado." My knees nearly buckled. I'd never been on one of those dating sites, but if I were, I would request an alto. Each word—each syllable—punches above its weight, transforming simple sentences into melodic swells and paragraphs into operatic scores.

Alto's hair was pinned back, and she was dressed in black, as was all the help. A shirt a size too large failed to conceal an attractive figure. I couldn't place her age within ten years, but her eyes and posture indicated she wasn't attending her first dance. Her name tag read Suzette. I asked Suzette if she'd worked the house before.

"I have." A man shuffled his feet behind me. He could wait. "Mr. Carlsberg is quite the party man," she added. "Big parties, little parties, formal parties, casual parties."

"Big dog. Little dog," I said.

"Do you like my hat?" She cocked her head and tented her hands above her head.

"I do. What's the agenda?"

"It's the same mopey song," she sighed, lowering her hands. "The band's good to eleven thirty. Bar closes at midnight. Men with cigars congregate outside. Women who smell like money start the night erect and poised in their high heels. By closing time, their posture is teetering from the booze."

"You have a beautiful voice. Want to marry me and have six kids?"

"Golly, that's sweet of you. I think I'll pass, but thanks for the offer."

"Why the heavy muscle at the front door?"

She gave that a second and then came back with, "Rumor is, Mr. Carlsberg—he's a defense attorney—doesn't play well with other children."

"Does he hire someone different every time, or do those two hounds come with the property?"

"Why so curious?"

"Making conversation."

"You do that as well as cook, clean, and screw under the moon?"

"A man of many talents."

She gave me a coy smile and said, "Those two are always here. They didn't come with us. They used to check our food when we first started here. Still do, but not as thoroughly."

"Check your food?"

"Take a peek under the aluminum foil, rummage through the utensils and stuff. But they know me now and don't check my booze boxes. The booze is my little town, so I don't pay much attention to the rest of the city."

"Jake, look who I found," Kathleen said from behind me. I pivoted around and faced her and Sophia Escobar.

"Always a pleasure, Sophia." I gave her a peck on the cheek as I moved off to the side. The man behind me stepped brusquely up to the bar.

Sophia was a Colombian aristocrat: olive skin, high cheekbones, and hair that matched a shuttered coal shaft. She'd previously lived four homes north of Carlsberg before

I put her cheating husband in jail for human smuggling. Fortunately she didn't take it personally. At least she hasn't yet sent a *sicario* after me.

"Likewise, Jake," Sophia said with a warm smile that I never trusted. "But don't just stand there, gorgeous, buy us something."

"Soft or hard."

Sophia turned to Kathleen. "Matter to you, K?"

"Let's do old-fashioneds tonight," Kathleen said.

I waited my turn and then asked Suzette for two old-fashioneds. She placed them on the bar, caught my eye, and said in her deepest voice, "Old-fashioneds all around." I nearly fainted. She handed me her business card. "If you ever want anything catered, I'm *passionate* about my job."

I took her card and stashed it in the breast pocket of my sport coat, next to my fluttering heart.

The three of us drifted outside. Carlsberg was in command of a group of men who surrounded him like golden retrievers. I needed to meet him but didn't want to force it. I wasn't worried—my little harem would turn heads.

Kathleen, Sophia, and I took up positions by a white gate leading down to the docks, where a pair of WaveRunners rested high on a lift. They were snuggled under black covers that fit them like designer jeans. Next to them was a thirty-something-foot cruiser. Its name, *Final Voyage*, was scripted across the transom. I wasn't sure I'd head out to the gulf on a boat with that name.

After a few minutes, Carlsberg broke free and marched up to us. He went straight to Sophia, vaulted up on his toes, and planted a kiss on her cheek. He inquired how she was "getting along." Guess they knew each other.

Sophia made introductions. Kathleen greeted him with a sparkling smile that would shatter midnight. Every time she meets a fellow human being, a contagious smile floods her face. Not me. To the contrary, oftentimes, when I meet someone, the room darkens. I'm working on that, but I'm not on any timetable.

Carlsberg's handshake was soft and clammy. He was a man who saw no reason for the act. If Carlsberg was surprised that the person he'd requested a file on was now planted in front of him, he hid it well. But he had no reason to believe that I knew he'd received my file. Perhaps he received dozens of such requests a month and had simply passed it on without giving it a glance. Regardless, I lived across the bay, so if he'd done background check on me, my presence wouldn't be alarming.

Carlsberg said to me, "What a fortunate man you are. A stunning woman on each elbow."

"Too bad I'm not an octopus," I replied. "You and Sophia used to trick-or-treat together?"

"Pardon? Oh yes." He glanced up at Sophia, for Carlsberg was a short man whose surroundings swallowed him in, and the lady from Colombia towered over him. "We had many a good fundraiser together, didn't we, dear?"

"To the days," Sophia said and tipped her tumbler in a mock toast.

"The days," Carlsberg repeated, his eyes steady on Sophia, as if some secret were passing between them.

Carlsberg's neck was soft and curved up to his chin like an inverted hill. Despite hosting the affair, the knot on his tie was sloppy, as if frumpiness was a dedicated style. His diction, though, was precise, which made his speech an incongruity to his appearance. Such unassuming men hold supreme confidence. They inherently have no interest in anything other than their intellect and words and are quickly bored with the superficial prattling of other people. Their veins course with explicit goals that are achieved through the dullness of routine.

My veins course with Irish blood. I wanted to choke his blubbery white neck and demand who wanted to see my file. That card was always on the table, but once played, it took all the other cards off. Nor could its success be guaranteed. He might have more hired guns than the two at the door. I didn't need additional legal trouble.

In lieu of my barbaric desire, I opted for a civilized, "Are you deeply involved with People for a Floral Florida?"

"They're a fine organization," Carlsberg said, his voice dulled with disinterest.

"Not a ringing endorsement."

"What is it you do, Mr. Travis?"

"I'm remodeling my house. And you, Bernie?"

"We're involved in a myriad of projects, as well as tax and legal work for a number of individuals and their companies. Do you live around here?" Despite his questions, he spoke as if his primary interest was the termination of the conversation.

"Cheap seats, across the bay. What companies are you involved in?"

"Privately held concerns. We prefer flying under the radar. Who's doing your remodeling?"

"My left and right hands."

He gave that a second. "Thank you for coming. We appreciate your support." He dismissed me, quickly assessing that he had no interest in my kind. He gave me a brief smile that was no more than a frown that had inadvertently flipped upside down.

89

"My pleasure," I said. "I have a soft spot for preserving Florida's beaches. My family used to vacation on Vanderbilt Beach."

"Oh?" The slightest hint of uneasiness crept into his eye.

I kept my eyes drilled to his and leaned into his space, just enough to register. "Thirty years ago. Do you know the area?"

"A little north of Naples, correct?"

"You don't need me to validate your knowledge. And you? Who do *you* know who has memories of Vanderbilt Beach?"

His eyes were cold. "I'm afraid I don't follow your questioning." He shifted his attention to Sophia. "Sophia, do come around more often. Kathleen, it was a pleasure meeting you."

He waddled off but didn't get more than a few steps away before being engulfed in another conversation.

Kathleen said, "That was a pretty good shake."

"We'll see what falls on my head," I said.

"Or what the wake washes in."

"Am I missing something?" Sophia interjected.

"No, my dear," Kathleen said and took her arm. "Jake's been struggling with metaphors lately—it's something we've been working on. Let's go see what trouble we can get into, shall we?"

They strode off, arm in arm.

I circulated throughout various rooms, struck up conversations with the help, and never let hors d'oeuvres go unappreciated. After a while, Carlsberg gathered the crowd around the pool and thanked everyone for attending. As he started into a monotone speech about People for a Floral

Florida, I took the opportunity to slip up the spiral staircase. A minute later, after poking my head into three bedrooms, I unlocked a door that led to a study. It was the only door that had been locked. The slim key was still on the doorframe above the door, likely left there from when the house was constructed.

I entered the room and silently closed the door behind me. A panoramic wall of dark windows looked out on the Gulf of Mexico. Pictures and framed diplomas on the opposite wall came into focus. The wood file cabinets were locked, as was the desk, which was the size of my truck. Behind the desk, a bookshelf held photos and an assortment of memorabilia: a small brass cannon, an elaborate business-card holder with no cards in it, and a crudely carved wood monkey flipping me off. There were numerous pictures, all framed in black.

One picture that caught my eye was of several men, all smiles, standing on a rickety dock. A younger but still pudgy Carlsberg was in the front left. He was the only one in long pants. A wiry older man in the middle held numerous good-size snooks. The tip of a lighthouse was in the background. It looked like the one at Egmont Key, not far from my house, but I couldn't be sure.

I took a picture of the picture with my phone. I snapped a dozen more pictures and then quietly shut the door behind me, remembering to lock it.

I tolerated the rest of the evening. When the first guests started to peel out, I confiscated Kathleen from Sophia and announced that we were on the early shuttle.

We pulled out of Carlsberg's drive and crossed back over the drawbridge. As we crested the high bridge leaving the mainland, the pink hotel, built on the beach in the Roaring Twenties, was illuminated under the round night sky as if it were in a snow globe. Upon seeing it, Fitzgerald wrote that it was "surrendering its shape to the blinding brightness of the gulf." I don't think it surrenders anything, day or night.

"Learn anything?" Kathleen asked.

"No. You?" I'd instructed her to be inquisitive when meeting anyone who knew Carlsberg.

"He's divorced. No children. He entertains—which is another word for business—constantly. People come and go, Monday through Saturday, starting at ten in the morning. In the evening he prefers his women to arrive around seven and leave around ten. Thursdays and Saturdays only. They never spend the night. Brunettes over blondes. Once, he had two together but never again. Stays clear of drugs and caps out at two drinks a night, never before six or after nine. Lights out at ten. Oh, and he has an encyclopedic knowledge of college football."

"Busy girl."

"Most of that's from Sophia's shopping crowd. Ready for the best part?"

"You and Sophia and me—"

"In your little-boy dreams. After he left you—you know—when you confessed that Mr. Right Hand and Mr. Left Hand were doing your remodeling, and you shrunk in his eyes like you didn't even exist?"

"Little shitball."

I gunned through a yellow light onto Pass-a-Grille Way. It was late, and Andy's Ice Cream Parlor, on the ground floor of the hotel, was closed. Tucked deep in its freezers was black cherry vanilla ice cream. Sleep well, my love. Sleep well.

"A venerable grease pit," she said in agreement. "But our little grease pit took out his phone and made a call no more than five minutes after he broke away from you."

"Extra pepperoni?"

"How much do you love me?"

"Tell me you overheard the conversation."

"I did."

"And?"

"I could barely understand a single word."

"Where are we going with this?" I asked her as my truck dipped sharply on the uneven pavement.

"Sophia, dear. Do you know she went to private schools in Colombia?"

"No, but I assumed."

"Carlsberg said, 'He's here, and he knows,' and then he hung up."

I nodded as I slowed down for another bump. The road, like my house, was torn to shreds. The pavement, in parts, had sunk three feet over the decades. The road, sidewalk, and a hundred ancient Washington palms were all being replaced. The project was scheduled to take five hundred years. They were behind schedule.

"How does this come back to Sophia?" I said.

"I only studied Russian for two years. Sophia is fluent."

"He spoke in Russian?" I doubted many of Carlsberg's clients spoke the language.

"He did."

"And Sophia knows the language?"

"She was required to learn English and an elective. She chose Russian. She claims it's the best language to make love in."

"Listen, angel, that's what I was getting at earlier."

Kathleen leaned over to me. Her hot, liquored breath melted the right side of my face. *"So mnoy lyubov'yu,"* she whispered in a bedroom voice, her tongue flicking my ear.

"Does that mean what I think it means?"

"Da."

"You know—I speak a little Russian myself."

"Do you?" she said, pulling back with mock surprise. "Let's hear it."

"Yabba dabba doo."

"That's cartoon, silly."

"So you think, baby. So you think."

12

"It is the Egmont Key Lighthouse," Morgan declared. He sat cross-legged on the ten-by-ten deck at the end of his dock, conducting his morning meditations. He was shirtless, and his hair was pulled back. The moon talisman hung around his neck. I rarely interrupt his solitary time, but there I was. Again.

"You sure?" I'd given him my phone with the photo I'd snapped last night in Carlsberg's study.

He shadowed the phone with one hand. The early-morning sun twinkled through a thin yellow cloud. A steady southeast blow created a jagged stucco surface on the bay, and white caps reflected the sun like tinsel.

"No doubt," he said. "Judging by the angle, this was taken at the end of Cabbage Key, across the road from the gulf. Great piece of land—still totally wild. I've often wondered why it's not developed, although it's perfectly fine as it is." He handed my phone back. "Know anyone in the picture?"

"Pudgy pants is Carlsberg, the man who hosted last night's gala. I'm going to head down there. See if anyone knows him."

Morgan closed his eyes. He let his breath out slowly and straightened his back. A dolphin blew off to our starboard side, followed by two more. He paid no attention.

The sun broke free of the cloud just as the breeze died. As I walked down the dock, the swelling ball of heat pressed on my back like a hot iron. It didn't escape me that the guru in my life was not a mythical figure at the end of my dock but a real person one dock over.

AT THE END OF Cabbage Key, three craftsman-style homes were spaced out on the non-gulf side. They looked original—likely put up in the forties or fifties—and backed up to a pond that had no access to larger water. The last house was a good two hundred yards from its nearest neighbor. The gulf side was fenced with tangled mangroves and was undevelopable. I started with the house at the end of the road. According to the research I'd done, the structure occupied several acres. It was secluded from the other houses not only by distance, but because the street curved into a dead end. I parked my truck on the street where the road gave way to sand.

I walked over to a flatboat that was shrouded by mangrove branches and tied to a dilapidated dock. The boat was clean despite being docked under the mangroves. Someone used it regularly. The Egmont Key Lighthouse was visible above the mangroves.

I crossed back across the street to the house. It had white siding with dormer windows. A wide-planked covered porch wrapped around the front as well as the north side and appeared to continue across the back. The inside of the house was likely half the footprint of the outside. Two palm trees, thin like wands, each hugged a front corner, their fronds clattering in the wind. The ground was seashells and tufts of grass.

A series of muffled blasts thumped the air. I hit the ground. I started to get up, and another burst sent me back to the crushed seashells. A squadron of screeching gulls flew overhead, seeking refuge in the airspace above the Gulf of Mexico.

"Sons of bitches and mother of whores!" An angry but weak voice floated from the rear of the property.

I hugged the circumference of the house until I reached the back northeast corner. The backyard was flat Florida scrubland that fronted the stagnant pond. A dozen or so palms arched over the still water from its muddy edge. A man not much wider than those palms, and bent in a similar manner, stood at the end of a dock. His hands, at ten and two, were on an antiaircraft gun mounted on the dock.

Another smattering of gulls attempted to land on the far side of the pond. He spun the gun around and let a few rounds rip, tracking the birds as they scattered over the house.

"Come over here, son," he commanded as if he were expecting me. "I'm gonna hit the head—stomach's been bothering me all morning. Remember to give them a little lead—shoot where they're going, not where they're at."

He scurried off the dock and into his house. The screened door bounced a few times behind him.

The dock was reinforced with six-by-six posts driven into the muck. The gray gun—complete with its armor plate, should the birds decide to mount a counterattack— was bolted to two three-quarter-inch pieces of plywood. I didn't know much about antiaircraft guns, but I put this one as a relic of the sixties, maybe before. Its barrel was muzzled with a homemade silencer.

He came up beside me a few minutes later.

"Good Lord, I feel better," he said.

His button-down shirt was faded, and his ripped cargo shorts needed a box of Tide, but he was clean-shaven. His thin gray hair was neatly combed over his spotted head. His blue eyes sparkled. He wore a pair of blue-green Pegasus running shoes with low-cut white socks. A wide-brimmed hat shielded his face from the sun. The hat was old, the shoes were new.

"What year is your pistol?" I asked.

"It's a '53 ninety-millimeter," he replied. He leaned over and opened a dock box. "Last of its kind. After this, they went to guided missiles." He glanced up to me and flashed a sly smile. "That would hardly be fair to the birds, now, would it?" He pulled a string of ammunition from the box, considered it, and placed it back. "You don't look like any of those city guys they sent out here before. You some new neighbor here to file a complaint?"

"No, sir. I would never walk uninvited onto a man's property and complain about his vintage ninety-millimeter antiaircraft gun."

He nodded as if I'd passed some test. "Know much about them?"

"Got us through the Second World War. Dropped planes and stopped tanks."

"And in retirement, an excellent antibird gun," he informed me triumphantly. "I'll be honest, though: some Russian MiG gets lost, or a misguided Ivan finds my land—that'll be a day I'll remember. Yes, sir. Me and Sally-Mae," he said, patting the gun, "would have us a party. She knows she was built for more than gulls."

"Jake Travis." I stuck out my hand.

"Walter MacDonald." He pumped my hand. "But everyone calls me Mac. The last guy who called me Walter, I killed him. Oh," he waved his hand, "it had nothing to do with him calling me that, but it's a good story and a true one."

"Pleasure, Mac."

"What can I do for you, Jake?"

"Tell me everything you know about Bernard Carlsberg."

He paused, and his eyes narrowed. "You didn't come here to kill me, did you? 'Cause if you did, I'd rather know right now."

"No, sir—"

"Get it over with, know what I mean?"

"I'm here on my—"

"Single one to the head, Jake, would do just fine."

"—own accord. Just—"

"I knew this day was coming."

"—seeking information."

He processed that and added, "Where did you say you were from?"

"Didn't. Only bridge off of Pass-a-Grille."

"Mud Island, right? That's what they called it before that developer christened it 'Vineyard by the Sea.' Put a sculpture of his dog on the bridge. Can't think of his name, though—the dog, not the developer."

"You've been here for a while."

"For a while?" He gave me a dismissive shake of his head as if he couldn't explain, nor would I comprehend any answer he might proffer. "Yeah, I got roots. I came in—Major Lee—that's the name of that dog. My mind just pops around by itself nowadays. Remember—you might be too young—those popcorn machines that had a glass bowl on top and you could watch the popcorn pop? Older I get, that describes my mind. Just popping and pinging all over the place."

"Can't say I remember them," I said, surveying the land. "Nice piece of property. Yours?"

"Bought it in the fall of '62. Day after James Meredith was escorted onto the campus of Ole Miss. Own all you can see, including the two houses you drove by on your way in. I rent them out. One next to me, though, is empty now. I'm particular about whose money I take. You did say Bernie Carlsberg, right? Lives up the trail from me?"

I nodded.

"You law, Jake?"

"No."

He rubbed his chin. "Why does a man from Mud Island have questions about Bernard Carlsberg?"

"My sister was abducted and murdered thirty years ago. I think someone's trying to bury the case. That person may be using Carlsberg to gather information."

He held my eyes just for a second and then said, "I'm sorry about your sister."

He reached into the dock box and took out an oiled towel. He rubbed down the gun, taking the edge of the towel into the crevices of the firing mechanism. He rubbed it more than I imagined was necessary. He dropped the rag back into the box.

He stared into the box and said, "I knew sooner or later that son of a bitch would cross paths with the wrong man." He shut the lid and latched it. He stood and said, "You look like a fine wrong man. Might I suggest some beers?"

"You know him? Carlsberg?"

"I do."

"After you, Mac."

As we stepped onto his back porch, he turned to me and said, "How'd you find me?"

"I tripped upon a picture in Carlsberg's study. Buddy of mine who knows these waters recognized the Egmont Key Lighthouse in the background."

That seemed to satisfy him. He continued into his house, where he went straight to an old refrigerator with a pull-down handle. I wandered into the living area. It was an authentic Florida conch home with buckled plank floors, a tongue-and-groove ceiling, and planked walls. I wondered if planked walls would work in my pad. The sparse furniture was clean, as was the floor. A bookcase dominated one wall, its sagging and weary shelves groaning under the weight of reams of books. A staircase to my left led up to a loft. I gazed up. She gazed down at me from behind a thin rail. I took a second to make sure I saw what I thought I saw.

She was a life-size cardboard cutout of a young woman. She wore tight bell-bottomed jeans and nothing else. Her breasts peered over the edge of the rail, her chestnut nipples round and dark. Her brunette hair was thick and curled at the end where it rested on her shoulders. Her skin was neither black nor white, her lips were rouge, and her eyes dark blue with eye shadow. Her expressionless face conveyed a serene boredom with everything below, as if she'd achieved a Zen state and accepted that everything she'd ever known was not worth knowing.

Mac handed me a bottle of Michelob. That back of his turtle-skinned hand was mapped with veins.

"What's your friend's name?" I asked him.

"Lady." He glanced up to her and raised his bottle in a solemn toast as if something invisible passed between them. "But that's only because I got her in '75—that's when that song came out. You know who did that?"

"'Lady'?"

"Yeah."

"Styx."

"*That's* it. Couldn't remember that the other day. That kernel just wouldn't pop. With an X, right? Her name was supposed to be temporary." He shrugged. "Truth is, Jake, I don't really know who she is. Hefner gave her to me. We used to represent him back then."

He took a seat in a recliner. A side table next to his chair was littered with books and a folded edition of the previous Sunday's *New York Times*. The crossword puzzle was off to the side. It appeared he was only missing a few words. I sat across from him on a leather couch that enveloped me like a hungry lover. Lady loomed over us.

"How do you know Carlsberg?" I asked him.

"I founded that firm he runs. His daddy and I. After the war."

"Yet when I told you I was here to learn about Bernard Carlsberg, you reflexively asked me if I was here to kill you."

"That's because of Bernard's daddy."

"I don't follow."

He took a draw from his beer and, like Lady, looked bored with it all. "Jonathan Carlsberg was the last person to call me Walter."

"And the barrel of your Colt .45 the last thing he saw?"

"Luger P.08. My brother brought it home from Aachen—krauts didn't give that place up easy. November, '44—know much about it?"

"October, I believe. It was the first city on German soil captured by the Allies."

"October—that's right. Nasty little skirmish. He went on to Hürtgen. Said it was even worse. You never want to fight people in their own country."

"He survived?"

"Spenser? Oh, he had no problems with war, but peace tripped him up pretty bad."

"Carlsberg?" I said to put the conversation back on track.

He took a pull from his beer. "Jonathan Carlsberg was a swindler and a cheat. He deserved that bullet as much as any man could."

"His son, Bernie, doesn't hold it against you?"

"Hold it against me? It accelerated his rise up the firm's letterhead. Bernard Carlsberg is the only thing in this world colder than dry ice. Can I get you another?"

"Do you insist?"

"I do."

He grabbed two more beers from the refrigerator. He handed me one and then moseyed over to the shelves. He pulled out a book and held it up. It was William Manchester's war memoir, *Goodbye Darkness*.

"You ever read this?" he asked me.

"I have. A memoir that's part fiction."

He paused, as if considering my affirmative answer.

"All memory is part fiction, Jake," he reprimanded me, as if I'd disappointed him in some manner. I repositioned myself in the couch like a chastened student. He raised the book. "This copy is signed. That part where Manchester pees in his pants after he kills the Jap? There's nothing truer in this world than that—fiction or not. God pity the man who can make that statement. That was me, in the war. Kill and piss. But when I put Jonathan Carlsberg in the ground? I couldn't care less."

"You in the army?"

"Navy man," he announced proudly. "How old do you think I am?" He placed the book back.

"Older than I think."

"Ninety-two," he announced with pride. "We bombarded Iwo, Peleliu, and Okinawa. I was a medic, and we'd collect bodies off the water. Had to battle the birds for them. Ever see a bird go after a man's eyes, and the man is still alive but too weak to do anything—just bobbing there in the water or lying in the sand, the birds pecking away, taking his eyeball out piece by piece?"

He raised his bottle up to the ceiling and took a long draw. He wiped his mouth with the back of his hand.

"Been killing them ever since, although I've stepped up the pace this past year. But enough about me. Why do you want to know about Jonathan Carlsberg's inbred son?"

I told him everything. Strange. I'd held it in for so long and then went blabbering my sad tale to anyone with a set of ears.

When I finished, he asked, "And you think someone told Bernie to get your file?"

"I do. A Russian. Or someone who speaks Russian."

"State Department?"

"That's correct."

He considered that and then said, "You never asked me why I killed my partner."

I took a sip of beer.

"He was a snake," Mac said. "Would represent anyone for anything."

"That's not why you killed him."

"No, son, it's not. There is only one reason to take another's life. I killed him because he was about to shoot me. I was the faster draw. He said, 'Walter, I hate to end it like this.' He went for his gun, but mine was already in my hand behind my back."

"You were both packing? What did you do, anticipate a disagreement over vacation days?"

"No," he replied as if he'd taken my remark seriously. "We were starting to represent some bad people. I'm talking about people who killed to get what they wanted. I didn't want anything to do with them. I'd also heard he'd gotten wind of my dissent and had been instructed by his clients to settle the issue, once and for all. I don't seek confrontation, but I answer the door when it knocks.

"We were both bright enough to pick our clients, but like a moth to a flame, he was drawn to the insidious side of the human soul. Of course, that side pays four times as much as anything else. I wanted to turn our clients over to the law; he wanted to take their money."

"And his son?"

"That apple never even fell from the tree. This was a little over thirty years ago—a month after the *Challenger* blew up. You know the old joke, right? What's NASA stand for? Need Another Seven Astronauts." He shook his head. "Little Bernie told me that one. He was only a few years out of college, but age was never a deterrent to his level of expectation. Cocksucker took over. You met him, right? Cold. The intellect's there, but at the cost of everything else. Little pudger and I made our peace. I left the firm and promised not to sing. He promised not to bring charges. But he's not who you're looking for."

I leaned forward, my elbows on my knees. "Who am I looking for?"

"Apparently a client who speaks Russian."

"Know of any?"

He scratched his chin. "I did hear that one of the firm's longtime clients used some Russian oil money to patch the bleeding during the financial crisis a few years back."

"How can I access the list?"

"What list is that, Jake?"

I stood in frustration and walked toward the stairs to the loft. While the rest of the house was well tended, the steps were coated with dust, as if no one had bothered to visit Lady in years. I spun around to Mac. His eyes were waiting for me.

"The list of Carlsberg's clients," I said, unexpectedly struggling to control my voice. "Your old firm. Do you have a way of accessing that information?"

"No."

"Names in your head?"

"It was a long time ago."

"Know anyone there who can sneak it out? I'll pay."

"No, no, no, don't do that." He waggled his finger at me. "That would just tick them off, get us both killed."

I blew out my breath. Garrett and I could hit the house when Carlsberg was away. Take his computer and hope we could break into it. It was a low-probability plan, but I didn't see an alternative. I glanced up at Lady. She was a knockout, centerfold cardboard lady.

"You have anything that haunts you, Jake?" Mac said from behind me.

I turned. "I killed a Catholic cardinal by accident. That's good for a few nights a week."

Good God, man—your life's become a confessional booth.

Mac nodded in sincere appreciation. "That's a good one, all right, although I think a dead priest is a step in the right direction. The older I get, the less control I've got over my memories. But my dreams are always about those damn birds. Every night they come and peck out the eyes of living men. Hell, I can't wait to get up and get to work—on the gun, I mean. I don't remember what I had for dinner last night, but those birds never left me."

"What else can you tell me about Carlsberg's current practice?"

"You know I didn't really mean that about the priest."

"I know."

He took another sip of his beer. "I don't blame you for not having much interest in the musings of an old man. I barely keep my own interest." He chuckled at his comment and stood. He padded over to me. His shoes were unnaturally large and sturdy for his diminutive and frail figure. "Your sister went AWOL thirty years ago, right?"

I nodded, getting a glimpse of where he was headed.

He continued. "We, the firm, don't have a lot of client turnover. We represent family businesses from one generation to the next."

"We?"

"I sold to Bernie after I plugged his daddy, but I kept twenty percent. He's offered me ludicrous amounts for it, but I refuse to sell, mostly to irritate him."

"But you don't know the particulars of Russian money being used to bail out one of the firm's clients?"

"Don't get testy on me. A lot of what the firm does is on a need-to-know basis. In most cases, you're better off not asking and not knowing. We worked with our own clients; the people you're asking about weren't mine. Give me a day. I'll write down what I know. Your man may or may not be on my list. I wouldn't be surprised either way."

"I'll make certain there are no repercussions."

He laughed and touched my shoulder. "I'm ninety-two, remember? That repercussion word has lost some of its oomph with me."

"Tomorrow morning?"

"Not before nine. I might be fishing."

I thanked him for the beers and headed for the front door.

"Say good-bye to Lady," he said.

Maybe Mac only had one paddle left in the water. I'd find out tomorrow if that was good enough to resurrect a client list from three decades past.

"It doesn't appear that you ever go up the stairs," I commented as I turned back to him. "The two of you not on speaking terms?"

He gave that a few beats and then said, "You know she's cardboard, don't you?"

I nodded. *Do you?*

"You're right—I don't go up there," he admitted. "You don't want reality to shatter your dearest dream."

"Your bird dreams?"

"No, Jake. That's the dream that sets me apart from other men—that haunts me—like you and your Catholic bird. I'm talking about the universal dream. The dream that every man takes to the grave with him."

"What might that be?"

"My wife's been gone over forty years. That's a long time—doesn't even seem like the same life."

His shoulders shrunk as his age manifested itself. He eyes gazed past me and settled on his books, as if in some manner they were responsible for a mystery he could never solve. As voluminous as his hefty books were, they were no match for the frail man in front of me.

"You still dream of her?" I asked.

His eyes found mine. "I do," he admitted. "No matter how old a man gets, no matter the good or bad he's seen or done, he always dreams of the girl his heart loved the most." He paused, as if his thoughts had exhausted him. "If you ever wondered what the end looks like, my new friend, now you know."

13

I am not yet forty, so I can't validate Mac's comment, but there are two things I know: art imitates life, and life is anticipation.

And there is no greater anticipation than the false dawn—the brightening of the sky before sunrise. It was ten minutes before the coned top of the sun peaked over the eastern horizon to see if we were still hanging on. I'd finished my death run and was anticipating the next segment of my rigidly structured mornings: water, three rounds with the punching bag until my arms were on the floor, more water, shower, coffee, breakfast, and beer—all in an attempt to cleanse my system of yesterday's abuse. Flush and reload. I was mortgaging my body—but I'd worry about that later.

I rounded the back corner of my house and spotted Colonel Janssen, my former commanding officer, sitting at the end of my dock.

The previous time I'd found him there, he confirmed that an assignment he dispatched me on had gone slightly askew. Instead of killing an assassin who was known to disguise himself as a Catholic cardinal in Kensington Gardens, I had plugged an actual cardinal. Although it was no fault of mine—the cardinal had used me to end his life— my act haunted me. The cardinal was a scratchy presence in my dreams, like a song that was long over but the needle wouldn't lift off the record. I'd come to believe that my role in his assisted suicide represented far more than the actual deed and that it said as much about me as it did him.

I was eager to get back to Mac's place. When I'd left him yesterday, I told him that I'd be there around nine. I didn't want to get my hopes up; I wasn't sure what to believe from the man. He'd said he'd been in the navy but then professed—when he'd held up Manchester's book—to know about killing a man with a gun. *Kill and piss.* Few navy men saw hand-to-hand combat. For all I knew, he was going to present me with a list of Looney Tunes characters and insist that Shropshire Slasher was my man.

I rinsed off under my outdoor shower, changed into shorts and a faded pink button-down silk shirt, poured myself a cup of coffee—not Mickey and the gang—and strolled to the end of the dock. A pod of dolphins to my left rolled lazily to the surface, one after another.

I took a seat comfortably away from Janssen on the opposite end of the bench. A red folder rested between us. Janssen, clean-shaven and immaculately groomed, was dressed in tan slacks, a blue shirt with a button-down collar, and loafers. A navy-blue blazer was draped over the back of the bench. He was inside the Beltway wherever he went. His skin was pale, and his ears protruded from the sides of his head just a tad too far. He had as much business sitting on the end of a dock in Florida as I did working in a skyscraper in Manhattan.

"I would have brought you a cup," I said, "but I missed the memo."

"Why are you suddenly interested in your deceased sister?" Janssen spoke in a medieval font, moving his lips awkwardly. His manner of speech made it nearly impossible to focus on his eyes, since his mouth demanded attention.

Saltwater Cowboy, a black center console with four outboards, roared by the end of the dock, scaring the bay like a surgeon's scalpel. I waited until the noise dissipated and then said, "Someone's trying to pin her abduction and murder on a man named Leonard Hawkins. He conveniently washed up less than a mile from here."

"Hawkins's DNA was found in your sister's evidence bag," Janssen said. That told me he'd been briefed on what had transpired. "Tell me about Bernard Carlsberg."

"The Pillsbury Doughboy?"

"Why were you there?"

"I've become a conservationist. If the sea really does rise two feet in the next hundred years—take a look around, Colonel—I'll be a Louisiana swamp."

His jaw tightened, and he gazed back out over the water. "Has that sandbar always been there?"

"It has. It's only visible at low tides."

The sandbar was east of the red channel marker. A dozen or so birds were milling around its edge, pecking at fish.

"And high tide?" Janssen asked. "When the shallow water can't be seen?"

"Many boats have spent the night there."

"Hawkins killed your sister," he said, turning to me. We had just completed the longest string of small talk we'd ever engaged in.

"Her body was never found. Are you telling me something new?"

"No. I—"

"Why are you here?"

He ignored my question and came back with a variation of his previous question. "Why were you at Carlsberg's?" He rolled up his sleeves. The sun was taking its first peek at us, and it was in an angry mood.

I took a sip of coffee. "I'd offer you breakfast, but I need to get going. Got a big remodeling project under way. Boss gets mad when I'm late."

He leaned in, elbows on knees, and drilled his eyes to mine. "I got a call from a friend."

"State Department?" I asked. He squinted at me. That was enough confirmation. "Let me guess. A friend of a friend."

"You want to tell the story, or me?"

"Give me the last page."

He gave that a moment, and I wondered what options he was considering. "Leave Carlsberg alone."

"Long trip for a short message."

"You hear what I said?"

"Something about you'd be happy to speak to the local women's group this Tuesday on the perils of beach—"

"Your goddamned attitude is—"

"All you're going to get until you come clean," I said. "Tell me the last thing you were hoping you wouldn't have to tell me, or I'm back to hanging drywall."

"Your sister's gone. You need to forget her."

"That was your freebie, Colonel. One more like that, and your ass is in the bay."

He nodded and gave me an uncharacteristic smirk, as if he understood the full implication of my comment. He was not a man to make unforced errors or speak needless words. I like to think I'm the same.

"I can't help you," he said as he stood. I did likewise. I didn't like the man being above me. "From what I see, Hawkins is your man. I don't know why you insist…" He bobbed his head and furrowed his eyes. "You visited him, didn't you? You and Garrett? Goddamn, boy. I should have seen that."

I took a drink from my mug.

Janssen said, "You don't buy that he's your man because you left him fighting for his last breath, and he never spilled. Now you're pressing Carlsberg because you found out your file's been passed to him. Don't interrupt me. I'm guessing your buddy Applegate had a hand in that." He stepped into me. "For the record, I ever prove that, his career's in the shitter. Forget Alaska; he'll be reassigned to the slums of São Paulo. You think of that next time you milk him for information. Look at me."

I'd been gazing out toward the drawbridge, where a large cruiser was idling, waiting for the bridge to raise. I looked at him, as instructed, and was immediately ticked at myself for doing so.

He said, "You want the ending?"

"All ears."

"I could be a factor of five from the source, so we won't get anywhere beating that rock. But the message was clear. Undiluted. I'm to take you off. Dismiss you from payroll. Do whatever I can to halt your revengeful solo quest into your past. Convince you that your sister's killer is dead."

"You didn't catch a plane for that."

"No. But I did for this: don't let it come back to me. I didn't recruit you to roll over, and you're no good to me if you've become that type of person. Someone's making calls, summoning in favors. That indicates that whoever abducted and killed your sister is not only still at large but is a well-connected operator, not some stiff doing life in a zebra outfit. This is an act of someone who's built himself a life and has the means to protect it."

I nodded in agreement and said, "You're on your own today, aren't you?"

He stepped even closer. His breath smelled like mint. His left eyelid drooped over the corner of his eye.

"I hope you find who murdered your sister," he said, "and pour battery acid down his throat. But it *never* comes back to me. Understand? As of now, you believe and accept that Hawkins killed your sister. You are not in pursuit of anyone. That's what I'll report."

I saw the man in a new light and was grateful for his visit. But that didn't necessitate, however, that I show my appreciation. "You're here so you can say you convinced me that Hawkins is my man," I said. He nodded and backed off, as if his task was complete, and he'd successfully conveyed the purpose of the meeting. "Who *is* my man?" I might as well throw it out there. No harm in asking.

"I don't—"

"Who?" I said forcibly. I stepped in to him, giving him a taste of his own tactic.

"I do not know," he reiterated, without yielding an inch. He used every muscle in his mouth to form each word, as if shorter words required greater mechanical effort.

I thought of asking him if he had any information on Mac—Walter MacDonald—but went in another direction. "Carlsberg's client list?" I picked up the red folder on the bench. "You brought it because you know I'd choke every last molecule of oxygen from him."

"That was here when I arrived."

"Your conscience clear now?"

"Crystal. It's yours that's always been a Louisiana swamp."

"Appreciate the insight," I said.

"Careful, you're in shallow water in this one."

"What did you do, grow a heart?"

"Garrett will only work with you."

14

I did a quick search on the list Janssen had provided me. It was a smorgasbord of business owners, hedge-fund operators, and lobbyists. There was nothing overtly criminal about any of them. The list was likely a red herring, intentionally given to me to set me off on the wrong path. Maybe that was the reason for the red envelope. Janssen had likely left it to cover his tail and knew I wouldn't take it seriously.

Mac wasn't home when I pulled up in my truck at 8:58 a.m. The flatboat at his dock was gone. His front door was unlocked. I entered and helped myself to a beer. I'd forgotten to set Tinker Bell; therefore, I wasn't officially cheating on her. Besides, I was invoking the aforementioned Island Early-Morning Drinking law.

I raised my bottle to Lady. "'When you're with me, I'm smiling,'" I said. She was a handsome woman. A man could love a woman like her, as long as he didn't get too close. The thought struck me as more universal than I intended. I erased it with another swallow of beer.

I wandered outside to Sally-Mae. The barrel was sun hot but not action hot. Mac hadn't yet taken his revenge on the birds. A white egret landed serenely on the far side of the pond. It seemed an unlikely creature to warrant such wrath. The air was still and quiet. It had a calming effect on me, like a witch's tranquility potion.

"You have breakfast?" Mac called from the back porch. He held a pair of sea trout in his hand. He'd surprised me. People don't usually sneak up on me. That was a tribute to the character of his property.

"No," I said as I joined him. "At least nothing like you're proposing."

We went inside. He filleted the fish, while I oiled a veteran iron skillet. I scrounged around in his cupboards and pulled out a bag of flour, cornmeal, salt, and pepper. I dumped some flour in a flat pan and mixed in the salt and pepper.

"Would you like me to fry it in the cornmeal?" I asked him.

"No. I keep that mainly for cush-cush. Let's keep it simple. Dice up that tomato," he instructed me. "I like it sautéed on the fish."

I found a mezzaluna knife with worn wood handles and let the knife work its magic, dicing the tomato into machine-precision cubes.

"You know your way around the kitchen," he observed.

"I do."

"I admire that. No woman?"

"Best one in the world."

"And she lets you do the cooking? That was the arrangement we had. 'Course, it's more common now. That wasn't the case fifty years ago."

He poured a little whole milk over the fillets and handed them to me. I patted them with the flour and lay them in the skillet, which greeted its prey with a spitting hiss. Bits of grease flew out and tingled my arm. I sprinkled the tomato cubes around the sides of the fish.

"Tell me about your girl," I said out of conversational obligation, but then I realized my question stemmed from genuine interest. I'd been anxious to compare my list with his and see who surfaced. Thirty years. It could wait for a breakfast of fresh trout with a ninety-two-year-old man.

He acted as if he were considering my request and then said, "She was my world." He opened the refrigerator. "You want another?"

"I'm fine."

"I like what you did."

"What's that?"

"Walk in and help yourself to a beer. I don't have any friends left who would do that."

"I didn't mean to take advantage of your hospitality."

"You didn't. People who walk right in are the best. You can't teach folks to do that. Good friends remain a mystery to me—you can't go fishing for them. It either clicks or it doesn't."

"Your girl," I said.

He cracked open a beer for himself. "I saw her from across a crowded room—you know, like that song goes? I didn't run to her side, but I certainly skedaddled. It wasn't just her looks, it was...well, you should have seen her." He took a drink. "You going to flip those? That skillet runs hotter than Sally-Mae does after firing off nine yards."

I flipped the fillets and stirred the tomatoes, while he opened a cupboard and carefully took out two plates. He seemed slower and more frail than yesterday, but I dismissed it. I hadn't known him long enough to gauge what a normal day was for him.

"It was the way she smiled at everyone," he continued. "The way she talked and looked at other people. We married a year later. She died the day before our twenty-third anniversary. Leukemia. She was trying to finish All Creatures Great and Small. Never made it. She was worried about Tristan. Wasn't sure he was cut out to be a country vet."

"I'm sorry for your loss."

"She told me to move on with my life. But you only love once and just pretend to do it again. Besides, I don't even know if they make them like that anymore."

"They do," I said as I plated the fish.

"You know this?"

I handed him his breakfast and said, "'Once you have found her, never let her go.'"

"Don't you forget that. Ask her to marry you?"

"Not yet."

"You need to move that up your priority list. A man should never be afraid of his next step, or he will surely falter."

I felt an unidentified swell of emotion. I couldn't remember the last time I'd been the recipient of a fatherly comment. I had no place to file it. We took the fish to his back porch. He nodded at the red folder that I'd left on the table when we'd gone in the house.

"What have you got there, Jake?"

"Supposedly a list of Carlsberg's clients."

"Working both ends, I see."

"Casting far and wide."

"Where'd you get it? A disgruntled employee?"

"No one you would know."

"What did you say you do again?"

"I didn't."

"No, you didn't. You mind?"

"Go ahead."

He opened it and took a bite of his fish.

"Nothing beats trout straight out of the water," he said. "You got connections, I'll give you that."

He closed the folder and tossed it onto the crushed seashell ground. A few loose sheets of paper partially slid out.

"You're not impressed," I said as a fact, not a question.

"On the contrary." He took another bite of the trout. "You cooked it just right."

I pulled out a vacant chair and propped my feet on it. "Someone giving me the cream off the top and nothing else?"

"You know what I instituted at that firm when I ran it?" His question was rhetorical, so I let it go. "Keep it where no one else can find it." He pointed at his head. "The ol' noodle. That way, when someone comes sniffing around, they got nothing. You know that book I showed you yesterday?"

"Manchester's?"

"Could you go get that? This heat is already getting to me. I don't know how many early-morning fishing trips I've got left, at least in the summertime."

I rose and returned with the book. He opened it, pulled out a single page that had been torn from a notepad, and handed it to me.

"If Carlsberg is protecting someone," he said, "he's likely one of these men."

It wasn't much. Five meaningless names were freshly scrawled on yellowed hotel stationery from the Park House Hotel, Galway, Ireland.

"You needed time to do this?" I said. He'd told me during the conclusion of our first meeting to "give me a day." It didn't look like a day's work.

"Naw," he said with a knowing smile. "I was shoveling puppy shit. What I needed was time to make sure you are who you say you are."

"Who am I? I'd like to know."

"I'm not sure. That makes two of us. But your story, about your sister, checked out."

I thought he was going to say something else, but he didn't. I held up the paper. "What am I looking at?"

"Those names you brought that I tossed on the ground? Those are legitimate relationships. I'm sure the firm's moved on to that, if for no other reason then to cover the scum." He nodded at the sheet in my hand. "These names pay the bills, and some of those bills got blood on them."

"How long has it been since you were active in your own firm?"

"Don't go second-guessing me," Mac admonished me. "That has nothing to do with it. Those are family names. We represent them into the grave and beyond. By then we have our claws in the next generation, not to mention the businesses. Of course," he said with a chuckle, "they have their claws in us as well. That's the way those relationships survive from one generation to the next. Each party understands MAD: mutually assured destruction. We can bring them down, and they can force us to shutter our shop. I foresaw that decades ago, when Jonathan and I had our little spat."

I wasn't sure how factual his claim was but decided not to contest his statement. "Where do I start?" I said, studying the sheet.

"Start, middle, and end with Russell Alexander Brackett—although the first one's been in the ground the last four decades. Don't worry, though; there's two more of them. The family never wasted time debating names. All the Bracketts were Russell Alexander Brackett, with a roman numeral tagged on the end."

I waited for an explanation, but, instead, Mac announced that he had to "hit the head." He was fond of that phrase. He shuffled off in his bright Nikes and nearly lost his footing at the door stoop. A great blue heron glided in on the far side of the pond. It quickly became motionless, waiting for any movement in the water to seize its attention. I couldn't hunt like that—frozen and waiting for someone to make a mistake.

"Sorry," he said as he shambled back to me a few minutes later. "My body's not what it was even a few months ago. A man can tell. I'm getting to that point where I only need my weather app to show the next six hours."

"Done with green bananas?"

"George Burns was a funny man."

"You have any family?" After I asked, I remembered that he'd told me the other day that he had no one to leave the property to.

"My wife and I never had any children; it wasn't to be. But life was plenty full—we were close to my family. I had nine siblings, including two sisters named Mary, a brother we called Nancy, and a French poodle that embarrassed my mother to death by barking only at black people. But I'm the last of the Mohicans. Got a battalion of nieces and nephews—they would just subdivide and sell. Been after me for years to do that. My heart would shatter in my grave if that were to happen."

"What—"

"Funny thing is, Pierre was black himself."

"Pierre?"

"The poodle."

"What would make you happy?" I said, but I wished I'd asked him his wife's name.

"I always thought this would be a great place for the indigent: the homeless souls who need to get their bearings and catch a quiet breath before tackling America. My father was a stowaway on an American freighter out of Belfast. My wife's father jumped out of the back of an army truck during the Bolshevik revolution when they were rounding up dissenters and Jews. To this day, I got a soft spot for those seeking refuge from distant shores. Unless you're a Native American, you're a descendent of immigrants."

I caught myself gazing out over the reflective water. I turned my attention to him. His contemplative gaze was waiting for me.

"Brackett," I said and then was upset that I didn't comment on his statement about his family.

He paused a few beats and then said, "Russell Brackett Senior. Like I said, he stepped off the carousel a long time ago. He was an outstanding individual. Smart and gracious—he was a man who won you over with his courteous manners and impeccable words. He started an oil company, Brackett Oil, and, by any measure, did an admirable job of expanding while mitigating his risk.

"He built a ranch in central Florida. Used to be a hunting lodge, but he later turned it into a family retreat. Middle of godforsaken nowhere. You go to the end of a road—there's some watering hole there, but its name escapes me—then take a right where an old barn used to be. It's another twenty-two miles past that. Nothing but dirt and tread marks, but you run smack into it. The family still owns it, I believe."

"And his son?" I'd finished my beer and wanted another one.

"That was the direction on an invitation: 'Go twenty-two miles after the road ends.' I'll never forget that. His son, Russell the Second, was born two quarts down. He destroyed men with a sneer on his face. Killed careers, ruined marriages, reneged on promises for a thrill and a buck. It all came too easy for him. But Lady Luck smiled on the family fortune. His instincts were flawless. He took the oil money and bought up the west coast of Florida."

"He's my guy?"

"Nope, gone too. His liver couldn't take the pounding and checked him out about—my gracious God, it's been over twenty years. He died the same day the 99 year lease expired and the British handed the keys of Hong Kong over to the Chinese. Russell Brackett the third runs it now. Took over as a young man and never looked back. Goes by his middle name, Alex—less confusion that way.

"They say the first generation builds the business, the second runs it, and the third spends it. That wasn't the case with the Bracketts. They got the number two and three slots reversed. Just because his father checked out early didn't mean number three—Alex—would grow up fast, but he did. He married some woman from Russia. I heard she was an American who studied over there."

"He likely knows Russian."

"Not as uncommon as you think," he observed, his eyes steady on mine.

I thought of Sophia and ceded him the point. "When the third Brackett ascended the throne," I said, "you'd been out of the firm for about ten years."

"I own twenty percent, remember? They fear my block. I could threaten to sell to their mortal enemy. They tell me what I want to know. Always make sure the coffee's hot when I go to board meetings. They've been harping on me to give them first right of refusal, but they blew that salient negotiation point long ago. A colossal mistake."

"How old is Alex?"

"Your sister disappeared thirty years ago?"

"About." The blue heron took flight. It wasn't the most patient example of its species.

"He's around fifty now. Give or take." Mac gave a slight shrug of his left shoulder, as if to dismiss the whole line of conversation. "I killed that man again last night. Did I tell you about him?"

"Kill and piss?"

"That's right. Sometimes I just forget what I've told people. He didn't have any eyes; the birds had already pecked them out. I told myself—in my dream—that I didn't really kill him. How can you kill a man with no eyes? Then I woke up, because I knew I was trying to talk myself into something that wasn't true. Pretty cruel you can't even do that in your dreams."

"How did you come to engage in hand-to-hand combat?" It had been bothering me since he'd first told his story.

"This was Korea. By then I was with the Naval Security Group. Code work, mostly. But on account of my medic background, I volunteered to go ashore when the Chinese emptied their bowels on us after MacArthur crossed the thirty-eighth parallel in October, '50. You know what bothers me?"

"No."

"When I got back to my ship? I was more ashamed about peeing in my pants than killing a man. I used to think I'd get over that, but now I know I own it to the grave. He would have killed me if I weren't the more decisive of us two, but that old saw dulls with age. Now all I do is wonder about his family and how they received the news."

"Do you feel that way about Jonathan Carlsberg?"

"No."

"Why not?"

"I don't know. Maybe because I knew the type of man I was killing. I've given up thinking about it. You're allowed to do that at my age."

I let a few seconds pass and then asked, "Who else on the list should I focus on?"

"Steinberger, Raguso, Plueddeman—I wouldn't waste my ammunition on them. Not until you exhaust the Brackett family. What do you think of this land?"

He'd caught me gazing over the pond and into the underbrush and wild palms, heavy with coconuts.

"I like it," I admitted. "I live on open water. This is..." I wasn't sure where to go with my thoughts or where they were leading me.

I looked at Mac and was surprised to see his eyes Velcroed to mine. He wiped the back of his hand over his forehead. He hadn't stopped sweating since he climbed out of his skiff.

"Let's go inside, old man," I said. "We'll turn on the AC. You're too hot."

I stood and helped him to his feet. But instead of taking a step, he steadied himself on my arm.

"The Bracketts?" he said.

"Yes."

"They don't pee in their pants."

"Inside."

I took him by his arm, and his thinness startled me. I couldn't imagine how he had the strength to reel in a feisty trout, let alone fire Sally-Mae. I closed the windows and cranked up the wall AC unit. Mac collapsed into his leather chair with deep creases that, like a flytrap, swallowed him in. The AC struggled to come to life and settled into a rhythmic thrumming in which every third strum came out as a prolonged wheeze. I went to close the back door.

"Leave it," Mac said. "I like some fresh air and natural light. I don't care about the bill."

I wrote down my cell number and Morgan's as well. I explained that Morgan was a good friend and told him that if either of us could do anything for him, not to hesitate to call.

"I don't need your charity," he replied with an unexpected bite. "But you can go to the top drawer over there— below where you got the salt and pepper earlier. That's it. Bring that to me, will you?"

I handed him his Luger P.08.

"Thank you. I like to keep her clean," he said and picked up an oiled rag on a coaster. He rubbed the barrel of the gun. "You never know when your dreams cross over."

"Why did you advise me not to waste my ammunition on anyone else on the list?"

"To save you time."

"You're not sending me on a vendetta against your old nemesis, are you?"

It had occurred to me that Mac might be using me for his own purposes. The manner in which he'd zeroed in on the Bracketts and summarily dismissed the other names suggested that he might be holding something back.

He gave me a steady gaze and twisted his thin lips into a smile. His teeth were in remarkably good shape. "I don't blame you for that line of thought, Jake. You don't have any particular reason to trust me. No. I'm not sending you on a suicide run." He gave me a devilish grin. "I am, though, sending you into the gates of hell."

"Pity hell."

"Yes." He narrowed his eyes. "Pity hell." He placed the oiled rag back on the coaster, taking care that it didn't touch the wood surface of the table. "I barely even remember being that cocky. You want to know, don't you, why I think the Bracketts might in some manner have knowledge of your sister's abduction?"

"It would help."

"A couple of connections might pique your interest. Recall that I told you one of the firm's clients tapped the Russians for a loan in '08? That was Alex—Russell the Third. His father had previously forged a relationship with a Russian family who had an oil-exploration and manufacturing company. As I recall, the family also had some sort of diplomatic status in the States."

"How far back does the relationship go?"

Mac squinted, as if doing so would help his memory. "I'm not sure, but I know it was before Gorbachev introduced perestroika to his comrades. In May of '85, Gorbachev gave a speech in Leningrad and admitted what the rest of the world already knew: Russia had been tolerating unacceptable living conditions for too long. Russell the Second entertained Russian clients at the Masters that year. I remember because Bernhard Langer won—he was the first German to do so. So there's your modern-day Russian connection that's got some deep roots. Maybe coincidental, maybe not."

"You said you had a couple of connections."

"I did. Recall, also, that I told you Russell the Second, with his brilliant business acumen, bought up the west coast of Florida. He constructed and purchased hotels. Put family members in charge."

"Any one in particular I would have interest in?"

"The Vanderbilt Reef Motel."

15

I left Mac cooling in an armchair after chastising him for letting himself overheat. I insisted he stay inside during the sun's high hours, although I wasn't foolish enough to believe he'd do anything other than what he pleased.

Instead of turning left onto Pinellas Bayway off 676, I swung right and onto 275 south. The police report from the time of my sister's disappearance didn't mention the Bracketts as owners of the Vanderbilt Reef Motel, nor had it ever occurred to me to research the property owners. I assumed they had cooperated with the investigation but, as business owners, petitioned the police to keep publicity to a minimum. They couldn't have been pleased when the Matilda moniker took flight.

I crested the Sunshine Skyway Bridge a few minutes later. Fishing boats skimmed the water below me, their wakes trailing like threads on an ironed blanket. I hit Garrett's secretary Mary Evelyn's number. Mary Evelyn was an ex-nun—an item I'd picked up only recently from Garrett. Her parents were missionaries who'd fled Cambodia shortly before the Khmer Rouge took power. She was aware that Garrett and I took assignments from Colonel Janssen and derided the notion that she might harbor any issues with the morality of our deeds.

She also put Google to shame.

I gave her the names on Mac's list and told her to start with Brackett. She signed off with a courteous, "Certainly, Mr. Travis." We had an ongoing battle in which I tried to get her to address me by my first name. The missionaries' daughter was a focused opponent.

Two hours later I pulled into the side parking lot of the Vanderbilt Reef Motel. It was the first time I'd been there since the day my sister disappeared. My previous forays into finding my sister's killer hadn't required a return trip...or so I told myself.

The area around it, once a muggy and mosquito-infested tract of land, now supported some of the priciest houses and condos on Florida's west coast. Russell Brackett II might have misjudged his liver's capacity to hold liquor, but he did not misjudge American's post–World War II infatuation with, and insatiable appetite for, the Gulf of Mexico, once mosquitoes were eradicated and central air conditioning became as common as lightbulbs. As I walked away from my truck, a surface cloud of steam, the aftermath of a morning shower, rose from the parking lot and swirled around my feet, like a tempestuous lover trying to pull me back to Middle Earth.

My memories of the motel were snapshots of happy images that served as a prelude to a tragic ending. Like an osprey's talons gripping my mind, the final scene came to dominate my childhood years.

Sit here. Don't move. When did you last see her? What did she say? No, you didn't do anything wrong. It's OK you didn't go to the room with her. Did she talk to anyone? Sit there a little longer. We'll tell you.

My parents had planted me in the lobby as the police questioned the hotel's guests. I'd sat in a red chair across from the ice cream freezer—the same freezer that my sister and I were allowed to extract one treat a day from. The taste of raspberry and vanilla ice cream on a stick covered with crunchy chocolate has never left me. It is the taste of long ago and of what I lost.

I remember this, too: the ice cream freezer didn't give a damn. It just stood there. I didn't understand that for a long time, and when I did, I wish I hadn't. Sometimes you're better off holding a question than trading it for an answer.

Except for the footprint of the land, the hotel was foreign to me. Deep pockets make good property managers, and the two-story hotel had done an admirable job of holding on to its 1960s' charm. The smooth stucco exterior looked like a Chris-Craft at an antique boat show, better than the day it entered the showroom. Despite its attractiveness, the hotel seemed disproportionate to the influence it had upon my life.

A uniformed bellman opened the door and welcomed me. There was no ice cream freezer. I marched through the lobby like a thoroughbred with blinders on, which was my method of keeping my emotions in check. I flew out the back door to the pool, the Gulf of Mexico, and the heart and soul of every beachside resort: the outdoor bar.

Cassie, from Mississippi, planted herself in front of me and said, "What will it be?"

I gave her a look and said, "Why are employees in Florida required to wear name tags stating their place of origin?" It's a question I've asked before, having never received a satisfactory answer.

"That's a good one," she said as she tilted her head. "I dunno...maybe because it adds to the mystique that you've arrived at your final destination. I mean, everybody with a wandering heart eventually finds Florida. It's the home of secondhand American dreams and middle class fantasies. The last southern exit before you leave the country."

She was a bar soldier—her hands on her hips and a dishtowel draped over her right wrist. Behind her, golden bottles of booze rested at various levels to allow the bartenders to efficiently select the ones they needed. Every bottle held a dream. To my left, the Gulf of Mexico glittered silver and white, like a stage curtain backdrop.

"Where in Mississippi?" I asked.

"Little hamlet you've never heard of—Holly Springs."

"North of Faulkner country."

"Listen to you," she said with a complimentary nod.

"I'll take a fish sandwich, iced tea, and beer."

"You got a better theory on name tags?" she asked.

"It's to remind them where to return to if it falls apart."

"Like a luggage tag?" she said.

"You nailed it."

She spun around to prepare my iced tea and beer. I got out my phone and scooted the high barstool closer to the counter so my elbows rested comfortably on the edge. Mary Evelyn had just sent me an attachment, addressed to "Mr. Travis." I opened it.

The Bracketts controlled Calusa Land and Development, a privately held company with extensive holdings in Florida. The Calusa Indians inhabited southwest Florida before the Spanish wandered in. They were known as fierce warriors. That was hardly surprising, considering the hostile Spanish had promptly set out to methodically seize their land, rape their women, and kill their children. Now they sell trinkets on the side of the road to tourists from Ohio, who in their wildest dreams, would never stop at a roadside stand in their native state and buy something from a descendent of the Iroquois.

Florida isn't just another state; it's a foreign destination within the contiguous forty-eight, a magnet for the venturing romantics who aspire to travel abroad without ever leaving home.

Mary Evelyn uncovered that Calusa Land and Development had recently, as Mac indicated, received an infusion of money. They had overextended and, during the financial crisis of '08, required additional capital to fend off creditors. The creditors, despite being initially on the ropes themselves, coveted the company's real-estate holdings after they found themselves flush with cash from the government bailout. The banks wanted to call in the loans and unload the properties after the markets recovered. That wasn't on Alex Brackett's agenda.

He found a guardian angel in Kopeysk Petro and Machine—KPM. KPM was a Russian holding company, gushing with oil money. Mac had heard that Brackett hooked up with the Russians, and he assumed it was the same group that Alex's father had befriended decades ago when glasnost kicked in. I had no way of proving that, nor was I certain that it mattered.

Sophia had overheard Carlsberg speak Russian into his cell, telling someone that "He's here, and he knows." I imagined the State Department would have an interest in Kopeysk Petro and Machine as well as dozens of other Russian corporations. Any relation to my family, however, eluded me. Mary Evelyn indicated that her research hit a wall at that point.

I hit Special Agent Natalie Binelli's number. I left a voice mail. She rang back two bites into a tough piece of overcooked mahi-mahi.

"I just got them," she said after I greeted her by asking if she had the DNA results yet.

"Licenses?" I said.

I had sent her an e-mail with the plates that PC and Boyd had collected at Carlsberg's fundraiser. Morgan had reported that no one had arrived or left by boat that night.

Binelli said, "I'll send them to you, but I don't see anyone of interest."

"Type in Kopeysk Petro and Machine."

"Spell it."

I did.

"OK," she said. "What about it?"

"Who runs it?"

"Hmm…guy by the name of Peter Omarov."

I started to spell it. "O-M—"

"Only maids and robbers order vodka. Why?"

I explained the tentative connection between Carlsberg, the Bracketts, and Omarov.

"The theory," she summarized, "is that Carlsberg represents the Brackett family, who—maybe, maybe not—have a long-term relation with Omarov's family. That relationship intensifies in '08, when Omarov wired funds to Alex Brackett to shore up his bank loans. The Bracketts own the Vanderbilt Reef Motel, which may, or may not, be coincidental. Meanwhile, someone is trying to put the padlock on your sister's case. Carlsberg speaks Russian into his cell, and that leads you to believe that Omarov is somehow linked to your sister's abduction."

"Close enough."

"And what, you think Omarov was sunning himself in Florida thirty years ago?"

"Beats Siberia." I took a sip of iced tea and let a piece of ice slide into my mouth. I cracked the ice and asked, "Anything else about Omarov?"

"He's got heavy rubles invested in Ukraine. I don't really see anything of substance."

"Any connection to the State Department?"

"They don't put out press releases on those things. We can assume that Omarov is intimate with people in State. They'd covet his relationships and network in Ukraine. But life is murky up here in government land. It could be that half of State cuddles up to him, and twenty-five percent of them want to hang him by his nuts."

"The remaining quarter?"

"Strictly in the game for the benefits."

I asked her to keep me in the loop, and we disconnected. I tilted my head to catch a slight breeze from one of the corner fans that dropped down from the ceiling. The fans were connected to thin hoses and blew a light mist over the bar. They hummed gallantly against the humidity, creating a dissonant tone with the music coming from the speakers.

"Another one?" Cassie said as she nodded at my beer— or my iced tea, as they were beside each other.

"Just the bill," I replied.

She swooped off the empty iced tea glass. "What's your name tag say?"

"Jake from Saint Pete Beach."

"What brings you here?"

"Heard the food was good." I brought up the picture of Alex Brackett on my phone and held it up to her. "Ever see this guy?"

She gave it a hurried glance and then came back to me. Her eyebrows scrunched in toward her nose. "Why?"

"I'm supposed to meet him here."

"Sorry," she said, shaking her head.

"You been here long?"

"Started at nine this—"

"How long have you worked here?"

"Oh, let's see." She curled up her left lip and squinted her left eye as if that side of her face was intertwined. "Two years, going on three this October. My first day was Halloween. I was Cinderella. I changed clothes at midnight—right here behind the bar. That got me some heavy tips and a testy letter from management."

"Do you know the owners?"

A phone call from McGlashan interrupted our meandering conversation. He asked if I had time to talk. I replied that I was in town, and we decided to meet at a Starbucks on Tamiami Trail. I popped him a few questions, and we disconnected. Cassie asked me if I wanted the charge to go to my room. I gave her cash and told her my plans weren't finalized, and I didn't know if I was staying there or not.

"Looking for good hotel food and DNA?" she quipped.

"Excuse me?"

"On the phone. You've been asking people about the DNA. Is he the guy you're supposed to meet here?"

"Sure." I didn't owe her an explanation. "But we changed venues."

"Most of them come by once a year."

"Who?"

"The owners. You asked, remember? They're some big-time family. This was one of their first properties, and they hold some kind of reunion here. Every January."

I slid forward in my seat. "You ever work it?"

"No."

"Know anyone who has?"

She hesitated, and a girl squealed from behind me, followed by a splash of water.

"Talk with Chase," she said. "He's been tending bar here for over twenty years. He only works the sunset shift now—that's the best tip money, over the shortest time." She cocked her head. "Why does that information make me think that you've decided to stay?"

"Have a good day, Holly," I said as I slid off the stool.

"Safe sailing, Pete," she said to my back.

I didn't go to my truck. Instead, I wandered up to room 214. A family was strolling down the outdoor balcony that fronted the rooms. A girl dragged a coral-green raft as she skipped and sprinted her way toward me. Her father instructed her in a stern voice to hold the raft up, since it might tear. I wanted to tell him to forget the damn raft and to grab his daughter's hand and never let go.

I wondered if *Matilda*, in some unexplained dimension, was still resting on the bedside table in the room. It was a bullshit thought, and I felt stupid for letting sentimentality sneak into my mind. I kept my head down and my feet moving, careful not to loiter, since that might have been a trait of whoever took her all those years ago, and I didn't want to be viewed with cautious parental stares.

My memories were buried so deep I had to dig for them, for they had been sequestered by my mind so as not to harm me. They were hidden in my muscles. My skin. My bones. Only the dark and locked corners of my brain could release them. But there, at the motel, they broke free.

"Let's eat it from the bottom up," she said the morning of the last day. The last time we had ice cream together.

"Bottom up?" I said.

"Sure. Why do we always start at the top?"

My sister and I sat in the shade on a bench by a trash can outside the motel's front door. We ate our raspberry and vanilla ice cream on a stick, starting from the bottom. As I licked it, I recalled Jimmy Banfield telling me on the final day of school that my sister was hot. I didn't like him saying that.

"I think," she'd said after a slurp, "you start at the top because the thick chocolate at the bottom is like a cup. It holds the ice cream as it melts, before you can get to it." She took a lick. "Also, I snatched an extra dollar from Daddy. We can split a third one."

"Lick from the same stick?"

"Sure."

"How?"

"Diddly-doo-diddly-dee." She smiled and flicked the end of my nose with her finger. "Diddly-you-diddly-me."

I took a large bite and thought how cool she was.

It was a nonsense, toss-away moment, one of countless millions. It was never meant to last forever. Never designed to assume such a sacrosanct position. But it grew in stature and now makes me fear the commonality of everyday life. For what trivia sleeps, only to be sparked by a tragic event and vaulted into timelessness?

16

Detective McGlashan was at a table by a window when I strode through the door at Starbucks. His body spread beyond both sides of the chair. He was not a guy you wanted to see squeezing down an airplane aisle and eyeing the middle seat next to you. A sweating clear-plastic cup of iced tea rested in front of him on top of a soaked napkin. He stood, and we shook hands. His handshake was always good for an extra second. That was an endearing trait of his.

I was searching for who might have checked out the evidence bag on Hawkins. McGlashan had previously stated that except for Detective Melissa Dendy, the file hadn't been touched in nearly twenty-five years. My theory was that someone had first gotten to the bag and planted the evidence implicating Hawkins *before* Dendy dusted it off. That person could lead me to whoever had abducted my sister.

I claimed the chair across from him and asked, "What do you have?"

"Tallahassee," he replied.

"A state agency?"

He pushed himself up in the chair. "Over a year ago. Someone knocked on our door. Said they were working cold cases at the state level. Two men. Flashed IDs. Said they worked for the state prosecutor's office and wanted to get a heads-up on what cases might be reopened. It made sense to us. The state's been trying to put a dollar sign on their cold-case liability. What they might owe to some lucky bastard, they stuck away for thirty years for a crime he didn't commit, while he laughs his ass off because we never fingered him for the six he did."

"There was never a conviction in my sister's case," I said. "Why would they care?"

He took a sip of his iced tea. "They wouldn't. But it wasn't just your sister. They checked out a dozen or so. Had them all back within two days."

"They ever talk to Dendy?"

"They did not, nor was there any reason to. Dendy, and Estep—the junior detective assigned to assist her—hadn't even been assigned the case yet."

"You told me there was no record of my sister's evidence being checked out."

"We recorded everything that went out. It all came back. There was no evidence that your—"

"Then how do you know they had it?"

He pawed his cheek with his right hand. "They requested the lady who keeps the records not to record that they peeked at your sister's. They claimed that particular investigation had already been reopened, and due to the problems we had with Rutledge, it might jeopardize the operation." He flipped his hands. "They knew our weak point. They played it."

Rutledge had been a rogue detective who had given McGlashan's office a black eye. I could see how someone would use that angle, but that didn't dampen my frustration.

I said, "Ethel the gatekeeper fell for that?"

"Her name's Chalene, and she did nothing wrong. They were smooth. Confident. They were also bogus. The agency on their business cards was fraudulent—phones were dead a day later. Numbers were untraceable. We turned the whole mess over to the FBI."

"What made you suspicious of them?"

"We're not idiots."

I let that slide.

"You got to have some trace," I insisted. "Some direction to send me."

"Nothing. We—"

"A couple of smooth talkers knock on your door, skirt out with evidence bags, and you sit here scratching your chin?"

He shoved his cup a few inches, as if to get it out of his line of fire. "You want a taste of my world? We got a deputy who was first to respond to a young woman's suicide call. He was too late. A neighbor happened to drop by—said she'd been concerned with the young lady's mental condition. She found our deputy—"

"No."

"No, what?" he asked, angry that I'd interrupted him.

"I don't want a taste of your world."

He rolled his tongue over the front of his top teeth. "I don't owe you any of this," he said.

I gazed out the window and allowed him a moment to diffuse. "You have no incentive to open an investigation that makes your office look like the middle act of a three-ring circus."

"We done here?"

"Your best guess?"

He skipped a beat, as if to register his discontent. "Could they have planted Hawkins's DNA in the bag, and then our cold-case detectives open it a few months later? Sure. But there's no way of knowing. I had my guys dust it—no prints, nothing. The bag's clean except for Hawkins's DNA. Case closed. Someone got in and out without a trace."

"Cameras?"

"Pardon?"

"You record traffic in and out of your building. Do you have pictures?"

He nodded his head in approval. "We turned it over." He stood, and I did likewise. "What I just told you?"

"We were never here today," I said. "You said they knew about your issue with Rutledge. Almost has to be an inside job, doesn't it? One government agency impersonating another."

"That's our theory. And that's why we're not wasting time on it."

"One more. You ran Hawkins's DNA against other cases from the time. Any matches?"

"No. I would have informed you." He gave me a courteous nod and turned to go out the door.

"McGlashan," I said to his back. He turned around. "I appreciate it."

He gave me a cowboy tip of the head and turned back to the door. He opened it just as a girl with a laptop came in. She smiled timidly at him and went to join a young man wearing a tweed tartan cap at a corner table.

I went to the counter, ordered an iced tea to go, and stared at the guy in the tartan cap. I pondered the possibility that a government agency might have been behind the elaborate and risky scam to pin my sister's murder on an innocent man. It fit with Janssen visiting me on my dock. But would my government kill Hawkins and threaten Red? Or was that the act of another government?

"Can I help you?" the man in the tartan hat said.

"Pardon me?"

"Is there something I can help you with?"

"No—we're good. Nice hat."

I walked outside and the afternoon heat sucked me in like fire breathing in oxygen.

I wished I'd shown McGlashan more gratitude than my gimpy parting comment.

17

Alcohol is sex without rapture. It takes you to the edge of all your desires—and leaves you there, dripping with heat and struggling to breathe. It is both soaring anticipation and hollow disappointment. It is consistent on both fronts.

Chase, the sunset bartender at the Vanderbilt Reef Motel, was putting the finishing touches on a rumrunner, crowning the rim of his magnum opus with pineapple and orange slices. Men in button-down shirts and thick watches and thin, well-dressed women with erect postures circumscribed the bar. I ordered a Jameson on the rocks and scooted my stool back so I could cross my legs. It was hot, and I prayed for a breeze.

I kept expecting something to stir within—a ghost to pay me a visit or a tsunami of feelings to awaken my emotionally deadened soul—but I was numb. The Vanderbilt Reef Motel was just another beachfront motel. Maybe our life is not the great continuum we think it is but, rather, separate frames of a film. The pictures of holidays and traditions do nothing more than fuse together random events and create the illusion of fluidity.

I took a sip of liquid foreplay. But it was just whiskey and not the sacred answer I always hoped it would be.

Chase had a trimmed beard and buzzed gray hair. He moved quickly while preparing drinks and then relaxed when presenting them to his patrons. I pitched him a few easy questions about the hotel and his tenure there. He talked with both hands on the bar, as if he were steadying himself. When he learned that I'd been there as a child, he said, "You can share some memories with Eve. She's been nesting here for at least that long—probably longer."

I wasn't sure I wanted to talk to Eve, Adam, or Jack Shit that evening. The whiskey was quickly taking me inside, where something new was brewing: I didn't want to just kill the man who had abducted my sister. He would need to suffer, to offer me an empty prayer for a quick death, to know it was me who was sucking his life away.

"She works here?" I asked Chase, keeping my eye on the prize.

"No, sir," he replied, bending over to wash a glass. "She's a club member. They're local people who pay dues to use the property. All the motels and hotels do it, but we jumped on that wagon early."

"Any chance of Eve coming by the next day or so?"

"She's here right now. She has a glass of wine around the fire and watches the sunset nearly every night. I wait on her myself."

"You cover the fire pit?"

"Just her."

I waited for further explanation, but he clammed up.

"She easy to spot?"

He replied to my pressing with a reassuring smile. "Everyone finds Eve."

I ambled, drink in hand, toward the edge of the boardwalk and onto the sand.

Several gas fire pits were strung out on the beach just beyond the boardwalk. Each had an arrangement of chairs and couches surrounding it. A family of four occupied the center fire pit. The mother and her daughter were tickling their phones with intense concentration, occasionally laughing and exchanging words. The pit to the left was home to two skinny men with fat cigars. The farthest one to the right had a sofa with a couple snuggled together on one end of it.

Three chairs were across from the couple. Eve was in the chair closest to the water. The gulf was flat and placid. Remnants of waves lapped up on the beach like exhausted messengers from a distant land. They died softly, surrendering both their form and purpose to the welcoming sand.

A long-stemmed glass rested on the table to Eve's left. Her legs were crossed, and her arms extended elegantly along the armrests. She wore a tan sleeveless dress and sandals. The light from the fire flickered on her face, casting shadows where age had started to collapse her skin. I put her somewhere between fifty-five and seventy-five, which is an open swath of life, although with a week of neglect, the upper number would manifest itself. The chair next to her had my name on it.

She was in midsentence, talking to the young couple.

"…and after that, dears?"

"We're not certain," the man said. "Where is it you suggest?"

"Louie's. It's intimate, and the clam sauce on the spaghetti is second to none." She turned her head to me. "Greetings." She nodded and gave a coy smile at the couple. "The Lady and the Tramp are formulating dinner plans. Where did you sail in from?"

"The bar."

"It is a *lovely* port, isn't it?"

"The best. Jake Travis." I offered her my hand.

"Eve Davidson," she said with a puff of gusto, as if she were pleasantly surprised to meet someone who presented his name in such a traditional manner early in a conversation.

"And you, Eve?" I said. "What port's banner do you fly?"

Her eyes were of many colors, and her face was creased with fine wrinkles, as if each one were a story line. Her blond hair was splayed with white and gray, although the color scheme seemed well tended to. She relaxed deep into the cushioned chair and emitted the calmness of someone who was at ease with herself. I envy such people. In a wasted effort, I crossed my legs and tried to mimic her sanguine posture.

"This is my home port," she said.

"Although you've wandered far," I said.

She considered that. "Is 'wander' your best word?"

"Enlighten me."

"I'm open to suggestions. Wander carries such an anchorless connotation."

"Sojourn?"

"Yes," she agreed. "But in the old sense."

Snuggle Girl peeped in from her corner of the couch. "I read once that we're all tourists, even in our homeland."

"There you have it," Eve concurred.

"You come here often?" I asked, eager to learn if Eve had been around during the time of my sister's abduction.

"Nearly every night, when I'm home."

"You're not a guest." I knew she wasn't, but I threw out the observation to prod her into talking about herself.

"She's a tourist," Snuggles added before Eve could answer.

"I'm a member of the ocean club," Eve said. She swept her hand over the fire pit and beach. Her open palm was suspended toward the darkening waters of the Gulf of Mexico. "This…is my parlor."

"And a majestic one," I observed. "I'm not advocating this, but at two stories, I'm surprised the wrecking ball hasn't found it. It's surrounded by—"

"Florida ugly," Eve interrupted me. "That's what smothers this ensconced jewel. Concrete pillars blocking the sun. People piled on top of one another, their sheltered dreams having taken them south and then high into the air. At dinner, they all tumble down the elevators, pile into their German and Japanese cars, choke the roads, and pay exorbitant sums of money for mediocre California wines and fresh Florida grouper that's farm-raised in Panama. This motel is the pearl within that crusty shell."

"To paradise," I said and raised my glass.

"I've never been to California," Snuggles said.

"To *our* paradise," Eve said, keeping her eyes on me.

Her glass was nearly empty, so I asked, "May I get you another drink?"

She landed a warm smile. "Why, thank you. But, no, Chase will take care of me. He knows my pace. I rely on him to make sure I don't outdistance myself."

The young couple excused themselves after thanking Eve for the dinner recommendation. After they left, I asked Eve if she would mind if I lit a cigar.

"Only if I can suck on it."

Things took off pretty fast after that. I didn't want her to know of my personal connection, so I told her I was doing an article on missing persons and heard that the Matilda case had recently been solved.

She took a drag from my cigar and handed it back to me. "It's a shame those things are bad for you. I've done a lot of things they say are bad, and I haven't regretted a single one. I've done some good things too, I suppose, but in the end, I find such things boring and hardly worth the memory."

"Were you an ocean-club member during those years?"

"What years?" she said flatly.

She was toying with me, but I didn't know why. "During the Matilda case."

"What publication do you write for?"

"Freelance."

She studied me for a minute. "You blew it at the opening," she said.

I hadn't given her credit for such a good memory. Her eyes of many colors narrowed, and now they were eyes of many emotions—sadness, pity, even fear—but that might have been the alcohol, for why would she fear me? She brought the wineglass up to her lips but kept her gaze hard on me.

"Travis, right?"

"Guilty."

"Tell me, have you talked to anyone else from that day?"

"No."

My answer seemed to relieve her. Her eyes died on the flame. A sea breeze flicked a few renegade strands of her hair.

"Look over your shoulder," she said. "See the diving board? There used to be a cabana there. It had a solid wood roof, with grass tacked on it for authenticity. We'd just gotten back from two weeks on the other side of the pond. I was sitting there, reading the British edition of Vogue.

It was a hideous cover. Christy Turlington swathed in a ghoulish combination of purple and blue and red and yellow—it just made no sense at all—and then those ridiculous shoulder pads mounted on her. It was as if women's fashion was turning into the bastard child of a football player and an impressionist's color palette.

"My palms were greasy, as I'd just put sunscreen on before taking a walk on the beach, but then I decided to read a little more. I remember that day. That magazine. Those shoulder pads. I remember all that because I remember you, Jake Travis. And I remember your sister."

18

My supplication was answered as the air finally stirred, as if my sister had been beckoned into the conversation.

"You were here that day?" I got the words out before the implication of her statement fully registered with me. Not only had I never talked to anyone who remembered my sister from that day, but I'd begun to wonder if any of it was even real.

"I was here with Allen, my husband, nearly every afternoon. We would read, walk the beach, chat with the tourists at the bar, and listen to the employees gossip and unload their troubles."

I didn't know where to start, so I went with the standard, "Tell me everything." She countered with, "Why are you really here?" and I shot back, "I seek the man who murdered my sister."

"You seek the man who murdered your sister," she repeated, giving my words her own cadence and meaning bred from her life and experiences. "And that garbage about being a writer and the case being solved?"

"Garbage."

She fidgeted with her hands, uncertain whether to place them on her lap or on the arm of the chair. She settled for her lap. She didn't strike me as the type of person who needed to touch herself for reassurance.

"Yes, well, I can see why you threw it out," she said. "Why start your hunt now, or is our coincidental meeting already late in the game? It is coincidental—is it not—our meeting?"

"It is," I said. "The case was reopened due to DNA testing. Another drag?" I offered my cigar to her.

"Really, dear, I'm one and out. I just liked the line."

I snuffed out my cigar, having lost interest in it. She brushed back another few strands of riotous hair, although her movement seemed more of show than of necessity.

"I would not have remembered the day," she said, "if she hadn't gone missing. But she did, and that froze the clock." Her eyes came back to me. "You both scampered in front of me, she in the lead in a green bathing suit. Afterward, everybody was asking if anyone remembered seeing the girl in the green bathing suit. I told the police that was the last I saw of her. How old were you?"

"Seven." *Nearly eight.*

"You know, or were told, that the police questioned everyone?"

"I've been told."

"Well, I can assure you they did."

"Did you see any unusual-looking men hanging around that day?"

She studied the flames as if they were a haven, or at least a refuge, from looking at me. She glanced back at me and crossed her arms in front of her as if she were cold, even though the evening air was still summer thick.

She said, "I'm sorry, your question?"

I repeated my question.

"That was the line they pitched to everyone," she said with resolve, as if she'd regained her bearings. "If I'd noticed anyone *acting* unusual, I would have told the police. As far as anyone *appearing* to be unusual—it's a motel. By nature, outside of the help, it's a collection of people who don't know each other."

Something in her last words struck me as odd, but my thought flared out like a shooting star.

She reached over and squeezed my arm. "I felt *terrible* for your parents. As the day wore on..." She shivered and withdrew her hand. "Allen and I went to the bar like we always did, but it seemed wrong. At first everyone thought she would appear, that she was just in a friend's room. We heard all types of rumors and speculations. None of them panned out.

"They struck the gong at sunset, as they always did, but it was *so* inappropriate. It sounded like a death knell. The paper dubbed it the Matilda case. It took a while for the motel—the staff, the people who worked here—to get over it." She shook her head in disgust. "Tell me about you."

"Bits and pieces remain—like a shattered antique mirror that, even if you pieced it back together again, would never be any good."

"Hmm...what a lovely summation. Not to belittle your tragedy, but at some point in our lives, we all need to move past that mirror. Is there a fresh lead?"

Hesitancy had crept into her tone. I shifted my weight.

"Not a lead," I said, carefully measuring my words, for I sensed Ms. Eve Davidson was clutching cards close to her chest. "More like a diversion. The man who was the prime suspect floated up dead. He left a confession. But he was framed. Someone, with money and power, pinned it on him to permanently close the case."

"His name?" she rushed out.

"Leonard Hawkins."

She straightened up in the chair, reached for her glass, but then folded her hands in front of her. Again, she spoke to the flames. "They are the same, are they not? Money and power?"

"One does beget the other."

"So…your mystery man. He is not a drifter—not someone who lives on the fringes of society."

"No."

"I assume they ran background checks on the guests. Anyone show up as a person of interest?" Her voice floated, as if her mind were plotting a different direction than her words.

"Years ago. No one warranted further questioning."

She was silent, and I took the opportunity to sneak in a drop of whiskey that wasn't there. On the gulf, a distant light shown on the horizon, and I wondered what size boat it was and where it was headed. Chase popped in and asked Eve if she would like another glass of wine. She declined, and he turned his attention to me.

"Sir?" he said.

"Unto the breach," I said.

"Put it on my tab, Chase," Eve told him.

"That's not nec—"

"It's nothing," Eve said as she placed her hand on the back of mine.

Eve's glass was empty. The hour was late. The conversation had run dry, yet she sat. I remembered the flash thought I'd had when she said, *Outside of the help, it's not a collection of people who know each other.*

"How long's Chase been here?" I asked.

"What? Oh, that's a good one. Twenty years, maybe?"

"And before him?"

"I don—"

"Who was the bartender that day?" The abruptness of my voice surprised me.

"I don't..." She leveled her eyes at me. "Are you a violent man, Mr. Travis?"

"That's an odd question." "But a simple one."

"Yes."

"Good. At least my senses aren't deceiving me, for they tell me you are not interested in conventional justice for the man you're seeking. Your honesty will earn you mine. Hugh Ellison was the bartender. Hugh died a few years back. He was a wonderful man. He would have my bloody mary waiting for me on Sunday mornings: horseradish that curled my tongue, fresh celery that cracked like ice, and pepper to raise the dead."

"What was the gossip?"

Chase deposited my drink and collected the old glass.

"I changed my mind, Chase," she said.

A couple claimed the empty couch across from us. The woman crossed her legs, and her short skirt disappeared into the fold of the couch, as if she had nothing on but a shirt. Chase explained that their barmaid would be by soon.

"It is a bit awkward," Eve admitted, "waiting only on me. But we don't give a damn."

I said, "What did you and Hugh talk about while you nursed your bloody mary and chewed your fresh celery the Sunday following Thursday, June 18, 1987?"

She reached into her purse and took out a silver cigarette case. She shook out a cigarette.

"Allow me," I said as I leaned over with my cigar torch.

"Thank you, although that thing might incinerate me. I indulge once a day."

I lit her cigarette. She inhaled deeply, crossed her legs, and threw her head back. She blew out a stream of smoke that wafted into the night and then was confiscated by the wind, like a mother grabbing a naughty child. She froze in that position, her neck curved and suggestive as the lines of age flattened out. She inhaled, and her chest rose and then fell against her dress.

Chase circled back with her drink. She lowered her head and took the glass as if it were an extension of her world.

"I've not spoken this to anyone," she confided to me.

"I've been spilling my guts to everyone with a pair of ears. Try it. It's refreshing."

"Allen's been gone for eight years." She took another drag from her cigarette. "We never did the children act. We were too into our friends. Ourselves. The world. We had a wonderful life: sailed the oceans, picnicked under the Eiffel tower." She fluttered her hand as if decades of life were nothing more than the wind slipping through her fingertips. "You can't imagine. Our favorite thing to do was to sit in the sand, right out there." She raised her hand. The suspended red glow of her cigarette created a red dot in the black night. "He would read to me at sunset. Voice the great words of our language as the sun gave up the day."

Her arm dropped as if she could no longer support its weight.

"When I was a little girl, I wanted to be the ocean— to float under the sun by day and sleep under the moon by night. To have the waves gently massage my body. But

I thought I needed more. Vanity is a terrible disease—a lurching and destructive animal."

I wanted to ask her again what the rumor mill was the week following my sister's abduction, but like a fisherman with a prized catch on the line, I needed to be careful. I sensed she could jump hook at any moment.

"I cheated on Allen," she said, knifing me a look, as if it were my fault. "Do you think I'm a bad person?"

"You told me you didn't regret—"

"Who cares what I say?" Her voice was thick with wine. "Certainly not me. He was the only man I ever loved. He died of a massive heart attack. So odd—guilt and pleasure in the same bag. But guilt is permanent, and pleasure is transitory. No one tells you that. Have you ever cheated on your woman?"

I thought of Christina, a woman I'd recently assisted. "Physically or emotionally?"

"Oh please."

"No."

"Bastard."

"I'm sorry you lost him."

"I thought I might find another man—it's really not much fun on your own—but I fear love too much."

"Fear love?" That was a new one for me.

"If you really love, you live in fear of losing it. It is only if you have never loved that you do not fear love."

I inhaled a wisp of whiskey as her words created harmony out of my feelings for Kathleen.

"You know," she said, "this is a family-owned business."

"The Brackett family. I'm well steeped in their history."

"Are you, now?" she said, mocking me. "Thirty years ago, they used to rotate family members through this property, like a training ground. They've gotten quite big, as I'm sure you know—being 'well steeped' and all. But this motel holds sentimental value. Do you find me attractive?"

Her mind was wandering away from my question of what the gossip had been the Sunday morning my sister disappeared. I decided not to push her.

"Pardon?" I said.

"Don't pretend you didn't understand the question. Answer me."

"You are an attractive woman."

"Oh God," she said, smothering a laugh. "That is so polite it hurts. You hold your whiskey well, Mr. Travis. I was slipping away. Me, Miss American Airlines, 1981. That earned me January on the calendar and the envy of eleven other beautiful women.

"I could see it in the shattered mirrors you mentioned earlier. A line here, a freckle there. Youth cracking while I slept, vanishing behind me like a runner who could no longer keep the pace. Age dragging me forward as if I were a dog with its four paws planted on the ground. I was afraid that a young man would never want me again. Afraid of drifting on the ocean of middle age, knowing that one day I would wash upon a foreign shore that I could never leave. Didn't someone say that youth was too good for the young?"

"George Bernard Shaw."

"I'll better him: Youth is the magic lantern of life. Mine had extinguished itself, but the glow lingered. Look at us, sitting here pouring alcohol into our bodies, but you have no interest in me—oh, don't protest, a woman knows. 'Attractive for my age' is what I've become. I needed to flirt with youth one last time, to taste its bittersweet fragrance.

I seduced him." She took a sip of wine and put her glass down. "Is it really refreshing, spilling it all?"

"A real laxative."

"And you've told strangers?"

"Blabbered it to the gulls. Who did you—"

"A member of the owners' family." She rolled over my words, her gaze above the flames, as if the past resided there. "He was my Mrs. Robinson moment. One wild and drunk toss in an air-conditioned motel room on a steamy summer day. When I walked out? I was mad with an exotic concoction of guilt and pleasure, as if I'd crossed a threshold. A real woman of the world. But I also knew I'd hurt Allen. Hurt us. I thought I'd liked the pain—but it became a stranger I'd invited into my body. It would rear its ugly head on its own schedule.

"It never happened again. Although he told me he was assigned to the motel for another three months, it was not to be."

I remained silent. When fishing, you need to let the big ones exhaust themselves.

"That's it, my dear. The official word was that his rotation ended prematurely, because they needed him at some other property."

"Who?" I demanded.

"I'm not—"

I leaned in to her and grabbed her arm. It was like grabbing a broomstick, and I thought of Mac's arm when I'd steadied him, afraid that he might fall.

"You're hurting me."

I released my grip but kept my eyes locked to hers. "He was a pool boy," she said. "Keep your judgmental eyes to yourself."

"Did you have sex with him the afternoon my sister was abducted?"

"No. Not on that day. Our tryst happened two days before your sister went missing. He told me he would be here for another two months, and then—*whoosh*—he was gone."

"You said three months."

"Two or three, what does it matter?"

"You tell me."

"Fine, dear. I will. Do you really want to know what Hugh Ellison and I discussed that Sunday morning?"

"Tell me."

"How quickly the family whisked Alex Brackett away after your sister went missing."

"Your fling was with Alex Brackett, the man whose family owns the property?"

"If the employees knew the golden boy was banging a guest, the Brackett family would have had a nightmare on their hands. An even bigger one than they already had. And once the police started asking around, it would have been hard to keep the lid on."

"How old was Brackett?"

"What does it—"

"How old?"

"I don't know. Twenty-something."

"Anything about him strike you as odd? As capable of abducting a young girl?"

"Alex? No," she replied with a nervous laugh. "He was as harmless as a lovebug."

I leaned back. So Eve had a fling with Alex Brackett. Big deal. She turned her head out toward the gulf.

"Did he say anything else to you? Even if you think it was inconsequential."

"Pardon?" she said, with her head still turned away from me.

I repeated my question.

She looked at me and said in a husky voice, "You want to know what he said when he was fucking me?"

"I didn't—"

"Oh Eve," she said, "listen to yourself." She touched my arm. "I'm sorry, little boy of so long ago, but you see, he was learning Russian that summer from a friend. When we made love, he spoke to me—"

"Who was teaching him Russian?"

"His Russian friend."

"What Russian friend?"

"Don't sound so alarmed, dear. There was a man—a boy, whatever you call twenty-somethings—staying here that summer. He was a friend of the Brackett family and attending school in the States. I assumed his family were diplomats of some sort. He and Alex were close. Alex was learning Russian from him, something about needing to know it for the family business. Word around the bar was that Peter the Russian needed a stronger leash."

"Was that his real name? Peter?" *Did Omarov and Alex Brackett go back that far?*

"I was just using it in the generic sense, but now that you mention it—I'm sorry, I can't say for certain."

"What do you know about Peter the Russian?"

"Not much, I'm afraid."

"Anything?"

"Hmmm. More of an impression, really. How shall I say this? After World War Two, the French accused the British of walking around Paris as if they owned the world and the Americans of walking around Paris as if they didn't give a damn who owned the world. That was our man called Peter. He walked as if he didn't give a damn. Diplomatic immunity is a seductive drug for a twenty-something-year-old. Talk around the bar was that he started drinking before noon and liked the girls."

"Did you ever meet him—the Russian?"

"Meet him? No. See him? Yes. It's not like I kept track of him. There was another boy-man as well. He was a college friend of Alex and Peter. I don't recall his name—French, or something. He seemed more reclusive. The dark and bookish kind."

"The Russian's last name?" I asked.

"Sorry."

"The police question them?"

"I'm afraid I'm not the one for that question."

"When the family comes around for their annual reunion every year, what's it like seeing Alex Brackett again? He's the family patriarch now. Do you two talk?"

She pushed her wineglass across the table, as if to distance herself from the glass. I wondered if she'd already regretted what she'd divulged to me.

"Those reunions aren't as well attended as you might think," she said to the glass.

"How so?"

She raised her eyes to mine. "Alex Brackett, despite becoming the patriarch of the family, apparently has a strict aversion to family reunions. As far as I, or anyone, knows, he has never again set foot on this property."

19

When I set foot on my property the following morning, Detectives Rambler and Yarborough arrested me for the murder of Leonard Hawkins.

"We've got a witness who put you in his neighborhood, snooping around Hawkins's windows the night before the medical examiner said he died," Rambler explained after I asked him what grounds the charge was based on.

"That's the basis for an arrest? You admitted that you believed I had nothing to do with his murder," I reminded him.

"We have a witness," he repeated, but the weariness in his voice exposed his lack of conviction.

"And I have a solid alibi," I protested. I had no idea what I'd been doing that evening, but between Kathleen and Morgan, I was with one of them. "What have you really got?" I challenged him. "A jailhouse snitch you picked up on a drug charge who spilled, unsolicited, that he saw me? Little late in your career to be wasting time on a bogus collar, isn't it?"

"In the car, beach bum," Yarborough said and clucked his tongue. "We're booking you. What do you think of that?"

"I'm being booked by an autistic cow?" I said, recalling Red's description of Yarborough.

"Whatyasay?"

"I'm looking into holistic vows."

Yarborough challenged my eyes for a moment, as if deciding to revisit my earlier comment.

"Bogus or not," he said, "you'll still get a pleasure cruise down Gulf Boulevard from the back seat of an unmarked. I'll drive real slow. Might have to pick up my laundry on the way."

"What's it like getting up every morning with a broom up your ass?"

"Damn convenient," he said, bobbing his head. "When I do my Elvis thing, I get to sweep up buckets of shit like you. Let's go."

I wanted to volley back a smart-aleck reply so he wouldn't win the point, but I held my tongue as Danny Gilliam's words came back to me: *Unless you're the victim of a crime, you never talk to the police.* My half-baked comments had certainly done nothing to enhance my predicament.

They fingerprinted me at the station—which I suspected the ruse was about—and stuck me in a holding cell. I asked if I could renew my resident parking pass while I was there, but my earnest question went unanswered. I stepped into a cell, and the metal door clanked behind me.

There's a misconception that jails stink like a gorilla's armpits and are stuffed with tattooed rapists, sodomists, and arsonists, who nailed their girlfriends to trees and that, in the middle of that zoo, a bar of soap lies on the floor. That may well be, but not in my little town. My cell was tidy and clean, which, considering the disarray of my own establishment, was an upcharge. It was empty, except for a tabloid newspaper with a special section on Hollywood stars. It rested on the opposite bench. No language on planet earth can adequately describe the depths of my dis-interest in Hollywood and its incestuous offspring.

I stared at it.

It stared back.

After a thirty-minute face-off—it was a tough rag—I picked it up.

I put it down.

I picked it up again.

It was as if I had no choice but to read it, to view over-weight—or anorexic—celebrities on some exotic spit of sand, to learn who was mad at whom, who was drinking too much, and who was having someone else's baby. It wasn't all make-believe—I did learn that Princess Diana was not only alive but also tending sheep in Austria and that Dolly Parton had given birth to an alien baby. It was agony. I read every word. I gladly would have traded it for the stench of gorillas' armpits and a bench lined with tattooed rapists, sodomists, and arsonists who nailed their girlfriends to trees.

Eve.

I wasn't sure what to do with the information I'd gleaned from her. Neither was I certain that I was done with her. Alex Brackett never again showing up at the hotel seemed odd but certainly didn't implicate him. I found my inter-est, and imagination, drifting more toward Omarov. Was he the Russian Eve spoke of? Did Alex Brackett and he go back that far?

Three hours later, a sergeant with a paunch and a bored attitude arrived. He unlocked my cage and declared me free to go. I told him I hadn't been served lunch yet. Paunchy shrugged, locked the door, and whistled "Yellow Submarine" as he walked away. My own damn fault, but I didn't care.

"We lost your lunch," Paunchy said a thin hour later as he unlocked my pen for the second time. "Dinner's in three. Your choice, frat boy."

Four hours of solitary with a Hollywood rag had done me in. I was disoriented and mumbling to myself. I'd been gnawing at my fingernails and scratching the walls. I'd grown a four-week beard. I stumbled past him toward the front door, landed a solid stare at his gut, and said, "Sweet Jeebus, there's my lunch."

"And I can eat it any day. Not that way, hotshot. Over here."

He handed me my phone and took off. I'd texted Garrett when we arrived at the station. I checked my messages and saw that he had booked a flight and was in the air. He also said he'd let McGlashan know that I'd been brought in.

Paunchy led me to a conference room with an oval table and five chairs. An air vent high on the wall rattled, and the linoleum floor was close to its historic preservation date. I took a seat in a brown leather chair that had a patch of black electrical tape on the seat. Fifteen minutes later, Rambler strode in with doughnuts with white icing and two cups of coffee. He handed me a cup as a peace offering. He took a seat across from me and scratched his chin. I scratched my armpit. That's what gorillas do.

I took a sip of coffee and said, "Where's squirrel's dick?"

I leaned back in the chair. The damn thing nearly toppled over, and coffee spilled on my shirt. Rambler suppressed a smile and then shook his head, as if I was a bad act he was tired of. I uprighted my chair and placed my mug back on the table.

"Out collecting more nuts," he said. It was a good comeback. Sometimes the other guy gets one in.

"Riding his broom horse?" I said, not willing to accept defeat.

"I don't like being used," he replied, ending our dance.

"Nor do I. Lemme guess, your snitch changed his mind?"

He nodded. "I also got a call from a Detective Patrick McGlashan of Lee County. He vouched for you, although he said a hemorrhoid would be less painful."

"He's part of my warm and fuzzy friend collection." I could no longer resist the doughnut's cosmic pull. I took a third of one in one bite. "Why do you give two shakes?"

He shifted forward in his seat. "About your smart mouth? I don't. Leonard Hawkins was murdered. His killer is out there, taunting us. Trying to pin it on you. I represent Hawkins."

"You're bending over backward for the man with enough pedophile smut on his hard drive to sink an iCloud?"

"I talked to people who knew him," he said. "His girlfriend claims she saw no evidence of his behavior. I'm entertaining the possibility that his computer was tampered with."

"'Entertaining the possibility,'" I repeated his words. "You go full throttle, don't you? She tell you that someone paid her a visit?"

He rolled his tongue inside his cheek. "Who?"

"Hawkins's girl," I said.

"You met her?"

"Maybe."

He leaned across the table. "She clammed up with us. What did she say to you?"

"You first. You got one shot, and then I walk. Tell me who's punching you like a busted remote control."

He rubbed his forearm and said, "The snitch got a new attorney two days ago. High-profile guy, way beyond the snitch's level."

"Bernard Carlsberg," I said as I finished the doughnut. He placed his elbows on the table. "You get around. Why did Bernard Carlsberg want to put a scare in you?"

"You think I scare that easy?"

"Tell me what Felicia Hayes told you."

"Who?"

"Hawkins's girlfriend. Thought you said you knew her."

"Red," I nodded. "I never caught that fireplug's name."

I thought of Red strumming her guitar in her garden. Whether she'd admit it or not, she lived with the constant fear that her intruders would return. She might even welcome sharing her knowledge with the police. Once she talked to the police, Hawkins's killers would gain no advantage by harming her. I was talking myself into what rational minds would do, although I knew I was not dealing with such minds.

I explained to Rambler what Red had confided to me about the men who'd paid her a visit. I gave him a description, down to the split fingernail. He was old-school and would occasionally jot down a note in a small spiral notebook. He nodded a few times, as if he were internally processing the information. I impressed upon him that Red was afraid for her life and urged him to treat what I told him delicately so as not to infuse her with panic. Rambler thanked me for the information.

"Just trying to help," I said as I stood. He also rose. "You got my fingerprints, right?"

He nodded.

"Don't waste my time," I advised him, "if they show up at Hawkins's house."

"I would have thought you'd worn gloves."

"I did."

I walked out of the room and through the front door. I breathed in the sunshine as I hit a wall of heat. A car chirped from down the block. I summoned Uber but entered the address of a restaurant a few blocks from the police station. It beat having someone pick me up at the jail. Five minutes later, a Kia that had never known a car wash pulled over to the sidewalk where I was standing.

"I collect a lot of folks at this restaurant," the woman driving the car said when I climbed into the back seat. She smelled like strawberries. "Usually, though, it's around the early-mornin' hours."

A backpack was on the floor. I nudged it over to the other side with my foot. It was heavy. I kicked it.

"They open that late?" I said.

"Heavens, no. People get hauled in to the police station—it's just around the corner—for rowdy behavior. Too much drinkin' 'n shit like that. They don't want to be seen gettin' picked up there, so they call from this place. This is the first restaurant on Corey past the cop house. People can be so small and pathetic sometimes. Know what I mean?"

"Real cowards."

"Gutless. That's a nice shirt, but it looks like you got coffee on it. If it's new, I got a stick in my purse—probably get it out."

"Just spilled it in the restaurant."

"Honey, they don't open till four. You can go ahead and move that backpack if you need more room, but I'd appreciate it if you don't kick it again."

20

That evening, Garrett, Morgan, Kathleen, and I ate Caribbean lobster on the outdoor table. A passing cloud obscured a waxing gibbous moon. Orion was in the east, its belt barely visible because of the lights on the bridge across the bay.

I'd trimmed the pleopods, or swimmerets, off the lobster tails—the first pair on the males is larger—butterflied them, rubbed the meat with olive oil, and placed them on the five-hundred-degree grill, meat-side down. On the way back from jail duty, I'd asked Strawberry—my Uber driver—to pull in to a bakery. I'd gotten two loaves of French bread and given one to her. Morgan contributed conch chowder that had simmered for hours. Kathleen pitched in three candles in small glass bowls, not much larger than shot glasses.

We baptized the lobster meat in melted butter, bathed the bread in chowder, and rinsed our souls with fine Bordeaux—except for Garrett, who stuck with water. For a moment, everything was fine. Then, as I'd been prone to do numerous times a day for the past thirty years, I remembered my sister, and the light, once again, dimmed just a bit.

I was afraid that one day that light wouldn't dim, and her life would have lost all relevance. I was fighting that as much as anything I'd ever fought.

Binelli had called earlier and told me she'd just received the DNA profiles. There were two profiles from Hawkins's house. One was Hawkins's, and the other was unknown. We assumed the unknown profile was Red's. I thanked her. It had always been a long shot.

It hadn't been hard to confirm that Eve's Russian was Peter Omarov. Coupled with what Binelli had previously told me about KPM as well as what I'd gathered from publicly available information, I learned that KPM was the child of Nikolay Omarov, a contemporary of Russell II.

Nikolay had served as a special attaché to his government's embassy in Washington for seven years. His son Peter had attended the University of Virginia at the same time Alex Brackett had. That helped to reinforce my faith in Eve, since she'd mentioned that Alex's Russian friend was attending school in the States at the time of my sister's murder. Nikolay had died eleven years ago, leaving the company in his son's hands. Considering that Mac had stated that the Bracketts had turned to the Russians for money after the financial panic of '08, I assumed that Alex Brackett and Peter Omarov were still close.

Peter Omarov, who Eve said drank before noon and liked the girls, had become my number-one suspect. I had nothing hard on him, but someone had to fill that slot. Might as well whack a Russian.

"Let's pay him a visit," Garrett said. We'd been discussing Bernard Carlsberg, who, due to his representation of the Bracketts, might be a geyser of information on Omarov. I'd previously provided a synopsis of my conversation with Eve Davidson.

"And telegraph to whoever's paying his bill that we're on to him?" I said.

Garrett grunted.

Kathleen asked, "Why did Carlsberg orchestrate your arrest?"

I dipped a chunk of bread into conch chowder and then quickly put it into my mouth. A drop landed on my shirt, next to the coffee stain.

After a few chews, I said, "Maybe he figured I went through Hawkins's house, and now that they got my prints, Rambler would fall for it."

"The purpose of that being?"

"Keep me off the trail."

"But he—Rambler—didn't fall for it," she said with a note of worry.

"He was used once. He's not my friend, but he's no longer the enemy."

"He's a cop," Garrett reminded me.

"Alex Brackett never returned to the Vanderbilt Reef Motel," Kathleen said. "Perhaps Omarov is guilty, and Brackett's been protecting him. The associated guilt has kept him away."

"Or he has a strong aversion to family reunions," I added.

"The question always bothered you," Garrett said, "and this answers it."

"What question?" Kathleen asked.

I let some Bordeaux take its time washing over my tongue. I wished I had a cigar to light. I didn't necessarily want to smoke one, but I ached for the ritual of unwrapping it, clipping it, and torching it. It's a cheap prop that makes me feel as if I am in control of my world.

"What has bothered me," I said, "is how did my sister's abductor get her off the property without somebody seeing

them? Two people abducting her addresses that. One for
the act and one for the lookout. Maybe Alex Brackett had
a hand in covering it up. Maybe he went to his family and
was told to forget what he saw, for the sake of the business.
Between Omarov's diplomatic immunity and the Bracketts' participation in the cover-up, it's no wonder the police
were stymied by my sister's murder."

"Brittany," Kathleen corrected me.

"Kopeysk Petro and Machine," Garrett cut in. "What
do we know?"

"KPM's controlled by Omarov," I said, addressing Garrett's question, which conveniently allowed me to duck
Kathleen's jab.

"He sounds like a character out of Doctor Zhivago,"
Kathleen said.

"It's likely his ancestors migrated up from Kazakhstan," Morgan pointed out. He'd just returned from the
kitchen with another bottle of wine. "Kopeysk sits on top
of Kazakhstan and was part of the Soviet Union until 1991.
It's not far from Chelyabinsk, which is a major metropoli-
tan area."

Morgan, who spent his entire youth on his family's
charter sailboat, possessed an encyclopedic knowledge of
geography and history. He had a genuine interest in the
people of the world, their land, and the governments that
determined their personal freedom. He'd recently mounted
a large map on a wall in his home that lacked the fine lines
that separate one political system from another. Above the
map, a sign read, "When one suffers, all suffer."

I have a sign in my garage that reads, "No working during drinking hours." I'd recently taken it down and placed
it on a shelf under paint cans. I did that shortly after Mor-

gan put his map up and I started volunteering in the thrift store—but those events had nothing to do with my action.

Garrett said, "KPM has oil operations and manufacturing operations in Ukraine. When Putin got the urge to expand, KPM found themselves on the wrong side and scrambled to appease both the Ukrainians and Putin. The collapse of oil in '15, coupled with the slowdown in China's growth rate that year, crimped profit margins. Omarov shifted toward armament production."

"He took his scrap-metal business and plowed it into swords," I added.

"Conflict and war," Garrett pointed out, "know no recession. They sell hardware to anyone with currency. That's what's made them a business of interest to State. Omarov likely serves as a liaison between Washington and Putin. In return, both parties turn a blind eye toward his armament catalog."

Hadley III vaulted out through the cat door. She hesitated, as if she had no clue as to what to do next, and then bounded onto Kathleen's lap. Kathleen started stroking her. She purred in deep contentment, deliberately folding her front paws underneath her.

I raked my hand through my hair. The politics of today had nothing to do with the disappearance of my sister thirty years ago. On the table, the candles danced in their glass bowls, creating a pale reflection on the glass. The reflections moved in opposite direction of the flickering flame, the two of them joined together in an ordained and failed effort to rid themselves of each other. Unrelated but the same. An unshakable shadow.

Kathleen took a stab at the silence. "If Omarov is associated with Brittany's disappearance, and Omarov is involved in negotiations between DC, Ukraine, and Moscow, then *all* parties—the Russians, the Ukrainians, and the State Department—would desire the case to remain closed."

Garrett picked up the thread. "When word comes out that Brittany's case has been reopened, they take offensive action. Maybe Omarov's DNA was in the room. How would that play out?"

I stood and said, "The State Department needs help in Ukraine, or it desires a simple favor from Putin that's immaterial to us. They require a middleman, and Omarov is their boy. He informs them that if they're going to pump him for help, there's a small matter they can clean up for him—a crime he committed long ago that has no statute of limitations and is being brought back to life because of DNA testing.

"State—or some combination of State and Omarov—makes Hawkins take the fall and then puts me behind bars for taking out Hawkins. It's speculation, but it fits. My sister's death is permanently swept under the rug."

"Brittany," Kathleen said again.

"Brackett?" Morgan said. "Do you think he even knows what Omarov is up to?"

I shrugged. "There's no telling how close Omarov and Alex Brackett are."

"Your bet?" Morgan asked.

"Keep it simple," Garrett said, jumping in front of me. "Brackett covered for Omarov thirty years ago, and they've been tied at the waist since '08."

I grew weary of the speculative discussion. I topped off my wineglass and strolled to the end of the dock. A great blue heron that had been stalking the sea grass took flight with a protesting squawk.

I sat on the bench as the red channel marker beat like a mariner's heart. In the distance, beyond the pesky marker and the drawbridge, a cruise ship closed in on the Sunshine Skyway. On board were hundreds of people, drinking, eating, and enjoying one another's company. Their troubles trailed like a distant wake as the ship idled west, chasing the sun. A dolphin blew in the night, and then another. *That's all we got*, I thought, *nothing but air.*

The vibration of the dock indicated that it was Kathleen who was coming to join me. Garrett was heavier, and Morgan was not one to intervene during moments of solitude.

"Brittany," she said as she stopped beside me.

Oh, suffering shit, I thought. *Buckle up.*

"What did you say?" Kathleen asked.

"Nothing. What about her?"

She hesitated and then said, "You still refer to her as 'my sister.'"

"I don't need you on your high horse tonight." I was shocked at the sharpness—and galactic stupidity—of my words. I knew better than to go one-on-one with her. It was a suicide mission.

"Wouldn't hurt you to pony up every once in a while," she shot back.

"I have virtually no memories of her."

"But you have them."

"'Don't eat food off an old person's plate, or you'll get old.'"

"Come again?"

"She used to say that—at our grandparents' house. That's what I remember from my sister. 'Don't eat food off an old person's plate, or you'll get old.' I believed her."

"See. That's—"

I spun around to her as my uncensored words tumbled out. "What's the curtain call here? Welcome a new person into my life? Maybe place a gift at her grave on her birthday every year? She's gone. Brutally murdered a long time ago. Left in a ditch to rot. I barely remember her. The only thing I feel is the burning desire to introduce myself to her killer and grant him a slow death. That's the closure I get from this."

Somewhere around the gift-on-the-grave quip, I'd thought of pulling in the reins. But thinking doesn't cut it.

"When's the last time you even went?"

"Where?"

"Her grave, Jake. The family plot."

"I don't know."

"You don't know." Kathleen said as a statement, not a question.

"It's like staring at my failure."

"Oh, that's just brilliant. You think putting the man who killed Brittany in a pine box will disenthrall you from the chokehold your childhood has on you? That's your trumpet blast?"

"It's a start."

"This isn't about faceless revenge; it's about you."

"Bet accordingly."

My self-loathing retort was a wasted effort, for it fell on her back as she stormed off down the dock. Sometimes, that girl is just too damn luminous for me.

I turned back around, and the mocking channel marker was waiting for me. A rising wind lifted the smell of the bay. It was soft and moist, like a woman's body when she first gets out of a hot shower. I took in a deep breath of the air flecked with salt. I was close. I could smell it. Him. My sister's killer. I'd never been this close before. What if I blew it? I inhaled more air, as if to instill myself with confidence.

I got a good whiff of just how close I was the following day. Fortunately, Danny Gilliam's son Austin and his partner, Kenneth, along with my pickelhaube floor lamp, stepped forth and likely saved a few of my teeth from being knocked out.

21

"Can you cover the thrift store for thirty minutes?" Morgan asked over the phone.

I was at the counter at Seabreeze having breakfast. Kathleen's departing salvo played in my head like an incessant song. *This isn't about faceless revenge; it's about you.* To compensate, I'd ordered double bacon. I do that when I feel sorry for myself.

"Sure," I told Morgan. "What's up?"

"I'm at the DMV. The wait was longer than I thought. I should be there within the hour. Life's out of town and won't be back until after closing."

Life was a Jamaican man whom Morgan had recently hired to assist in the thrift store. I told Morgan not to worry, and we disconnected.

Peggy dropped off scrambled eggs to the man two stools down.

"Pepper?" I said to him, reaching for both the salt and pepper shakers.

"No, thanks," he said. "I'm good."

No pepper on his eggs. I'd seen his kind before. He reminded me that, ultimately, humanity is a tragedy. I asked Peggy for the bill.

"It's the same amount every time," she said. "Why waste paper?"

"Double bacon."

"That's right. Trying to sneak one in on me, aren't you? You ask that girl to marry you yet?"

"Been busy." I placed a twenty on the counter.

"Don't look it to me." She scooped up my plate. "Coffee to go?"

"I'm good."

"So you think," she said in a tone that I didn't need over breakfast.

She rang out my twenty and stuck the change in her apron. She snatched a coffeepot and was making her way down the counter as I slipped out the door. The thrift store was less than half a mile down Pass-a-Grille Way. I fired up eight cylinders, lowered the windows, cranked up the air, and caught sixty seconds of the Allman Brothers blowing out twelve speakers as the truck snorted down the street. A four-door sedan that had trailed me down the road slowed. I thought it might pull into the parking lot. Instead, it crept past and swung into the deserted bayfront lot on the opposite side of the street.

The shop's hours were posted on a sign in the front yard: nine to twelve Tues., Wed., Thurs., and Sat. We were missing the letter *W*, and the sign had an upside-down *M* for Wed. People leave donations at the door when it's not open, and it had been closed the previous day.

I reached across a cloth armchair and stuck the key in the door. I lugged the chair inside—it wouldn't last, it was in decent shape—and flipped on the lights as well as the wall-unit AC. The best the mighty warrior would do was to keep the temperature from rising too rapidly.

Morgan had the place looking sharp: clothes along one wall, household goods in two aisles in the middle, and larger items, where I placed the chair, against the wall opposite the clothing as well as across the back.

A dining set with four chairs that had been there when I last worked was gone. My floor lamp with the pointed tip, what Kathleen had referred to as a pickelhaube, stood by the side of the antique cash register. It had a "hold" sign on it. I knew someone would appreciate its beauty. A stack of four plates was on the counter. There was no sign on them, and I presumed they needed to be stocked. An original 1976 Farrah Fawcett poster in like-new condition was on the wall behind the counter. A sign underneath it stated, "Not for Sale."

Two muscular men came through the front door. One went straight to the clothing on his right. He was stout and had cords of muscle curling out of his T-shirt and up his neck. *Like a pine tree you snip off at the top*, Red had said. The other man, who was much taller, drifted through the middle of the store, occasionally examining a coffee mug or plate. He was the driver of the car that had pulled into the deserted lot.

It wasn't unusual to have men arrive together, since our policy was "you buy it, you load it." Couches, beds, and tables require men and a truck.

But these men had come in a sedan.

The shorter man stayed close to the door. His friend, who wore a loose-fitting jacket, worked his way toward me. Not many men wear jackets in Florida in the summer. Despite his effort to appear nonchalant, the man moved with purpose. I usually pack but wasn't that morning, since my intention had been to grab a quick bite at Seabreeze and then head over to see Mac. I was eager to see what, if anything, he knew about Peter Omarov. Also, his shortness of breath last time I left him seemed more serious than he let on.

The taller man selected a coffee mug and approached me. Red had said that the two men who'd come to her house had foreign accents and that one was "notably" taller than the other. She'd mentioned a tattoo as well, but that wouldn't be any help. I positioned my floor lamp to my right. I kept my hand on it. If a coffee mug was his weapon, I was in good shape.

I took my left hand and knocked the stack of plates off the counter. I kept my attention on the man. When the plates shattered on the floor, his eyes never left mine. I knew, and we both knew that the other knew. He placed a Saint Pete Beach cup on the counter. I wanted to steal a glance at his hand to confirm a split fingernail but didn't dare allow my eyes to fall from his.

"You going to pick up the plates?" he asked in a slight accent. Russian.

"Why don't you do me that favor?"

"How much for the mug?"

"A million rubles."

"Seems a little high."

"Sentimental value."

"For a mug?"

"Belonged to my sister."

He twisted up the left side of his lip. He started to reach into his jacket pocket. I grabbed my lamp with both hands.

Two more men, in the midst of a heated argument, burst through the front door. The man in front of me turned his head slightly and nodded at his partner. When he faced me again, I had the point of my floor lamp, the pickelhaube, leveled at his chest. Both my hands were on it.

"Interesting," he said. "You think you got a chance with that?"

"Hand out of your jacket. Slow."

"We're only here to deliver a message."

"Know how to use a phone?"

"We find personal contact makes a greater impact."

"Both hands."

His eyes digested my last comment as the commotion approached him from the rear. He withdrew his hand from his jacket.

The arguing duo was closing in fast. I recognized Austin Gilliam and his partner, Kenneth, from the picture that Danny Gilliam had showed me of the three of them when they went on their $300-a-day drinking extravaganza at the Epcot Food and Wine Festival.

"We need another floor lamp," Kenneth proclaimed, "like we need another cable company in our lives."

"And that's an open mind?" Austin countered. "OK. So it needs a new shade, but it weighs a ton, and you could spear a—oh my God." Austin focused on me. "Careful. That's sharp, you know."

"This man wanted to buy it," I explained as I lowered the lamp. "But we honor our hold tags."

"Do you ever," Austin said in singsong appreciation. He tilted his head to Kenneth. "I told you, the guy who runs this place—Morgan, like Captain Morgan, you know, the rum? He keeps a tight ship. He told me he'd hold it for me."

"What's your message?" I said, ignoring Austin and Kenneth and keeping my eyes locked on the man in front of me.

"Jailhouse snitches are a dime a day."

"Spell it out."

"Your sister's gone. Nothing good will come from your efforts."

"Who sent you?"

"That's not your concern. This is: step aside."

"Says who? My government or the Russians?"

He cocked his head. "I like your girlfriend."

"I see you on the same street as her, and I'll—"

"Relax. You no sense of humor?"

"Ahem," Austin said, clearing his throat. "I don't know if you guys are rehearsing a play or what, but—"

"Five hundred for the mug," I said. "That's as low as I'll go."

He held the mug in front of me. He had a split fingernail. "You know, how many mugs does a man really need?"

"I mean, I've got my favorites," Austin said with nervousness edging into his voice. "Don't we all?"

"It's a little hard to play a guitar with a split nail." I gave him the same line Red had told him.

It took a second to register, but when it did, he granted me a solitary nod. "Throw flowers on her grave and walk away. Do it for your woman."

He turned and walked leisurely toward the front door, as if he were daring me to stop him. Halfway there, he flipped the mug into the air without turning his head. It landed on the top shelf and took out several glasses and plates. They tumbled and shattered on the floor. His partner trailed him out the front door, neither of them glancing back. Morgan entered the door as they were leaving.

"The line was horrendous at the DMV," he said. "But I was already there, so...what happened?" He stared at the broken glass.

I said, "You want to explain it, Austin?"

"Sure...I'm sorry, have we met?" Austin studied me as if my face was a mystery.

"Kenneth told me your name."

"I did no such thing," Kenneth protested.

"How else would he know?" Austin asked.

"I don't know, ask him."

"You ask him."

Kenneth looked at me. "*Do* I know you?"

I said to Austin, "I met your father. He was a little stupefied, but he had a hell of a time with you guys at the wine and food festival."

"Told you," Kenneth said, slapping his partner on the shoulder.

"The broken glasses?" Morgan said with a rare note of irritability.

I glanced at Austin. "Want to take a stab at it, Austin?"

"Sure. I think...I'm sorry, your name?"

"Jake."

"Pleasure. OK. 'Take a stab'—that's good. So...I think this is what happened. Those men meant to do harm. They threatened Jake, who I believe is missing his sister. Jake, sensing danger, was using my—*our*—floor lamp, or to be precise, its point—"

"Pickelhaube," I said.

"Excuse me?"

"The point. It looks like a pickelhaube; the pointed helmets the Germans wore in the Great War," I said, giving him the same explanation I'd given Morgan when he first encountered the lamp.

"OK. Fine. Jake was using the pick-el-haube as a weapon. I tried to keep the banter light, hoping to diffuse the situation, but honestly—I was starting to think it would have been a great day to sleep in. Oh, and there was something about Russian and fingernails, but that totally zoomed over my head. How'd I do, Jake?"

"You did all right." I handed him my floor lamp. "It's my lamp. I donated it to the store."

"Get *out* of here." He took it from me. "What possessed you to buy it in the first place? I mean, it is an unusual combination: a weapon with a shade, although that shade's not long for this world."

"It's so ugly it's pretty."

"That's ex*act*ly what I said," Austin exclaimed. He shot Kenneth a triumphant look and then came back to me. "So why did you get rid of it?"

"I knew you'd appreciate it more than I would."

"OK. That just makes no sense. There's no—"

Instead of listening, I darted outside to make certain our unwelcome visitors weren't waiting to ambush us and perhaps get a better look at their car. They were gone. I'd wasted time in mindless conversation—not that it would have made a difference. I stood in the middle of Pass-a-Grille Way as the heat radiated off the blacktop, and felt bad for bringing disarray to Morgan's store. I turned back toward the store.

"Let's clean it up," I said, striding through the door as if I were in charge. The three of them ignored me. They were already hard at it.

I half-heartedly joined the effort. I felt like Pigpen, the character from Charlie Brown's world, who always trailed dirt wherever he went. But I trailed trouble, danger, and busted kitchenware.

22

"It's known for being formal," Kathleen said. "I believe you need a tie to walk in the lobby."

"Listen, pigeon. I see a tie walking in the lobby? I'm done with the booze."

"You know what I—forget it."

It was two thirty on the same day. We'd learned that Peter Omarov was attending an international oil and gas symposium at the Greenbrier Resort outside White Sulphur Springs, West Virginia. He hadn't been hard to discover. Garrett had spotted an article in the *Wall Street Journal* that listed the speakers, and our boy's mug shot was there. Garrett's law firm was able to secure two invitations, and each came with a guest ticket. I didn't question Morgan when, shortly after closing the thrift store, he barged through my door with his duffel bag.

Our flight was in two hours. Kathleen was cramming items into her reluctant bag, resting on the foot of her bed. She was teaching a summer course but had managed to rearrange her classes to allow for a few free days. Morgan was grabbing sandwiches to go, and Garrett was waiting in my truck. I never made it over to Mac's to see how he was feeling or to question him about Omarov.

"What's the plan?" Kathleen asked. Instead of waiting for an answer, she stepped away from her suitcase. "You can take it now." She treated a full suitcase like poison oak.

"Try to get a little one-on-one quality time with Omarov," I replied. "There's no sense pressuring Carlsberg. He's just a conduit."

"And how do you plan to get your tête-à-tête?"

"Clueless."

"That always leads to the most interesting endings."

We flew into Charleston, rented two cars, and curved through the countryside draped with blankets of green that smothered the rolling foothills of the Appalachians. It was handsome hill country, a symphony of landscape that was neither flat nor sharp but gently curved, like a full-bodied woman who gave you no choice but to sit back and appreciate.

Mary Evelyn had booked a cottage for Kathleen and me as well as one for Garrett and Morgan. We planned to shadow Omarov the first day, see what type of muscle he surrounded himself with, and then confront him the second day. The details beyond that were a bit sketchy. If the two men who'd jumped me at the thrift store were present, then that would complicate matters.

The four of us relaxed on the restaurant's veranda having drinks before dinner. We reviewed the coming days' schedule and activities. The mornings were limited to PowerPoint presentations by experts, none of whom had foreseen the nearly 70 percent peak-to-trough collapse of oil prices. Still, they would pontificate behind the podium and confidently predict the future price of West Texas crude, while bored attendees counted the minutes until they were free to chase little white balls over the resort's manicured golf courses.

Morgan's head was buried in a resort pamphlet. "We're in fly-fishing heaven," he said without looking up. "They have morning and afternoon excursions."

He flipped the brochure around and showed us a picture of a stream meandering through a dense green hall of trees and wild bushes. Sunlight sparkled on the water.

"Enjoy it," I said, taking a drink of whiskey. "We don't all need to shadow him for the day."

"I think I will."

"I spotted his foursome when he came off the course," Garrett said, steering us back to business.

"Anyone I'd recognize?"

"Was the short guy in the thrift shop bald?"

"No."

"Unlikely. One appeared to be a bodyguard—but he doesn't fit your description. The other two were Americans."

We'd spent the better part of the previous hour discussing ways to get close to Omarov. It had been a futile effort. We did learn, courtesy of the maître d', that Omarov and his entourage had reserved a corner table on the edge of the patio for seven o'clock that evening.

"Anything come to you yet?" Garrett said to me.

"Still thinking."

"No plan, no results," he reminded me. As if it was my fault we hadn't cooked something up.

"Sometimes you need to let it come to you," Kathleen said.

She laid waste to the patio. She wore a devastating scooped-neck white dress that I'd never seen before. It had a puffy flower pattern and was sculpted to her body. Her lips were rose red, her eyes sea green, and her blond hair was piled high atop her head. She had on stiletto heels that forced me to stand on my tippy-toes. The spikes surprised me—she wasn't a fan of high heels. A string of white pearls hung low on her chest. She looked as if she'd just gotten done doing a photo shoot for the resort—circa 1960s.

She hiccupped.

"Excuse me," she said.

"And if nothing comes to us?" I said.

"Ye of little faith." She shifted her attention to Morgan, who was still lost in his pamphlet. "Mind if I tag along?"

He glanced up. "Fly-fishing?"

The three of us stared at her. Kathleen had never shown any interest in fishing. She had treated previous overtures to join Morgan and myself on fishing excursions with puzzled amusement and courteous negative replies normally reserved for those who occupy lower stations in life.

"It is beautiful here," she said. "I can't sit in a spa for two days."

His face brightened with anticipation. "I'd be delighted."

"How is it different from regular fishing?"

"Fly fishermen try to replicate the fish's natural bait," Morgan explained, eager to have a student. "Most of them tie their own flies. That, in itself, is an art. You cast by whipping the line over your head and land the fly close enough, and soft enough, that the fish reacts to it as if it's a real fly, or a bug, that's hit the surface of the water."

"You trick it," Kathleen said.

"You get the fish to react instinctively. But like all fishing, much of the joy is in the environment. Fly-fishing is totally different from being sixty miles out in the gulf or standing at the end of a dock."

A puffy-nosed man, two tables over, in a black suit and a crooked polka-dot tie kept eyeing Kathleen as if she were a lollipop in a store window.

"You get the fish to come to you," I said, my mind racing in a different direction.

I took a drink, crossed my legs, and gazed into Kathleen's eyes. "You look splendid this evening," I complimented her.

"Thank you."

"A real insect."

"Pardon?"

"A hell of a fly."

"You should have pulled up with 'splendid.'"

I laid out my plan.

"You're joking," she said when I'd finished.

"Will she be safe?" Morgan wanted to know.

"Do it now," Garrett insisted. "Tonight." He glanced at Kathleen. "Correct me if I'm wrong. You'll be too nervous if we think on it. Besides, assuming he shows tonight, this might be as close as we get to him. If we fail, it doesn't necessarily preclude us from making another attempt."

"Now?" Kathleen said. "How do we even do it?"

"Garrett and I will move over a few tables," I said. "It's still early. Most of the people here are afternoon drinkers. The place will turn over for dinner."

"And if he doesn't bite?" she asked.

I flipped open my hands. "Then you'll embarrass yourself in front of people you don't know and will never see again. Your call. If you're not comfortable, we walk."

She rolled her tongue over her lower lip. "I suggest you two men leave," she said flirtatiously. "My lover and I have a few things to discuss."

"You good?" I directed my question to Morgan.

"I've got the easy part."

"You sure you're OK?" I said to Kathleen.

I was having second thoughts about getting her involved. There was a part of my life that I wanted her to remain as far away from as possible. But I'd come to realize that wasn't practical. The hell with it: I was never fond of the word "practical." It is a dull and stupid word. It leads to predictability, forgone conclusions, and death by boredom. It even sounds...practical.

"Excuse me while I freshen up," she said.

She stood and sashayed away. My moment to cancel the plan, exercise practicality, and keep her from harm's way sashayed with her.

I again approached the maître d' and this time requested another table two removed from ours. He checked his seating chart as if it were a five-star Sudoku—he was tiring of me—before finally granting my wish.

The late-afternoon bar crowd hung up their glasses. The dinner assembly filled the tables, and the transition was complete. Only two original four-tops remained. Garrett and I relocated to the new table, as Omarov was due any moment. Kathleen returned and sat across from Morgan. A woman in a white shirt and a black apron came out and lit the tiki torches surrounding the patio.

"I'm nervous," Morgan confessed to Kathleen.

"As am I," Kathleen said. "You know you're the last person in the world I would ever slap."

"I know. But let's do it right—let me feel it in the morning."

Morgan had on a beige sport coat over a white shirt with a wide-patterned collar that he'd produced from his T-shirt-infested closet. His hair was tied back in a ponytail, and his left ear was pierced. He stuck out from the usual corporate crowd, who would assume that he was nouveau riche. More than one set of wandering female eyes had already pretended not to stare at him.

"On the patio," Garrett said, but I didn't look.

A few seconds later, Omarov and three other men passed our tables on the way to their corner table. He looked like the pictures I'd seen, but he moved with a confidence that a photograph could never capture. Some men demand attention by their mere presence. Omarov was such a man.

None of his companions were the two men who'd paid me a visit in the thrift store, although one had a similar build as the shorter man. He was stout and looked as if his best opportunity for gainful employment would be wrestling horses with a traveling zoo. The other two men appeared to be corporate warriors. They smiled with shallow ease and private pleasure.

"Remember," I said, although I wasn't sure anyone was listening, "let him get a few drinks in himself."

Garrett and I struggled with banal conversation. Neither of us possessed the talent, or appetite, for small talk. Kathleen faced Omarov, and he made her within a few seconds of sitting down. Every man, upon entering a room, scans his surroundings and instantly identifies the attractive women. That is a genetic trait we have no control over. Like a dog sniffing another dog's ass, it just happens. We're dogs.

Kathleen had little competition. A redhead a few tables over had a bedroom smile and a body to warm Lambeau Field in January. But when she laughed, she brayed like a donkey. It was unfortunate for the well-heeled crowd that her world sprouted an abundance of humor. Corporate couples dotted the rest of the veranda. Some of the men had neglected to take their name tags off, or perhaps they needed a not-so-subtle reminder of who they were. The women were pleasantly and appropriately dressed but nothing to get too excited about. Everyone worked hard to fit in.

One older lady, not particularly attractive, caught my attention. She sat bolt upright in her chair and held her head high. She was dressed elegantly and made no attempt to hide her age. Her focus never wandered from her companion, nor did her hand ever touch the bowl of her wineglass. The dog comment aside, I find myself equally drawn to class as I am to sex. Perhaps even more.

Omarov was a straight-up liquor man. He was into his third drink when Garrett stood and left. I stuck to water after my initial whiskey. Kathleen had already downed two glasses of chardonnay. That was her safe quota. She was working on her third, which was her tipping point. She and Morgan were frigid with each other.

She hiccuped again. She better get it under control. It could be a deal-buster.

"You can't keep it zipped, can you?" she accused Morgan. Her voice turned a few heads.

"And you're not without guilt?" he shot back.

"Christopher and I are done," she scowled at him. "I've told you that."

Christopher? Wasn't he that biology professor who followed her around campus like a motherless kitten and showed up at her class readings? The dweeb who corrected me when I called him Chris at the faculty Christmas party at Island Grille?

They went silent. That was good—you don't want the fish to know it's not a real fly. Kathleen sat erect, her spine well off the back of the chair. After a minute, Morgan crossed his legs, slumped, and said, "Really, love, I don't know why we do this."

"Because you love me, dear, remember? You love every woman who smiles back at you. Problem is, you end up *fuck*ing half of them."

It was the first time I'd ever heard Kathleen utter a swear word. The couple next to them gave her a punishing stare.

"Careful, snug-bug," Morgan said. "You may wish to tone down your language. It's hardly appropriate."

"Appropriate? Did you even hear what I said?"

"What do you want me to say?" Morgan gave an indifferent shrug. "I get a lot of smiles. They dig me. But your math's off. I only pump half of them; the other half like sucking the tube."

Sucking the tube? Morgan had never uttered a crass comment in his life. They were both in virgin territory.

Kathleen's arm flew across the table. She slapped Morgan hard on the face. The sound stunned me. The chattering conversations of the other tables fell silent.

"You may leave," she told him in a cold but controlled voice.

Morgan, his cheek blossoming red, abruptly stood and tossed his cloth napkin on the ground. "I'm getting another room," he announced, which was the only line I'd given him. "You're on your own."

He marched out, keeping his head up. Around us, conversations started back up. It had been a good show. I stole a glance at Omarov. His eyes were on Kathleen. The waiter dropped by and inquired of Kathleen if "everything is all right." She instructed him, with the propriety and demanding tone of a disgruntled monarch, to clear the table and to "Please pick the napkin up off the ground." She crossed her legs and took a sip of wine.

He bit ten minutes later.

Omarov moseyed over to Kathleen. He parked himself beside her and said, "In my country, a man would never leave a woman alone at a table." His speech carried only a hint of accent.

"What country would that be?" Kathleen asked as she tilted her head up to meet his gaze.

"The country of manners. Is your friend not returning?"

"Let me guess," she said with a sarcastic note, "you'd like to keep me company?"

"I was thinking more of unpinning your hair and seeing how far down your back it flows."

She gave that a second and then kicked the chair opposite her with her foot. "Have a seat, thinking man."

"Peter Omarov," he said and pulled the chair out farther before seating himself.

"Julia," Kathleen said.

"Your...friend. He is in the oil business?"

"He's in the ego business."

"He is not very bright."

"You're being kind," Kathleen said. Or maybe it was Julia speaking.

"On such a splendid night, a man would be a fool to leave you."

"On any night."

"Naturally. I was just referencing the summer evening."

"Peter?"

"Yes?"

"It's been a long day, and I'm sure you're a charming conversationalist. But I don't have the energy nor the interest in the game. I'm leaving. I know no one here, but a woman must insist on decorum, even under false pretense.

Please return to your table, and wait at least five minutes. I'm South Carolina. First one in off the path."

"Perhaps you've mistaken my intentions. I'm simply a man of manners. It was not my wish to take advantage of you."

"Unlikely. But it is my intention to take advantage of you."

"Women's rights."

"Down, correct?"

"Excuse me?"

"My hair," she replied in a lascivious tone. "I believe you prefer it down."

He gave a rumbling hum of anticipation. "Whatever you are most comfortable with."

Kathleen stood. "And Peter?"

"Yes?"

"I—hic—haven't mistaken a thing."

She swaggered off the patio and into the restaurant, her arms swinging and her hips pounding to a silent and primitive beat. Half a dozen pairs of eyes followed her out. Somewhere a donkey brayed. I kept my eyes in the opposite direction as Omarov wandered back to his table. He exchanged words with the men at his table. One of them smiled. I wanted to bash his teeth in. A few minutes later, Omarov and his horse-wrestling companion rose and walked off the veranda.

I followed.

I stayed well back, as I didn't want to arouse suspicion. The canvassing oaks shadowed the evening landscape and made the ground darker than the sky. Garrett was already at his post and texted me: *in the room*. I picked up my pace. The horse-wrestler was loitering outside the door of our

South Carolina cottage. The front porch that connected the row of cottages was deserted.

"Excuse me," I mumbled as I stumbled past him. I fumbled in my pocket and took out a cigar. Turning back to him, I said, for I always yearned to deliver the line, "Listen, old chap, you don't have a light, do you?"

He started to reach into his pocket when Garrett, with the butt of his revolver, clipped him behind his right ear. His eyes widened and then clamped shut. He tumbled into my arms. A couple exited the cottage next to us. The woman, wrapped in a striking yellow scarf, studied us as her male companion firmly closed the door behind him.

"Too much vodka," I said quietly.

Garrett and I each placed an arm under him. We walked our dead weight around the corner and propped him up under a tree. Garrett handed me my gun. I dashed to the back of the house, where Garrett had left the door unlocked. I entered silently and was greeted by the sound of Kathleen moaning.

Doesn't sound fake to me.

Omarov's back was to me. He had Kathleen pinned against the wall by the front door. Her hair was down.

"Slow down, Manners," she let out in a breathy voice as she broke away from a kiss. "We've got all night."

"And I plan to use every second of it on you," Omarov growled.

He buried his head into her chest. He yanked her dress off her shoulders, and his mouth latched onto her left breast as if he wanted to swallow it whole. Kathleen rolled her head back.

I flipped on the light. Kathleen's eyes popped open.

They'd been shut?

"What the...?" Omarov said, spinning around. "Who are you?"

"The man whose sister you murdered thirty years ago."

He ignored my opening gambit. "How did you get in here? Dimitri," he shouted. *"Dimitri!"*

"Dimitri won't be joining us this evening."

Kathleen pulled her dress back up on her shoulders. She raked her hand through her hair a few times and stepped away from Omarov. She headed for the back door.

"Kitten," Omarov called after her. "You were in on this?"

She faced him. "You lied."

"*I* lied?" he spat out. "You are the deceitful one. Tell me how I lie."

"You were *not* a man of manners."

"You tell me, before this man—he is your man, is he not? I recognize him from the restaurant. You tell me that you did not enjoy Peter. Then the three of us will know that you lie. Tell him, Julia, that you did not act."

"My—hic—name is not Julia," Kathleen said. She promenaded out the back door.

Omarov's head bobbed in approval as he watched her leave.

"If I were you, my friend," he shifted his gaze to me, "I would search no more." He pounded his chest twice with his fist. "*That* is a woman."

"Take a seat," I said.

Instead, he strolled over to the bar cart and dropped ice into a glass. With his back to me, he poured himself a drink and stirred it. He turned and said, "What is it I can do for you?"

Omarov didn't look at me so much as he aimed at me. His nostrils flared when he breathed, like a racehorse chomping at the bit. He was a large man: not muscular, but in bone structure. His hair was piled back off his forehead like a pompadour. A thin pink scar under his right ear traced toward his cheek like a hairline crack in a fine china dish. It wasn't new, nor was it old. His skin was thick, and it made the lines around his eyes fold in like a blanket. His face was his autobiography.

"Sit," I said.

"I prefer to stand."

I pulled my gun.

"We both know you have no intention of using that. I can't divulge information if I can't breathe. Nor do you have a silencer. Put your toy away."

"What if my reward is in heaven?"

"A man would not leave a woman like that for heaven." He took a deliberate drink from his glass. "Besides, you do not strike me as a mindless jihadist."

"We never do."

He blew out his breath. "I do not believe you. But, for the sake of your woman, who claims I have no manners..." He sat on the end of the couch and crossed his legs. "Now, what can I do for you, Mister...?" He opened his palm up toward the ceiling.

"Travis. Jake Travis. Know the name?"

"No. Should I? What was it you said about your sister? Right after I inhaled your woman's left breast. It was like a melon right off the vine. I'm sure I left my mark on it."

"My sister disappeared in Florida. The Vanderbilt Reef Motel. Nearly thirty years ago. You were there. You and

Alex Brackett. You took her. The Brackett family covered for you. And if you don't think that after thirty years of living with that, my reward isn't in heaven, then you are one dumb Russian."

A glint of nervousness flashed in his eyes, but this wasn't his first antagonistic conversation. He scratched his chin as if he were trying to dig something out of it.

"I know the girl you speak of—in my memory. I am sorry for your loss. But it was neither Alex nor I. I suggest *you* have a seat, Mr. Travis."

I took the seat across from him. When did obedience become a trait of mine?

"Dimitri," he said as he studied me. "You do not seem overly concerned that he will barge in on us."

"That won't be happening."

"We have a saying in my country: 'Trouble never walks alone.' The athletic black man at the table with you, he is with you, too, no?" I held his eyes with mine, and he continued. "Tell me, not that it matters, but are you two acting on your own?"

"Versus?"

"You are a man comfortable with trickery and guns. To me, that indicates government."

"What happened to my sister?"

"Do you really not know, after all these years?"

"I don't ask questions I have an answer to."

"Perhaps you are the type of man who would employ such a method to learn if another were telling the truth."

"Tell me a tale."

"Very well." He took another sip of his drink and uncrossed his legs. He leaned in toward me. "But I am afraid your little charade this evening is for nothing. What is that American phrase? 'You are barking up the wrong tree.' It was not I who grabbed your sister."

"Who did?"

"David LeClair," he said, as if the answer were obvious.

"I never heard of him," I said, although Eve's voice rang in my head...*a college friend of Alex and Peter. I don't recall his name—French, or something.*

"That does not surprise me," Peter Omarov said. "And now, my tricky friend, you will never forget him, for I am sorry to tell you this, but David LeClair has been dead for thirty years."

23

It had never occurred to me that the man who had abducted and murdered my sister was dead. How could I kill a dead man? Why the massive cover-up and effort to pin my sister's death on Hawkins if her abductor was already dead? Unless more than one person was involved. I didn't necessarily believe Omarov, nor did I necessarily *not* believe him.

"I'll tag along," I said. "Who was LeClair?"

"He was a friend—a long time ago. He was not a bad man, but a good man who did a bad thing—the day he took her."

"I'll verify everything you say," I reminded him.

"Brittany. No? Was that her name?"

The palm of my hand on my gun started to sweat.

"Yes. I see it in your eyes. She *was* your sister. I thought you might be a hired gun. Worse—you are a soldier with heart in the game. Pity. Such men are prone to errors. You should be careful, my friend. Emotions are the enemy of the mind."

"LeClair," I countered.

His chest rose and then fell, as if that particular breath was a great effort. He considered his drink and placed it squarely on a coaster on the end table. One of his fingers held a gold ring that looked like a radial tire with a cousin of the Hope Diamond mounted to it.

"You have talked to Alex Brackett?" he asked.

"You're the first batter."

I instantly realized my unforced error. I didn't want Omarov to know whom I had or had not talked to. No matter. I assumed he was lying, and he likely knew that. Still, I wasn't thinking fast enough. My feelings were bogging me down, as if in a dream when you're running but can't move your legs.

"David LeClair was our friend," Omarov said. "You know my father was attached to the Soviet embassy at that time?"

"Go on."

"I was, what, twenty-two? The three of us—Alex, David, and I—were students at the University of Virginia. Have I told you anything you don't know?"

"Leave no stone unturned."

"Yes. Well, fortunately for you, I understand your American idioms. We can skip the preliminaries. David LeClair had a dark side, and I do not wish to sound boastful, but he was taken with my lifestyle. My privileges. He wanted to impress us."

"Us?"

"Alex and me. Alex came from money. And I—" He spread his hands. "What can I say?"

"That you're a worthless Russian thug."

"I understand your hate. What happened does not represent the best of me. I offer no excuses."

"LeClair," I said to prompt him.

"He snatched your sister. Do *not* shoot the messenger. I would feel much easier if you would put your weapon down."

I put my gun on the table to my right.

"David, as I said, was trying to impress us. He had no money, so he resorted to other means. My position is defenseless, but for the record, I was a young playboy with carte-blanche privileges. I knew it was wrong, and I can only say that today I am ashamed of my compliance."

"Skip it. What did LeClair do?"

"I am sorry, Mr. Travis. Your sister died that afternoon. On her bed. He was too physical with her. He choked her. It wasn't his first—nor do I suspect, his last—such encounter with a young woman. We—David, Alex, and I—went to Russia shortly thereafter. The trip had already been planned, although my father accelerated it."

"I don't believe you."

"Of course you don't. But there is a difference between not believing and not *want*ing to believe."

"Where did LeClair die," I said.

"In Russia. A head-on collision. Both drivers."

"My sister's body?" My voice came out in monotone as Omarov's previous assertion about what I wanted to believe started to take root.

"You want to know?"

"I asked the question, didn't I?"

"David had her body out of the motel and in the trunk of the rental car before anyone knew she was missing. She was small. He dumped her into a room cart that was outside the door, under the dirty sheets. This I got later, understand? Neither I nor Alex was aware of any of this at the time. I was at the bar, and Alex," he scrunched his face, "was likely mounting a hotel guest."

"What did you tell the police?"

"The truth, and then a lie."

"The truth?"

"That we saw nothing."

"The lie?" Omarov had slipped into the plural pronoun, as if he were speaking for Alex Brackett as well.

"That we didn't know what happened to your sister. We did. David drove off with her body long before the police arrived. He disposed of her, came back to the motel—this was after the police left—and told us we needed to go."

"He told you what he did?"

"He did."

"You didn't tell the police?"

He shrugged dismissively, his left shoulder rising and falling. "Again, I will not defend our actions. Alex had a family business to protect. I was the son of a Russian diplomat. We were young. We made mistakes that day. Our decisions would not have brought your sister back. Both our fathers wanted us out of the country as quickly as possible."

"They knew?"

"They didn't ask."

"But they knew."

"They didn't ask."

I stood and said, "Nice story. You just make it up, or have you been waiting to deliver your lines for years?"

He rose as well. "I am sorry for your sister. I truly am."

"Where's her body?"

"I cannot help you there."

"You're lying."

"I understand your—"

I picked up my gun and was on him before he could react. I thrust the barrel under his chin.

"You don't understand shit," I said. "Where did he bury her?"

He smiled weakly, as if we both knew we could trade lies and insults all night but that doing so would serve no purpose.

"I told you. I do not—"

"The three of you cruised around Russia drowning in vodka. He told you everything, you sick pig. *Where did he bury her?*"

His eyes hardened, but his voice remained calm. "I do—"

I pressed the barrel hard into his throat. "I can pull the trigger now and never lose a wink of sleep."

The leading edge of fear crept into his eyes. "I didn't ask," he gargled out. "I might be a sick pig, but I am not a stupid one."

I eased up on my gun.

"Even if he had told us," he said, "what is there now? A housing development? A twenty-story condo?"

I backed off and felt strangely empty. What if this was the end of the road? *Then why the elaborate cover-up to frame Hawkins for her murder?* If David LeClair's DNA was in the room, that would lead back to Omarov and Brackett being part of the cover-up. Maybe even accessory to murder. It made sense. Worst yet, maybe that's all there was to my chase. I placed my gun back in the shoulder holster inside my jacket.

I gave the conundrum to Omarov. "If your lie stands," I said, "why is someone trying to pin her death on someone else?"

"Who did they try to pin her death on?"

"Leonard Hawkins."

"I do not know who you are talking about."

I leveled my eyes on his. "You want to do this? Stand in front of me and tell me you don't know anything about Leonard Hawkins? How he confessed to abducting and killing my sister? How Bernard Carlsberg, your attorney, called you and told you I crashed his party? How the two men who killed Hawkins paid me a visit at a thrift store the other day? You lie about all that, then you lie about everything else you just told me. Your choice."

He studied me as if he were unsure of his next step. Just as I had earlier, he had committed an unforced error, and both parties knew it.

"Your sister is gone," he said, as if those four words would settle our differences.

I took that as an admission to guilt for the laundry list I'd just recited to him. "Who, besides you, wants to bury this? Brackett?"

He stuck out his lower jaw and methodically bounced his head a few times. "I can think of a dozen," he said. "But you are asking the wrong man. You know that I have certain business interests in Ukraine, no?"

I arched my eyebrows.

"I am instrumental there in helping your country and my country save face. I can surmise that if this came out—what David LeClair did, and my proximity to him at the time—then your country might fear such a revelation would derail our efforts. Your efforts in digging up your past may cause my character to be besmirched. Perhaps I—or those who protect me—have engaged in misguided attempts to convince you that the past is best left sleeping. My apologies, but do not lay it all at my feet. You might consider looking at your own government for the source of your problems. Now, I must be going."

He headed for the door.

"If I find you're lying. If I find that in any manner you hurt her…"

He pivoted and took several steps back to me.

"What? You'll set your vixen upon me again? Please, Mr. Travis, come to my country next time you want to talk. I'll show you how a true whore moans."

My right fist flattened his nose. It wasn't a full blow, as he was too close to allow me to take a big swing. Omarov staggered back as blood spurted from his nose. He caught himself on the arm of the chair. He took his right hand and massaged his face. He got blood on his fingers. He sucked them in his mouth to clean them off.

"That felt good, no?" he said as he bobbed his head in appreciation of my swing. He gave me a cynical smile, his white teeth crimson with bright blood, like cherry sauce on vanilla ice cream. "Not as good as when your woman stuck her tongue in my mouth."

He turned and strolled out the front door. He left it open.

24

"**H**e's lying," Garrett told me over breakfast the next morning. "He gave you a dead man and made him for the crime."

"I didn't see the advantage of pressing him. We'll need to verify his story and check out David LeClair."

"His parting comment, again?"

"Some lame apology about my sister." We'd been over the previous night numerous times. I'd lost track of how many endings I'd fabricated.

"I thought you said he mentioned that earlier in the conversation."

"He repeated it going out the door."

I didn't know why I lied to Garrett, other than I felt bad for what I'd had Kathleen do. She, on the other hand, couldn't have cared less. "It's just a boob," she'd told me the previous night. "Guys go bonkers for them." When I told her about Omarov's parting salvo, she quipped, "What was I supposed to do, shake his hand? Besides, Julia's her own woman."

Julia and I were going to have to schedule a date night.

I wasn't going to verify Omarov's statement about David LeClair at the Greenbrier. Garrett and I checked out. Morgan stayed back to fly-fish for two days once I assured him that I had no immediate role for him. I impressed on him to stay clear of Omarov. Kathleen's sincere desire to experience fly-fishing would have to wait for another opportunity.

IT WAS NINE THE next morning. I was at Mac's house, although there was no sign of him. During my previous visits, he'd been outside during that time of the day. I rapped on the front door, waited, and rapped again. I tried the doorknob, but it was locked. I scooted around to the rear. It was also locked. I pounded on the door, gripped with worry about him. Finally, Mac opened it, his eyes confused in sleep. He was shorter without his Nikes on.

"Jake? I'm just getting up. Been tired lately. Come on in. Grab a soldier if you'd like, but I don't think I will."

I passed on the beer and instead fixed him eggs, toast, and coffee. I explained my meeting with Omarov and the information I'd accumulated on the man.

"Your woman did that for you?" he interjected.

I flipped an egg and the yoke broke, bleeding yellow lava in the pan. "She did. And with a little more enthusiasm than I envisioned." My voice carried a note of irritation. I blamed it on the broken yoke.

He chuckled. "Who's the other fellow again?"

"David LeClair."

"Omarov sounds familiar, but I'm not sure about LeClair. What's your next step?"

"I need to verify Omarov's story."

"And then what?"

"Pardon?" I handed him his breakfast as a gull screeched outside.

"Where's the end of the road?" he said.

"If LeClair checks out, I'm likely done. Sorry about the yolk."

"Why don't you go up there and move Lady. You'll find some files under the boards she's standing on. Maybe there's something on this LeClair fellow."

"I thought you said you kept it all in your head?"

"No. I said I keep it where no one else can find it and then tapped my head. You assumed I didn't keep files. Take a dull knife with you. You'll need it to pry the boards loose."

I left footprints in the dust on the way up the stairs. I picked up Lady—she was remarkably light for a full-figured woman—and gingerly set her down. Her backside was dull and brown. Her attractiveness was measured by the distance in which she was viewed, for the closer you got, the less you believed.

I jammed the knife between two floorboards and worked it underneath one. The board came up with ease. A bulging eight-by-ten envelope was curved between the floor joists.

"Go ahead. Open it," Mac instructed me when I joined him downstairs. "Before I left, I copied a few files. Never hurts to have a little blackmail insurance. That folder is Carlsberg's clients. Omarov, if he's anywhere, should be in there. I'm not sure you'll find anything to advance your cause, but you're welcome to take a look."

"I appreciate your help, but why now? You could have given this to me previously."

"You judge people instantly. I don't."

"What am I supposed to do?" I said, failing to keep the irritation from my voice. "Keep coming back and earn a little trust, gain a little knowledge each time?"

"No. But I don't fault you for your attitude. That's all I got right there. You could have called me, instead, you came over. I know what you're doing. I appreciate you checking in on me."

"It's Lady I'm after."

"Aren't we all? How'd she feel?"

"Fake."

"Now you know why I don't go up there."

Most of the content was legalese, and some of it pertained to Nikolay Omarov, Peter's father. Two-thirds of the way through the stack was a picture of Peter Omarov and his fraternity brothers at the University of Virginia. It was in a State Department brochure that boasted of an exchange program between the Soviet Union and the United States. I glanced at the names: Peter Omarov, Alexander Brackett, and—next to Omarov, back row, fourth from the left—was a young man with his eyes set deep within his face. His features were partially shadowed by the white-pillared brick building they stood under. He appeared to be squinting, or perhaps he had small eyes. He was the only one in the picture who was not smiling. I traced my finger along the bottom to track the names that correlated with the positions in the photograph.

David LeClair. Roanoke, Virginia.

"Found you," I said and handed the picture to Mac. "Brackett, Omarov, and LeClair were in the same fraternity."

Mac gave it a cursory glance and then said, "Keep it. You need to track down LeClair's family and see if you can verify what Omarov told you."

I cleaned up the dishes and asked Mac what his plans were for the day. Perhaps getting a glimpse of my motive, he assured me he was going to stay inside and do some reading as well as clean out his study. He padded into his study, and I followed to get him situated.

The study was a paper-strewn room with books and folders scattered around as if a tropical storm had blown through. The desk, however, was remarkably clear. It faced a shaded back window that looked out to the porch and the pond beyond. It was a desk one could accomplish great things at or at least lose all excuses.

I left him flipping through his mail, and humming a tune.

As I drove away, his parting instructions to hunt down LeClair's family reverberated in my head. It seemed more of a command than a suggestion. I couldn't help but speculate that Walter MacDonald knew more than he let on and that, like a shrewd and sagacious wizard, he was gently piloting my journey.

25

David LeClair's parents, according to public records, divorced soon after their only child failed to return home. I located an address for his mother and father in Roanoke. They lived on opposite sides of town. The flight schedules were a nightmare, so I'd hopped in the truck and drove straight through. I'd gotten in to Roanoke around nine, checked into the first hotel I tripped upon, and then camped out at the nearest bar. I would have been wise to have been more selective on both establishments.

If LeClair, as Omarov had maintained, had a record of soliciting underage girls, I couldn't find it. He seemed a straight-up young man who, after graduation, received a one-way ticket to Russia.

I arrived at his mother's home at 8:30 the following morning. Spreading street trees shielded the front yard from the sun and shaded the buckled sidewalks. A swing anchored one end of a front covered porch, and a wicker table with two chairs held down the opposite end. They were like warring furniture, each with territorial rights. I swung open a screen door and then had to chase it so it wouldn't bang against the house. The wood front door had a crescent-shaped piece of glass at the top. It looked dark inside. I gave the door a few sharp knocks. I repeated my action, but my effort was fruitless.

I walked around the side of the house and peered through the window of the detached garage. No car. A red Toro lawn mower had grass crusted to the side of it, as if the lawn had been wet the last time it was used. A nativity scene was haphazardly stacked in one corner. Mary was lying on a bag of triple-processed black mulch. Several plastic sheep were lined up against a wall. No sign of Baby Jesus.

I left and killed an hour fidgeting with my phone and sipping coffee at a McDonald's. When I again pulled up against the curb in front of LeClair's mother's house, a gold Honda CRV was parked in the driveway.

I presented myself at the door.

"Elinor LeClair?" I asked when a lady tentatively opened the door.

"Yes?"

I told her my name and that I was investigating the disappearance of a young girl many years ago and wondered what she could tell me about Peter Omarov. I don't know why I didn't tell her that the young girl was my sister, other than I felt like keeping it at a distance. Sometimes I feel as if I'm observing my life instead of living it.

Her face torqued with worry.

"I just have a few questions," I rushed out, afraid she might slam the door in my face. "I won't take much of your time."

"Are you with a law-enforcement agency?"

The formality of her question caught me. "No, ma'am. I'm—"

"Then come on in."

I followed her into a modest living room with a brick fireplace with brass-trimmed glass doors on the far wall.

A grandfather clock stood guard in the corner, like a tired old sentry who'd given up seeking relief from its post. The place was clean and neat, although I'd be surprised if a piece of furniture had been introduced to the room since Jimmy Carter was president.

"Coffee?" she asked. Then, as if forgetting herself, she tacked on, "Please make yourself comfortable."

"Coffee would be fine. Thank you."

Her hair was tied in the back, which was unusual for a woman of her age. She had on just the right amount of makeup to let one know she took care of herself. Music played softly from the kitchen. Behind me, the clock measured the day in seconds. The silence between the ticks was louder than the ticks themselves.

I took a seat on a flower-patterned chair. Elinor slipped into the kitchen and soon returned with a tray holding two cups. She presented the tray to me, and I took a small cup steaming with coffee. The handle was too small to be of use to me. She placed the tray on a table and then sat on the couch. She folded her hands on her lap, displaying no interest in her coffee cup.

"You're not fond of the police?" I said as a question.

Tick.

Tick.

Tick.

"They're OK," she finally said.

Her voice sounded older than she appeared to be, and I wondered how that had happened. Her eyes flicked to the front picture window and out to the street. Maybe she wasn't ready for business chat yet. Maybe she wasn't even there.

"I notice your name is not the common spelling," I said in an attempt to ignite the conversation.

"I was named after Thomas Jackson's first wife," she said, granting me her attention.

"Stonewall Jackson?"

"Yes. My father liked Confederate generals. Elinor Jackson hemorrhaged to death a month after giving birth to a stillborn. She was only twenty-nine."

"It's a pretty—"

"She's the daughter I never had. We talk in my dreams. We both need each other."

"Are you the daughter or mother?"

"I'll ignore the implication of your tone, Mr. Travis."

"I meant no offense."

"You might think me mad, but it works for me."

"I understand."

"You most definitely do not."

The conversation stalled like a sailboat in the doldrums. The ticking clock reminded me that I had but one chance with Elinor. It was slipping away.

"He was a great general," I said in an attempt to catch a favorable wind. "Both her and his death were tragic."

"So few people, especially northerners, understand the goodness in a Confederate's heart. That bothers Elinor. Do you understand?"

"I'd like to think I do."

I'd give Ms. Nutcase another minute and then jerk her mind out of the war between the States.

"He was a kind and wonderful husband," she continued. "I think he saw his Elinor as he was dying...while he lay delirious on that Sunday afternoon in Clarksburg and said his last words on this earth."

"'Let us cross over the river and rest under the shade of the trees,'" I said.

"Isn't that beautiful?"

"One for the ages."

"I'm surprised you know it."

"A schoolboy's memory."

Tick.

Tick.

Tick.

"Those police didn't bend over backward with concern," Elinor said, her eye resting peacefully on mine.

"How is that?"

"Why do you think Peter Omarov had anything to do with some young girl—when would this have been?"

"Thirty years ago."

"Hmm...pretty far back." She tilted her head. "Why your interest?"

"I've been retained by the family."

She hesitated as if she were questioning whether to pursue that or not. "And why me?"

"I understand that your son was friends with Omarov and Alex Brackett in college. The young girl disappeared at the same motel the three of them stayed at after graduation."

I reiterated that I would appreciate any information she had on Omarov or Brackett.

Her eyes wandered past me for a brief moment and then returned. She took a sip from her coffee. Her hands trembled, and she quickly put her cup down, as if she didn't want me to notice.

"They were close, Alex and Davie. Best of friends, really. I never cared for Peter, though. You know he was Russian, right? But educated and raised, for a good part of his early years, in America."

"Do you know much about their time together in Florida?"

"Not really."

I expected more, but she remained silent. *Did she not know?* "That's where the young girl went missing," I said to prompt her.

"What do you mean 'went missing'?"

"She was never seen again," I said in a curt tone. Either this lady could help me or she couldn't.

"My David had nothing to do with that girl's death."

"I didn't say she died."

"I know all about it," she said sharply, as if I'd missed something.

I leaned forward. "We're discussing the Vanderbilt Reef Mo—"

"I know what we're discussing. The police asked my husband and me all sorts of questions. They weren't that interested, if you ask me. Just going through the motions. Said a girl was abducted, and they were tying up loose ends."

"Your son didn't have any history of arrests, did he?"

"Davie? He was an Eagle Scout. Are you implying that he had anything to do with that girl's disappearance?"

"No, ma'am, not in the least. When did the police come around and visit you?"

"Which time? They came twice, although I'm not sure you'd call the second visitors policemen."

"When was the first time?"

"Two, three weeks, maybe, after they returned from Florida. But the boys were in Russia by then. One of the policemen sat in that very chair you're in now. I had no idea what they were talking about, carrying on about some girl disappearing in Florida. They seemed satisfied with my ignorance, although they were mighty interested to know if Davie had said anything to me or communicated with me since he'd left for Russia."

"Had he?"

"No."

"Did he act strangely—different in any manner—between the time he came back from Florida and when he left for Russia?"

She pondered that. "It's hard to tell. I thought he kept to himself more than usual, but it was so long ago. All I got now is memories of memories, and even those are starting to melt away. Memories are like a hard piece of ice. You think it will last forever, but then you realize it's melting away, and nothing in the world can stop it. I can thank Elinor for that. She was the first one to point that out to me. She said that even in heaven, memories melt."

"Tell me about their trip to Russia."

She landed a hard look, as if she were discouraged that I hadn't offered a conciliatory remark on her definition of memory being molded by an apparition of Stonewall Jackson's first wife. She massaged her cheek with her hand, momentarily cast her eyes to the floor, and then looked back at me.

"They—Davie and Alex—were going for two months. Tour the country after graduation. I thought it would be all right, Peter's family being with the government and all." She raised her eyes up to me, although her head was still down, like a weight she couldn't lift. "Then I got the cable. You know they still send those?"

"Cables?"

"At least they did back then."

"Did it provide any details?"

"That he had died in an auto accident. Someone ran straight into him. That was the end of our marriage. It wasn't strong enough to withstand that cable. You plan on dropping by Beaufort's—he's my husband—place as well?"

"I do. This was after the police came?"

"That's right. Save yourself the time with Beaufort—he's out for a week. Fishing over at Pickwick Lake. He has a friend in Waterloo, Alabama. Goes there once a year. He's not due back for a few days. Allow me to show you something."

Without waiting for my response, she stood and went up the stairs. It was rotten luck that I wouldn't be able to question her ex-husband, but there was nothing I could do. I tried to shrug off my disappointment, but it clung to me like a nasty cold. It would necessitate another trip to talk to LeClair's father and hear his version. It might not have been necessary if Elinor were playing with a full deck, but that wasn't the case.

I trailed her up the steps. She opened a door to a bedroom, and we stepped in. A poster of the rock band REM was on one wall. A young Michael Stipe was behind the microphone. A movie poster for the Bond film *A View to a Kill* was above the bed. I walked past her and toward a narrow bookshelf. Graham Greene's *The Human Factor* and *Our Man in Havana* were leaning against John le Carré's *The Little Drummer Girl*.

"He read these?" I said, still looking at the books.

"I believe so. Why?"

"Heavy stuff."

"He was always…quiet. Maybe even mysterious, although that comes across as an odd way for a mother to describe her son."

"Is there anyone else I should be talking to?" I asked, gazing into the room and realizing a beat too late that it was the wrong moment for that question.

Elinor ignored me. "The young man who once lived in this room? He *loved* Virginia: the cicadas in the afternoon, the kudzu vine choking us green every summer, the winters just cold enough to make you appreciate the warmth but not so cold as to chase you south. The sweet smell of the viburnum blossoms in the spring. He didn't know these things—he was too young—but they were part of him."

Something about her voice made me realize that she wasn't always a seventy-something widow who had outlived her only child. She too had once been a younger person, with dreams and aspirations plastered on the walls of her mind. She paused. I remained silent, not knowing what to say and feeling anything I did might be construed as disrespectful.

"I did try to tell him," she continued, "when he was young, about the Viburnum? He couldn't get the name right. We settled on calling it 'verby.'" She paused and then said, "I told you the police came twice."

"You did."

"'Police' probably wasn't the right word. The second time, about a year later, two men in nice suits knocked on my door. They said they were with the CIA. They wanted to know if Davie had communicated anything to me—like if I'd received anything from him postmortem. I told them no."

"Had you?"

She gave me a stern look. "No."

"Did their questions mimic the police who'd come a year earlier?"

"At first. But then they got into Davie's past. Wanted to see his room—walk around the house. Get to know what he was like as a boy. I found out later they even knocked on the neighbors' doors, asking about him. I don't know why they would care. I asked them to investigate his death. Told them that Davie was such a careful driver. Know what they told me?"

"No."

"The other guy wasn't."

"Is there—"

"They thought that was funny. The man who didn't say it? I could see him suppressing a laugh. I see him today—standing in my room and trying not to laugh. That ice never cracked. Never melted. I'd take a blowtorch to it if I could, but that would just seem to make it stronger. Colder."

Her face twisted in pain, and she brought her hand up to her mouth. The Westminster chimes of the grandfather clock a floor beneath us reminded us that it was a quarter to the hour. It played out like a sorrowful solo in an empty auditorium. She punched out her breath and straightened her back, as if she were preparing for a charge.

"I have a favor to ask you," she said with unexpected resolution in her voice.

"It'd be my pleasure."

She turned and took the stairs back down to the first floor.

"I really don't know much about Peter Omarov," she said over her shoulder. "Never saw him, or Alex, again. I understand that Alex stayed in Russia for some time before coming back and then returned several more times, but I lost track of it all."

We entered the kitchen. She opened a white kitchen cabinet, took out an envelope, and turned to me. "I never understood that—why he kept going back to Russia. But they—Alex and Peter—were college friends, and Davie told me once that he thought their families were connected in some manner. Maybe it had something to do with that." She held up the envelope in her hand. "I believe we have two unanswered questions."

"You asked me if I could do you a favor."

"And you inquired—one and a half times—if there was anyone else you could talk to."

"Is there?"

She handed me the envelope and then plopped in a kitchen chair, as if the envelope were a baton, and she'd successfully completed her hundred yards of the relay and, with a final and exhausted push, had passed it on to the next runner.

"Rachel," she said.

"Pardon?"

She nodded at the envelope. "You need to talk to Rachel. I haven't gotten around to depositing that one yet."

I opened the envelope. It contained a recently dated handwritten check for $1,000, payable to Elinor LeClair. The payer was a Rachel Haverford, 895 Bethel Church Road, Townsend, Tennessee.

I pulled back a chair across from her and took a seat. "Tell me what this means."

"I haven't a clue. She was David's longtime girlfriend in college. She doesn't go by Rachel, though. Everyone calls her Dusty. Or at least they did then."

I recalled her comment about not getting around to deposit the check. "How often do you receive one of these?"

"Every month."

"For how long?"

She looked at me, her eyes begging for forgiveness. I answered my own question. "Nearly every month since David died."

Her lower lip quivered. She reached out and took a napkin from a wood holder in the middle of the table and dabbed her eyes. I went to the counter and pulled a Kleenex from a purple-flowered box and handed it to her. It would be softer than a napkin.

"I'm sure I'm a mess." She straightened her back. "I *am* a mess. I needed—I *need*—the money. We didn't have much, and after the divorce, it was even less." She shook her head. "It started about a year after he died. I knew it wasn't right. But I'm not sure I want to know." Her eyes nailed mine. "The favor I asked you?"

"Yes?"

She shuddered, and I felt bad for her. I spoke so she wouldn't need to. "Find out who is sending Rachel—Dusty—money every month, and why she is passing it, or part of it, on to you."

"Thank you. My daughter can't help me with that, but she told me one would appear who could."

She held on for a second, and although I hardly knew Elinor LeClair, for that second, I was her biggest fan, her most ardent supporter. Then her head collapsed in her hands, and she sobbed as if everything inside her had broken at once.

I went to get another Kleenex. Outside her kitchen window, a bluebird dipped its peak into a birdbath. The water was clear, as if it were rinsed and filled daily with a garden hose and not left to accumulate leaves and debris from the towering trees. The grass was freshly cut. A track of black mulch encircled the yard. Flowers, like a fallen rainbow, lay along the edges of the mulch. A concrete patio held a table and four chairs. The patio was clean, not a clipping or a twig on it. Our surroundings are so particular. So organized. It's our insides that are a web of turmoil and disarray, a noisy prayer of what we want to be. It's a shame we can't take our lives and cut a little grass, spread a little mulch, plant a few flowers, and make ourselves what we thought we'd be when we were young, and the river and the shade of the trees were far away.

26

A seven-foot bear towered over me at the front desk in the Laurel Valley Cabins rental office in Townsend, Tennessee. Fortunately, it was dead and stuffed. Otherwise, I'd have to teach that bear a lesson. A poster for Dollywood was behind the bear. Dolly looked good. Dolly always looked good. The jailhouse gossip rag had indicated that her life was as put together on the inside as she was on the outside. That was before she delivered an alien baby.

"How long you be wantin' to stay, honey?" the plump lady behind the desk asked.

"Night or two."

"Our minimum is four nights this time of the year."

"Sign me up."

"How about if I charge you for that and then credit you if you need to leave early—family emergency, or somethin' like that. They allow me to put that in."

"I appreciate that."

I'd driven over from Virginia, clocking lost miles on the truck and searching satellite and Pandora stations as well as my own playlist for a melody to match my mood. But that song had yet to be written.

Elinor LeClair knew something wasn't right about her son vanishing into Russia, but she couldn't resist the money and was afraid her curiosity would be the end of the gravy train. She'd made a silent pact with the devil not to vigorously question her son's true demise in exchange for $12,000 per year. I'd come along at the right time, as her guilt had been drowning her for years.

Rachel Haverford—Dusty—likely hadn't seen David LeClair since he boarded a 747 to London and then on to Moscow, nearly three decades ago. Elinor said her son and Dusty had discussed marriage. She'd also informed me that David once brought Dusty, Omarov, and Alex Brackett to the house for dinner. That confirmed that they all knew one another. Maybe the money had nothing to do with David LeClair, but I needed to verify what Omarov had told me. Besides, you always follow the money. Perhaps the lucky nickel would shine some light on how three college chums of thirty years ago factored in to the murder of my sister.

"Bear's Den OK?" the lady behind the counter asked. She wore silver cross earrings that dangled on each side of her head.

I jutted my chin out to the stuffed bear. "I'm not taking that big boy's cave, am I?"

"Heavens, no. We just call it that. It's about a mile from here. Has a nice little stream that runs behind her. I think you'll like her a lot. I been here my whole life, and I can tell you there ain't no prettier place in the world than God's country right here and no prettier little cabin than Bear's Den. It gets five stars from people who stay there. Most all of them are repeat customers."

She smiled when she talked, and I wondered if her life was really that good. If *any* life could be that good.

"Bear's Den it is," I said.

"Okeydokey, honey. Here's your key."

She handed me a key, along with a brochure stuffed with flyers on area attractions. She reached over the counter and picked a piece of lint off my shirt.

"There," she said, "that's better."

I asked her where a grocery store was and thanked her for her time. She wished me a blessed day. Thirty minutes later, I unlocked the door and placed a plastic grocery bag on the counter, where it instantly lost its shape. I stuck my meager items in the refrigerator and checked out the wide stream off the back porch. The water was clear. It reflected the rocks and trees as if it were a liquid mirror. Stones jutted from the riverbed, and the water slipped effortlessly around them. Nothing impedes water in a stream.

I sat in a rocker and brought up directions for 895 Bethel Church Road on my phone. Twenty minutes later, after traversing mountain roads that had me repeatedly downshifting the truck, I pulled onto the gravel driveway next to the crooked mailbox of number 895.

There was no house.

The address was there, but the dwelling was long gone. A brick chimney rose out of the weeds. It reminded me of the third pig—the one who built his house of bricks—but this pig only did the fireplace. Queen Anne's lace and yellow trillium covered the ground, and invasive honeysuckle bushes with trunks as thick as trees rimmed the area where the house had once stood. Front brick steps, buried with rolling years of October leaves, led to nowhere.

I climbed out of the truck and paced the dry land. It had been a long time since any structure had occupied the ground. Yet someone was using this address to send money to Elinor. Maybe Dusty lived here once. Maybe she'd pulled the address out of thin air. I went back to the truck.

I sat in the truck, and for reasons that only Christ knows, the sign that hung behind Dr. Honaker, my adolescent shrink, popped into my head: *When I let go of what I am, I become what I might be.*

I turned the key.

"SOMETHING WRONG, SWEETIE?"

I was back at the rental office. *I been here my whole life*, she'd gushed to me. I explained to Ms. Happy that I was looking for Rachel Haverford of 895 Bethel Church Road but that nothing was at the address.

"First of all, she don't go by Rachel. Second of all, if you don't mind me askin', why is it you're wanting to see Dusty?"

"I'm a friend of a family she used to know a long time ago, the LeClairs."

"Name sounds familiar. From around here?"

"No. Roanoke, Virginia."

"I know where Roanoke is." She gave an indifferent shrug. "You can find her at the Down Yonder. 'Bout eight miles toward town."

"She works there?"

"Owns it. Dusty's a good woman and a hard worker, I'll give her that, even if it is Satan's work. We don't see her in the Lord's house as much as we'd like."

"I thought, 'Wherever you live, I will live.'"

Her forehead crinkled. "Pardon?"

"Old Testament. Ruth, I believe."

"Have you found Him?" she said with expectation rising in her voice.

"No. But I got a line on Princess Di—rumor is she's on a sheep farm in Austria."

She gave that a second and then said, "I doubt that. Poor girl. She was too good for that royal family."

I thanked her for her time and left.

The Down Yonder was less than a dozen miles west on Lamar Alexander Parkway, closer to Maryville. I pulled into the parking lot, killed the engine, and sat in the truck.

I'd been doing a lot of that lately.

I was a far poke from the Vanderbilt Reef Motel and felt as though I'd dragged the Gulf of Mexico with me. I hoped my actions were a circle and would eventually lead back to my sister, but there was no guarantee. Maybe I was on a straight line and burning time. I punched out my breath, got out of the truck, and marched, with manufactured energy, through the front door and smack into night.

The sun's light is rarely a patron of bars, and the Down Yonder was no exception. I gave my eyes a second to adjust. A mute jukebox stood against a wall. Two pool tables, like immovable fortresses, were in front of it, their cue sticks stiff at attention on a rack next to the jukebox. I took a stool at the bar and ordered a beer from the bearded bartender. He wore blue jeans and a black long-sleeve shirt. Under his beard, his skin was smooth. The beard made him look a good ten years older than he likely was. A sign under a corner TV read, "I lost my religion, but I found my gun." Under that, a sign stated that no hippies were allowed at the bar after 8:00 p.m.

A couple of stools down from me, a man did a thousand-mile stare into the magical bottles behind the bar. A cane leaned against his barstool. A dog snored under the stool, its nose nestled next to a ceramic bowl of water.

Halfway through my beer, I said to the bearded bartender, busy tapping a keg, "Is Dusty coming in this evening?"

"Who's asking?"

"Me."

"And you are?"

"Friend of Elinor LeClair."

"Never heard of her."

"Maybe Dusty has."

"You would need to ask her that."

"That's why—"

"I got it, Billy."

I turned and faced a woman in tight low-rise jeans and a white long-sleeve shirt with the cuffs rolled. A trio of buttons were undone, revealing a pale chest. Her hair was the color and smoothness of the sand on a beach after a wave washes over it and then recedes back to the water. The ends were layered, with the longest strands touching her narrow shoulders. She could walk into MoMA in New York on a Sunday afternoon or a football stadium in Mustang, Oklahoma, on a Friday night, and she'd fit in either place. I had a hard crush on her.

I stood, took a few steps, and extended my hand. "Jake Travis."

"Dusty Haverford."

Her handshake was business firm, and her voice had a rasp on the edge of it. She had the cutest damn pug nose this side of the Mississippi and north of El Salvador. She had me by a good ten to fifteen years, but they looked like damn good years to me. She was one wink away from putting me on my knees.

Hello, Tennessee.

Dusty said, "How'd you find me?"

"Lady at the rental office," I replied, realizing that Mac had asked the same question.

"Margot?"

"Didn't catch her name."

"Sugar sweet and smiles all the time?"

"Almost disturbing, isn't it?"

She curled up the corner of her lip. "'Round here we call that the Jesus smile. Margot's been trying to get me to church for years to meet him."

"How's that coming?"

"He can find me—after all, you did. Although I am surprised it took someone like you so long to come about."

"Concerning?"

"You said you were a friend of Elinor."

"We've met. I'd appreciate a few minutes."

"Let's get it over with." Dusty looked past me toward the bearded bartender. "I'm going to place some flowers on my parents' grave." She refocused on me. "Like to tag along? Cemetery's up in Cades Cove. Not far from here. We got some time till it's dark. This time of year, the day just hates to leave, and before you know it, it comes right back again. You can ride along or follow. Suit yourself."

"Dusty," the bartender said, "why—"

"Don't worry," she dismissed him. "I'll take Bud."

With that, the snoring dog perked up and struggled to its feet. It was some sort of bulldog mix. Its jaws looked like they could tear a barstool off its steel plate.

"Let's go, girl." She glanced at me. "You don't mind, do you?"

"No."

"You got a dog?"

"Cat."

She laughed and planted her hands on her hips. "Men don't have cats; they have dogs."

"She thinks she's a lion. Besides, women don't name their girl dogs Bud."

"Yeah? She always looked like a Bud to me. You know—ready to blossom at any time. All that promise yet to burst out. Shows how much we know about each other. I do need to tell you, though."

"Yes?"

"Two words from me and Bud here will be at your neck. You OK with that? 'Cause I really do want to put flowers on my parents' grave."

"I'll ride shotgun."

"Hand me a pack, will you, Billy?"

A minute later, I was sitting in the passenger seat of her F-150. A bouquet of fresh flowers rested on my lap and a cold six-pack of Coors Light between my knees. Bud adjusted her drooling snout so that it rested on my thigh. Dusty kept one arm on the wheel and the other cocked outside the window of her truck, her elbow sticking out like a V. She whistled "Levon."

I like a woman who whistles.

27

Cades Cove Road, in Great Smoky Mountains National Park, is a single-lane, winding piece of asphalt that snakes between expansive fields lined with split-rail fences, trees, and log cabins with stout front porches. Cobwebs of streams and narrow riverbeds dodge the road. It is routinely traversed by tourists who, having never seen a deer—or possibly even a tree—take to the hills of east Tennessee in pursuit of nature, only to suck up enough fumes to shorten their lives by the equivalent of a pack a day.

Cars fell in line behind us, and Dusty was soon tailgating a silver sedan with Pennsylvania plates and a bumper sticker that read, "One Life. Live It."

"Why do you write a check to Elinor LeClair every month?" I said. It wasn't a subtle opening, but Dusty didn't strike me as a woman who dented easily.

"Some people," she shook her head. "Be nice if they lived it a little faster."

"LeClair," I said.

She knifed me a look. "You don't do foreplay, do you?"

"I've come a long way."

"And you aim to do a bold dash into the past?"

"I do."

"That's one place you've got to take slow. We have a saying around here: the longest road leads to the begin-

238

ning. It's a tricky road on account of that 'beginning' stuff packing so much weight."

She took a sharp right turn into a gravel parking lot of a one-room wood church. As we crunched to a stop, Bud stretched her front legs out and emitted a muffled yelp in her sleep.

"You got the beer and flowers," she said.

Bud leaped off the seat, and Dusty slammed the door a split second later. It was a well-choreographed move, and I wondered how many time they'd done it. I tagged along, past the church and toward a small cemetery that sat on the edge of the woods. Beyond us, Cades Cove expanded into an undulating green valley with a train of cars working their way around the edge like a choker on a woman's neck.

"I'll take one, please," Dusty said as she stood over a headstone. I started to hand her the flowers. "A beer."

I popped two can lids and handed her one. "When did they die?" I asked, sensing she needed a little warm-up before diving into business. That's me: Mr. Sensitive.

She took a healthy swig and said, "My father went three years ago, June. My family was originally from this area. Plot's been held for years. Never sure I liked that—some piece of ground moaning my name." She kicked some dirt. "That'll be me someday."

I noted on the tombstone that her mother had died years before her father. "Your mother?" I said.

"Died when I was a little girl. Brain hemorrhage. Daddy said she was scrambling eggs and whistling 'We're All Alone' by Boz Scaggs, and she just fell over."

"I'm sorry. Do you have much memory of her?"

"Not really."

"It's a pretty song."

"It is. I find myself whistling it a lot. That used to bother me, but no more."

"Maybe it's not you whistling."

She smiled at me. "I've considered that."

"Any siblings?"

"Played solo my whole life."

"Your father raised you?"

"More than that. He was my best friend."

I dipped my head toward his marker. "I'm double sorry," I said.

"A buddy of my daddy died, and he wanted his ashes spread over Tellico Lake. They both loved that lake—thought that snail darter stuff was government at its worst. Daddy was a pilot, and he took off by himself. Twenty-three minutes later, his plane did a swan dive into the lake. The only thing they could figure out is that when he tossed the ashes out, they flew back into his eyes and blinded him."

I coughed up some beer.

"Shit...I know," she said, cutting me a knowing smile. "I swear—life is death doing stand-up comedy."

"David LeClair," I said and instantly regretted it.

She cut me an angry look. "Are you not paying attention? You go sit in the church, drink, and ponder patience. I'll get you when I'm ready."

I sulked off over the hard ground and to the church. I recalled Red talking to her mother, Beak the Kiwi Bird, and decided there was a boatload of life that I didn't understand. Or maybe missed. Or wasn't paying attention. Or was stolen from me by whoever took my sister. That's it, you sorry schmuck—put the blame elsewhere.

A plaque outside the door indicated that the church had been built in 1902. It had uneven plank floors and wood pews. It was cool inside, as the trees at the edge of the woods hung low over its roof, shielding it from the sun and trapping the night air inside. I took a seat in the back and took a long pull from the beer. A single pulpit was on the right side. I didn't understand people gathering one morning a week to hear a man speak from that position. Who put him in charge? I thought I should text Kathleen to let her know where I was. But the truth was, I had no clue where I was, and that was growing on me.

An older couple walked in and conversed in hushed tones, as if they'd entered an inner sanctuary where only solemn voices should be offered. They padded around the sides and then left.

"Open your eyes, Jake-o," Brit whispered one day in church. We sat next to each other.

"Shhh," my mother admonished her.

"Your eyes, Jake-o," Brit said in a barely audible voice. "When everyone bows their heads in prayer? Open your eyes."

"Shhh."

We did. We held our heads high and gazed around us as the congregation dipped their heads in submission to an unseen god. I don't think I'd ever done anything in such defiance, before or since. When the group's monotone "Amen" closed down the Lord's Prayer like the final word of a funeral dirge, Brit's eyes caught mine. They danced with glee, for we shared a great secret.

Dusty walked in and took a seat in the bench in front of me, a few feet down toward the center. Bud lumbered in behind her, grunted, and collapsed on the floor.

Dusty said, "I brought you another."

"Thank you."

I reached over as she twisted around and handed me a can of beer. A shaft of evening sun flowed through a window and died on her smooth and flawless chest. My eyes got stuck at the junction where her shirt touched the gentle slope of her breast—on the thin piece of cloth that had that tantalizing honor. I was momentarily sick with desire.

"You can start now," she said. Her voice was soft and quiet, like the air in the church.

I flashed my eyes up to hers. She was waiting for me. Had she known I'd been staring? She turned back toward the altar and draped her long arm along the top of the pew. Her suntanned wrist held a collection of silver bracelets. I wondered how far we could run. Despite my devotion to Kathleen, it was a thought I had no control over, for I have no armor against the shock of a woman's eyes on mine. An incurable pain would slide in and out with ease at the slightest smile or barely perceptible glance. At such times, I fear that life is unattended—that it is no more than a series of unfilled dreams, delusionary romantic quests, and empty ejaculations of the heart.

If there's a heaven, I'd like to meet all the women my eyes have ever caressed and loved and ask them if they too, if even for the briefest and immeasurable amount of time, felt that unmistakable tug. And if they all said no—that my heart was nothing but a piñata for them to playfully swat—then I would pray that the last woman in line would lie out of kindness and sympathy.

"Why don't you start by telling me about the money?" I said. I was struck by how my words had nothing to do with my thoughts.

"I didn't go looking for you."

"I'm *look*ing for the man who abducted and murdered my sister thirty years ago."

"I'm sorry about your sister. Where does your interest in Elinor come in?"

"I think my sister's death and the money are related. Why the check every month to Elinor?"

"I was told to."

"Told what, by whom?"

"To send half the money every month to Elinor. You know her son, David, and I were...this is all so stupid, like another life ago." She took another drink. "We were in love. College love. That's the bud of love—the sweetest love there is. Although I'd be the first to admit that every morning I wake, I know a little bit less than I did the day before."

"Who sends you the check?"

"You want to tell the story?"

I took a drink of the new beer. It wasn't as cold as the first.

Dusty said, "A couple of our friends came with money. Looking back, I see how that tainted our view. David and I? We'd be lucky to pull enough money together for dinner at Captain D's."

"Your friends have names?" I wanted to make sure we were talking about the same people.

She puffed out her breath. "Me, David, Alex Brackett, and Peter Omarov—Alex and Peter were the money men."

"Which one sends you the money?"

"What makes you think—"

"I'm guessing one—"

She bolted from the church. Bud grunted in protest— likely not pleased at having to leave the cool church—and then limped out. Her right rear quarter wasn't in sync with the rest of her. I felt bad for pushing Dusty, but I didn't care. I was searching for the man who killed my sister, not collecting friends. Besides, I was ticked at myself for getting caught staring at her.

I finished my beer and went out to find her.

She was sitting on her mother's grave. I took a seat next her, on Dr. Harry Fowler's headstone. I thought it more polite than sitting on her father's grave.

"He was born, raised, and died in Cades Cove," she said.

"Who?"

"The man you're parked on. Doc Fowler. He loved this valley. He could point to the cabin where his great-uncle lived. Another one where his grandfather lost his prized cow to a bear and the twins to the Spanish flu. Tell you about all the weddings in that church, the funerals, the baptisms, the Easter it snowed. All the births and funerals." She took a drink from the Coors can. "Mother Earth spinning like a revolving door."

"It's a nice—"

"He was my uncle. Taught at Maryville College. That man was always at peace with the world. That's a hell of a thing to do—to witness so many go through the swinging doors of life and never get mad at the doors."

I wished Morgan were there. He was better with people than I was. I ripped the lid of another Coors.

"Would you like me to relocate?" I said.

"Pouf." She blew out her breath, and her bangs rose and fell back into place. "I'm sitting on my mom, aren't I?"

The meadow still held the fading light, but a haze was forming over the fields like a damp silk blanket, and the stream of cars had dwindled down to a few late stragglers.

Our backs were to the woods, and a chill emanated from the trees as if it had been cloaked in there all day. Now, as the light retreated, it slithered from its hiding place and crept into our pores.

"There was a man," she said and then looked at me to make sure I was following, "about eight, maybe nine, years back. He came into the Down Yonder. Nice guy. We got to talking. Name was Daniel. You believe that?"

"Believe what?"

"That his name was Daniel."

"Don't know why I wouldn't."

"That's the point, why wouldn't I? Besides, it's a pretty name. Lyrical. One of the prettiest men's names you can come up with. I don't usually drink with the patrons, but he was a smooth talker. We were getting along just fine. Suddenly he put his mug down. He tented his hands real calm-like, rested his chin on his hands, leaned in, and gave me that deep look."

She took another drink. "See that haze there?" she said, jutting her pug nose out toward the meadow.

"I do."

"Doc Fowler used to tell me, when I was a little girl, that that was God tucking us in at night, and telling us that everything's going to be all right."

"I'm sorry."

Dusty furrowed her eyebrows. "For what?"

"For whatever Daniel said to you."

"You got some dirt on your shoes, don't you?"

I nodded.

Her cheeks puffed out with air, and she continued. "He gazed into my eyes and said that if I ever told anyone where the money came from, he would have to kill me. He said that would be a painful thing to do, seeing as how I had the prettiest nose he'd ever seen, but he'd done it before, and he'd make it as painless as he could. Thing is, I never told anybody. I don't even know how he knew."

"I—"

"What devil's womb did he come from?" Her body trembled. "So I'm a dead woman telling you this. But I've been dead so long—taking that money and all—I figure I won't know the difference."

"I can—"

"Daniel my ass," she said. "What cardboard god created this world?"

I recalled Red telling me that she had gotten dressed up to go out to dinner with Hawkins at the Blue Marlin, only to get bad news over tomato bisque soup that tasted like a cloud. Maybe the key to life was to maintain low expectations. I wished I had some ice to crack on. I always think better cracking ice, and despite the haze settling down over the meadow, the fog in my mind was starting to lift.

"No one's going to kill you," I said to her as she stared straight ahead. "Dusty, look at me."

She did. Her face was tight, her jaw clenched as she fought to hold herself together. I wanted to find Daniel and let Bud chew his balls off.

"You didn't do anything wrong taking the money. No one will know you spoke to—"

"You don't know that," she said angrily, although I didn't think it was directed at me. "You're going to find who took your sister from that motel and blow this thing wide open. I know it. I live with the fear of someone like you every time the door to the Down Yonder swings open and a stranger walks in. Why do you think I came with you? I told you I wanted to get it over with."

I let a quiet moment pass before I continued. "I've got a place you can hide until this passes."

"This passes? Honest to God, did you just say that? These things don't pass—it's who we are."

We were quiet for a moment, and then, in the silence, I said, "I never told you my sister was abducted from a motel."

28

Dusty didn't skip a beat.

"I knew soon as you dropped Elinor's name," she said in an exasperated tone.

"How did you find out?"

"About what?"

"My sister."

"The police. After the three musketeers shipped off to Russia. They questioned me and then told me everything that happened."

"David didn't tell you?"

She answered by puffing out her breath. "He didn't say diddly-squat. Just clammed up. I knew when they came back from that motel that something bad had happened. Don't give me that look. I figured Peter or Alex got caught doing drugs or something. Peter, on account that he thought he was a Russian prince, always lived on the edge. I didn't like him as much as David did. They fell for that 'I could care less' attitude."

"Peter Omarov told me that David abducted my sister, choked and killed her in her bed, stuffed her in the trunk of his car, but no one knows where he buried her."

Her mouth dropped open.

"Un-be-liev-able." She said it as if she were driving a stake into each syllable, although she combined the last two. "He said Davie did that? Son of a bitch. I always knew Omarov was dirt. David couldn't press his own weight. He was the student editor of Meridian—the school's poetry magazine. Please tell me you didn't fall for that."

"I didn't."

"Oh my God, you did, didn't you?"

"I did not," I reiterated.

She hung my eyes with hers and then, showing me mercy, dropped eye contact.

Any belief I had in Omarov's statements was fading faster than the day. I'd been a fool to let him go. Had I had my sister's killer in the room and failed to act? The thought made me sick. I couldn't ride myself now. There'd be time for that later, but my insides were starting to twist.

Dusty said, "He got real quiet when they got back from Florida. I forget the name of the hotel they stayed at."

"The Pink Shell," I threw out, to make sure she was being straight with me. After all, I'd been sucker punched before.

"No. That wasn't it. Some name like…a college."

"Vanderbilt Reef Motel?"

"That's it. He just—what the heck? You testing me to see if I'm lying?"

"I need—"

"Eat shit, Jake."

We shared a few bars of silence, and I wondered if she was really mad. I didn't think so, but I offered up an insurance payment. "I'm sorry. I needed to make sure."

"No, you're not."

"Not what?"

"Sorry. Don't ever fake sincerity. Men suck at that."

"I—"

"The three of them went to Russia, glasnost and all. They took off early. I never saw any of them again. I got a call from Elinor a few months later that David had been killed in a car accident. Head-on collision."

"Did David ever contact you from Russia?"

"No."

"Wasn't that odd? Being in love and all."

"Don't make fun of—"

"I'm not. I'm just—"

"Damn odd. We'd made plans to write, and he was to call me, but nothing happened. I wrote to him. I often wondered what happened to those lost love letters." She took a drink. "Lost love letters—listen to me."

"Did you ever see or speak to Omarov or Alex Brackett again?"

"Just told you, no."

"You said you never saw any—"

"Same difference. I tried to call Alex when I heard he was back. He and David were best friends, although David always thought Alex was trying too hard to impress Peter. But I never got hold of him. I left my number, but he never called."

"The checks?"

She considered that while Bud stood, ventured a few steps, and then slumped back down on a flat, and likely cooler, gravestone.

Dusty said, "About a year later. Two thousand dollars a month. A note with the first one had instructions that it be split anonymously with Elinor."

"Did you call her?"

"I told her it was coming and what the note said."

"Brackett?" I didn't make Peter Omarov as a man to make amends.

She answered with a nod.

"What did you think of that?" I said.

"What *do* I think? His family was rich, and he was trying to help us out."

"Alex Brackett's been sending you two K a month for the past—"

"Twenty-eight years and counting. I paid off the Down Yonder with my half."

"And you never heard from him?"

"Like panning mud for gold. He never returned my phone calls or letters. I went to a couple of reunions to see if I could run into him, but as far as I can tell, talking to my friends and all, he never set foot in Charlottesville again. To be honest, I assume he still sends the checks. Some time ago, there stopped being a payer—you know, in the upper-left corner? I just figured he'd wised up and no longer wanted his name associated with it."

I mulled over a picture of Alex Brackett that was forming in my mind. He never returned to Vanderbilt Beach nor attended a college reunion. Instead, he paid an indulgence of $2,000 a month to be split evenly between his deceased best friend's girlfriend and his friend's mother. Guilt money.

And Hawkins? Who was trying to pin my sister's murder on him? That might be my own government, in collusion with Omarov, doing what it could to close the case. It was a weak-legged theory, but it was all I had.

I drained the last can. I wasn't sure how that happened. I was sure of this: I needed to talk to Alex Brackett and find out why he was sending money before I did a final assault on Omarov. I had to make certain a different story didn't surface. I doubted Dusty was lying to me—I saw no motive, but I'd apparently severely misjudged Omarov.

"Thank you," I told Dusty. The haze in the meadow had turned to steel blue. It reflected the remnants of light in the western sky and looked like the clouds below you when you gaze outside an airplane's window.

"For what?" Her quizzical eyes searched mine.

"You didn't need to tell me any of this."

"Don't flatter yourself. I did it for me. I can't carry this weight anymore. I need to move forward, except it's hard when no road opens up."

"Cut a new path."

"That allegorical macho talk never did much for me. Besides, now that you've come, I fear he will as well."

"The other Elton John song?"

She smiled in recognition. "Yeah."

"You're a damn good whistler."

"Thank you. Daddy called me his little teapot."

"Did you ever marry?"

"That's a subtle shift."

"Just curious."

"No. That card hasn't been dealt yet. Are you thinking that David's death and your sister's murder are connected?" she said, doing her own hard shift.

"I am."

She let out a low whistle. "Wonderful. That means you're poking the hornet's nest."

"Come with me." I stood. "I've got a safe house you can stay in until it blows over."

"I just can't—"

"You can and you will. Next time you work at your bar, you won't worry about who's coming through that door. I bet you can't even imagine that."

"I don't—"

"I said, 'I bet you can't even imagine that.'"

"No." She wiped a tear from her eye that I never saw coming. "There's a load of life I can't imagine anymore."

She gathered herself and arranged some flowers beside the grave. "I don't like putting them in a vase; they're too far away like that. I want my parents to smell them."

"Your father never remarried?"

"No." She kept puttering with the flowers. "I urged him to, but he said it wasn't that easy."

"Eight ninety-five Bethel Church Road," I said.

"What about it?" she said, still positioning the flowers.

"There's nothing there."

"Sure there is, dummy. A chimney."

"There is that."

She straightened and brushed her bangs away from her eyes. A smudge of dirt remained on her forehead.

"David and I saw that property decades ago. Just like that. A chimney. We used to drive down from school to visit my family. I always knew I'd come back here.

"I'm a damn banana peel. You know, when you peel the banana and the peel starts to go brown the second it leaves the banana? That's me when I leave east Tennessee. I miss the smell of burning brakes when zigzagging down the side of a mountain. The way clouds kiss the trees. Roads that have water running next to them and bloated-cucumber tour buses hogging the pavement."

"Where God and guns are first cousins," I added.

She granted me an approving smirk. "It is a bit incestuous around here. But I like a place where roots run deep. We thought it would be a neat thing to do someday— build a house around that chimney. I tracked down the owner and bought it from her." Her left shoulder rose and fell. "I doubt David and I ever would've walked the aisle. He always seemed to be holding something back, like you only ever saw part of him. Still, I'm not ready to let go of that dream just yet."

"Maybe that's just the way you remember him."

"I don't think so. Doc Fowler used to tell me that memories were largely distorted recollections of the past. As I grew older, I understood what he meant. We tend to make up our memories; he called it *faux souvenir*—false memory. He was telling me to search for the true ones. He never cared much for David—sensed something a little off-kilter in him.

"I still believe that someone's out there for me, and that dream guards my life, and...holy cow, girl, listen to you. I can't believe I'm spilling all this to some junior Chippendale who rode into town just this afternoon."

"I've been spilling my guts for weeks," I said. "I'm likely contagious. You don't think memory is ice, do you? That it melts over time?"

She tilted her head and cracked a smile. "I didn't make you out as a man who goes inside himself very often, but that type usually runs the deepest."

I shrugged.

"No," she said. "That implies that at one time it was hard and true, and no part of life is ever like that. We just like to think it was."

She looked as if she were going to tack something else on; instead, she walked past me and toward her truck, which was now a dark shadow in the empty parking lot. Bud grudgingly rose and followed her.

We didn't speak on the way back to the Down Yonder. When she placed her truck in park, I said, "I'll be by at eight. I'd like you to come with me."

She popped a few questions: Where were we going, who would she be staying with, and how long might she be gone. She gave it a final silent moment and then said, "Tell you what, handsome, if you see me, I'm coming. Otherwise, don't slow down. Let's go, Bud."

Bud jumped down. She swung the door shut, and they both headed into the bar.

I got into my empty truck and headed to Bear's Den.

THAT NIGHT I SAT in the rocking chair, drank Jameson that I'd brought from Florida, and smoked a cigar. The Smoky Mountain stream rushed over the rocks, and I wondered why it was in such a hurry. Is it running to or from? I tried to put it all together but failed. My sister was long gone; she was dead longer than she had been alive. Crossed that line years ago. She died on youth's doorstep, her glory days waiting for her like a canceled party. I argued with myself about how that affected me. Both sides lost. I was finally done with the night and wondered if Dusty would be waiting for me at eight the next morning.

But the night wasn't done with me. The cardinal paid me a nocturnal visit.

"You're back," I said. It was my voice, but I didn't speak. *It's a dream, you idiot—wake up. No, wait. See what he has to say.*

He held my sister in his arms, her own arms dangling at her sides. She wore her green bathing suit. He stood in front of me as clear as the water in the mountain stream. Behind him was the birdbath from Elinor LeClair's backyard; next to it, a torn army tent, like a Confederate soldier might sleep in. The flap was open, and inside a man was tapping a keg of beer. Dreams are so screwed up.

"She's with me now," he said in a monotone.

"Let me touch her," I said.

"You can't feel her. She's a ghost."

"You're a ghost," I retorted like a child. I reached out, but my hand swatted air.

"What are you chasing?" he asked walking toward me.

He went straight through me, like water ignoring a rock. And then, as dreams can do, everything changed. My sister was sitting on a lakeshore, her feet touching the edge of the water. Several people were off to her left side under a weeping willow tree that failed to reach the ground. No one was to her right. I wondered how she got there. I thought I should go sit next to her and say, "Hi, Brit," and she would smile and say, "Hey, Jake-o." But I didn't. Instead, I sat at the end of the line, far away from her. She was talking. I wanted to move and sit next to her. I didn't. I knew I was dreaming, and I had to make my move before I awoke. Then the chiseled edges of the dream faded, and it collapsed. As I came out of it, I fought to keep it alive, to give myself another chance to get up and go sit by her.

I told myself that I had tried to sit next to her. But I was out of the dream by then and knew I was lying. My inability to act ashamed me. Nothing tramples you like shame.

I bolted up in a sweat. I heard water, but it wasn't the still waters of the bay outside my house—*my house, Jesus, it's a mess. I've got to put it back together*—no, this was water with purpose. A stream. A cabin. I got up, turned the AC on high, stripped off the underwear, and collapsed, spread-eagle, onto the bed.

Why hadn't I sat next to her?

I pretended to go back into the dream so I could sit next to her, to make things right, but we can't do that.

AT EIGHT THE NEXT morning, after fixing bacon and eggs, I pulled into the Down Yonder's deserted parking lot and came to a stop beside Dusty. And Bud. She opened the back door and tossed in a brown suitcase as well as a backpack. "Go on," she said, and Bud hopped in the back seat.

"I'm glad you decided to come," I said.

"Cut a new path and all, right?" she said with a nervous glint in her eye.

"You made the right decision," I added, wanting to reinforce her actions.

She climbed into the front seat and slammed the door. Dusty Haverford didn't lack muscle around a car.

"I'm not sure I have a choice," she said. "I can't run, and I sure as hell can't fear every man who walks through a door. I'd end up a crotchety, spidery old thing. Besides, I could use a little R and R. You enjoy your little stay in our slice of paradise?"

"It is God's country." I put the truck in gear and swung out onto Lamar Alexander Parkway.

"Learn anything?" she asked as she snapped in her seat belt.

"Don't fry bacon in the nude."

She crinkled her little pug nose. "That is something we all discover on our own."

29

We pulled into Mac's sandy front yard a dozen hours later. I could have driven to the bottom of the earth. The road didn't ask anything of me, and Dusty Haverford fit well in the passenger seat. A man can do a lot worse than driving around America, sitting high in a truck with a woman beside him and a dog in the back. Just before we got out, our eyes locked. Perhaps we each expected the other to turn away, but neither did, and we shared a wordless stare. It tasted a hell of a lot like our moment in the church.

As we stepped out of the truck, Mac shuffled out to greet us. I'd called him on the road and asked a favor of him. I'd told him I needed to stash someone for a few days, or maybe longer. He said he'd have dinner waiting.

"Mac, Dusty. Dusty, Mac," I said, making the introductions.

"Pleased to meet you," Dusty said, sticking out her hand.

His eyes twinkled with pleasure. He took her hand more so than he shook it. "You like fresh trout?"

"Smoky Mountain?"

"Not unless it's lost. Saltwater trout, make you forget you ever saw those blue ridges."

"I don't know about that, but I'll give it a try."

"Who's your friend?"

"That's Bud."

"He kill birds?"

"Bud's a she, and she probably will."

"Good. Let's go get some food—for Bud too. I got a job for her in the morning."

Mac never let go of her hand as he led her into his house. I followed, like an afterthought, with her suitcase and backpack.

Inside, I went to Mac's refrigerator. "Want one?" I asked him.

"Sure—"

"About time you offered," Dusty said, cutting Mac off, and they both laughed.

Dusty, Mac, and I sat on his back porch. We wolfed down trout, rice, and Italian bread in olive oil. When I left them, Mac was explaining Lady to Dusty—he remembered Styx—and Dusty was telling Mac to get off his feet and to allow her to do the dishes.

I entered my house, and Hadley III immediately darted out the cat door in the screened porch. It's nice to be missed. I'd called Kathleen somewhere in the middle of long-ass Georgia and given her an update. Morgan was due back from the Greenbrier the following day.

Although I knew it wouldn't remodel itself, I was disappointed that my house was still in shambles. I rued the day I'd caught the remodeling bug. Hadley III slinked back in, as if she were embarrassed by her earlier behavior. I fixed her a plate of the old trout left from a week ago. She sniffed it, cut me a dissatisfactory look, meowed, and moped away. I should have brought her fresh fish from Mac's. I'd text Morgan and ask him to give her some fresh fish.

Garrett had called right after we crossed the Georgia-Florida line. We briefly discussed our next move and made plans to meet at Seabreeze for breakfast the following day. I couldn't talk freely with Dusty belted in next to me. His call had interrupted our conversation, in which she was flabbergasted at my encyclopedic knowledge of Hollywood gossip. I insisted that I had no real interest in it, and she insisted I obviously did. She goaded me that star gazing must be a trait common to introspective men who liked cats.

THE NEXT MORNING, I did five punishing miles on the beach. I'd not shaken my dream from two nights ago, when my sister was sitting on the edge of a lake. Not only had I declined to sit next to her, but I had also lied to myself by saying that I had tried. Picasso said everything you can imagine is real. She was there. I know it. *Why didn't I sit next to her?*

I failed, again, to rip a hole in my Ringside leather punching bag. My body bled sweat on the concrete garage floor as I circled the bag, jabbing it with uppercuts and combinations. I wondered if my body would ever tire of my mind and landed a high kick in retaliation for the meaningless thought.

Garrett was already at the counter at Seabreeze when I took the stool beside him. The *Tampa Bay Times* was folded next to him. I gazed at the tide schedules and also noted that we'd lost a minute of sunlight over the previous four days.

We ordered breakfast. I filled him in on my conversations with Dusty and asked him if he'd found an opening for us to approach Alex Brackett.

"He's in Chicago," Garrett said, taking a drink of water.

"Doing what?"

"Some annual lodging conference at McCormick. He's speaking."

"You got this, how?"

"Mary Evelyn."

"Who are we?" I shoved my mug toward Peggy. She refilled it while exchanging gardening woes with the woman next to me.

"We're owners of three Radissons," Garrett said.

"They still in business?"

"Evidently. If they check our credentials, it falls apart. But we're not there for the duration."

I took the corner of a piece of toast and wiped my plate with it, sopping up yellow egg yolk. I washed it down with hot coffee. I glanced again at the weather page on the back of the sports section. Last night's low was seventy-three. The high for Chicago was seventy-eight. There was an ocean of humidity difference in those five degrees.

My plan had been to loiter around east Tennessee and then drop in on Beaufort, David LeClair's father, when he returned from his fishing trip. That fell apart when I decided to whisk Dusty off to Florida. LeClair's father would have to wait. I didn't want to miss an easy shot at an audience with Alex Brackett. The more actors in the play I talked to, the better my chances were of uncovering the truth.

"You think Dusty's straight with you?" Garrett said.

My mind flashed through Red, Mac, Eve, Omarov, and Elinor. "Of the whole cast, she's as straight as they come. I can't envision an ulterior motive for her."

"If we could envision correctly, we wouldn't be sitting here." He reached for his wallet. "Plane leaves in three hours."

Four hours later, from 39,000 feet, going the opposite direction from the day before, I gazed down at Georgia. Up and down. Back and forth. Looking for my sister. In the air. On the ground. In my dreams. Stirring the ashes of my youth and chasing the glory days I never knew.

30

We checked into two rooms at the Warwick Allerton on the corner of Michigan Avenue and East Huron Street. The Allerton was a Jazz Age survivor in tip-top shape. Garrett always stayed there when he was in town for business.

In the morning, I took advantage of the cool air and did seven miles on Lakefront Trail on the western shore of Lake Michigan. Chicago's in the eastern sliver of the Central Time Zone, and sunrise was at 5:37. I was on the path at 5:45. The sun was already shining its ass off. I dodged bicyclists as I ran north, past Oak Street Beach and Castaways. Garrett, running possessed, passed me coming back. The man refused to sleep.

Breakfast was fourteen-dollar eggs and a six-dollar orange juice. Afterward, I Ubered a car from my phone. As we waited, the summer wind, finding no clear path, echoed off the tall buildings, like the water in my Smoky Mountain stream caressing the rocks. There was no such breeze while I was running. At 9:45, Garrett and I were sitting in a conference room, where Alex Brackett was scheduled to speak on the challenges of going from a regional motel or hotel operator to a national one.

Brackett took the podium at the precise time. He was a well-spoken man and tossed out a few mistakes he'd made along the way. That got the auditorium laughing and positioned him as someone who preached from experience. I took notes. You never know.

Did he remember Eve, or was he a man who had so many notches in his belt that he took pride in the names he'd forgotten?

After his speech, eager attendees approached him on the stage and battered him with questions. I milled around the crowd and then queued up behind a man with a black sport coat over navy-blue pants. I granted him the benefit of the doubt and assumed his closet light had been out. He thanked Brackett for his speech and proudly pointed out that he'd heard him in Maui a year ago. Brackett reciprocated with a few sincere questions about the man's properties. He was fully engaged when addressing others, as if there was nothing more in the world he would rather be doing, and there was no one in the world more interesting than the person in front of him.

After black-and-blue dawdled away, I stepped into Brackett's space. He had an angular build, and his posture evinced an air of aristocracy, although I knew from listening to him speak that he did not shy away from self-deprecating humor. Such people are frustrating to me. They seem to have mastered both themselves and their environment with simplicity and grace. I, on the other hand, feel like coarse sandpaper trying to navigate through a world of silk.

"Mr. Brackett?"

His eyes flashed a hint of recognition but quickly clouded over, as if he'd gone inside and into lockdown mode. "Yes?"

"Three questions. Do you really think that, at four properties, it's necessary to have a dedicated manager for each unit manager to report to? That's heavy overhead."

His eyes narrowed, scrunching the skin between his eyebrows. He hesitated but then tumbled out his words. "As I said in my speech, if you want to go to five and beyond, you need that person to be your springboard."

"That's right." I nodded, as if acknowledging my own mental lapse. "You'll need to forgive me. My mind was drifting, having far more interest in questions two and three: Was David LeClair's death accidental, and does your monthly check to Dusty adequately atone for your sins of covering up the abduction and murder of my sister?"

His breath escaped him, as if he'd taken one to the stomach. His jaw tightened. He shifted his weight. Murmurs boiled from behind me.

"Mr. Travis," he announced with a tone of finality. "Am I correct?"

"I see you're still in contact with Peter Omarov."

He let that go and said, "I've been expecting you. Shall we find someplace to have lunch? I can do my part to impress upon you the urgent need for that operator once you've accumulated four properties. Although, despite that being your lead question, I sense your interest in that topic is less than genuine. Now, what do you say we grab a bite?"

Brackett had a car with a driver, and he insisted the three of us pile in. We voted unanimously for alfresco dining. His driver made a call. Fifteen minutes later, we had a covered outside table in the corner of Purple Pig's patio, just off Michigan Avenue. The air was refreshingly light and less humid than in Florida. That was countered by the smell of kitchen grease and petroleum fumes that were married into a single urban scent.

Purple Pig's patio was packed.

"It's really a zoo here," Brackett said as the waitress passed out menus. "But the food is innovative, and I know the owners."

He stood, took off his sport coat, and draped it over the back of his chair. He repositioned himself in his seat. He sat straight, like the tallest bottle on the liquor shelf.

"I get so tired of posh hotel restaurants," he said. "Nothing wrong with hotel food—it's certainly put bread on my family's table. It used to be overpriced mediocre food. Now it's overpriced good food."

Brackett's hair was just starting to gray. A cowlick on his left side swirled a tuft in the opposite direction of the rest of the hair. It was like a blemish on an otherwise perfect head, but even the blemish was good. His voice carried an air of both command and ease, as if he could move seamlessly between a board meeting and the kitchen staff.

"Tell me why you were expecting me," I said. I assumed that Omarov had gotten to Brackett, but I might as well hear it from him.

"I think you know," he replied, unbuttoning and rolling up his sleeves. "Peter Omarov gave me a call."

"What did—?"

"Sorry to interrupt," the waitress said, bombing our conversation and not the least bit sorry. "Can I get you gentlemen something to drink?" Garrett stuck with water, and Brackett asked if he could "please have an iced tea." He then thanked her for taking the order. His earnest consideration made him a hard man not to like. I followed him with an iced tea and beer.

"What did Omarov tell you?" I asked Brackett.

"That you were a desperate man who would find his way to me."

"Your take on that?"

"I think you're a man who is desperate for answers, and deservedly so."

Brackett had a disturbing way of gazing at me, as though he was trying to take me in, yet, at the same time, keep me away. I hadn't noticed that trait while he answered questions after his presentation.

Our drinks arrived. As the others ordered, my eyes wandered to an office building. Through a window, I saw a woman in a lipstick-red dress bend over a desk to collect papers. The framed window, with her in the center, looked like an Edward Hopper painting. Her brunette hair tumbled along with her head. She scooped it aside as she straightened out and left the office. I never saw her face. *What would she be like in the passenger seat?*

"What happened to my sister?" I said to Brackett, annoyed with myself for being so easily distracted.

"Peter told you."

"I don't believe him."

"Suit yourself."

"David LeClair wasn't the type of man to abduct an underage girl."

"You never knew David," he observed, "but you're right. He wasn't that type of man. White powder, however, made him that type of man."

I didn't defend LeClair any further. Instead, I said, "Tell me about your last day at the Vanderbilt Reef Motel."

"It was exactly what Peter Omarov told you."

"Repeat it."

He did. Like a well-rehearsed scene. At the end, he added a caveat. "Of course, if ever questioned by the police, I will deny what I just told you. The only thing I know about your sister's death—what everyone knows—is that a deceased man named Leonard Hawkins has been erroneously charged."

"Why would he confess to a crime he didn't commit?"

"I don't know."

"Are you going to step forward and clear Hawkins's name?"

"It would bear no meaning."

"It would be the right thing to do, assuming your story isn't fabricated."

"I am not going to get involved," Brackett said in a definitive manner that left no reason to pursue the line of questioning.

I kept my eyes on Brackett but jutted my chin toward Garrett. "See this man?"

Brackett asked, "What about him?"

"I've known him most of my life. But if he and I were to relay an incident we were involved in twenty—or even ten—years ago, our stories would not sync as neatly as yours and Omarov's do. That's where you made a mistake."

Brackett squirmed in his seat as a siren shrilled down Michigan Avenue.

"Traumatic events," he said, "are seared in our brains. LeClair's drug-induced, unintentional killing of your sister and his subsequent fatal accident certainly qualify as such an event. Our minds are especially anchored to our youth, when the world is new and intense. We have clarity of recollections from decades past but are clueless about what we did last Friday. I understand you…uh…engaged in a bit of scheming to get Mr. Omarov alone. Correct?"

I decided not to contend his winded dismissal of my challenge to his memory, nor contend how events are seared in our minds. Far from crystal recollections, after my sister died, my memories were more of a blur than a photograph. My youth was a horse that had been shot out from underneath me. After that, the world existed in pretense only.

Brackett continued. "Peter Omarov, although educated in the United States, is Russian. Russian money. Russian blood. On the contrary, instead of questioning my regurgitation of the facts, you should consider yourself quite lucky, Mr. Travis, that he came to me."

"How so?"

"So I could persuade him that killing you was not an acceptable means of retribution in this country."

"I'm touched."

"You should be."

I leaned across the table. "Are you threatening me?"

"No—"

"Why are you friends with such a man?"

He pursed his lips. "Our families have a history," he said with calculated words. "In '08, he provided us capital to ward off the barbarians. We found ourselves overextended and somewhat exposed when the credit markets became dysfunctional." He leaned in to me. "We are just now in the final, and delicate, stages of paying off that obligation."

"Perhaps having an operator to oversee every four properties wasn't such a wild idea."

He hesitated, reclined back in his seat, and said, "What is it you want from me, Mr. Travis?"

"Jake."

"What is it you want from me, Jake?"

"Why do you send Dusty two thousand dollars a month?"

"You've met her?" he asked, his eyes widening.

"According to her, your recollection of LeClair is a pile of donkey dung."

"She wasn't there."

"You knew LeClair better than his lover?"

He started to reply but screwed his mouth shut. I'd decided not to say anything about Eve and was glad Dusty was tucked away at Mac's place. Word had to be getting out that she was talking. Although I believed it was Omarov's man who had paid her a visit, it was possible that more than a single force was working to bar me from my past. Such forces might be withholding information and action from one another, as they were all acting in their own self-interest. Omarov and Brackett likely shared secrets about both my sister's and LeClair's deaths. Throw in political and generational business interests, and it was a tangled and sticky web, spun with decades of deception.

Brackett flipped open his hands, as if to dismiss our previous exchange. "David LeClair *was* straight," he said. "But the drugs twisted him. Dusty might have insisted that he did nothing other than the occasional joint. That, I can as*sure* you, was not the case when he took off with us that summer. But I felt—I feel—a sense of responsibility. The checks go out automatically. It's the least I can do."

"Real hero, aren't you?"

"Listen, I don't expect you—"

"Why one check? Why not one to Dusty and one to Elinor?"

"I don't really know. Perhaps convenience. When I did the first check, I planned to send them for a year or so." He frowned and looked sad, as men do when faced with their own poor decisions. "I didn't foresee how quickly the years would turn into decades."

"Tell me about Leonard Hawkins."

Our lunches came, and Brackett politely asked for another iced tea. Two women with Nordstrom bags took the table next to us. The one in black jeans kicked off her high heels. Her toenails were painted. They reminded me of pink roses you would see in a bridal bouquet. Would Kathleen carry a bouquet? Where would we get married— assuming she said yes?

"Hawkins," I said, snapping my mind back to the subject. I wanted to test his earlier casual dismissal of Hawkins being framed.

"We can only conjecture," Brackett said with a note of resignation.

"Bullshit. You were aware they put his nuts in a vise. Who's the mastermind who wanted to keep your name clean and put me in an orange suit? Omarov? Carlsberg?"

"I have not the slightest clue what my attorney is up to. That being said, I hardly think Bernard Carlsberg had anything to do with Leonard Hawkins's troubles."

"You speak Russian?"

"A little." He adjusted his posture.

"Did Carlsberg call you the night I dropped in on his party?"

"I don't know what—"

"Someone tainted the DNA evidence at the Collier County sheriff's office. Someone sent two thugs to kill Hawkins and threaten his girlfriend—"

"I don't—"

"Carlsberg sure as hell didn't dispatch those same two goons into a thrift store to issue me a warning. My bet is, the only thing he actively participated in was instructing a jailhouse snitch to finger me for a crime I didn't commit. That leaves Peter the Thug—the man you're in bed with."

Brackett dabbed his lips with his napkin. He had proper, even effeminate manners around the table. Two pens were clipped next to each other in his shirt pocket. Russell Alexander Brackett III would not get caught without a writing instrument. He was a thorough man, organized and prepared. A man who likely picked out his tie the night before. A tie he was certain he had not worn the previous two weeks.

"I had nothing to do with the laundry list you just aired," he said. "Your guess is as good as mine."

He took a drink of iced tea, placed his glass down, and interlocked his fingers, rubbing them against the back of his hands.

"Peter," he said, "is from a powerful family. The State Department is interested in keeping his name clear. One would think the easiest way to achieve that would be to make certain that the events of the Vanderbilt Reef Motel either stay buried or are in no manner connected to him. In that light, perhaps it became necessary to create a diversion—someone else to take a fall for the crime."

Garrett cut in. "Who in the State Department?"

"I'm only offering a theory."

"You're offering a cover-up."

Brackett ignored Garrett's accusation. His eyes flicked from Garrett to me. "Peter told me enough to know that I prefer ignorance. He's involved in high-level negotiations between our government and that of Russia and Ukraine. He's in Kiev as we speak."

"You're working overtime," Garrett said, "to pin the blame on a faceless bureaucratic ghost."

"Suit yourself." Brackett let his breath out. "My stab at it? Your government, which I believe you serve, Mr. Travis, is not pleased that you're poking sticks at Peter Omarov."

"When did you initially return to Russia?" Garrett asked.

"I'm sorry?" Brackett seemed thrown off by the question. Garrett, who wasn't fond of repeating himself, held Brackett's eyes with his own. Brackett scrunched up his face as if to physically dismiss the question. "About three or four years after my first visit."

"Why?" Garrett asked, his eyes hard on Brackett. Garrett never dropped eye contact when talking to someone.

"Why what?"

"Did you return?"

"To visit."

"Who?"

"Peter, of course."

"Where did you go?"

"I don't know—"

"Did you stay with Omarov?"

Brackett pushed himself up in his chair. His eyes darted around the patio. That was new for him. "Yes, I stayed with Peter. I saw some sights. We—"

"What time of the year did you go?" Garrett asked.

Brackett seemed flummoxed by the attack. He paused, glanced again at his watch, and then calmly replied, "Early summer. Is—"

"What did Brittany Travis look like?"

Brackett's face shimmied. "I don't know what you're—"

"Answer the question."

Brackett took a breath and leaned back in his chair. He took his hands off the table and started to reach for his face with his right hand but then lowered it and flattened it down the side of his body.

"This is most inappropriate," he said. For the first time, his voice lacked resolve, and he seemed emotionally vulnerable. "Is there anything else I can do for you gentlemen? I need to get back to the convention."

"Where's your searing memory?" Garrett said.

"I've been more than generous with my time."

"One more," I said. "David LeClair's death."

"A tragedy." He glanced down at the table and then quickly back up at me as if he were glad for the shift in topic. "A head-on collision. David died instantly."

"The other driver?"

"The same."

"Convenient," I said.

He paused a moment and then announced, "I assume you can both hail a cab from here."

He stood, and I did likewise. He leveled his eyes at me. "I am terribly sorry about what happened to your sister. You have my heartfelt apologies for...what subsequently has happened to you."

He thrust out his hand in a theatrical move. I took it by instinct.

"The economy's picking up," he said. "The travel industry is back to pre-'08 levels." He continued to hold my hand. "We've managed to restructure most of our loans."

He studied me like a teacher waiting patiently for a student to comprehend. Remembering what he'd said earlier, I said, "When are you clear of Omarov?"

"Soon." He held my eyes, as if to add weight to his answer.

"Shall we talk afterward?"

He looked at me like a caged dog, with both uncertainty and hope. "I have a ranch in central Florida. Perhaps you can drop by sometime." He pumped my hand one last time. "Best of luck to you, Jake."

He held my eyes as if he were going to say something more but then quickly dropped his gaze as if he were suddenly embarrassed. He strolled from the patio in an uncomfortable gait, clumsily slipping past groupings of people waiting for a table. I reclaimed my seat and took a drink of iced tea, letting a cube of ice slide into my mouth. For a man with two pens in his pocket and a flawless Windsor knot, he'd fumbled his exit like a gymnast who soars through the parallel bars but then stumbles on the landing.

"What was with the hard line?" I said to Garrett.

"Everything the man said was scripted. I wanted to get him off-road."

"We believe him?"

He grunted. "Some men make excellent liars—not because they lie so well to others but because they've lied so long to themselves."

I rested my head in my propped-up hands, closed my eyes, and massaged my temple. I popped my eyes open when someone bumped my chair.

"David LeClair," I said, straightening up.

Garrett said, "Likely murdered by a man who was informed that he was about to die. He could go out penniless, or money would be given to his family if he took someone with him. A perfect dead end."

"Our chances of proving that?"

"Zero. Think they're working together?"

"State and Omarov?"

He nodded.

"Possible. Problem is, it doubles our troubles." I glanced where the lady in the red dress had been. The office was empty.

"What's nagging you?" Garrett said.

I let my eyes linger on the empty office before shifting them back to Garrett.

"Brackett seemed to vacillate between pinning Hawkins's death—and my troubles—on Omarov or throwing the whole mess on the State Department. And the reference to paying off his debt to Omarov—what was he getting at?"

"That Omarov's got him caged, and he can't wait to spring free of the man," Garrett said.

"And he wants me to know that," I said. "Why?"

"So we can discredit everything he said."

"Meaning we flew up here for nothing."

"Not really."

"How so?"

"Beautiful run this morning."

31

David LeClair's father's home in Roanoke had white siding, black shutters, a gray-floored front porch, and a newspaper by the door with a ladybug crawling on it. I picked up the paper, flicked off the bug, and bruised my knuckles on the heavy wood door.

It was ten on a stuffy-hot Saturday morning in July. I'd arrived in Roanoke the night before and booked a room at a different hotel than the flophouse I'd stayed in when I'd visited Elinor. Elinor had told me that her ex-husband was fishing for a week and was due back a few days ago. I thought of calling first, but that would have given him the opportunity to run if he didn't want to talk with me.

Garrett and I had flown back to Tampa, and I had, again, climbed into my truck. I'd told myself that the flights were bad, but the truth was, the mindless hours on the road were good for me. Ever since I'd had the beer in the back of the church in Cades Cove—when Dusty came in, and the softness of her breast in the evening sun quieted my restless world—I'd had a burning desire to step away from it all. To be by myself. I wasn't sure why. Perhaps it was because, instead of feeling like water in a sink swirling around toward a drain with no control, my quest into my past felt more like a rushing stream tumbling over rocks. Or the wind dodging buildings. A mad rush to get somewhere I'd never been. I didn't know if I was running to or from. I needed to cut the pace. Slow it down.

I had always assumed that in the end—after I'd killed the man who killed my sister—I would be at peace with myself. After all, I would have slain the demon. Freed my chained soul. Attained my innermost desires. My theory was that once my past was mended, I could cultivate a life of order, like Elinor LeClair's backyard. I suspected that was wishful thinking—even borderline stupidity. Still, there had to be a finish line. Some sort of mental box I could close and then place on a shelf, having successfully mastered its contents.

What if that was not the case?

What if killing the man who killed my sister was nothing but a climax with no lasting effect? What if the epiphany is that the past is not a conquerable object but an active ingredient to the present, an impenetrable riddle rising each day like a well-rested sparring partner—a permanent and indissoluble component of who we are?

An invisible rudder.

I knocked again. I turned my back to the door. Two girls rode by on bicycles, swerving between peaked cracks in the sidewalk. The girl in front rang her handlebar bell. The girl behind rose off her seat and pumped hard to catch up, her shoulders swaying from side to side. On the other side of the street, a trio of mothers walked briskly with a horde of children in the same direction as the young cyclists.

I started to stroll around to the back.

"I don't believe you'll find anyone home."

I turned as the mailman ascended the steps.

"No?"

"You don't know Mr. LeClair, do you?" he asked.

"I do not."

"He's a bit busy today."

"Know where I can find him?"

He stuffed a handful of mail into a metal box with a flip lid that was mounted to the front of the house. "The park."

"Where might that be?"

"Follow the crowd. He'll drop in. Oh, I almost forgot. Merry Christmas," he chuckled. "Happy New Year too."

Nutcase. No wonder the government's broke.

I strolled down the sidewalk and took a left where the trio of mothers had gone. I soon found myself in a park buzzing with children. Tables with tents circled the perimeter of a playing field. Parents were grouped around, talking among themselves. Most of the men were around my age, but there seemed to be nothing, or no one, whom I could relate to. I was a stranger in a strange land. At the far end of the park stood a statue of a man on a horse. He was frozen in the blazing sun with his right arm raised, holding a sword. It looked like a crucifying position in which to spend eternity.

I found refuge, and cupcakes, in a shaded pavilion run by the First Covenant United Methodist Church Women's Club. They had red and green glitter on the frosting. I helped myself to a second one and then stuffed a ten into a canning jar. It was Christmas in July, and all the proceeds went to Toys for Tots. I loitered around similar booths that either provided tented shade or were under antebellum trees. Several large bins were stuffed with packages of toys. I bought a green Christmas tree cut-out cookie from the Girl Scouts and chatted with a lemonade lady about the weather. We agreed that it was a better turnout than the previous year, when the threat of rain had dampened attendance. I admitted I almost hadn't come last year, and she confessed to the same. I kept my eyes sharp but saw no one who was even close to LeClair's father's age, who, I assumed, was pushing eighty.

A plane droned overhead, and the children starting scurrying toward the open playing field. A figure jumped from the plane, and the chute opened. Santa Claus, looking like a red berry under a white drink umbrella, drifted down into pandemonium. *He'll drop in.* He hit the ground with a thud.

An hour later—that's two oatmeal-raisin cookies, one chocolate-chip cookie that was still warm and mushy, a cheese-and-ham sandwich that the Baptists just nailed, and three of Mrs. Cooper's award-winning gingersnap cookies—I approached Santa as he tugged off his hat behind the pavilion. The crowd, like a wave receding from the shore, was returning to the places they were from. They did so with as much excitement, chatter, and haste in which they had only recently arrived.

"Water?" I asked, extending a sweating, unopened bottled water to him.

His jolly eyes met mine. "Thank you." He took the bottle and unscrewed the cap.

"How long have you been jumping?"

"Forty-second year." He took a swallow. "Did it for my son's Cub Scout troop. Didn't know then that it would be a lifetime gig." He peeled off his beard and shed his heavy red coat. His head was shaved, and perspiration dotted his skin like tiny crown jewels.

"I'm sure your son appreciates your time."

He shot me a glance I couldn't discern. "Oh, I lost him years ago. But it's a good cause. Keeps me fit, I'll tell you that."

"Jake Travis." I stuck out my hand, and we shook. His hand was warm and damp.

"Beaufort LeClair. Thank you for the water. Hope your kids enjoyed the show."

"I don't have any children."

"What brought you to bedlam? Not that you need kids to support Toys for Tots."

"I'd like to ask you a few questions about your son."

He eyed me slowly, as if he were unwinding our conversation and scanning for something he might have missed.

"What about him?" he asked. His voice was guarded but not as suspicious as I would have thought.

"I don't think his death was accidental."

"Your name again?"

I told him.

"That doesn't mean anything to me. Who *are* you?"

"I'm looking for a man who abducted my sister thirty years ago. I—"

"*I* don't want to hear it." He shoved the water into my chest. He let it go, and I caught it after it fell a few inches. "You can tell Alex Brackett that he's a lying son of a bitch, and don't be sending anyone around to see me."

He started to walk away. "He *is* a lying son of a bitch," I said to his back. "But I need your help to prove it."

He turned and stared at me. "My son's been gone for thirty years."

"I know that."

"Why now?"

"It's a long story. Why did you call Alex Brackett a lying son of a bitch?"

"'Cause he is."

"OK. *Why* is Alex Brackett a—"

"I know what you're asking, but I'm taking a shower first."

He stalked off in the direction of his house. I followed, although I pocketed two more of Mrs. Cooper's award-winning gingersnaps along the way.

32

Beaufort LeClair and I sat in rockers on his covered front porch. A pair of sweating beer cans rested in pools of water on the table between us, like silos in a flooded field. An oak tree with a gnarled trunk sprouted from his front yard. It shaded a good chunk of the lots on either side of him. It was likely a direct descendent of a tree that was around when the Virginia territory was named for the Virgin Queen, Elizabeth I. A squirrel ran up its trunk, and another hopped from one branch to another. The oak's side branches were thick enough to support a housing project. I thought of all the life in that oak tree and then of my skinny coconut palms. One oak tree is a thousand palm trees.

A ceiling fan whipped the air that was filled with the fragrance of flowers. The early-afternoon heat was giving birth to clouds that looked like dirty cotton balls in the sky. I'd just given Beaufort LeClair, a man whom I'd only recently met, my life's story. There, but for the grace of God, went I, blabbering my woes to anyone with a set of ears and an unfortunate penchant for using them. After thirty years of silence, it was now a sad day for anyone unfortunate enough to make my acquaintance.

Beaufort put down his beer can. "I'm sorry about your sister. I never imagined that I'd meet any of her family members. That had to be a tough thing, growing up."

"It was the only thing I knew. Why did you tell me Brackett was a liar?" I said, suppressing a gingersnap belch. Or maybe it was the oatmeal cookie. Things were getting a little mixed up down there.

"What do you already know?"

I explained that I'd met with Brackett and Omarov but kept the details vague. I also mentioned my visit with his ex-wife, Elinor. He listened without comment. I left out the part about the money. Nor did I tell him that Brackett and Omarov pinned my sister's death on his son. My guess was, that version was Brackett's and Omarov's harmonized script. I wanted to know what Beaufort knew, without divulging everything I'd been told.

"That's about right," he said when I'd finished. "First the police came by. Like Elinor told you, they didn't break a sweat. But then, about a year later, the CIA—you know, 'Catholics, Irish, and Alcoholics'—came a-knockin'. We were starting to put it all to bed, and they fired it up again. We—Elinor and I—thought that was odd. After all, the cow was out of the barn by then. How is she?"

"The cow?"

His eyes lit up, and he smiled. "No, goofus, my ex-wife."

"Doing well. She said you were on a fishing trip; otherwise, I would have dropped by earlier."

Humor often endears a person to you, and Beaufort still smiled at my silly retort. "She tell you about her daughter?" he asked.

"Stonewall Jackson's first wife?"

"Elinor's doing her best. I don't pray much, but I do pray for her. Her mind's been sailing away for years."

"We each deal with the past in our own way."

"That's kind of you," he said. "I hear her friends are starting to drop her. Lose a bit of your mind, and you'll see who your true friends are."

I waited to see if he would offer anything more about Elinor. After a silent moment, I repeated my question about why he thought Brackett was a liar.

"He told me David was on drugs in Russia," he said. "That's what led to the crash. No way would David do any of that. I told those CIA boys that, but they weren't too interested."

"What *were* they interested in?"

"I asked them that. They said it was just the usual follow-up. You know, an American killed in Russia. But it was all smoke and mirrors. Their real interest was twofold—whether we had received any messages after he passed and what his boyhood was like. The hell they cared about his childhood for, I could never figure out."

Elinor LeClair had also questioned why the CIA was interested in their son's early years. I knew why the CIA made such visits, but I didn't dare share my speculation with Beaufort.

I gave him the same line I'd tossed out to his ex-wife. "Did he act strange—different in any manner—between the time he came back from Florida and when he left for Russia?"

Beaufort took another draw from his beer as his eyes tracked a red SUV crawling down the street. My eyes followed his. It was a street where the postman walks, where girls pedal bikes with bells, and where mothers and children stroll together under the protective shade of majestic oaks teeming with squirrels. A Sunday morning kind of street.

"Those Buicks are sharp in red," he said. "My car's got 75,000 and change on it. I've been considering getting a new one. Act strange?" He glanced at me. "Maybe a little. I was working long hours back then. Probably not around as much as I should have been. A parent can get a lot of miles off that line. Bury a lot of indifference.

"David was always a little withdrawn. Quiet. He wasn't here long when they came back from Florida. Then the three of them jetted off to Russia. I was more than a little nervous about that. But, with Omarov being a diplomat and all, I figured he'd be safe. Elinor and I...we didn't last too long after that. Some people think I left her 'cause her mind wasn't right, but that's not true. Truth is, I almost *stayed* because her mind wasn't right."

"I'm sor—"

"That bugs me, you know? Folks thinking one thing when the opposite is true."

"That's on them, not on you."

"She tell you David was adopted?"

"No."

"Not surprised. We couldn't have children of our own. When we told him, he didn't take it particulary well, got a little reclusive on us. Not sure he was ever the same. But then, again, I don't know how he would have been at that age anyway."

I recalled Elinor describing her son as "mysterious," although she admitted it was an odd thing to say. I was getting an image of David LeClair, and it was veiled in fog, even to those who loved him and knew him best. Perhaps he saw himself as a character from one of the novels he read as a youth. Men and women whose only sense of home comes from being lost. Who kept their world tight inside themselves and believed that a higher calling trumped any obligation to a fellow human being.

"I'm sorry things didn't work out for you," I said and wondered if that was really my best effort.

"Oh, I'm doing fine," Beaufort said. He shook his head. "The past is like nature; it abhors a vacuum. The best way to deal with that is to stay busy. He still pops in my mind every day, but I focus on the positive times. Put Miracle-Gro on them."

So far Beaufort hadn't given me anything other than David LeClair had been adopted and was likely an introvert. That didn't make him a killer. Brackett had tried to convince me that it was the drugs that had sent LeClair down the dark path.

"You're positive your son never did drugs?" Rain started pelting off the sidewalk and street. It had no rhythm or cadence, as if it were unsure of itself.

"Not a chance."

"You sure?"

"A wise man is never certain," he said. "I'd be surprised if he was into drugs. But I've been surprised before. You said Elinor told you about Dusty, right? I'm not sure those two had a wild seed between them. They planned to go back to her home, somewhere in east Tennessee. She was a nice girl. I often wonder what happened to her. She would have made a fine daughter-in-law."

"I met her."

"You did?" His face brightened.

"I did."

"How's she doing?"

"Just fine."

"You see her again, tell her I say hi. You do that for me?"

"I will."

"She really doing OK?"

"She is."

"Married?"

"She is not."

"Don't forget. You tell her I asked about her."

"I will."

I wanted to press him for something more but wasn't sure what direction to go. I reminded myself that this wasn't my first foray into solving my sister's disappearance. There was a reason I'd come up short every other time. I took another sip of aluminum beer and returned to my earlier question.

"Alex Brackett," I said, a little louder. The rain had ramped up to a steady, steel-drum pounding.

"What about him?"

"Does your conviction that he lied about the incident in Russia stem from something more than faith in your son?"

"That's well put, Jake. You think I let it go with a telegram? Hell, no. I hired a private detective to look into my son's death."

"Elinor never—"

"You're not married, are you?"

"No."

"There are some things you don't tell your spouse—divorced or not. The urge to protect is always there. I never found out much, only one little thing, but I didn't want her to know I was digging around. Who knows? Maybe we did misjudge our son."

"I don't think so."

He stared at me as if he were trying to take me in. "Ask you something?"

"Go right ahead."

"You really are that girl's brother, aren't you?"

"I am."

He nodded. "How long you been on this road?"

"Only one I know."

The rain stopped. The air was crisp and clean, as if the weather had declared a truce with itself. In Florida, the rain imparts no freshness to the air. It's sticky and hot on either side of it, for the rain is not a divisor but an interlude. Northern rain is different. It cleanses the day and resets the humidity.

An ice cream truck looped through neighboring streets, its repetitive song slicing the cooling air. I'd recently read—courtesy of my jail time—the obituary of the man who wrote the jingle. All things considered, it wasn't a bad thing to leave to the world.

Beaufort scratched his nose with his finger, stood, and went into the house. He returned with two more beers and a blue folder.

"The official report," he said, "was that David Beaufort LeClair was hit straight-on by another driver, and they were both dead at the scene."

"What one little thing did you find?"

"Take a look." In a single motion, he took a sip of beer and set it back on the table. He was not a man to waste calories taking in wasted calories.

I picked up the envelope, opened it, and studied the file. A year after David's death, Beaufort had sent two men to Russia: the investigator and an interpreter. It was a wise move. Beaufort could always look back and know he hadn't taken it lying down. There was value in that. The investigator, a retired detective from Salisbury, Maryland, had found the other victim's family. They had little to say about the accident, although he reported that the mother of the young man who drove into David's car told him: *He had no choice. Please forgive him.*

I repeated those words to Beaufort and then said, "That's your little thing?"

He nodded. "At first," he said, "I didn't know why they'd say such a thing. Then I saw it. Forgive the driver of the other car. *He* had no choice but to kill himself and my son. Maybe someone had something on him, and he died to save his family, but I never learned more than that."

My insides were boiling over my decision to believe Omarov and let him go. I had played the whole thing backward. I should have talked to all the other players first and then approached Omarov.

"I showed this to Alex Brackett," Beaufort said with a weary voice. "Didn't show it, actually, but told him about it on the phone. He told me to forget it. 'Dumb Russians don't know what they're talking about.' Said it was an accident. Said he was dead and to let it go. Wanted to know why I was snooping around in the first place. Got cruel on me. That was unlike him. He was always a well-mannered young man. I got the feeling he was sweating through the phone lines. But what could I do? He was lying. He knew. I knew. God in heaven knew. You don't think that man— what's his name, Hawkins—did it, right?"

"That's correct."

"You think someone else was at the motel that day and got your sister?"

"Possibly."

"And that might be related to David never coming home?"

"Another possibility."

"Then may the four horsemen of hell ride on your side."

His tired eyes rested on mine, but then he shifted his gaze to the street, as if he found solace there. I wondered how many hours, how many years, he had sought answers from his Sunday-morning street.

"That's a nice thing you do," I said. "Parachuting into that crowd."

"You know why I do that? All dressed up like Santa in the middle of the sweltering summer heat every year when the air's hotter than a cast-iron skillet in a bonfire?"

"Toys for Tots?"

"No," he snorted. "Don't get me wrong. It's a great charity, but it's not worth a Santa suit in July. I started, like I said, when David was a Cub Scout. He would be down there waiting for me. It was a hell of a thing, floating down into all those happy and eager faces. And one of them belonged to me. I'd jump down, year after year—see how high up I could spot him. David always helped out with Toys for Tots, even while he was in college. That's why I still jump. When I'm floating down, my boy is still there. I wish I could just float forever."

Beaufort took a reflective communion sip of beer. "It always gets me—how hard the ground is when I land."

33

"Tell you what, Luther," the man with a salt-and-pepper braided beard said, "that gives a whole new meanin' to rentin' your beer."

His beard was a thin cord that ran down his front like a bolo tie. He wore a black vest and had a red, white, and blue bandana covering the top of his head. I'd decided to call him Sergeant Pepper, although I never voiced that.

"My name ain't Luther," the man said.

"Is now."

I was doing my version of floating down forever by sharing rounds with a group of Vietnam vets, with a few token Korea vets drizzled in—one being a man not named Luther. After leaving Beaufort, I'd jumped on the road and decided to take the long way home. What the hell. I might as well marry the figurative and the literal—see what little bastard that produces.

Across from a gas station in Lynchburg, Virginia, stood a joint called The Red Blonde. Its sign had a faded picture of a woman whose voluminous hair, due to sun and age, was neither red nor blond. A dozen or so Harleys were scattered around the parking lot. One of them had a sticker on the back that read, "Vietnam Vets, We're Not Fonda Jane." Seemed like a nice family place to grab some grub and a beer.

I was aching to celebrate the latest failure in my life: I'd let my sister's murderer walk. I should have shot Omarov at the Greenbrier and testified that he was raping Kathleen. Fat chance. There was no way I would drag her through that pile of lies. Still, all those years, and when it was finally there in front of me, I choked. Time to hammer that home. Ride the big train off the cliff.

I'd told my new BFFs that I'd done time, and I asked if I could join their club. They enthusiastically accepted me, proclaiming that they needed younger blood.

"Nirvana, baby," Sergeant Pepper said to the man not named Luther. "You damn near see it go through you now. You done it, Luther—you have stripped it down to the simple life."

"I tole y'all my name ain't Luther."

"Luther!"

Riotous fists of beer mugs were raised toward the black ceiling. The man not named Luther had brought attention on himself, as he'd just announced to his buds that his proctologist had said he might have to carry a bag for the rest of his life.

The war stories flowed fast with the booze: one man was on his second new knee, another his third girlfriend— that drew a chorus of boos from his friends, who reminded him that he'd previously declared he was done with the game. The conversation segued from macular degeneration to a promising new drug for prostate cancer. Those vets quoted drugs like an Alabama tent preacher quoting scripture. We drank to elevated PSAs and the Bay of Pigs. We cursed motherfuckin' ISIS and raised a glass to the Stones, Cream, Grand Funk Railroad (*I'm your captain, baby. I'm your captain*), and the hands-down, flat-out king of the open road, Bob Seger. We decided it was impossible to listen to "White Rabbit" without craving a joint and unanimously agreed that a woman in bell-bottoms still flew our flag. After a few hours of such worldly proclamations, Sergeant Pepper asked me where I was headed.

"Florida."

"Fuckin' A," he said with a solemn nod, as if the mention of my home state pretty much capped it all. Long, straggly hair trailed out from under his bandana. "That's a fine direction to be headin' to. What brings you up here?"

I told them. Burned their ears off. Even told them about the bird I capped. What's next? Daytime TV? I was becoming a Hollywood rag, the very thing I detested in life. My barroom confession quieted the group and, like a hard rudder, turned the conversation.

"That there's a big hole you got to fill, Junior," Sergeant Pepper said, holding my eyes with his. "We all got those."

Someone said, "You know what my therapist said to do with holes in my life? She said to—"

"You don't see no therapist."

"Don't you go shittin' on my story, Luther."

"My name ain't—"

"She said to pour beer in those holes."

"Barroom therapy?"

"Ain't no better kind, once you cross that moral line."

"The bigger the hole, the more you drink."

"I think we're all fucked."

"May the bird of paradise fly up your ass."

"That'll fill *that* hole."

"That'll do it, all right."

"I tell ya, this country's got a few holes that need fillin'."

"No politics, T-Rex. You know the rules."

"Yeah? Smoke this in your pipe. I saw that family again last night. Walkin' like the livin' dead after a 52 showered 'em with yellow jelly. Me mowin' them down to end their misery. You wanna tell me you got sumthun' to plug that hole?"

The room became quiet. I sensed it was not the first time the group had approached the edge of the cliff.

"You done?"

The man called T-Rex gave that a second and then replied with a courteous, "Yes, sir. I am."

"Then buy me a beer."

"Y'all ain't got no sympathy."

"Would it do any good?"

"Moral line, my dick."

"You said you was done."

"Yes, sir."

We broke up around nine, which, they all agreed, was the new midnight. It ended on a somber note when one of the men, to settle a pair of contentious arguments, confirmed, via his phone, that Farrah Fawcett was indeed dead and that Ursula Andress's voice had been dubbed for the entire James Bond film *Dr. No.*

"How'd I miss that?"

"Fawcett or Andress?"

"Fawcett, dim-nit."

"She checked out the same day as...uh...what's his name? That pervert who liked little kids."

"Michael Jackson," I said.

"Yeah, that asshole."

"That wasn't even her frickin' voice?"

"Who?"

"Andress."

"I thought we was talkin' about Fawcett."

"We was, but we ain't no more."

"Not according to this. Says they dubbed her voice."

"Frickin' Hollywood."

"Bet it was her boobs, though."

"Really? Not even her talkin'?"

"Nope. They scammed us all."

"And that, dear gentlemen, is the story of 'Nam."

I received multiple offers for a bed, but I lied and told them I had a room booked. I did drive to the hotel but never got out of my truck, except to water some bushes. I woke with another crick in my neck. Same place. Most injuries—body or mind, it doesn't matter—never leave you. They hide in bushes, eager to jump you when you least expect them. That's why, every opportunity I get, I piss on those bushes. I was helping the world get over its injuries. I was also getting sober, which seriously messed with my new, and improved, take on the world.

Breakfast was on the road. It was the crumbs of what at one time had been Mrs. Cooper's award-winning ginger-snap cookies.

The next stop was Savannah. I'd had no intention of exiting there, but Kathleen called and inquired if I'd learned anything. I told her I met my soul mates and that, like me, they knew the healing power of alcohol—how effortlessly it filled the holes. I informed her that I was going to grow a beard, tie a knot in it, and asked if she would be my woman if I provided a truck, a dog, and a Bob Seger cassette. She told me to get it out of my system before I got back. I explained to her that she was missing the point; that I'd become a bona fide roads scholar. That I'd entered the inner sanctuary of life and had discovered that drinking like a heathen grants you a dance with lady immortality. She hung up on me. Tough shit. That babe would never know what she missed. Garrett rang and reminded me that unless I found Omarov in a bar, I was wasting my time and his. After that, I switched my phone off. Friends—piff, who needs 'em?

In Savannah, I tripped—damn doorstop was raised, where the hell's the Disability Act when you need it?—into a yuppie watering hole in an ancient downtown building. A hot dog and Fritos, along with a beer and a double Jameson chaser, made the world a better place. Not a bad combo, but I missed the bikers.

Omarov.

I'd let him go. The biggest play of my life, and I blew it. I doubled down on the dog and Fritos. I tried to do the same with the booze, but the bartender cut me off.

By then, my three dearest friends had joined me: Me, Myself, and I. We were yakking the shit off one another's ears. Our posse crashed the next dive. I ordered two thumbs on the rocks, explaining to the chick behind the counter that I was drinking for four. Two drinks later, when Chicky informed me it was my personal quittin' time, the four of us hit the joint around the corner, where someone had sacrificed money to a jukebox to hear the Indigo Girls. We lasted an hour there, but then Myself and I got into a contentious argument about—ah, hell, I don't even remember—and they tossed us all out on the street. The next bar had an atomic clock ticking off the nanoseconds to Saint Patrick's Day.

In Savannah, Georgia.

Frickin' Irish. Let's blame it on them. They cover the world like a thin layer of gunpowder. They also lay claim to a chunk of my lineage. That might be why I wake up every morning itching like a pipe bomb ready to blow.

I gave my neck a break and checked into a motel that had a section of its parking lot cordoned off for a car show. I was in no condition to appreciate classic cars. I headed straight to my room. It smelled like new carpet.

Like a boat that had slipped its anchor and become unmoored, I drifted aimlessly in the night, my dreams and memories fusing to form a collage of self-pity, self-flagellation, and self-loathing as the dragons of emotion feasted on my wasted and weak mind. Hard liquor will screw you six ways from Sunday.

"You need to brush your hair, kiddo."

We were at the zoo viewing Christmas lights. I'd taken off my hat, as it wasn't that cold.

She ruffled my hair. "I wish I had a mop like that," she said. I couldn't imagine me having any advantage over her. Having anything she could possibly want.

THE NEXT MORNING, I felt my head. Could've sworn she'd touched me last night. Right...there.

I sat on the side of the bed. If I got up, I would need a direction, and I didn't know what direction that would be. The hotel room drapes hung like iron curtains over the windows, blocking any attempt by the sun to see if I was going to answer the bell. I know that pecker missed me. I got up and took a peek. The world was stupidly sunny and bright. Green all over the damn place. Flowers under the first-floor windows were bathed in early-morning yellow and white, their smiling little prissy petal faces rising up to greet me as though I was their pissant play buddy. I closed the drapes and slumped back down on the edge of the bed. There was no joy in the sun. My world was winter. *Oh, for God's sake, man. Pull out of it.* I flung open the drapes. I endured a long run and followed it with a cold shower. The binge had always worked before—it cleaned me out and allowed me to move on. One time, that note might come due. I'd worry about that later. I wolfed down a hearty breakfast—it's amazing what $12.95 still buys—and read the local paper as if every word counted.

When I was walking to my truck, an early-morning group was already milling around the classic cars. A blind man with a cane felt the fins of a '57 Chevy. He smiled as he ran his hands over her smooth and hard steel. He fondled the chrome plates. Another man was beside him. They were talking. I wondered if the blind man had ever seen and if the world had ever known a sorrier and more ungrateful SOB than me.

I hightailed it back on to the interstate—that great vein of American freedom that provides sanctuary and forgiveness for all who ride her. By the end of my Bob Seger playlist, it had all faded behind me as if it was never there, but this remained: life is a small town on a phone app, a white space of nothing, until you zoom in. Then it appears, and the more you zoom in, the bigger it gets: streets, schools, the post office, a Dairy Queen, a cemetery, a bar. For just a second, your senses explode: the smell of cookies, the scream of children rushing out of school, the peal of a church bell on a hot weekday afternoon, the laughs, the potholes, the talk in the barbershop, a first kiss, a blind man's touch on indifferent metal, the confession of a man who killed a family after napalm only did half the job—that bagful of disparate stuff that packages itself as life and demands that we treat it with great profundity. But zoom back out, and it sinks away. It's gone. It disappears back into white space, too small to register in the grand scheme of things. You wonder if that's a clue, but you're too damned tired of it all to give it further thought.

I ARRIVED IN SAINT Pete Beach late in the afternoon and went straight to the hotel beach bar for an early dinner. My stomach was Dachau empty.

I noticed him after the woman wearing the white safari hat left, although, like the lingering touch of my sister's hand on my head, the scent of the woman remained.

34

The hotel was a pink Moorish structure built in the
1920s by an Irishman from Virginia, named after a
character in a play by a French dramatist that was turned
into an English opera, and is set in a city named for its Russian counterpart.

I wondered what the man not named Luther would say
to that.

My stool faced the north pool, and the Gulf of Mexico
was to my left. Dark clouds hung low in the sky as if their
weight was too great for them to stay aloft. The air needed
to rupture to rid itself of moisture, but it couldn't come.
Instead, it kept itself on the brink, pressing and threatening to splatter everything at any moment with an eruption.

A woman in a white swimsuit cover-up, and a white
cloth safari hat with a black band around it, came up next
to me. It was a nice hat. Put a hat on a woman, and she
owns the world. She smelled of sunscreen layered over perfume. She ordered two rum punches. I pulled my cap lower
over my eyes.

Steven, the bartender, presented Safari with two drinks,
each garnished with fresh fruit. The woman scrawled her
name on the chit, pirouetted, and headed off toward the
south pool. I took a sip of iced tea and tried to remember

the last time I'd changed my boat batteries. They don't last long in the suffocating heat.

"Sold my first house," Steven declared as he placed a beer and an iced tea, neither of which I ordered, in front of me. I didn't have the heart to tell him I didn't have the stomach to drink the beer.

"Good for you," I said. Steven had recently gotten his real-estate license. There are more realtors in Florida than people. It's tough math, but it's true.

"Except management told me I'm not supposed to talk about it on the job," he said. "Anything to eat?"

"I'll take a burger, medium."

"I'll take a cold draft," the seat next to me said.

I hadn't noticed him when he'd sat down, but now his body occupied a place that was still hostage to the scent of another person, for the sunscreen and perfume stayed on like rain.

He was dressed in long pants, a short-sleeve blue shirt, and loafers with frayed tassels. His graying hair was buzzed short. He didn't wear sunglasses but had a natural squint, as if his eyes were used more to filter out the world than to let it in. Black skimmers are like that. The birds' eyes are slits that are designed to keep the sand out. I don't think I registered his eyes when I first noticed him. But afterward, when I tried to reconstruct when he had first taken the seat, I recalled the frayed tassels on his shoes and that his eyes, which reminded me of black skimmers, rendered his face soulless. He cut me a glance. I ignored him.

Resort guests straggled in wearily from the beach, looking as if they'd lost a battle with the white-hot sun. They never came in from the beach with the speed and gusto in which they'd hustled out in the midmorning hours.

I nursed my iced tea, occasionally glanced up at the TV screen, where the Rays were protecting a one-run lead in the eighth, and tried to contrive a plan to again bump into Peter Omarov. The problem was, we couldn't find him. He'd dropped off the radar. I'd blown my chance. Here I go again. Iced tea, though, couldn't do the damage of alcohol. It's like comparing a popgun to a howitzer.

"You follow them much?" the man next to me said, staring at the TV.

"The Rays?"

He nodded.

"Not much into sports."

"Me neither," he said. "Baseball's a math game played out on a field. I never got it. Some guys, though? They swear by it."

My eyes tracked a young mother with high-school legs and an ounce of cloth covering a few strategic inches of her body. Two children trailed her like obedient ducks. She was lecturing them on hot-tub etiquette. My mother wilted away on a hospital bed with an IV tube turning her arm ice blue. I remember staring at it and thinking how unnatural it looked, but at least there was color, for I was soon to learn that death is white and starts at the fingertips. Here's another lesson before my first kiss, courtesy of my mother: Life leaves fingers first.

"You from around here?" the man asked.

"I am."

I glanced up at the TV to indicate my unwillingness to talk. The batter had two strikes against him. *Just like me.*

"Washington, DC, myself."

I caved in. "What brings you to the beach?"

"Business."

My burger came. I repositioned the sliced onion and then cut the burger in half. I took a bite. I took the plastic lid off the ketchup cup and fished around in the white ceramic bowl for the crispiest fry coated with salt grains. I dipped it in the ketchup. My stool mate drifted away in his beer, occasionally looking up at the game he professed not to have interest in, and then said, "How was your hot dog?"

I took my time, wiped my mouth deliberately with the napkin, and said, "Which one?"

"Pardon?"

"I had two hot dogs." I drilled my eyes into his. "Which one are you referring to?"

"Either."

"Let me guess," I said, placing the napkin down. "You rode into town to convince me to lay off Peter Omarov. My sister's dead, so move on. Omarov's boys in the thrift store didn't impress me, and now it's your turn at the plate. Good cop, bad cop. Do it for God and country. Problem is, when you mix those, you get horseshit."

As I'd rambled on, I searched my mind for any recollection of someone trailing me in Savannah, but I drew a blank.

He held me with his eyes, although I wondered how he could see out. "To the contrary. I am no friend of Peter Omarov."

"And you are who?"

"Oh, you know me. From what I understand, you know me as well as anybody."

"Enlighten me."

He took a drink of beer, placed it neatly on its cardboard coaster, and said, "LeClair. David LeClair."

35

"I 've been expecting you," I said.

That was skirting on a lie. I had my suspicions, but mainly, I said it because I didn't like anyone getting the drop on me, although he already had. Ever since Beaufort informed me that the CIA had paid him a visit a year after his son had presumably died, which was the same line his wife, Elinor, had given me, I'd been skeptical that David LeClair was dead. Such background checks were standard procedure for the agency to conduct on recruits.

"Oh?" he said. I expected his eyes to widen just a tad. Incredibly, they did not.

"Were you recruited before or after the so-called accident in Russia?" I asked.

He looked vaguely similar to the photos I'd seen of LeClair. Close enough.

"You're quite perceptive. It was after."

"Omarov and Brackett?"

"They might know," LeClair said.

"That you're alive?"

"More or less."

"Strange answer."

"Strange life. The party line is that I died. I have a new name now."

"They know you're with the agency?" I asked.

"Not likely."

"It was a yes or no question," I said.

"Such questions don't exist in my world."

"They do. You choose to ignore them. Your staged fatal accident in Russia?"

He pursed his lips. "It was unfortunate." He motioned with his left hand as if to discard a meaningless object. "But if I wanted to live, someone had to die."

"Two people died."

"No one accuses the world of being a fair place."

I was tired of my questions and took another bite of my burger. The onion was good—sweet and hard. But my appetite had vanished.

"I've heard everyone else's version," I said. "Give yours a whack. But in fair disclosure, you'll be lucky if I swallow half of it."

"They didn't need to recruit me. I—"

"Start with my sister, you fool."

"Of course. Pardon my insensitivity." He crossed his legs. "Omarov was the one with powder up his nose. He followed her to her room and then dragged her to our room. We were only three doors down. Then we—they—relocated her to an empty room. Brackett had a master key. He knew what rooms were empty. That's why the police never found her."

I didn't call him on his slip-up of "we" and "they." I'd long since given up hoping that any member of the college trio who was at the motel that infamous day would provide a truthful rendition of events.

"Where were you when this allegedly occurred?" I asked.

"On the beach. Rotating every fifteen minutes." He humped his right shoulder. "I didn't find out what had happened until I went up to the room. We left the motel the following morning."

"My sister."

"She fought. He choked her to death. I know it's no consolation, nor do I offer this as one, but it was not his intent. After he and Alex moved her body to the empty room, Omarov panicked. He stuffed her in a laundry cart and then into the trunk of his car."

"Where is she?"

"I don't—"

I spun on LeClair and squeezed his forearm. "Where is she?"

"I'm sorry." His calm words flashed me back to Brackett's parting comment: *Best of luck to you, Jake.* "He never said. I never asked."

I released my grip. "Bullshit. You asked."

He humped his shoulder again, as if a body motion was a sufficient substitute for words.

I said, "You're trying to pitch me that Alex Brackett was involved in the cover-up but not the crime?"

LeClair glanced up at the TV. I sensed he was deciding what road to take. I wondered what road he wasn't taking. He turned his head back to me, as if he were cognizant of not being caught drifting for too long.

"Alex Brackett," he said, "had nothing to do with the crime. When Peter grabbed your sister, Brackett was in a room having sex with an older woman. They'd started some torrid affair a week or so before. Same time, same room, every day."

Eve had told me it had been one and out with Brackett. Was she lying? Or had Brackett been playing the field and misled Eve to believe that she was the only fruit in the garden?

"The woman in the room," I said. "Did she know?"

"I doubt it. Why do you ask?"

"Curious. What time?"

"What time, what?"

"What time did they meet every day?" I said with impatience.

He shifted his weight on the stool. "I don't know. Early afternoon. Have you found her?"

I decided not to play the Eve card. "It's your fairy tale," I said as he eyed me warily. "How did you end up here?"

He scooted himself higher in the stool. "In Russia, I told Alex that we needed to turn Peter in to protect ourselves from possible charges. Peter overheard us and went to his father.

"The old man blew up. He had no choice but to leave Alex Brackett untouched, as the families had growing business ties. I had no such value, and as Nikolay eloquently explained to me, my knowledge doubled the risk. He could tolerate one bleeding heart knowing what his son had done, but not two. Nikolay gave me a choice: lead the life of a dead man, or be guilty of sending both my parents and Dusty to an early grave if I talked."

"Why not kill you?"

"Oh, trust me," he said, letting out a lighthearted chuckle as if the whole affair were mildly humorous. LeClair's teeth were a size too small, as if they were packaged with his eyes. "That was his first inclination. Alex Brackett—and, to some extent, Peter—put up stiff resistance, although I've always harbored doubts about Peter's sincerity. He seemed far more interested in positioning himself alongside Alex for the sake of appearances. "Peter's father arranged the accident. Two men died. I had no hand in it. Nor did I have a clue who they were, although I assume they were on the old man's short list. I was told to go back home and forget I ever lived. Do not contact anyone again, or they would meet a similar fate. And never mention what happened at the Vanderbilt Reef Motel. I was twenty-two."

"You fell for that?"

"I was twenty-two," he repeated, but I sensed there was more.

"He faked your death, put the fear of the devil in you, and let you go. Then what?"

"Nikolay arranged for a new name, passport, and driver's license."

"But you ended up in the spook business. That wasn't in the plan, was it?"

He chuckled. "I doubt the old man ever saw that coming."

"You're CIA?"

"Enough about me. Your turn. Unless you truly do possess the world's best poker face, why are you not surprised to meet me?"

I shrugged. "Lucky guess. The agency visited both your parents a year after your so-called death. They described it in a similar fashion: a standard government background check. My only question was whether you were alive or if the agency merely coveted your name. Tell me how that feels, Davie—that's what your mom calls you—letting those you love live hell on earth?"

"You think I—"

"Your father still does Toys for Tots. He dresses as Santa and parachutes into the crowd, hoping to see your face."

His jaw tightened. "I didn't have a choice. My actions, my *life*, keeps them alive."

"We all have choices."

"And who are you? That last virgin standing?"

"You're clandestine, right? You could take Omarov out and come clean. You think being adopted gives you a pass on love?"

"He made it clear. My silence for my life."

"That's caged you for thirty years? Peddle it to somebody else, pal."

"You sit here in paradise and think you can dance with the devil? You have no clue."

"Give me one," I said.

"I don't owe you."

"Nice talking with you."

He took a sip of his beer and then focused his slit eyes, like gun turrets, on my eyes. "I landed in Oregon," he said with a hint of anger in his voice. "I had my new identity. The first night back, I was sitting in a bar, alone. I knew no one. I got talking to a girl. She was some hot little number, legions above my pay grade. She was also the last thing I remember from that night.

"I awoke the next morning in a hospital, minus a kidney. The police questioned me, but I had no memory. An anonymous call had directed the police to me. They'd found me propped up in an alley. A week later, I received my missing kidney in a gift-wrapped box. A note said that it was a friendly reminder that if I ever talked, my mother's heart, or Dusty's, would be gifted to me as well."

"No one accuses the world of being a fair place," I said, throwing his line back at him. If it sounded harsh, tough. For all I knew, he was spinning lies faster than a black widow on Red Bull. I finally gave into the temptation and took a large swallow of beer from the plastic cup with the hotel's logo on it. It went down pretty good. Flush and reload.

LeClair pivoted slightly in the chair as if to ward off the outside world. "I planned my revenge," he said, with a calmness that chilled the air like a northern rain. "About a month after my kidney went missing, I went to the State Department with my sad tale. Less than a year later, after initially being underwhelmed by my suggestion, they put an offer on the table. I turned out to be a perfect agent, for I, as you kindly pointed out, was dead."

"You dropped the identity Nikolay Omarov arranged for you and became the third person in your life, despite your aversion to being number three."

"I believe I've now died twice in auto accidents."

"Not an easy accomplishment."

"Nor a path I'd recommend, but sometimes our options are limited, if not preordained."

"The Omarovs have dictated your life."

"They have," he said.

"Now it's payback time."

"And that, Mr. Travis, is what brings us to the intersection of our lives."

36

I thought I knew where we were headed, but I wanted more information. I would sort out later whether that information was factual or not.

I said, "I can see Omarov lying to me about you, but why Brackett?"

"Money."

"That's it?"

"Surely you joke."

"Any humor in the checks?" I pushed my plate away and cracked an ice cube that I didn't know was in my mouth.

He arched his eyebrows and asked, "What checks?"

"Dusty—remember her? Says that Brackett sends her two K a month. She passes half of it on to your mother— I'm sorry, the woman who raised you. She's been doing it since the year you skipped out on her."

He bounced his head a few times as if the information I'd just imparted to him was more than he could digest. He said, "Alex Brackett sends money every month?" It was unlike him to backpedal in a conversation.

"Three decades' worth."

I considered telling him that Omarov's man put the fear of hell into Dusty but decided I was better off listening and not talking. There's a reason we have two ears and only one mouth.

LeClair gave a slight shake of his head. "I've moved on. Married and divorced twice. That was another life ago. A shame that some people get their feet stuck in the muddy past."

"Your parents deserve better—not to mention your ex-wives."

"I never knew my true parents," he said bitterly. "You survive thirty years under a death threat from the Russian mob, then you pull a chair up to my table."

"Next time I talk to Elinor, I'll pass along your heart-felt gratitude."

"Don't meddle in my affairs."

"No problem, Sparky. I'll just stand by while you shit all over mine."

The singer, who had been on break, came back with an acoustic version of "Walk Away Renee." I liked the song. I made a mental note to stuff a ten in his glass jar.

"Who are you now?" I asked.

He squirmed in his stool and pulled out his wallet. He handed me a business card.

I glanced at the card: "Patrick James Manderos, Vice President for Centralized Intelligence and Analytics." Underneath that it read, "Leading the Way in Cloud and Data Storage."

"You didn't even bother to change the initials," I said.

He arched his eyebrows again. He was fond of that move, as if it were a substitute for opening his eyes. "There's only so much you can do with those letters."

I said, "Someone tried to frame me for the murder of Leonard Hawkins."

"Terribly sorry about that ruffian affair."

"You?"

"Not exactly."

"Exactly who?"

"It's complicated."

"Try me. I've recently mastered tying shoelaces."

"The agency is conflicted about what to do with Peter Omarov. He's important to our network. When the threat arose—due to DNA testing—that he might be linked to your sister, we scrambled to protect him."

"You scrambled to protect Peter Omarov?"

"Irony is the sharpest element, is it not? Omarov has both friends and enemies within the agency. I am of the latter group. My vocal minority didn't carry the day. They decided to pin your sister's murder on Leonard Hawkins. When that didn't stick, they tried to put your picture on the wall of the post office."

"Bullshit. Two Russian thugs, whom I've had the pleasure of meeting, punched Hawkins's card."

"We...synthesized the operations. Both sides participated."

"You're colluding with the Russians?"

"Not so much I, as others."

I took another drink from the plastic cup. If LeClair were lying, and he'd had a greater hand than he was indicating in Hawkins's death and the subsequent effort to pin it on me, then I'd doubt I would ever know. Nor did I care. It seemed a cavalier attitude, but I had little choice.

LeClair was a spook. By definition, he was not a man with singular objectives or loyalties. He was a self-dealing survivor, unencumbered by loyalties, who would claim whatever cause was most advantageous to him at any given moment. It struck me that he and Bernard Carlsberg were likely cut from the same cloth.

"And if they were successful?" I said, trying to keep my head in the moment.

"Well," he crimpled his face, "I suppose you would've taken a hit. But no harm, no foul, right? You've proven to be far more resourceful than we calculated."

"The DNA plant in the Collier County sheriff's office?"

"My associates," he said.

I believed him on that, since McGlashan had indicated that he thought his office had been scammed by a government agency.

"Anything else before I feed your face to the fish?"

"I understand you're a bit miffed," he said. "Omarov had his own playbook. The team who handles him wasn't pleased with that. Especially Hawkins's death. Omarov knew what he was doing. His actions forced us to play along. You never want to be the caboose. But Omarov was our point man in dealing with Putin on issues in Ukraine. We couldn't afford to have you mucking things up."

"*Was* your point man or *is* your point man?"

"That is the question, is it not?"

"He's fallen out, hasn't he? The team who handled him is discredited."

"I won't argue the word."

"He's no longer the engine," I said.

"Indeed not."

"An opportune time for revenge."

"All good things come to those who wait."

Steven stopped in front of me. I nodded at my beer, impressed with how quickly I could jump back on the saddle. I nudged my plate toward him, although I snatched one more fry as he took it away.

I needed to make sure that LeClair was really who he said he was.

"Eight ninety-five Bethel Church Road, Townsend, Tennessee," I said. LeClair actually squinted.

"Pardon me?"

"You heard me."

"What of it?"

"You tell me."

"Very well. There was a chimney that stood in the back of the house. We were going to take that chimney and build our lives around it."

I glanced at the TV that wasn't carrying the Rays game. Jim Cramer was interviewing a president of some company. The man looked like the singer Meatloaf when he was younger. *Real name is Michael Lee Aday. He suffered from depression and spent months holed up in his room.*

"Tell me about your room," I said.

He paused a beat and then said, "I left it with a poster of Michael Stipe—that's REM's lead singer—hanging over my bed. What it looks like now, I don't know. Do I pass?"

"No."

"Why?"

"Because you're a grade-A jerk."

"I don't see how—"

"We have a common enemy," I said, suddenly eager to get to the gist of his visit. "Omarov double-crossed the agency. He's no longer useful. The faction of your agency that was working with him has lost the board. They're turning the dogs on him, and what better dog to lead the sled than someone who has a thirty-year vendetta against him."

"Your words, not mine, although there's little I would edit."

"What did he do?"

"The minute details of global politics is not your concern—or mine, for that matter."

LeClair's voice had taken on an air of bored insouciance, like an English professor in his thirty-second year of teaching *The Sun Also Rises* who still has to put on the face.

"Omarov is engaged in cyberwar," he said, evidently deciding to toss me a bone. "He got caught in a crossfire between the US government and his own. He had a decision to make and—fortunately for you and me—he chose poorly." He leaned in toward me. "I understand you were warned to stay clear of Omarov. I assure you that's no longer the case."

"You don't sign those paychecks."

"I'm just pointing out that—"

"Have you talked to my contact?" Garrett and I never publicly mentioned Janssen's name.

"I don't know who—"

"You're out in the cold, aren't you?"

"Some affairs are too messy for words," he said.

"That's right—you don't do yes or no. Let's skip to the ending. For different reasons, we both want Peter Omarov dead. But killing him kills your parents and Dusty. Isn't that the inherent threat he holds over you? Or has that just been a convenient excuse for an ungrateful adopted boy?"

"I'll ignore your churlish accusation," he said. "That threat, I've been assured, dies with Omarov. As power weakens, parties change alliances."

"You're fabricating this to get me to kill Omarov and free you. To cancel the guilt you've been carrying all these years for not having the balls to do it yourself. Maybe you'll even pick up a fourth identity in the event that some of your coworkers are less than thrilled with your rogue actions."

"This will get us nowhere. You need me to find him."

I couldn't trust David LeClair, nor could I ignore his bait. Like the damn magazine in the jail cell, I *had* to pick it up.

"Enter Jake Travis," I said. "Let him take out Omarov and his merry men. If it goes to hell, I take the fall. You'll make sure it leads back to me so that if someone is left to carry out Omarov's curse, he'll gun for me instead of you. But it's even better, isn't it? If some faction of either government seeks retribution, it's my picture that pops up, not yours. It's a neat package, Davie. I'll give you that."

"Dissecting motives will not bring us together. You're certainly capable of ascertaining your risk."

"Keep that in mind."

"That leaves the central question," he said.

"Which is?"

"You in or out?"

"In."

37

I rode the hell out of the last twenty-four hours and was three-quarters dead.

When I entered my house, the odor of sawdust and stagnant heat greeted me like a squatter who had taken up residence. A familiar silhouette sat on the screen porch in the waning evening light. She was gazing out toward the blinking red channel marker and the rising drawbridge across the bay. I navigated through my plastic-covered possessions and out onto the porch. The rising plaster-white moon cast a shadow of the dock on the still bay. A palm frond lay on the concrete seawall. It hadn't been there the last time I was home, which was a different life ago.

Kathleen rose and said, "You can't—"

My tongue in her mouth cut her off. I wrapped my arms around her and brought her tightly to my chest. I kissed her like a rushing mountain stream.

I tore off our clothes, eager to ditch the mindless highway miles, the music I saw but could not hear, the lonely chimney, the man who was leeching on to my vendetta to fulfill his own, the empty holes of soldiers who had gone before me, and the soft glow of a woman's breast in a musty Tennessee church.

I lifted her and then clumsily laid her down on the outdoor carpet, our bodies wedged between the coffee table and chairs. A wineglass on the table tumbled in the process. It didn't break. I dove my head between her legs and got lost in her. After her fourth convulsion, she took me inside her. Like a great tree that had held on against a raging torrent, as if it were death itself, I fought pleasure. I finally snapped and lost all bearings and sense of purpose as I rushed madly into her, eager to lose my body into hers and wondering why I ever desired anything else.

"I didn't catch your name," she said as my breathing in her ear geared down from cardiac-arrest pace.

"McCrae."

"Like the poet?"

"Sure, doll."

Our moist bodies generated heat in the oppressive Florida night. I shoved away the table that had been pressing upon us, rolled over on my back, and stared at the sagging ceiling of the screened porch. *Not sure I got that leak fixed.* The rhythmic clacking of the useless ceiling fan was the only sound. It had been the sole witness to our bodies' eager and desperate attempt to taste the night and silently scream while others slept.

"Tell me, poet McCrae," she said, "would you like to know my name?"

"Not really."

She half-nudged and half-slapped me with her arm. "You haven't called for days."

"I did."

"That didn't count. You were drinking and battling demons. Any success?"

I rolled back on top of her and said, "I missed you."

"And I you. You were gone—"

"Just now—on my back. I missed you."

That brought an appreciative smile. She wrapped her legs around me and traced her finger down my back. "What now, brown cow?" she said.

"McCrae."

She rolled her eyes. "Of course. What was I thinking?"

I untangled us and went to the kitchen. I pulled out from under the sink—my ad hoc liquor cabinet—a bottle of twenty-year-old port that was next to a nearly empty Windex bottle. I poured a glass. On the porch, I rearranged a few cushions and leaned back against a chair. Kathleen snuggled back into me, her hot and sticky back fusing with my chest. We shared the port, while, in the distance, flashes of light brightened mushrooming cumulus thunderheads. For all their enormity and show, they would die out over land and never make it to the sea. The heat of the day was gone; tomorrow, the molecules would regather for another assault. A lone sailboat went by, its mast light a single dot of white gliding through the dark. Music came from the boat, but it was not meant to share.

I reached for my phone and put on Mazzy Star's "Fade into You." The soft, tinny sound reminded me of the thinness of the night and the vulnerability of everything we hold dear. Kathleen laid her head back on my shoulder. I wrapped my arms tight around her, like a leaf taking in a flower. We melted together—lovers the world would never know, for there is a reason that the dark claims half the day.

All the things you have loved will have a last time.

There was a last time you saw a friend whom you used to see nearly every day, but you never gave that privilege a second thought. A last time you drove your child to school or read her a book. A last time you saw a lover with whom differences couldn't be mended. A last time you viewed a sunset from a favorite balcony you thought you'd always return to. Kissed the girl. Heard a parent's last breath, although you only realized it by the absence of the next.

"It's OK," she said when I stopped and peered into the game room. *The pings and bells of the arcade pleasure machines were a siren to my ears.* "I'm just going up to get my book."

"You sure?"

"Beat it, Jake-o." *She punched my left shoulder.*

All the things you have loved will have a last time.

I drifted on the edge of sleep. It would take me in and then let me go, as if it was breathing me.

After a while, we got up and went to bed.

THE CARDINAL POPPED IN again that night. I've got to hand it to the guy—he doesn't play second fiddle.

My sister's body was draped in his arms. But we were at Kensington Gardens by the Peter Pan statue, and I knew that was all wrong. As he got closer, it wasn't my sister in his arms. It was Kathleen. He kept walking toward me, but he made no progress.

He said, "Once you have found her, never let her go."

"Crazy bird," I said. "You got the wrong girl."

The body in his arms was now back to being my sister's.

"You honor her memory," he said, "with the life of others?"

"It is the only way." *Who barfed up this junk?*

He let go. The body stayed suspended, like in a magician's trick. "Then you have failed."

Victor, a man I killed three years ago, was next to him.

"What are you doing here?" I asked Victor.

"Why did you kill me?"

"I didn't—"

"You did not even sit by her," the cardinal said.

"I tried," I said, and my pitiful little voice disgusted me. I wondered if he knew I was lying. "God knows I tried. Ask him. You two are close. Hit the head together." *Hit the head. Who says that?* "Ask him. Go ahead. I tried to sit by her."

But in my dream, I remembered that, in my other dream, I hadn't tried to sit by her. It was only when I was waking that I pretended to make the effort.

"I tried to sit by her," I pleaded to the cardinal. "God knows I tried."

"God knows I tried."

"God knows I tried."

"God knows—"

"Jake?"

"—I lied."

"Jake? Wake up, babe."

My body shuddered, and sweat rolled off my forehead. "You're dreaming, babe. You OK?" Kathleen brushed my hair with her hand. "You're sweating up a storm."

She got up and went to the bathroom, her naked body momentarily illuminated as the moon's voyeuristic light sneaked through the venetian blinds. She ran water in the sink and then leaned over me, placing a cool and damp washcloth on my forehead. Her hair formed a curtain around my face, the fine ends sticking to my clammy skin.

This time I was patient with her neck, her ears, her breasts. I ran my teeth over the thin, leathery scar on her shoulder, and my tongue traveled her hot skin before finally settling between her legs. After she shuddered, I laid my head on her moist and flat stomach, which held the stale, sticky scent of the previous day. As the ceiling fan cooled my back, and her breath raised and lowered my head like the moon swelling the tides, I dreamed of killing the man who killed my sister.

38

The next afternoon, Joseph Dangelo and I were sitting inside Mangrove's on Beach Drive in downtown Saint Pete. We'd opted for an inside table, as the hammering sun made a mockery of the outside umbrellas, scorching through their fabric like a broiler set on high. Dangelo, whom I'd tangled with previously, ran organized crime on the west coast of Florida, although he assuredly operated with the blessing of others. If I was going after a gangster, I wanted advice from one.

Outside, a man sitting on a bench emitted a cloud of smoke from his hookah pipe. Across the street, a woman carrying a grocery bag misjudged the curb. She nearly took a spill. Her recovery would have made the Wallenda family proud.

LeClair, through other people in the agency, planned to inform Omarov that I'd gotten wind Omarov was planning a family vacation in the States and that, furthermore, I was assembling a group of ex-GIs to mount an attack against him. LeClair had asked me for a location, saying he would feed it to Omarov. I'd given him one. He wanted to destroy Omarov by demonstrating that Omarov's organization had leaks that resulted in the deaths of his own men. In return, he promised to deliver the address where I could find Omarov. LeClair argued, in the event that I needed convincing, that my lucky encounter at the Greenbrier was one and out.

Dangelo sat facing the front, which put me in the uncomfortable position of having my back to the door. He was dressed in creaseless beige pants and an off-white short-sleeved silk shirt. A gold necklace circled his neck. He'd cultivated a gray goatee since the last time we'd met.

His bodyguard, a man named Chuck Duke, sat two tables away, cleaning his eyeglasses with uncommon thoroughness. The last time we'd been together, we'd parted on amicable terms. I'd referred to him as Tweedledum and his partner as Tweedledee. Duke, who proved to have more brains than I'd initially given him credit for, called me Alice. He acknowledged me with a nod.

The Four Tops' cover of "Walk Away Renee" played over the speakers. The singer at the hotel had performed it wistfully. I'd meant to leave him a tip but had forgotten. The little stuff just sticks to you. I wondered why the song was popping up in my life, but I knew. LeClair was likely using me, perhaps even leading me into a trap.

Walk away, Jake. Just walk away.

But I couldn't. I was trapped in a jail cell with my past.

"Say it again, my friend," Dangelo said.

"I need to take out a Russian mobster."

"What madness possesses you?"

"Revenge for the death of my sister."

"That is a good madness, although all madness is bad." He fondled his goatee as if to make sure it was still there. He took a bite of his grilled ham and cheese sandwich. He'd had the same thing when we'd met previously in Ybor City. He waited until he swallowed, for Dangelo was deliberate in both manner and speech. "This man—you are sure? He is the one who killed your sister?"

"I am," I said, with more conviction than I actually had.

"Why me? You are not a man who's a stranger to violence."

"Not all battles are won with blood."

He eyed me for a second as if I'd uttered an unexpected truth—or perhaps a truth he didn't think I was capable of—and then turned his attention to his sandwich.

I'd explained to Dangelo, without divulging any names, about the blackmail that Omarov had over David LeClair and that Omarov's death could possibly trigger a series of deaths, which LeClair could not tolerate. I'd gotten too close to Omarov, and LeClair had been forced to reveal himself to me. If not, I might have knocked off Omarov and inadvertently caused the death of both LeClair's parents and Dusty, although I no longer believed that to be a viable threat. LeClair never admitted as much, nor did I expect him to.

That was the A side.

The B side was that Dusty and company were not on LeClair's radar and that he couldn't care less about them. He was using me strictly for cold-blooded revenge. This was all assuming that the man who called himself David LeClair was, indeed, David LeClair.

"Do you trust this man?" Dangelo said, patting his mouth with a napkin. We were discussing LeClair.

"I don't trust you."

He chuckled. "May I assume he shares a similar disposition toward you?"

"You may."

"So you need to play two games: one, to work with this man in shutting down a Russian mobster, and, secondly, to do so in such a way that no one will retaliate. Correct?"

"That sums it up. I'll take a refill on my iced tea," I said to the waitress who had been ignoring us as she rushed by. She clumsily snatched my glass in midstride as if I were an inconvenience in her life.

"And if you perform, he gives you an address?"

"Correct."

"What if you perform and he ceases to exist?"

"It's a risk, but he has no motive for that play."

"But you do not wish to follow his plan, correct?" Dangelo asked. "What other objective do you have?"

"I need to protect my own."

"You want to cripple someone, possibly kill him, all without fear of retribution?"

"I do."

"You have a full menu."

"That's why I came to you for guidance."

He laughed. "I will disappoint you, for I am a bar owner."

"And I'm Alice, according to your confidant over there." I poked my chin toward Duke.

"Then a bar owner and Alice will discuss the dilemma."

Garrett and I had tossed the scenarios around into the previous night. We both felt that, with Hawkins's taking the fall for killing my sister, and his subsequent death, Omarov's threat over LeClair had likely lost its punch. I'd thought of pointing that out to LeClair but kept the thought to myself. LeClair was using me to rid himself of a demon who had controlled him for years and likely pulling my strings to advance his stature within the agency. I accepted that role, which left me no grounds on which to object.

Garrett and I had ruled out taking Omarov out with a sniper shot—assuming we'd know his location, which was not a given. Doing so would deny me the opportunity to hear him explain the last day of my sister's life without trying to pin it on LeClair. While I was 99 percent certain that Omarov was my man, that left 1 percent festering in my mind. I wasn't convinced that I'd heard the truth, or a credible facsimile of it, from any of the participants. I could only fantasize why they might be lying.

I did know this: if avenging my sister's death meant that my actions would kill innocent people, then I would never escape The Red Blonde.

The surly waitress dropped off my iced tea. She had a tattoo of a rising sun with a cross in it on her forearm. I picked up my empty plate and dropped it on the vacant table across from us. I was overcome with a sudden urge to chuck it all and head to a remote island with Kathleen. I'd been doing fine. Why risk sliding into a labyrinth?

I leaned into the table, and it tilted. "Tell me what I don't know," I said. "How would you handle it?"

Dangelo scratched his goatee appreciatively. I wondered if he grew it just for the sensation of feeling it. He leaned back in his seat, granting more distance between us. "This man—he wants you to eliminate his foe? Do his dirty work for him?"

I spread my hands.

"Do you know why," Dangelo asked, "you slap someone before you talk to them?"

"Bad manners?"

"My father once told me that you get better results from the respect of violence than from violence itself."

"Fine. I'll slap him before I kill him." I backed off the table, and it shifted again.

He gave me a disapproving look, pushed back his chair, and crossed his legs. "When I was a young boy growing up in Chicago, my father used to take me on his rounds. He was a collector. We'd go into bars, restaurants, Laundromats, and we'd leave with a little cash in a leather satchel that had been his father's.

"One man, his name escapes me—but he had white arms that were large and soft, like that of an old woman. I remember because I was afraid that my arms might grow to be like that. He was the kindest and most jovial of the men we would meet. He had a scar across his left cheek. My father would always spend an extra few minutes with this man. How's the family? Your health? That sort of thing.

"The man dropped dead one day from a heart attack. Another reason, I thought, to avoid fat arms. My father insisted that our whole family attend the funeral, even though it was not custom. The man only had a small bar. Nonetheless, I realized that my father considered him to be a true friend.

"I asked my father—you see, it had always bothered me why the man had such a scar. 'I gave it to him,' my father replied. I was—oh, twelve, maybe thirteen? He explained that the man didn't want to pay and that he had to be taught a lesson. My father told me that day that the respect of violence is a greater facilitator for business than violence itself. You do not teach a lesson if you kill the pupil."

I cracked another piece of ice that had been rolling around in my mouth during his soliloquy. "Perhaps your father felt remorse for his act," I said casually.

"You think?" he said, challenging me. "Then you do not understand."

"Your suggestion?"

"Don't mess with the Russian mob. Enjoy your beautiful woman. Let your sister go. You cannot undo a tragedy."

"Your second suggestion?"

He tented his hands. He raised and lowered his fingers as if they were lungs, taking in and letting out air. "I would toy with him. Show him you have no fear. Killing is easy. Respect is hard. Powerful men are not afraid of violence or death; they are afraid of men without fear."

"Then what?"

"I would either confront him or wait for him to make himself known. I doubt there would be any of the repercussions you mentioned. By scaring his organization first, you would have their respect. When he is gone, they would act in their self-interest—that being, of course, to fill the vacuum. The man who is setting you up—he wants you to kill?"

"Not in those exact words."

"Of course. But implied?"

"Yes."

"And if you don't, you show him that you are your own man, that you do things your way. You show strength to both sides, do you see that?"

I nodded. "And how would you do this?"

"That is for you to discover." He started to say something but pulled back. His eyes floated outside, where a young man in black pants and a bright-purple shirt limped by with the help of a cane. One leg was notably shorter than the other. The man's face was serene, but he walked with great effort.

I reached for my wallet.

"No. Allow me," he said. "I believe you paid the last time we met, at the hotel on the beach."

"I'd rather not owe you."

"I can say the same about you. May I ask you again—are you certain he is your man?"

"I am."

"So be it. But if you do this, carry the deed to the end, and then learn one day that it was not him—that you hunted the wrong man—you will lose your religion."

"I never had any."

"So you think, my friend. It takes as much blind faith to not believe as it does to believe, both in religion and in guilt."

"I didn't know you were so wise."

"Yet it was you who came to see me."

39

Eve Davidson was in the same chair she had been in the previous time we'd met. She likely thought she was in the tranquil waters of her life, where she no longer created a wake. I wasn't so certain. Even the smallest ripples travel a great distance.

I'd decided to make one more stop before a final assault on Omarov. LeClair had mentioned that Alex Brackett had nothing to do with the abduction of my sister, that Brackett was "having sex with an older woman." He'd asked if I'd found the lady whom Brackett was having a tryst with. I had steered the conversation in a different direction. But LeClair's piqued interest indicated that Eve, if she were the one in bed with Brackett that day, was more than a two-bit player.

Eve had given me a detailed statement about her whereabouts the afternoon of my sister's disappearance. She had denied that her fling with Brackett, days before my sister was abducted, had lasted more than one afternoon. But her description of that day was too precise. Like Omarov's and Brackett's versions, it came off as being finely rehearsed. She'd also done so with her eyes cast on the flame and avoiding mine. Her change of demeanor was odd. If Eve could provide an alibi for Brackett as well as LeClair, then that would leave one man standing: Peter the Russian.

I wished I'd thrown Eve's name out when Garrett and I'd met with Brackett, although he likely would have denied knowing her. Or, perhaps, he would have accused her of concocting a tale. I told myself to forget it. Life is a chess match; once your hand's off the piece, your move is sealed.

I'd been camped out at the bar, keeping an eye on the fire pit and waiting for a seat to open up next to her. She wasn't the same lady she was before. The week of neglect had taken its toll on her. She exuded a weary pallor as she sat slumped in the chair, her once-meticulously attended hair pulled haphazardly behind her head. She had not been engaged with the people around her. No Lady and the Tramp tonight.

The group sitting with her left. I approached her and took a seat. We were alone.

"Why do I think your return trip isn't particularly good news?" Eve said.

"You tell me, and I won't have to ask."

"I'm not in the mood," she said. She gazed straight into the fire, her jaw firm.

"The Vogue cover," I said. "That was good. Every detail of Christy Turlington's outfit neatly stitched into your mind. It's also a defense mechanism. A counterfactual reality you pounded into your head until you believed it."

She coughed out a nervous laugh. "What did you do? Get a psych degree in the past week? I don't need counseling or life tips from a lost soul like you."

"That is what you *wish* you were doing, right? Reading your Vogue and watching the boys go by."

"Careful. I can clam up fast."

I took a sip of watered-down whiskey. Ice cubes are not indigenous to Florida. A breeze teased the flame, and it flicked its yellow tendrils at us. It just as quickly lost interest, as if we were old news.

"Tell me," Eve said, "did someone squeal, or are you really that astute?"

"No one sang." I didn't want to get into it with her that I had spoken with LeClair and Brackett.

She turned to me. "*Really*? I don't believe you."

"Nor I, you."

Her face sagged with guilt-racked memories. "If I tell you, will you leave me alone?"

I took another pull from my whiskey.

"I see," she said. "Damn the torpedoes and full steam ahead, right? Let the old gal vomit up her memories, is that it?"

I placed my drink down and leaned in toward her with my elbows on my knees. "I'm not here to tear down your wall, but I need to know."

"Leave me alone," she said.

"I need—look at me, Eve."

"I don't want to."

"*Look* at—"

"Fine," she said whipping her face around to me.

"Tell me what happened."

"You won't understand."

"I'll try."

"Try?" she said in comical anger. "Try this: you and your shattered mirrors have no idea what it's like to be a woman who knows she's been caught. To glance over your shoulder and see that age is chasing you, and she's a bitch on a stick, and she's gaining at every turn, laughing at you in the morning mirror, stalking you in the corner of the shower, sleeping in your bed, adding pounds although you're starving yourself, and you just want the day—this day—to go on forever, and for the sun to never set, because regardless of age, your body still convulses with desire. You think you understand that? I assure you, little boy, you do not understand that at all."

"I'm not here to take anything away from you that you haven't already taken."

"Stop that stuff."

I leaned back in my chair, gambling that the time for earnest supplication had passed.

She shifted her weight and crossed her legs. She took a drink but kept the glass touching the edge of her lips longer than was necessary.

"I'd like you to leave," she said, lowering the glass.

"Not a chance."

"No...I suppose not."

She let her breath out slowly. She spoke with formality and avoided eye contact. "I did have the magazine, and it was exactly how I described it to you. When the police starting asking us where we were, I...lied. I told them I was in the shade reading the magazine." She glanced at me. "Oh, I'd seen your sister and you. Her green bathing suit and your blond hair. I didn't tell you that before, did I? That I remember your golden hair. What kind of old hag would you classify me as, then? But it wasn't from the poolside chair but rather from peeking behind a curtain on a balcony while having a postcoitus smoke. Is that what you want?"

"You were with Alex Brackett the afternoon she went missing?"

She shrugged as if, in the end, it was hardly worth the lies and the posturing. "An hour or so. It was our daily routine."

"The guilt song you played for me when we first met?"

"Oh, it's there. Tell me, at what point in your journey did you realize that you paint your own life, only to discover that you're a flawed painter?"

"This is your story."

"Your day will come. I wanted a lifetime of dedication to Allen, with a solitary indiscretion. It's a better picture that way, isn't it? I wanted to taste a drop of guilt on my tongue, not have it for dinner. That is how I choose to remember it. That is my painting. I made it up that day. I had to, you see, for we were discovered."

"Who discovered you?"

"Why? So you can verify?"

I leaned in toward her again, elbows on my knees. "I don't care about your love-pad with Alex Brackett. I'm after the man who took my sister."

She stiffened, as if preparing a counterattack, but then her body slumped.

"His French-named friend. He knocked on the door. Pounded on it, shouting Alex's name over and over. He knew Alex and I used the room. Alex cracked the door, and he burst in. He smelled like the beach." She glanced over to me. "You can tell when someone comes in from the sand. They wear the heat and smell of the gulf like clothing."

She focused, again, on the flames. "He said he'd gone back to the room to get another book and that Peter had done something terrible. He and Alex dashed out, leaving me nude in the bed."

She eyed me as if I might challenge her statement.

"What did you do?"

"I scrambled to pull the sheets up around me."

I expected more, and when nothing came, I repeated myself. "What did you *do?*"

She cut me a cold look. "I had no idea what had happened, understand? So save your judgmental eyes for someone else. You really want to know? I lay in the sheets and fantasized that another lover came in and then another, and they ravished me all afternoon while I lay with my head to the side and stared indifferently at the wall, listening to the gleeful sounds of the pool below. Are you satisfied now? Is that what you want?"

I'd harbored thoughts that LeClair was guilty, but Eve was now vouching for both LeClair and Brackett. LeClair had lied to me at the hotel beach bar when he'd told me that he hadn't known what had happened. I hadn't believed him—but I wanted him to think that I did believe him. His deceit went with the general theme; no one wanted to tell me the truth. It was as if they were afraid of it themselves. As if the truth defied traditional explanation—or, worse yet, there was no truth.

"You didn't tell anyone?" I said, more as an accusation than a question.

"Tell them what? I didn't know what they'd done."

"When the police came—you had to have been suspicious."

Eve swallowed and kept her eyes on the flames.

"Look at me, goddamn it."

She did not.

"*Did you tell anyone?*" I demanded again, my voice rising in the night.

She remained fixated on the flames. Her jaw quivered, and her hands tightened on the armrest of her chair. The waning light cast shadows across her face.

"You're the one," I said, "who told the paper you last saw her at three. It was only after the police were finished questioning everyone when they realized she was last seen at two."

She sniffled and nodded. "I told Allen I was running back to the house. If I told them I'd seen her at two, then it would..." Her voice trailed off as her eyes of many colors filmed over with tears.

The wind shifted, and the flame's tendrils were now forked devil tongues, lashing out and pulling her back into hell. Saint Augustine urged to never use the truth to hurt someone. I would have been wise to observe that credo, but I didn't care.

"You sad fool," I said. "You told me when we met that my honesty would earn me yours, and then you lied to me. You hid behind your self-centered deceit instead of helping the investigation. At that point, they might have been able to save her. She would be alive today. You understand that? You're as responsible for her death as the man who killed her. Do you *fuck*ing understand that?"

Silent tears tracked down Eve Davidson's cheeks as she sought refuge in the fire. Her body lunged, as if something inside had died. The world is full of pain, but none so great as the arrows we inflict upon ourselves.

I dropped my drink on the table and walked away.

40

The following evening, Garrett and I rendezvoused with LeClair on the rooftop of Hurricanes to finalize our plan.

We took a table by the edge, overlooking the Gulf of Mexico. The water was smooth and flat until it formed a line with the sky. Below, on Gulf Boulevard, a man rode his bike to Paradise Grille. His dog was leashed to the handlebars, its tongue flopping from the side of its mouth, panting to keep pace. Another man rode south on a motorcycle with a sidecar. His dog rode in the sidecar, its ears fluttering behind, its nose wild with the scents in the air.

"How can we be certain that Omarov will send his men?" I asked LeClair.

"We'll leak that you want revenge," he said. "That you plan on ambushing his family with your own militia unit. He's at Disney World with his wife, mother, and two daughters, both of whom attend school in the States. Your proximity will cause him great unrest."

"He'll buy that?"

"The threat alone warrants a reaction. How will you dispose of the bodies?"

"Cinder blocks and the Gulf of Mexico."

"What if he has a dozen men?"

"Blocks are cheap."

340

LeClair nodded. "This land—it is remote enough?"

"It is," I said.

"And you're confident that you can take his men out?"

"Drop by," Garrett said. He leveled his eyes on LeClair with a marksman's gaze. "We might make it a baker's dozen."

LeClair flinched. "We have specific roles that the other party cannot replicate. You will destroy the man who... hurt you. We need each other. You do see that, don't you?"

My eyes wandered again to the beach. The red-wafer sun rested on the horizon, its lower half already sacrificed to the sea. A Frisbee sailed the air above the beach, crested above the sun, and then floated beyond outstretched hands.

"He'll know it's a trap," I said, "and that the agency betrayed him."

"He will," LeClair agreed. "But his men will be dead, and his US assets will be frozen. For the first time, he'll be afraid. Furthermore, his contacts within the agency—I'm sure he's cultivated relationships that I'm not aware of—will be equally baffled and surprised. Omarov will hightail it back to Mother Russia."

"But not before you tell me where he is," I said.

"Correct."

"This is an elaborate scheme to engage us to do work for you," Garrett pointed out.

"It is," LeClair admitted. "You are free to track him down on your own. But know this: even if you do find him and kill him *before* you cripple his organization, that will likely trigger an act of retribution."

LeClair had been directing his comment to Garrett. He now turned to me. "You can also rest assured that he hasn't forgotten your unfortunate blunder involving your girlfriend. That was a sophomoric and immature act. You don't think his men will come after you? Swing away."

I'd come to regret Kathleen's involvement. My quixotic quest was generating bad decisions. I wondered if I was making another one now, but I was incapable of waiting. I didn't necessarily subscribe to LeClair's statement that Omarov's organization would seek me out if I killed him with a sniper's bullet. But it wasn't a chance I could take.

LeClair, perhaps getting a sniff of my dubiety, lobbied his case. "You do not bring down a bear with a single shot."

The bell rang at Paradise Grille, signaling the sunset. A faint round of applause rose from the beach. But from our vantage point, higher off the ground, the sun's coned top still arched over the horizon—it had yet to set. It's all a matter of perspective. What is so real and self-evident to one person is equally false to another.

"He has friends in your organization who have supported him," I said, trying to get back in the conversation. "They'll let this pass?"

"That is correct."

"How loyal are these friends?"

"There are no friends in diplomatic relationships, only shifting interests," LeClair lectured. "They will act in their own best interest."

"You'll give me his address where I can find him?"

"Yes."

"Where Omarov's men will be waiting for me."

"Not by my hand."

"And if you don't come through?"

"Then I imagine the two of you would put a target on my back. You must accept that I realize that and have every intention of fulfilling my end of the bargain. That I am indeed grateful for the role you—"

"What will you tell him?" I said, cutting him off.

"That you're sick with revenge for your sister's death."

"You're confident the agency won't kiss his ring one more time?" I said, revisiting my earlier point to see if I could trip up LeClair.

"The other side has taken the field."

"Let's hope so, for your sake."

LeClair squinted at me like a cyclops. The conversation had made a full circle. I thought of a few more questions, but why bother? I didn't trust David LeClair to split a loaf of bread with a starving orphan girl.

LeClair said, "The address?"

I gave it to him.

LeClair rose and gave a solitary nod. He strolled away with an ethereal indifference to all around him.

"He's the one who tried to pin Hawkins on you," Garrett said as a rumbling roll of distant thunder made the air tremble. "His plan was to put you in jail. If needed, he *might* have ridden in at the eleventh hour, saved your neck, and then unleashed you on Omarov. He's playing both sides."

"Goes with his union card."

"Did you tell him previously about our exploits at the Greenbrier?" Garrett asked.

"No."

"Then they're talking," he said.

"I know. But not necessarily directly."

"How so?"

"LeClair might have gotten the story from Brackett."

"They're talking," Garrett said, repeating himself in the event I hadn't caught the full implication of his words the first time around.

I took a drink from a new and cold beer. A car with a paddleboard on its hood crawled down Gulf Boulevard. I'd had difficulties focusing all evening. Instead of being focused, my mind was easily distracted. I was listening but not hearing, observing but not seeing. I was trapped inside myself, a passive observer to the world spinning around me.

I'd been in too many states recently—both mentally and physically. I just wanted to kill the man who killed my sister. But to do so without repercussions, and to make certain I had the right man, was taking a measurable amount of fun out of the game.

"You hear what I said?" Garrett demanded.

"You said he'd shoot me in the back."

"Don't forget it."

We formulated our own plan. For the first time since Leonard Hawkins washed up on the sand, I felt as if I were taking the lead.

We talked until the marbled sunset faded to total black, until the stars that had been there all day, although we could not see them, twinkled above us, and lovers entwined on the beach as one bid good-night to the cooling sand. Until Paradise Grille closed its doors, not to reopen until sunrise, when the smell of fried bacon would permeate the air, and early-morning joggers would leave the first footprints of the day. When young children with their fathers, and women walking together, would bend over and examine common seashells with innocent awe as if heaven itself had washed up on the beach and the angels had left their calling cards. When the municipality's truck would drive on the sand and collect the previous day's garbage. When the first beach umbrella, like a flag proclaiming the new day, would be staked in the sand.

It was time to stake my flag.

41

"You sure I can't help?" Mac asked as I tossed his over-night bag in the back of my truck.

"Already are. We couldn't do it without you," I told him. "You've got the perfect piece of land."

"And equipment."

"That too."

Before swinging by and collecting Mac, I'd been at a construction-rental business on Route 19. My truck had been loaded with a small pair of high-voltage lights for night work. They were now leaning against one of Mac's palm trees. The generator was being delivered.

"Don't worry about any damage to the house," Mac said, climbing in with considerable effort into the front seat of the truck. He fiddled with his seat belt. I resisted reaching over and fastening it for him. "She'll come through, especially if she smells a Russian. Sure I can't help?"

"Positive."

"What's the name of Morgan's boat again?"

"Moonchild."

"That's right. Got AC?"

"You betcha." I put the truck in gear and rolled out of his front yard.

"You've known him long?"

"Morgan? Ever since I moved in, five or six years back."

"He's an exceptional human being. You know, I don't remember the last time I was in a truck. Think we could mount Sally-Mae in the back and take her down to the keys? A lot of birds down there."

"A road trip?"

"I'd like that," he said. "I'd like that a lot."

I glanced over at him but was surprised to see him staring out the side window.

We planned to stash Mac on Morgan's forty-two-foot Morgan sailboat—the line of boats he was named after. Morgan docked the boat on an interior lot on a canal where the water was calm. Boca Ciega Bay was too large a body of water to keep a boat in the water. Not only could the wind do damage, but even on a calm day, a cruiser could leave a wake a Diamond Head surfer would envy.

When I pulled in, Dusty dropped a rag she'd been using on the rails and planted her hands on her hips. *Moonchild* had teak and mahogany trim that Morgan kept marble-glossy to protect it from the sun. I hadn't told her that David LeClair was in town. I'd eventually have to—I think—but I wasn't up to it. Besides, I wasn't totally convinced that LeClair was really LeClair.

I told Dusty it was getting close to midnight and that we were relocating Mac, since we needed his property. She asked me for details, and I told her that Mac would fill her in and that she needed to "just trust me."

"I don't trust men," she said.

"No kidding," I snapped back at her.

It was only two words, but they thunked to the ground with an unintended meanness.

Between LeClair's alleged car crash, her father—her best friend—crashing his plane into Tellico Lake and a man who called himself Daniel crashing the Down Yonder one night, Dusty was shell-shocked. She was a prisoner to her past, perhaps more so than I.

None of that excused my wounding retort. She took the back of her hand over her forehead to wipe away sweat. It was the same motion she had used at her parents' gravesite.

"You didn't need to say it…like that," she said achingly. Her eyes settled on me like a puppy who didn't understand why it had just been punished.

"I didn't—"

"Just finish this business, for both of us." She went back to her task, giving it far more concentration than it demanded.

There are few feelings in the world that shrink you faster than the feeling that you have let down the person in the passenger seat.

Driving away, I called Dangelo. I asked him if I could borrow Chuck Duke and Tweedledee, his two "associates." I knew such favors didn't come cheap, nor was I eager to jump into bed with the devil. But Garrett and I didn't see another viable option. We anticipated being grossly outnumbered. Worse yet, perhaps *we* were the ones walking into the trap. A deep chuckle reverberated over the airwaves when I popped the question to Dangelo.

"Certainly, my friend. It would be an honor."

One day, he would call in the favor. I'd worry about that later.

DUKE AND TWEEDLEDEE ARRIVED late that afternoon. I gave them the blueprint. Duke stroked Sally-Mae's barrel as if he were trying to get a rise out of her. "Poor Russians," he said. "You sure the neighbors won't mind?" He surveyed the area. "Not that anyone lives in these sticks."

"It won't come to that," I said.

"Too bad, Alice. Such an isolated spot is a perfect space."

Duke was a forward scout. Tweedledee, a lanky man who looked as if he could slice a field of sugarcane without breaking a sweat and whose eyes popped around in his head, covered the rear side of the pond. Duke's responsibility was to let us know how many there were and then to hustle back to support the front line. I'd told Morgan to stay on *Moonchild*. He didn't listen. Instead, he camped out in the mangroves by Mac's dock and made a bed on the bottom of the flatboat. If the Russians came by sea, then Morgan would sound the alarm.

We built a campfire every night at the edge of the pond. We placed two dummies in chairs so that it appeared as if two additional men were sitting around the fire. We stuffed sleeping bags with pillows. We littered the ground with empty whiskey bottles. I guzzled water for three straight nights.

We texted each other every fifteen minutes. LeClair had told us at Hurricanes that the agency, without Omarov knowing they had switched allegiance, would leak the position of the house to the Russian. They would inform him that I was gathering men before making a final assault on him and his family.

We tested the lights and positioned them. Garrett observed that a small light had to be on me or else the construction lights would blind Omarov's men. We maneuvered a yard spotlight so that it lit the gun but didn't impair my vision.

On the second night, we saw nothing but a shooting star that traced the sky like an angelic flare gun.

At three fifteen in the morning on the third night, my cell vibrated with a text from Duke: *suv unknown number.*

We had mapped out our positions earlier and each had a designated spot to report to. Garrett was south of me at a right angle. Duke would come in from the north but at forty-five degrees from Garrett so as not to catch any friendly crossfire. Tweedledee would stay put beyond the pond in the unlikely event that the frontal assault was a decoy. Morgan would be our escape messenger if our play never made it past the opening act.

Another group text came in: *they split, three and three, converging on house.*

I texted an affirmative reply. Duke would now reposition himself. My phone vibrated: *three in, three out.*

I didn't have time to reply. Stealthy shadows cautiously exited the back door of Mac's house. They were joined by two men coming around the north corner and the sixth man around the south corner of the house. They started toward the campfire and stuffed sleeping bags. They were about twenty meters out and converging with guns drawn when Garrett hit the construction lights.

I don't know what the Russkies were expecting, but I'd bet bottom dollar that in their worst nightmares, they didn't anticipate running into a refitted 1953 90 mm anti-aircraft gun.

"Drop the guns!" Garrett shouted. Not original, but it got to the point. He came out of the shadows holding an M27 Infantry Automatic Rifle.

The men froze momentarily. Then one hit the ground in combat position, while another ate dirt with his hands covering his head. That left four men staring at me as I stood behind Sally-Mae's armor plate. I lowered the gun barrel so that it was chest high. I swung it to my left, aiming directly at the man on that end. He dropped his weapon and flung his hands into the air. A man toward the middle barked out something in Russian.

"*Teper!*" Garrett barked out. The four remaining men went down.

I took my trembling hand off Sally-Mae's trigger.

42

At five that morning, we informed LeClair that, instead of tying the men to cinder blocks and sinking their lifeless bodies in the gulf, we'd opted to confiscate their weapons and disable their vehicles. After we took a picture, we sent them slumping down the road—two of them donning Mickey Mouse hats that Morgan had provided from the thrift store.

Garrett and I never considered letting LeClair manipulate us. For all we knew, the police would have been tipped, and LeClair's true purpose was to simultaneously destroy Omarov and put me in the electric chair. I didn't see that being a viable goal for him, but I'd been pinning the tail on the donkey since day one.

LeClair was ticked but not as much as I would have thought, considering he wanted Omarov's men dead. He begrudgingly accepted our actions, although he had no choice in the matter. LeClair gave me Omarov's suite number at the Disney hotel. I pointed out that we both knew Omarov would scuttle his plans in view of recent events, and I demanded that he tell me where Omarov was going to go, not where he was. LeClair insisted that he'd get back to me. He squinted through his slit eyes and signed off with, "Best of luck to you, Jake."

Why did people keep telling me that?

Omarov would receive an anonymous envelope with the picture. He would already know, due to the silence from his team, that the mission was blown. More disturbingly, he would also realize that he'd not only lost the support of the CIA but that they had mutated into his enemy. My bet? Omarov would seek me out to learn who had double-crossed him, recant his previous version of what had transpired thirty years ago, and inch me closer to the truth.

I would get my final opportunity to talk to him.

It would have to count.

I wanted to kill the man who killed my sister, not blindly kill the man who I thought killed my sister. Sitting on the porch the other night with my arms wrapped around Kathleen, I'd decided that holding on to what I had now was more important than avenging the past. I wondered if that thought could hold the field, for the other side of my bifurcated brain voted for the blind kill. In Vegas parlance, all bets were off.

No plan is without flaws. The men we encountered were likely hired guns and not part of Omarov's inner circle. Neither Dimitri nor the twins who had visited the thrift store made an appearance in Mac's backyard. Still, those three men knew that the organization they worked for had an internal leak in addition to well-informed enemies. They also knew that their organization had sent mercenaries into a trap. Good luck recruiting. They aided my cause by being alive more so than by being dead.

THE FOLLOWING DAY, MORGAN, Garrett, and I finished installing tongue-in-grove ceiling in the main room. Morgan pointed out that the roofline above my bedroom was raised. We tore out the bedroom ceiling, repositioned the air vents and the electrical box for the ceiling fan, and stuffed insulation up tight against the rafters. We were nearly done when Morgan was due back at *Moonchild* to pick up Dusty. He split. I told Garrett I had it from there. He went to Morgan's, where he was staying, to clean up.

I was dripping with sweat. Insulation was prickling my skin like tips of hot electrical wire. I'd just cut a beadboard for the bedroom ceiling, and the damn thing had splintered on the end. It was useless. It was also my last piece. I dealt with the setback by delivering a masterful combination of cusswords and then hunkered down on the plastic-covered couch and threw back a bottle of water. I got up, fixed a more appropriate drink, and enjoyed it under my outdoor showerhead. A pair of bickering crows, in the event I'd forgotten about them, clanked their claws on the aluminum gutter at the corner of the roof.

Kathleen rang as I trailed water back into the house. Picking up the phone, I juggled it with the whiskey while switching hands. I nearly dropped them both. The towel slipped off my waist.

"When's dinner?" she asked.

"Life-tip for for you first."

"Oh goody."

"You know that some days you're the hammer and some days you're the nail?"

"I've heard."

"Some days you're a split piece of wood."

"That type of day?"

"That type of day. Takeout fine?"

"Takeout's great."

I picked up the damp towel. It was imbedded with sawdust. I opened the door to the garage and tossed it on the washing machine. My shot was long and it slid off the side. I shut the door and headed to my closet.

I called Mac, who'd since gone back to his house, but he wasn't feeling well. Garrett opted out of dinner. He decided it was "idiotic" for us all to sit around the same table while we assumed that Omarov would exercise rationality. He was right, of course. Garrett never crossed his legs when in the passenger seat of a car. He stayed at Morgan's, where he would keep a watchful eye on the street and bay.

Morgan returned with Dusty. They brought takeout containers from Dockside, a fish shack on the channel before taking the bridge to our island. A few minutes later, Kathleen came in through the screen door holding Hadley III. The cat had been AWOL since breakfast. She was likely canvassing the neighborhood for a new home.

The four of us sat on the screened porch eating grouper sandwiches, although both Kathleen and Dusty ignored the buns. The sunset boats *Magic* and *Fantasea* sailed past the end of the dock. Their billowed sails, searching for the wind, stretched out toward the open waters of the gulf. Colored flags from different countries, high on the masts, flapped in the breeze. Groupings of legs dangled over the side. They would reach the mouth of Pass-a-Grille Channel just as the sun dipped into the Gulf of Mexico. *Magic* caught an extra puff and keeled over toward shore. A dolphin surfaced and flapped its tail hard on the water. It repeated the act several times. Hands pointed out from the boat, and people from the port side repositioned themselves on the starboard side as the captain let out more sail.

"Why do they do that?" Dusty asked.

Morgan said, "It's one of numerous ways—some say as many as thirty—in which they communicate to each other.

No one knows what it means. It likely means different things at different times."

"You've witnessed it before?" Kathleen said.

"Often while at sea," Morgan said. "I could never draw any parallels between the occurrences. Mac also told me he couldn't draw any conclusions."

"Speaking of—where is Mac?" Kathleen asked.

"He's not feeling well," Dusty said. "He's been tired lately. He asked me to witness a will."

"I'll swing by tomorrow," I said.

"You might want to do that." Dusty kept her brown eyes on me, and I wished she wouldn't do that. "You've known him a long time?"

"Not even two weeks."

"Really?" she said with suspicion.

"Is that an issue?"

"No. It's just that...he spoke highly of you. Morgan as well."

She cut a look toward Morgan, and I got the impression the two of them had previously discussed Mac and his will. They had been spending time with him.

"You two hit it off?" Dusty said to me, seemingly not content to close the subject.

"We did. Once he accepted that I wasn't there to kill him."

"I can see how that might impede a friendship."

"How's Bud?" I said, changing the subject that for some reason I was not comfortable with.

"Younger than springtime when Mac unleashes her on a bird," Dusty said. "That man does not like birds."

"Tell you why?"

"He told me everything. That's a nice piece of land he's got."

Dusty seemed bent on returning the conversation to Mac, but I didn't accommodate her. We finished our Styrofoam meal, passing around unwanted fish, salad, bread, and coleslaw until we were members of the clean-plate club.

The wine and the warm air mixed together to create a lethargic spell over us. I was in waiting mode, biding my time until Omarov contacted me. It was not a natural position for me. *Magic* and *Fantasea* quietly slipped past the end of the dock on their return voyage as if they were children out late and were trying to sneak back to their beds.

"Walk with me?" I said to Kathleen.

"Forever," she said with sincerity. My heart thumped like a dolphin's tail flapping against the water.

Maybe that's what it's all about.

43

Kathleen and I strolled hand in hand to the end of the dock. It was low tide, and the water seemed far away, as if it were ceding the earth to us. Across the bay, the headlights of cars traced over the Tierra Verde Bridge. They were silent travelers in the night, as the water molecules in the humid air absorbed the sound waves. When the air was cold, the sound waves would meet no such resistance, and you could hear the cars. Sight and sound, after all, are not travel companions.

Kathleen's hair was tied back, as it often was in the summer, although a few strands had broken free. She wore beige shorts and a white sleeveless shirt with the top buttons undone. A single gold chain no thicker than a fish line was draped around her neck.

We took a seat on the bench. She said, "Do you think Omarov will contact you soon?"

"I do," I said, eyeing fresh splotches of bird crap on the dock. Every day I hose it off, and every day the birds come. Some battles are fought, knowing you will never win.

"And you'll get a different story from him this time?"

"I will."

"And you'll perhaps kill the man?"

"I might."

"You get an A for brevity and an F for content."

"That's a C average. Not bad for me."

"And then what? You enter the realm of the gods as peace washes over you?"

"Don't forget chirping little cartoon bluebirds dancing on my shoulders."

"What if things went wrong, Jake? Then what?"

It is never a good omen when she uses my name.

"I would have killed six worthless Russian thugs."

"All with mothers and children. And that's who you are?"

"You'd be surprised."

"Save it for the locker room," she said with a hint of disgust in her voice.

"It would never have come to that."

A large cruiser came in from the gulf; its bow was proud and defiant, riding high over the water. Its rolling black wake crashed in the seawall, scurrying the birds that were high-stepping in the shallows looking for food in the sea grass. I wished I were the bow of a large cruiser, riding tall and defiant as I plowed the night water in front of me, scattering all that stood in my path.

Kathleen raked her hand over her forehead in a futile attempt to tame a few more strands of hair that a sudden gust of air had freed.

She said, "What was the plan? Shoot before being shot?"

"That's generally how it works, although Garrett likely would have beat me to it."

"Ahh, your guardian dark angel. I think part of you wishes you were more like him."

The red channel marker punched in for its graveyard shift. *Doesn't that sucker ever get a night off?* We were quiet for a painful moment, and then Kathleen said, "You ever keep score? The men you've killed."

"Does it bother you?"

"No," she said. "Does it bother you?"

"You give up keeping score," I lied. "You have to trust yourself and the decision you made at the time."

"You didn't answer the question."

"No."

"It's not that simple, is it?" she said.

"Reckon not much is."

"Who is Victor?"

"Never heard of him."

"Reckon you have, seeing as how you coughed him up in your dream the other night."

I punched out my breath. "Remember when I was trying to free those two kidnapped girls, Maria and Rosa, at Sophia's old house a few years ago? A man named Victor held us at gunpoint. His eyes—you could tell his heart wasn't in the game. I tried to convince him to leave, to save himself and let us go. He wavered. Maria said she had to use the restroom. He took his eyes off me and said, 'Go.' He dropped his gun. I shot him. But he was saying, 'Go. Leave.' Not just telling her to go to the bathroom. When he realized that I'd shot him..."

"You—"

"He was puzzled. Confused. His English wasn't good. He felt the mistake had been his—that he might have misspoken. I felt bad for him, thinking that he had caused his own death. I felt worse about that than I did for killing him."

"You romanticize your memories," Kathleen said. "He was a killer for hire. He might have let you go, reconsidered, and then shot you in the back. Maria and Rosa as well. They're alive today because of you."

"That's painfully nonsensical."

"Why?"

"You can't have it both ways," I said. "I'm a good guy for killing. I'm a bad guy for killing."

"I never said you were bad."

"No, you didn't."

"Besides, I don't care about the dead."

"That's good, because they're—"

"It's you."

Her hand was on my shoulder, and I wished she hadn't done that. It was my fault for opening my mouth. I'd dug the hole and had been spiraling into it ever since I dropped into The Red Blonde. Was The Red Blonde my preordained destination, set in motion thirty years ago, when I was seven—nearly eight? Was it really about my sister? Killing Omarov? If Kathleen and I were to marry...

You want the goddamned truth? It was never about killing the man who killed my sister. It was about killing my excuses so they wouldn't control me anymore. When I let go of what I am...

"You with me, champ?" Kathleen said, rescuing me from my drowning reverie.

"Front and center."

"What's the big door prize here? Everything becomes hunky-dory, and you march triumphantly into the future, forever unshackled from your past?"

"Don't forget the bluebirds."

"Babe, there is no big door prize, and birds crap all day. You, of all people, should know that."

"I want my money back."

"You can't exorcise your past."

"Think the Rays will make the playoffs?"

"Listen to me," Kathleen exhorted me. "We come naked into the world. It is the first prick of life, the first warmth of the sun's rays, the first drop of cold rain, that seal our lives and chart our course. We never return to them, for they never leave. They reside in the chambers of our hearts, from our first conscious thought to our last dying breath."

"I think my chamber's empty."

"Stop it, Jake. I'm serious."

"I'm the comic."

"'Comedy's just a funny way of being serious.'"

"Didn't a Russian say that?"

"Peter Ustinov," Kathleen said pointedly. "He was English."

"Same thing. Didn't he—"

"You're thrashing around in the dark, thinking that by killing Omarov, you will rectify the past. All you'll do is lose your excuses."

Does that woman know me, or what?

"When you see Omarov?" she said as a question.

"Assuming I do."

"Don't let your false sense of failure make you vulnerable to compromising yourself."

"You got to bring it down to my level."

"Don't abdicate who you are," she said, as if she were delivering a papal edict.

"You just said the first prick seals us."

"Your first prick was long before the tragic death of your sister. You have happy memories of her. I know you do. You chose to bury them."

"I wouldn't be so certain. I came out on the other side of youth; she didn't. That's who I am. That's what I owe her. Owe us."

"You have a duty to carry on as she would want you to."

"We done?"

"Close."

"I can hardly wait."

Kathleen paused and then said in a soft voice, "Brittany."

Hadley III cat-walked over to Kathleen. I was surprised to see her, as she wasn't fond of the dock. Her body was low to the ground, her eyes alert. Even the cat knew we were in dangerous territory—or she smelled blood. Mine.

"What about her?" I said.

"She fuels your Arthurian crusade to help others. Why you risked life and limb to help Maria and Rosa—two young girls you didn't know. She's why you went to the mat for Jenny Spencer when she was abducted, for Riley Anderson when she had no place to turn. Why you eagerly step up to the plate to be someone's last vestiges of hope on earth. Why, every morning, you run until you die."

"I think I'd prefer a lesser woman."

"She's why you don't want to have children."

"Got it figured out, don't you?"

"Tell me I'm wrong."

I almost asked her then, but I didn't, so what's the point?

44

With God's sweetest breath, she created summer mornings in Florida.

I ran on the beach as the moon hung low in the western sky like a nightlight in a nursery. It cast my shadow across the sand. A barefoot runner going in the opposite direction passed me. She danced like a ballerina on the line of the sand where the curved and sleepy waves made their farthest assault before thinning out and dying backward. Each of her footprints was a little weaker than the last as the wet sand filled in the indentations. I counted them. Twenty-eight. I quickened my pace.

At the house, I dove off the end of the dock and swam hard into the tide. A morning breeze—the remnants of a blow that had fired up the previous night and had teased Kathleen's hair—whipped the bay into a white-capped surface. On the return trip, I floated on my back and kicked as the tide carried me home. The high blue sky was cloudless, and the sun bathed me in all her bridal glory.

I showered the sticky saltwater off my skin, drank my beer instead of pouring it on my head, and went to Seabreeze for breakfast. I read two newspapers, and ate eggs, bacon, home fries smothered with onions, and buttered toast with grape jelly on it. Peggy kept the coffee hot. The windows were open, and the bushy geraniums splashed red flowers and green leaves beside the booths that ran along the walls. The growl of outboard engines clashed with the FM radio station that was playing classic vinyl through the speakers.

I love Florida mornings so much I could—

"Hey, dreamer. Nudge your cup over here so I can heat it up," Peggy said. I scooted my coffee cup toward her.

"You'll miss me," I said, although I hadn't a clue what prompted me to utter such a mindless comment.

"Has it come to that?"

She was a few weeks from retirement. What do you give a lady who's served you breakfast for years and never once busted your yolk? I asked her.

"There ain't nothing you can give me," she said, "that I don't already have or don't want."

"Million bucks?"

"Would screw up my life."

"Flowers?"

"I'd kill them faster than the desert sun. I got the blackest thumb in the world."

"Tickets to Disney World."

"That's so corny. I never been, though lot of folks love it."

"Hey, man. You Jake Travis?"

I pivoted my head. A young man in jeans and a red T-shirt was behind me. He smelled like cigarette smoke. I scanned the parking lot outside the windows.

"Who's asking?" I said.

"Are you Jake Travis?" he said again. He bounced nervously on the heels of his feet.

My eyes darted around the room to make sure he wasn't marking me for someone. Behind me was the kitchen. I wasn't worried about that but then thought I should be.

"If I am?"

"Here." He thrusted out his hand. "Some dude palmed me a ten to give this to you."

I instinctively took the envelope he held. He spun around and went out the front door. He picked up a half-burnt cigarette from atop a post, took a drag, and walked at a leisurely pace down the sidewalk. I sliced open the letter with a table knife that still had grape jelly on it.

It contained a folded sheet of paper with an address scrawled on it. It was the empty lot where Morgan kept *Moonchild* moored. Dangelo's comment ran hard in my head: *Don't mess with the Russian mob.*

I dashed out the door. The car next to me was backing out, and another was waiting to pull into its spot. I drummed my hands on the wheel as I waited. I called Morgan, but it went to voice mail. I finally swung out and raced the truck to *Moonchild*. I hit Garrett's number on the way there. It also went to voice mail. He was likely kite-surfing. I left a message.

Moonchild rested motionless at the side of its dock. I ran over to the sailboat and stepped aboard.

"Morgan? Dusty?"

The boat was empty. No notes. No sign of a struggle. No smell of food. I went down into the galley. Checked the bathroom. My heart pounded in my chest like it was clamoring to get out and join the search. My mind flashed through different scenarios of the consequences of my actions. None of them were good. I took the narrow teak stairs back up to the deck.

The tall man who had approached me at the thrift store sat behind the wheel. His partner was on the dock, squinting in the harsh sun. I didn't know how they'd gotten the drop on me.

"Nice boat," the tall man said.

"Where are they?"

"Who might you speak of?"

I took a step toward him. "Where are they?"

Morgan kept a fish knife under a starboard seat. I took a step toward it but foolishly moved too quickly.

"Amigo," the man on the dock shouted out, although in a slight Russian accent. I shifted my gaze to him. He opened his loose jacket to reveal a small cannon stuck in his belt. "Just in case you're stupid," he added.

"It's broad daylight," I said.

"Less chance of missing you."

"What do you want?" I asked the tall man in front of me.

"Our men were led into a trap."

"More importantly, your men walked out of the trap," I pointed out.

He nodded slowly and then spat at my feet. "One of them was my brother," he said.

"He tell you what a barrel of a US antiaircraft gun looks like?"

"He told me you didn't have the guts to shoot."

"I had nothing against your men. I want to meet Omarov again."

"Good thing my brother is alive. Otherwise, you'd be dead now."

"Where are they?"

"I'm sorry, who are you talking about?"

"My friends," I said and was ticked that I'd reflexively answered him. He knew who I was referring to.

"Friends." He mulled the thought over as if we'd gone off script, and he wasn't sure what to say next. "You think you scare Mr. Omarov? Think his men running will weaken him? Your action just excites him—makes his nipples hard. Such men are cheap. If these men are lucky, we will not hunt them down and kill them for being such cowards."

"Even your brother?"

"I have three more."

"They should have fixed your mother."

His jaw tightened. "It is lucky for you—and unfortunate for me—that we meet in," he gazed around, "such an open place."

"You want an exchange?"

"Pardon?"

"Don't play dumb. Where are they?"

He turned and faced his partner. "Ilyich, where did you say they went?"

"Who's that, Yuri?"

"You know, those two who were on this boat. The man with a ponytail and that tight ass he was with."

"How do you think she got in those jeans?"

"You stupid Russian," Yuri, the tall one, said. "It's not how she got in the jeans; it's how you get her out." Yuri turned back to me. "Apparently, we, or at least Ilyich, remembers seeing them."

I sat down in the shade of the awning that Morgan had mounted over the cockpit. I crossed my legs and cut a casual look at Ilyich standing on the dock.

"How's the sun on your lily-white Russian skin?" I said.

"Makes me even hotter for your woman."

"Paradise Grille," Yuri said before I could volley a reply back at his partner, which was good, because I had nothing in the chamber.

"What about it," I said.

"They are having breakfast at a place called Paradise Grille. It is on the beach. You know it? Yes?"

I looked over my shoulder. Morgan's two bikes were gone. Idiot. I should have noticed that when I first approached the boat, but I was in panic mode while listening to yapping voices in my head and thinking LeClair had double-crossed me. Or was it triple-crossed? I couldn't even keep score. That made it a tough game to win.

"What's the bottom line here, Yuri?" I said.

"The bottom line." He plopped down across from me on the wide-planked gunwale. "The bottom line," he repeated as if he were testing the words. "You choose poorly. You have fallen for a wild tale and are being used in a game you do not understand. We wish you no harm. Your friends are eating breakfast. Your girlfriend is sleeping downtown. Such a beautiful morning would not exist for you unless it was our wish." He paused as if he wanted his last words to sink in. "Mr. Omarov would like to meet you."

"He sent six men to kill me," I reminded him, although his words rang in my head like a victory bell.

He shrugged. "Business interests change daily. As a peace offering, a gesture of goodwill, we let your two friends live."

"When and where?" I said. "But you might want to tell your boss to change his tune. LeClair's story makes more sense than his and Brackett's tightly woven tale."

"'Tightly woven tale,' Ilyich," Yuri said over his shoulder. "You know what that means?"

"We're talking about that tight ass?" Ilyich replied.

Yuri laughed. "No. But I like the way you think, Ilyich. Try again."

"We get to kill him?"

"No, although that was my vote." Yuri leveled his eye on mine. "It means that everyone lies to you—Mr. Omarov included. He thinks it is now in his best interest to tell you the truth. To unwind the tale. You two will talk again."

"Let me guess. At his place surrounded by goons like you?"

"It does not matter to me. My job is to deliver the message. Who knows what my next job might be."

"Killing Hawkins's girl because she cooperated?"

"Who? Oh, her. No. You think she is that red between the legs? I would like to see that fire. Our threat to her was empty, as I'm sure you know, or you would not have mentioned her just know. Tell me, do you know how to tell the difference between a sincere Russian threat and an empty one?"

Ilyich let out a snort, as if he'd heard this one before.

"You can't," Yuri announced with pride. "That is why everyone fears the Russians. Even we have no clue what we might do."

"You killed Hawkins," I said.

Yuri gave me a thin smile. "I do not know who you speak of. But I know this: if I were there the other night, I would not have hit the ground."

I stood and faced him. "You didn't have the guts to show up."

"Mr. Omarov can smell a trap."

"How will he contact me?"

"Mr. Omarov has legal counsel—Mr. Bernard Carlsberg. He will reach out to you, as you like to say. Mr. Omarov is a legitimate businessman. He has much interest—money—in the United States."

"Your boss is finished. Both here and in Russia."

Yuri kept his eyes on me and said, "Ilyich, do you recall how we got the information that our men had been led into a trap, and their lives were spared? An antiaircraft gun, no? That is good. I give you that."

"Sorry, Yuri. I was still thinking of that tight and finely woven ass. I think we cut off the man's ponytail and take the girl. Can we do that?"

"Perhaps," Yuri said, keeping his eyes on me, as the riptide of the conversation had greater weight than the spoken words. "Tell him, Ilyich, how we learned."

"Mr. Omarov told us."

"Of course, Ilyich, but how did he come into such knowledge?"

"He got a phone call just as he was spreading syrup over his pancakes shaped like mouse ears."

"It is a disturbed country."

"Yet they think so highly of themselves."

"The phone call?" Yuri prodded him.

"I believe it was the Frenchman."

"Frenchman?"

"His name reminds me of that pastry the frogs are famous for."

"That's éclair," Yuri said with irritation. "Might he be the same man our friend here has associated with and recently mentioned when he spoke of a tightly woven tale?"

"I believe so. Mr. Omarov was at first surprised to hear from the French pastry. It had been a long time. But soon he was laughing—enjoying the morning, as he always does."

"Laughing?"

"Like some sort of joke."

"Perhaps Mr. Travis should have picked his friends more carefully."

"A man should not have friends."

"Not everybody can think like a Russian."

45

Was LeClair working with Omarov and double-crossing me, or were the Russians just trying to confuse me? Maybe Omarov laughed on the phone because LeClair told a mean knock-knock joke. One thing was certain: my level of cluelessness was stubbornly consistent.

After Yuri and Ilyich sauntered off the property, I raced to Paradise Grille. I flew out of the truck and came to a halt as I rounded the corner. Morgan and Dusty were finishing breakfast at a wood picnic table under the shade of an umbrella. A seagull was perched on top of the umbrella, its senses alert for an opening. I'd told Dusty she was safe and that I could protect her. Her trust in me would shatter, and deservedly so, if I barged in and told them who I just had a conversation with. I decided I'd tell Morgan later and let him decide whether or not to inform Dusty.

I told them I was driving out to get a newspaper and had spotted Morgan's bikes. Morgan gave me a curious look—I bought newspapers at the convenience store at the end of the street. He suggested we take a stroll down Eighth Avenue. When Dusty ducked into a shop, Morgan and I claimed a bench in the shade across the street.

I explained to Morgan the encounter on his boat. We were still debating whether to keep it between us when Dusty emerged from the store with a bag in her hand. She waited for a car to pass and then crossed the street. She had a natural swing in her arms that I'd not noticed before. We stood as she planted herself in front of us.

"Where's your newspaper?" she asked me.

"On my way now."

She hesitated and then said, "How's the fight against the Reich coming?"

"Our side's winning."

"And if we were losing?"

"Our side's winning."

She scrunched her upper lip. "You've been avoiding me. That tells me that things—"

"Are just fine," I said. The threat to Dusty was likely the last item on Omarov's plate.

"Don't leave me in the dark."

"I won't. You can head back to east Tennessee—if that banana peel is starting to brown."

She smiled, and her pug nose got even smaller. "I'm having a good time. I just want to make sure it's not a funeral dance."

I assured her again that she was free to leave, but recalling the pulpit in Tennessee, I wondered on whose authority I spoke. They pedaled back to his boat. I headed to a lumberyard to get a new ceiling beadboard to replace the one that had split.

At home, I cut the board, slapped a coat of white paint on it, and positioned it in the bedroom ceiling before the paint was thoroughly dry. I hit the switch for the overhead fan, and the bedside light came on.

"Wonderful," I said. I punched out my breath and headed off to kill the fuse and get a screwdriver.

My phone rang.

"Travis Remodeling. All jobs guaranteed late, overbudget, and poorly done."

"Mr. Travis?"

"Your lucky day."

"Bernard Carlsberg. I'm having a small party tomorrow evening and wondered if you could drop by. Say, seven? I've been thinking of remodeling my house, and I have a contractor you may wish to meet. Perhaps he can help you with yours as well, though I recall you indicated you had two local people assisting you."

"My pleasure, Bernie."

"And Mr. Travis?"

"Yes."

"No guest."

My phone went dead.

Showtime.

I located the card from Suzette, the bartender I'd flirted with at Carlsberg's house. Both the business number and her cell were listed. She had indicated that working at Carlsberg's was "steady money." I called the caterer, stated I was on Carlsberg's staff, and inquired what time they would be arriving the following evening. I was informed they would be at the house at six. The man on the phone also verified that, as usual, the staff would all be wearing black.

Suzette answered her cell on the fourth ring. I reintroduced myself to jog her memory.

"You're the guy with a girl on each arm, right? Yeah. What can I do for you, Old-Fashioned?"

I explained the favor I wanted from her.

"A...what is it?"

"Tackle box. It's for fishing. Mr. Carlsberg has taken an interest in the sport."

"Carlsberg? He looks like the dough at the end of the hook."

"I see you know your fishing."

"Older brothers."

"Sound OK to you?"

"Whatever. Sure, bring it by."

She gave me the address on Central where the caterer was based. I impressed upon her to keep it our secret, as I wanted to surprise him. She asked how big it was. I replied that it was a small box with a lock on it.

"A locked fishing box?" she said.

"Tackle box."

"How's he going to, you know, open it?"

"I'll give him the key when I present it to him."

"Blonde or brunette?"

"The key?"

"The girl, dildo brain. Which one are you bringing tonight? The smoky blonde or the Miss Universe brunette?"

"Neither."

"You think brunette wants a girlfriend?"

"Really?"

"Why not. You're dicking around with me. Tackle-smackle—I don't care what you call it. I can't afford to lose this job, you understand?"

"Understood."

"I don't know why I'm doing this."

"You don't have to."

"It's not drugs or anything, is it?"

"It's a tackle box. Fish stuff inside. Dough."

She hung up.

GARRETT AND I MET for lunch at Dockside. We took a high-top overlooking the channel. Across the water, a sprinkler system shot silent streams of glistening water over a bright-green lawn. Beams of sunlight created iridescent colors.

We were discussing our plans for the following evening. I'd explained Suzette's role. I planned to drop by the caterer's facility after 3:00 p.m. the next day. Suzette had indicated that no one would be there prior to that time.

"And if she doesn't come through?" Garrett asked.

"You're up."

"Why not have me lead off?"

My mind jumped to the sinking sun I'd witnessed from the top of Hurricanes. To the people on the beach, it had already dipped beneath the horizon. But at my height, it had still been visible. There is another view of everything that happens. Even in natural law, things are not what they appear. A different scenario regarding my sister's killer was coming into focus, but I was afraid to grant it quarters.

"The chimney," I said. I wasn't in the mood to debate Garrett's question.

"What chimney?"

"At Dusty's lot, in Tennessee. LeClair said it was at the back of the house. It's not. It's at the right side."

"A simple mistake. Thirty years is a long time to keep the position of a chimney right."

"And the poster," I said, angry with myself for not seeing it earlier. "LeClair said the poster of REM was above his bed. It's not. A View to a Kill is."

"Maybe he moved them."

"Or LeClair is not LeClair."

"You're trying too hard. It's best to assume he is who he says he is."

"And Omarov?"

"He killed your sister."

"I want the unvarnished truth," I said, "not the unvarnished assumption." That was a point of contention between Garrett and I.

"He's involved," Garrett reminded me. "At a minimum, he had a hand in her death."

"I can't kill him for that."

"I can."

"We're different in that regard."

"We used to not be."

I swirled my tongue around in my mouth.

"What's Trotsky's quote about war?" Garrett asked. "The one you're always twisting around?"

"I forget."

"No, you don't."

"'You may not be interested in war, but war is interested in you.'"

"You may be interested in morality," Garrett said. "But morality is not interested in you."

What a chum.

46

When I returned to my house, the street was still and vacant, like a Western town at high noon on the day of the big shootout. I collected the mail from my box—it was four or five days' worth—and walked over to the recycling bin in the back of the garage. After a cursory glance, I flipped all but one item into the bin. The keeper was a small hand-addressed envelope with no return address. I opened it.

Dear Mr. Travis,

Eve Davidson passed away last night. She took an overdose of sleeping pills. She seemed distraught after your previous visit. I'm afraid we had to arrange transportation for her home that night. I never saw her again, for she never returned to the motel. I will miss her, and everything gone that she represents.

She left me a note saying it had been a lovely cruise and to tell you she was deeply sorry.

Chase

I waited to feel something, but nothing touched me, for I was stuffed with emptiness. Had my words given her a sword to fall upon? There had to be more, but I couldn't imagine what that might be. Perhaps not. Who is to judge how heavy someone else's invisible suitcase is?

I tossed the note in the bin as if the longer I held it, the more it would impart guilt on me. I entered my home. It was a mess.

47

A t 7:30 the following evening, I presented myself at Bernard Carlsberg's front door. I winked at the observing concrete lions and gave my name to some stiff, who demanded to see my driver's license before checking my name off a list. Carlsberg was tightening his security.

Yuri met me inside. He invited me into the parlor off to the right.

"Arms up," he said.

I raised my arms.

"Where is your blond whore this evening?" he asked as he frisked me.

"None of your business." I was disappointed with my lame response, so I tacked on, "Where's Ilyich? Playing with his pistol?"

"Pumping his barrel, in case he needs it tonight. But that is unlikely, as your *shlyukha* is not available."

"We're done here."

"I hear her breasts taste good—soft yet firm. Like Florida grapefruit. That is what Mr. Omarov says when he sits with his friends and smokes cigars, drinks fine vodka, and tells them how your woman sucked his tongue."

"Breast."

"Pardon?"

"He only got one. A shame. The other was laced with arsenic. Such a beautiful plan, but I came in too early."

Yuri gave that a second. His eyes narrowed, and then his lips morphed into a tight smile. "Yes. She told Mr. Omarov that. That you come too early."

"Would you like to step outside?"

"Please."

I turned away as if I were going to leave the parlor. Instead, I squared my stance. I spun back around and threw my weight behind a right jab into his solar plexus. Yuri grunted, doubled over, and collapsed on his knees. It would be more than a few minutes before he was operational. I grabbed his left ear and gave it a half-counterclockwise twist. A couple wandered into the parlor and came to an abrupt halt at the site of Yuri moaning on the floor.

"You two lovebirds might want to stay clear of the crab cakes," I said as I strolled out of the room.

The party wasn't as packed as the previous one I'd attended. There was no live band, but the home's stereo system created a seamless string of melodies. The music was a faithful chaperone, following me as I made my way through the house.

Suzette was by the far edge of the pool with no edge. I fell behind a man who kept bobbing his head like Rodney Dangerfield.

"Old-Fashioned," she said with a smile when I stepped up to the bar. "Where are the Barbies?"

"Playing Parcheesi with the kids."

"That sounds fun." She handed me a Jameson on the rocks. "Too bad it's not true."

"What if I wanted something different tonight?"

"You're not that type," she demurred in her knee-knocking deep voice. "I got your bait thingy."

"Tackle box."

"Hmm. For Carlsberg the fisherman. Want it now?"

"Where is it?"

"Under the table. What's the plan?"

A line had formed behind me. I asked Suzette, "Did you say you needed help hauling a heavy box out from under the table?"

"Hey, big, strong man," she said in a perky voice. "Could you help me lift a box?"

I went around to her side and bent over. The black tablecloth nearly touched the ground. I partially pulled out a case of wine from under the table. I opened it. The tackle box was inside. I unlocked the box and took out my Beretta Pico. At five inches in length, it was the smallest gun I owned. I locked the box, placed it back in the wine box, and slid it under the table. I positioned the gun under my jacket, in my waist across my back.

I placed two bottles of chardonnay on the table. "On second thought," I said, "I'll leave it for later."

"Thank you," Suzette said to a man who stuffed a few bills into her tip jar.

"Did you hear me?" I said.

"You're getting it later."

"If I don't, tape the box and haul it out of here. Do not tell anyone that you brought it in. Never discuss what we've done. Deny that we ever talked."

"Ah, shit." Her face creased with worry. "I knew I shouldn't have done this."

"Do you understand what I just said?"

"Yupper," she said and sucked on her lower lip. "I did something stupid, and now it's too late. Good ol' Suzy-Belle. Screwing up my life for a smile from a guy."

"You'll be fine."

"Hell's bells I will."

I decided not to worry her anymore and parted with a worthless smile.

Carlsberg was ping-ponging from one conversation pit to another. I stuffed myself with shrimp cocktail, meatballs, and Bruschetta. I avoided the crab cakes. I texted Garrett and let him know that I had not seen Ilyich, and that I'd likely pissed Yuri off. He came back with, *do you need me in house?* I gave it a second and texted him back: *yes*. I couldn't afford to worry about Yuri mucking things up. We were already off the plan, and it was my fault. Garrett, like the help, was dressed in black and planned to enter through the kitchen.

Carlsberg approached me. I quickly swallowed a partially chewed piece of filet that was heavily flavored with pepper.

"Mr. Travis."

"Mr. Carlsberg." Neither of us offered a hand.

"So nice of you to drop by," he said.

"Wouldn't miss it for the world."

"I'd like you to meet a client of mine."

"After you, Bernie."

Carlsberg lumbered toward the spiral staircase. I had to curb my pace as I followed him. The Beretta Pico pressed against my back.

"Please," Carlsberg said as we approached the door to his study. Like an usher, he extended his arm toward the open door. "After you."

As I strolled into the room, I felt as if I were leaving one world for another and could never go back. I was suddenly overwhelmed with nostalgia.

My world wasn't so bad, was it? Why mess with it? I could be sitting in the quiet at the end of my dock right now, hearing the dolphins blow and watching the tide drift out.

Peter Omarov sat on the couch. He made no effort to rise. Yuri, slightly bent, stood on the far side of him. He pointed at me with his finger and squeezed it. Those silly Russians. Carlsberg walked past me and toward a bar cart. He fixed himself a drink. He offered to freshen Omarov's, but he indicated he was fine. I took a seat in a leather chair facing Peter Omarov. I started to cross my legs but then held back. It would be easier to stand and draw my weapon if I kept both feet on the ground.

I placed my drink on the table next to me and said to Omarov, "Where's Dimitri?"

"He has been demoted."

"Pastry chef?"

"I forgot. You wear humor like a Russian wears a hat. Yes, he makes cupcakes for me now."

"Perhaps Yuri can give him a hand. His ear is red and shining, like a treat from a French patisserie."

Omarov glanced at Yuri, but Yuri kept his eyes on mine.

"You may leave, Yuri," Omarov said. "Mr. Travis and I have some business to attend to."

"Straighten up, Yuri," I told him as he passed me. "You look a little slumped this evening."

Yuri landed a venomous stare and then closed the door behind him. I didn't know what Omarov's play was, but if he thought that by letting his guard dog leave, he would summon fairness from me, he was sorely mistaken. I was glad that I'd gone off script and told Garrett to enter the house. Having a force your opponent is not aware of is an incalculable advantage. While Omarov would recognize Garrett, I doubt he would have passed his description on to Yuri. If he had, it would not be a pleasant encounter for Yuri.

Omarov stood and strolled toward a window. He considered the darkening sky and then turned back to me. "I understand you met a man who calls himself David LeClair. Is this correct?"

"The name sounds familiar."

"You worked with him to set a trap for my men."

"Fine bunch of boys."

"You threatened my wife and daughters."

"LeClair told you that to flush you out. I never threatened your wife and daughters."

"He said you truly intended to kill them."

"David LeClair is a lying sack of pigeon shit."

Omarov snorted out a laugh. "Yes, he is. It is good that we agree on him. My father underestimated him all those years ago."

"Were you shocked when he revealed himself, or did he lie to me about you not knowing?"

"Shocked? I am not a man who is jolted by the unusual." He bobbed his big head in appreciation. "Was I impressed? Yes. But I laughed at him—he thinks this rattles me."

"He got his revenge."

"So you think. David and I reached an understanding. He is a free man, as is his mother and Dusty, although," he raised a shoulder and twisted his face, "that one never liked me. It was a meaningless threat. LeClair used it for convenience, to justify his life. He was adopted. You know all this, no? He is a muddled man with no country and, far worse, no soul."

"And you are penniless."

"I am afraid he was disingenuous with you. He agreed not to close my personal accounts. We—he and I—may need each other someday." He twirled his hand in the air. "Such is how diplomatic relationships exist. The world is gray, not black and white. I fear you do not understand such things, Mr. Travis. As I observed when we first met, you bring your heart into the arena. It does not belong there."

"It has its advantages," I said, defending myself.

"LeClair told me that you were supposed to kill my men, but you played with them instead. Mickey Mouse hats." A rumble emitted from deep within his chest. "I like that. A little goofy, no?"

"I followed my own plan."

"You like my comment? A little goofy?"

"Hilarious."

He studied me for a moment and said, "I changed my mind. You have no humor. Sad. Why did you not kill my men?"

"To give peace a chance."

Omarov ignored my gambit. "David LeClair," he said, "used you to grab power at the CIA and to discredit me in my homeland. This you do not know, for I am telling you for the first time. Putin is breaking into your government's e-mails. The hackers he uses? They are my men: Fancy Bear. Cozy Bear. All designed to break into our competitors' e-mails so we can undercut their armament prices. Putin hired my company to discredit his enemies. We engaged in *kompromat*—you know what I speak of?"

"Planting damaging and incriminating information on someone's computer," I said.

"Yes. We are accomplished in that area. After that, he thought I worked for him. But when he wanted to shut down the power grid to Ukraine, I refused. That was a crack in our relationship. Later, when he interfered with your presidential election, for he thought Trump was a man easily manipulated, he called and—"

"I have no interest in any of this."

Omarov waited a beat and then added, "You have no choice, my friend, in what has an interest in you."

I recalled my earlier conversation with Garrett and realized that paying attention to the grand scheme might not be as fruitless as I thought. Little late for that.

Screw it. I'm taking it home.

"My sister," I said.

"Yes. Your sister." He brought his hand up to his face and scrunched his cheeks together. "In time," Omarov said. "Tell me, what other lies did LeClair tell you?"

"None as big as the one where you claimed he was dead."

"Well," Omarov said, "it was a good story. I had to lie—not that I had any clue as to his career path—but the truth might have derailed negotiations far more important than your vendetta. As I told you, I could not risk my character being besmirched. But that time has passed. You ever play Russian roulette?"

"Why? Is it on the dance card tonight?"

"I've not played it. It is a stupid game, but it ends the charade. But I will play it tonight. I. Not you. I will take the chance."

He took a few steps toward me. The end table to my immediate left held a granite chessboard. Hand-carved onyx warriors silently anchored both ends. Each side stood at attention, prepared for a battle in which a commander could never blame, or claim, luck. He opened the drawer. I squirmed forward in my seat. He pulled out a gun. I reached under my jacket and wrapped my hand around the Berretta.

Holding his gun by the barrel, he placed it in the middle of the chessboard. It looked like a Salvador Dali painting— a metal thug of reality surrounded by abstract symbols. The kings and queens of the chessboard were relegated to what they always were—make-believe power. He backed a few steps away from the table and placed both hands in his pockets. Carlsberg crossed his legs and sunk into his chair as if settling in for the opening act of *King Lear*.

Omarov said, "It is loaded. Take it. Kill me."

"Tell me what happened at the Vanderbilt Reef Motel."

"Why didn't you kill my men?"

"I gave up butchering worthless Russians for Lent."

"Life's a laugh for you. An unfortunate trait the Americans inherited from the English."

"Another unfortunate trait is common law. Murder is frowned upon."

"It was a desolate piece of ground, and you are not a stranger to murder."

"It wasn't necessary."

"Ah...the truth," he said with a smile, as if we were making progress. "Tell me, are you any closer to this truth you seek about your sister now than when you started?"

"Everybody's exhausted their lies."

He bobbed his head. "That is not an answer, but I will help you: truth *is* exhausted lies. And who am I? The man who killed your sister, right? Yes. I see it in your eyes. But you have doubts, don't you?

"You want to know the truth? Your government has blinders on—all they care about is the Middle East. The rest of the world can rot in hell. Putin gets stronger by the day, and the unfortunate leadership vacuum in the United States doesn't know whether he is friend or foe. He is neither. Russians wear ambiguity much better than the Americans. Americans still see themselves as cowboys riding high on their horses. Into this trots, Mr. Jake Travis, looking for his sister. Do you see now what a tiny little man you are? Tell me, tiny little Mr. Travis, on this global stage, who gives a—what is the saying?—a rat's ass about your sister?"

"You do, Peter. Or we wouldn't be talking. I can put you behind bars for life."

"That would not be victory for you, and we both know that. I know why you didn't kill my men."

"Enlighten me."

"You have doubts." He took a quick step toward me. "You have doubts," he said again. "And that has brought you here to hear the truth—the exhausted lies."

My silence confirmed his accusation. I wasn't certain. For truth is a shifting policy, a sunset viewed differently. A nagging thought.

The truth? I had another theory. It had reached out and gently touched me at Dockside, where I recalled the sunset at Hurricanes and how a self-evident truth can be blatantly false. How natural laws themselves are open to interpretation. And, like a guardian angel whose charge had suffered too long, my theory—my wild and sick dream—had found a friend in my delusional heart, where it fanned the embers of hope.

Why did Alex Brackett, with such kind and sincere words, wish me good luck when we left the Purple Pig? You might not have an interest in the world, but the world has an interest in you.

Carlsberg took a sip of his drink as if he were content to be a passive observer. If I clipped Omarov, then I wouldn't need to worry about Carlsberg. Like LeClair, he was a survivor with no allegiance. Mac had described him as "the only thing in this world colder than dry ice." He'd gone on to say that Carlsberg had used his father's murder as a stepping-stone in his career. I doubted Carlsberg would shed a tear for Omarov.

Omarov said, "You think it...coincidental that after attempts to dissuade you from looking into your sister's disappearance, we no longer care?"

"We?"

"Your government and I. LeClair told me you know that his agency and I took turns dissuading you from your past. Our moves were not particularly synchronized, but such things rarely are. I feel sorry for you, Mr. Travis. LeClair has disappeared, am I right? Your passion to avenge the death of your sister has made you a blind participant."

"It got me an audience with you."

"Ah, yes. He promised that he would reveal me to you, but what value is that? For I am willing to expose myself to you, unarmed. Tell me, has it occurred to you that you have sought the wrong man?"

"I don't think so."

"Perhaps you should be having this conversation with Alex Brackett."

"He didn't kill my sister," I said.

"That's not what I implied."

"So he could tell me more lies?"

"Our business deal is complete. He has paid off my loan."

"Why does that keep popping up?"

"You do not see?"

"Enlighten me."

"He no longer gets paid to lie."

"We're done running in circles," I said, although something told me I should have lassoed his last remark. I rose from the chair. "Story time's over. One of you three killed my sister, and you'll be the first to discover that three dead men make my day."

"Then pick up the gun, Mr. Travis. By all means—be my guest. Pick up the gun."

I did.

Omarov stepped in to me. His eyes were clear, and the lines under them formed deep crevices in his skin.

"I am going to tell you three truths," Omarov said. His breath was stale and wet with liquor. "They do not sound right to you? You shoot. You think I'm lying? You shoot. You understand? We do it here and now. Then, one way or the other, we are done with each other. You leave my family alone. I do the same to your friends. Agree?"

"I told you I never threatened—"

"LeClair said you would kill my daughters," Omarov said.

"You believe him?"

"Why not? You do, no? Go ahead. Shoot, if you believe his lies."

"Peter," Carlsberg said, "you need to tell him—"

"Quiet, Bernard." Omarov's eyes had never dropped from mine. "We understand each other?"

"Save it, if it's the same recycled lies," I said.

"Oh no," he said with a chuckle. "I am talking *truths.*" He pounded his chest with his fist. "A Russian lives by his soul, and in his soul he does not lie. You want to kill the man who killed your sister. Am I right?"

I felt as if I were being unwillingly led down a path, but I no longer cared. I wanted it to be over.

"Time to remember your childhood prayers," I said.

"Why? You think death scares me? What is life without death? A dog with no appetite. The moon with no water to make love to. Death does not make me quiver."

"You're hearing your last words."

He punched me in the chest with three fingers. "*You* will be the judge of that. I tell you three truths, then I give you a charge. My truths: I sucked your woman's breast, I bit your sister's budding tit, but I did not kill her."

Our eyes locked for a suspended moment. I tossed his gun on the floor.

"You know I speak the exhausted lies," Omarov said as an ugly smile mutated his face. "Now I give you your charge: look elsewhere for the fate of your sister."

He turned his back at me and went to fix himself a drink. I pulled out my gun.

"Peter," Carlsberg said again. His eyes darted between Omarov and me while his fingers fiddled with the underside of the end table.

Omarov spun back to me. He saw the gun, and his eyes went wide with panic.

"Her budding tit?" It was my voice, but it came from somewhere I was trying to leave.

"She's…"

Peter Omarov never finished what he was saying, or I didn't hear him. I caught a reflection of Dimitri in the window, gun in hand, flying out of a closet and closing rapidly behind me. Carlsberg must have signaled him. The hall door flung open, and Garrett burst into the room, his SIG Sauer leading the way. Carlsberg shouted, but I didn't know what he said. Omarov reached inside his jacket. I couldn't kill Omarov and defend myself against Dimitri. I had to choose.

I squeezed the trigger just as a fire exploded in the back of my head.

I WAS ALONE AT the end of my dock. The world was quiet, and the tide was moving out. I was benumbed with a heavy sadness at the failure of my life, for I'd been no match for the promise; there'd been no glory in my dream.

I tried so very hard, but I could not hear the dolphins blow.

48

*L*ady God hovered over me. Her breasts were tanned, and her nipples dark and inviting. Her face was expressionless, and that was her identifying characteristic, more so than her smooth stomach that disappeared into her tight jeans. You could bow to her, worship her, tithe to her, love her, ignore her, die for her, and kill for her. She would take whatever you gave her, be whoever you wanted her to be, have powers that you alone could dream of. But on her own, her indifference was all she brought. She showed no pity, not even a tinge of amusement, which would only hint at a false sense of empathy. I reached up to touch her, and Mac said, "You do know she's cardboard, don't you?"

But it wasn't Lady who loomed over me; it was Garrett. His eyes searched mine with a mix of concern and quizzical amusement.

"You with me?" he said.

"We secure?"

"Pigs in blankets."

My head was splitting, as if someone had taken a machete and whacked it like a coconut. I knew there were layers of pain that hadn't had time to surface yet.

"You got clipped from behind," Garrett said. "Dimitri. I came in just after he took his gun to your head."

"He didn't shoot me?"

"Who?"

"Dimitri."

"No."

"If Dimitri was instructed not to kill me, then Omarov was likely telling the truth. He didn't kill my sister."

Garrett seemed to process that. I looked around and saw that we were at Mac's.

"Where's Mac?" I asked.

"Later."

Something about his reply made me want to question him further about Mac, but my mind was preoccupied with reconstructing the conversation I'd had with Omarov. Did Omarov suggest I talk to Brackett? Find her fate elsewhere?

I said, "How'd you get past Yuri?"

"With pleasure."

"Ilyich?"

"Earlier in the kitchen. What did Omarov say?" he asked with a note of concern.

"He insisted that he didn't kill her."

"He lied."

"I believed him."

"He's mendacious," Garrett said. "It's who he is."

"I don't think so. Not this time. But I shot him anyway."

"You missed. Nicked him in the shoulder."

"Really? From two feet?"

"Dimitri likely swiped you a split second before you squeezed."

"Where is he?"

"Omarov?"

I nodded.

"Last seen wrapped in a sheet and being loaded onto his boat, Final Voyage. Carlsberg didn't even flinch when his body hit the floor. Said he was more of a liability than he was worth. It wasn't Carlsberg's first dead body."

"Omarov's dead?"

Garrett nodded.

"You said I missed."

"I didn't," Garrett said, but he looked away.

49

I took a few days' reprieve from my usual routine of greeting the predawn hours by running, swimming, punching, and kicking the living daylight out of the dark until it finally surrendered and the day sprung free. I wondered if anyone on the planet knew that I, and I alone, was responsible for defeating the dark and harkening the light. If so, I've received no gratitude, and no one has yet to thank my wretched soul. People can be ungracious.

If I expected a serendipitous Godot moment, it never arrived. Not only had I not found my sister's killer but I was also succumbing to wild and fantastical dreams about what had happened to her. The fine line that separated me from the nuthouse was fading by the minute. I had nothing to base my theory on, other than it was the last explanation standing, which was one step up from throwing shit on the wall. No surprise there. Our lives are scored by the musician, choreographed by the dancer, rhymed by the poet, painted by the artist, filmed by the cinematographer, and immortalized by the writer, all in a vain attempt to disguise the randomness—and keep us from realizing that we are all just shit-tossers.

LeClair, or whoever he was calling himself now, had vanished. I felt bad for Dusty and never told her. It's always easier for those who leave. It's the ones who are left behind and surrounded by familiar props—the highways they traveled, the land they adored, the chimney that was to be the anchor of two lives joined as one—who are captive to the past. How do we escape when the symbols are still there, kept alive by *faux souvenir*?

I both loved and hated my sister, the tandem feelings fusing together to form a new emotion so tangible that I could move it from one pocket to the other. I didn't have a clue what to call it. I was ashamed of it. But wouldn't it have been better if she had never been born? Better for my parents? For me? I knew that wasn't right, but it was easy, and I do that sometimes.

Morgan drove Dusty back to Townsend, Tennessee.

Mac died of natural causes the same night my bullet missed Omarov from two feet. Garrett found him when he took me back to his place. Mac had drawn a new will. Bernard Carlsberg's secretary and Dusty had witnessed it. He left his property to Pinellas County, to be administered by Morgan and myself. His 20 percent of the law firm, estimated at around $5.5 million, was to be placed into a trust to operate the property, and Morgan and I were to serve as cotrustees. It was his wish that it become a camp for "those seeking refuge from distant shores." The will had explicit language that it never be used as a wildlife preserve. It was to be a human preserve, "dedicated to the most sacrosanct of all the species."

Morgan was excited. He had the money and the property to help the homeless and indigent poor—those who largely due to the time and place of their birth, had been condemned to a life of unending struggle. When I'd first met Morgan, he was an ex-sailor who was trying out his sea legs. His life had been picking up steam, gathering meaning and direction, rising like the morning sun with a sense of purpose, spreading light and warmth to others.

Mine, on the other hand, was like an eighteen-wheeler climbing a steep Colorado grade. At any moment I might strip the gears and slide backward, the weight and the grade more than I could bear.

I had never asked Mac his wife's name—the woman he dreamed of and once saw from across a crowded room. I looked her up. Gloria. I found a picture of the two of them on a sailboat as it keeled over off the coast of Siesta Key in the spring of 1964. The sun was on their faces. They were young.

Once you have found her, never let her go. Mac never did.

I wanted to be depressed, but I was too pig-headed to accept defeat. Tighten a noose around my neck, and I'll ask you what time the sun rises tomorrow.

From out of nowhere, I would hear Omarov say, *Go find your sister*, and then Alex Brackett would echo, *Best of luck to you, Jake.* I decided I'd give Brackett a jingle one day to, if nothing else, smother that last ember of hope and get on with my life.

He beat me to it.

KATHLEEN AND I SAT next to each other on the dock, our bare feet hanging over the water. The rising moon was full and begging for our attention. Soon it would sparkle on the water, creating a broad swath of light. From my dock, you could set sail and drift past the white cliffs of Dover, queue up at the Panama Canal, drop anchor off the southern coast of Italy, motor past the Statue of Liberty, or race out to the mouth of the gulf to catch a molten sunset. Each drop of water contains a little of that magic.

Kathleen wore a blue summer dress with spaghetti straps. Her hair was down, and it didn't bother me. Thin lines were forming around the corners of her eyes. I'd not noticed them before and wondered if I'd put them there. I liked them. They were like an artist's finishing touches.

Black skimmers flashed below us, their beaks slicing the glass surface of the water and leaving miniature wakes. They came in low from both directions, like fighter pilots. To our right, off toward the gulf, the sunset sailboats were crawling back from the gulf, leaving Shell Key behind them. The marinated scent of grilled steaks filled the air. I glanced down at Lynn and Sandy's house two doors down. They were standing over their grill, their two dogs hugging their sides. The tangy smoke mixed with the salt air, and I inhaled it like an aged cabernet when the cork is first popped.

Kathleen took a patient sip of wine, tilted her glass, and said, "How long has it been this time?"

It was an abrupt change in the conversation. We'd been discussing her upcoming fall teaching schedule.

"A week."

"And the consensus?"

"After one hundred and sixty-eight booze-free hours? There are no more answers found abstaining from alcohol than there are from indulging in it."

"Hmm. Might there be peaceful coexistence on the horizon?"

"Unlikely. Want a job?"

"Sure."

"Pick out the backsplash."

"I thought you'd never ask."

"Paint and trim as well."

"Anything else?"

"Swab the deck."

"Aye, aye, Captain." She took another sip of wine. "You talked in your sleep again last night."

"Words of wisdom?"

"Do you remember anything?"

I'd had a doozy. The cardinal and I were on a Ferris wheel together, and we'd left Kathleen on the ground. She stomped her feet like a child and whined, "I'm the one who wanted to ride a Ferris wheel, remember?"

Then the Ferris wheel transformed into a kid's coloring project, where you put paint on the center of a sheet and then let it spin, and the colors fly out in all directions. Mine was all red.

Omarov wasn't in the dream. I knew then that I'd made the right decision.

"Hey," she said.

I glanced at her. "You talking to me?"

"Do you remember the dream?"

"No."

"Why do I bother?"

Three black skimmers soared under our feet, their beaks kissing the water. Just as quickly, they were gone and out of sight. A thought flashed in my mind, but like the birds, it too had wings. A large fish splashed behind us, and I wondered what kind it was.

"How's Mac's old place coming along?" she said.

"Good."

"Don't knock yourself out there, champ."

"Be operational in a month."

"Settle on a name yet?"

"The Walter MacDonald Homeless Shelter and Refugee House."

"I'm sorry I never met him," Kathleen said.

"I just caught his last act."

"He obviously thought the world of you and Morgan. Interesting, isn't it? Sparks from one life passed to another."

I leaned over with my elbows on my knees and studied the lead-gray water. A thick leaf the size of a dinner plate drifted lazily toward to the gulf. The tide was close to running itself out. The pendulum was about to swing in the other direction. I raised my head and stared straight into the damn channel marker. A few rounds from Sally-Mae would take that sucker out. Maybe get the osprey that used my dock as a dumping ground as well. I wondered if some legal authority would have an issue with me mounting a 1953 ninety-millimeter antiaircraft gun on the deck of my dock.

Kathleen said, "Bum a light, buddy?"

I looked at her.

"So..." she said. "I'm just wondering...who really killed him?"

I'd previously told her about the last minute I remembered in Carlsberg's study. I'd confessed that I'd killed Omarov but that Garrett was claiming the bounty. She had deliberately avoided asking specific questions.

"I blew his head off," I said.

"Frontier justice."

"None better."

"Garrett's statement?"

"He's just shouldering it himself."

"I amend my previous comment. He's a guardian dark angel, offering his soul for immolation. Does it bother you?"

"What?"

"That you killed Omarov?"

"No. Bother you?"

"Not in the least," she replied.

"What happened to 'Don't let your false sense of failure make you vulnerable'?"

"Academic double-talk."

I let that slide, although I didn't fully subscribe to Kathleen's indifferent attitude. She struggled as much as I did but hid it much better. We live with the chaos of our own personalities, our minds thrashing with issues we never conquer. Irresoluteness is our chafing and identifying mark.

My only regret was that I blacked out before I emptied my chamber into Omarov's heart. *I bit her budding tit.* A statement like that sure as hell erases the moral line. Omarov gambled. He lost. That simple. Sometimes a cigar is just a cigar.

"Will Garrett come clean?" she asked.

"No."

"Why not?"

I shrugged my right shoulder.

"That, my friend, is not an answer."

"You never question a buddy when he's got your back."

"Even your moral back side?"

I shrugged my left shoulder.

Kathleen puffed out her breath. "Man-o-man, no wonder y'all make such good soldiers." I didn't know whether that was a compliment or a jab. "We both overthink it," she said. "You've been at ease this past week—content with yourself. You made the right decision. What's right is what feels good afterward."

"I thought you didn't like Hemingway."

"He had his moments. If Peter Omarov didn't kill Brittany, who did? LeClair?"

"He's the shadiest of the bunch, but lying Eve provided a solid alibi for both he and Brackett."

I hadn't yet told Kathleen that Eve had committed suicide. It was one of those things that the longer you kept it inside, the harder it was to let it out.

A boat hugged the far shore, its green starboard light nothing more than a moving dot in the blackness. I wondered if Omarov's daughters were eating Mickey Mouse-ear pancakes when they got the word.

Where the hell did that drop in from?

Kathleen unknowingly came to my rescue. "LeClair has disappeared, right?"

"No trace. The agency doesn't even acknowledge that he existed. He played me like a cat batting around a mouse."

"Don't be so hard—"

"Sometimes the dragon wins. LeClair, or whoever he is, was the mastermind behind it all. DNA and I came along at the right time."

"Your metaphor issues aside, what if that's not the case?" Her eyes were cast out over the water.

"Come again?"

She turned to me. "What if it was something else all along that brought Brittany's disappearance to the forefront, and not DNA? Something that ran congruently with the DNA angle but was overshadowed by it?"

"Such as?"

"I don't know, but you always say that focusing on one item comes at the expense of everything else."

"I've never said that."

"No, but you should have," she said with a sassy smile.

"Wanna fool around?"

"Everything was about Omarov," Kathleen said, ignoring me. "What if it was LeClair and Brackett who were working together? What if all of it would have happened anyway without the threat of DNA? Didn't you say that Brackett was in debt to Omarov and that he'd recently paid off his debt?"

My phone rang. I didn't recognize the number, which had a Chicago area code. I usually don't answer my phone unless I recognize the number. But for some reason, I picked up.

"Jake? This is Alex Brackett. I'd like to invite you up to my ranch, north of Ocala. We're having a regional meeting of hotel operators, and I think you might find it interesting."

"Still sticking by adding a manager after three properties?" I asked.

"Four properties. I don't believe you were paying attention that day. Tomorrow at seven. I'll text the directions. And Jake?"

"Yes?"

"We look forward to seeing you."

He hung up, like you do when you're nervous about making a call and you're glad it's over.

Kathleen said, "What was that all about?"

"What did you say?"

"What was that—"

"No, you twinkie blonde, before that, when I wanted to fool around."

She processed that for a moment and then said, "What if the DNA was just a red herring?"

My gaze gravitated out over the open water. I'd spent years searching for my sister's killer, banging into closed doors. And now, within a week, I'd received two phone calls, first from Carlsberg and now from Brackett, inviting me to come and explore my past. I recalled what Mac had said after he'd told me that the Bracketts had gotten the second and third slots reversed.

Had Mac known but couldn't tell me?

50

"You go to the end of a road—there's some watering hole there, but its name escapes me—then take a right where an old barn used to be. It's another twenty-two miles past that."

That's what Mac had said about the Brackett family ranch.

I thought of skipping my exit off I-75 north. Marry the road instead of Kathleen. Drop in at The Red Blonde. Have a beer with Dusty at the Down Yonder. For the truth was, I was tired of my yesterdays. Morgan believed the past was like the rudder of the boat: always behind you but directing where you go. Kathleen said we come naked into the world, and it's the first prick of life on our skin that seals our lives. Eve called youth a magic lantern. I think the past is like a dog trying to shake off water. You just keep shaking and shaking and shaking. Finally you lie down, still wet.

Enough of the mental ranting.

I was done blaming my sister for my parents' deaths. She had no hand in it. I was finished fingering her for every little personality flaw that flared up in me. For every empty bottle of whiskey. Every wound that didn't heal. Every violent act I committed, only to sit in a confessional booth, crank up the remorse, and pretend I didn't know what I was doing. For pretending my past were a malevolent force

I was powerless to counter. Damn convenient, that murdered sister turned out to be.

I swung into a fast-food joint and sat in the parking lot eating a cheeseburger and fries and slurping diet sugar water. I ached for the endless vagabond Georgia highway. I was stalling but didn't care.

Mac's words describing Alexander Brackett III came back to me: *married some woman from Russia.* I'd been too focused at the time on the Brackett family lineage and had gone with Mac's dismissive statement: *I heard she was an American who studied over there.* Had he held my eyes while saying that? Had he paused afterward? Who knows? Memories, after all, are not only fiction but also change over time. They are stories that are never finished, for we continually edited out memories.

I went in and used the restroom and splashed water on my face. There weren't any paper towels, only a busted blow dryer, and for some reason, that deflated me as much as anything. Something else to throw in my jail: the sorry-ass son of a bitch who replaced towel dispensers with blow dryers. I wiped my face with my shirt.

The paved road ended with a simple metal guardrail stretched across the road. To the left was a bar. A neon sign said, "Westfall's End of the Road Saloon." Mac had said there was a watering hole there, but he couldn't recall its name. A few pickups were in the parking lot, along with a rusted Chevy Tahoe that had duct tape holding up its rear fender. A Confederate flag was plastered to the rear window. A bumper sticker read, "You can pry my gun from my dead hands." A smiley face was next to it.

To the right—where, according to Mac, an old barn used to be—nothing was left but stone steps. They were hanging on to the last bit of air before being completely buried with growth. Next to them, a packed dirt road disappeared deep into Florida wasteland. A crooked road sign said, "Long Road." Mac had said that the Brackett family ranch was twenty-two miles past the end of the road. I reset my odometer. Clouds swollen with rain darkened the early-evening sky.

The road was straight. It knew where it was going.

At three miles, I remembered that Beaufort wanted me to say hi to Dusty for him. I was disgusted with myself that I'd forgotten and made a mental note to tell her.

At four, I thought that if hope springs eternal, then I was running on eternity's fumes.

At seven miles, I accused myself of being an indentured servant to my past despite my proclamation of being done with it. Not to belabor the point, but just because you're done dwelling on stuff doesn't mean that stuff is done dwelling on you.

A pounding thunderstorm hit me at eight miles, the rain pinging off the roof and hood of the truck. At 8.9 miles it was over and quiet, and in the quiet I remembered that I wanted to get Peggy tickets to Disney World. Also, I never paid for my last breakfast. I had dashed out to rush to *Moonchild.*

I read the message in my side mirrors: "Objects in mirror are closer than they appear."

At ten miles, I reminded myself to call Rambler and let him know that I believed it was the Russians—Yuri and Ilyich—who had taken Leonard Hawkins's life. I doubted he would ever find them.

At fourteen, I couldn't stop wondering who Bernard Carlsberg had called the first night I'd met him. I punched through six satellite stations and then killed the noise. The music rolled off me as if I were cloaked in a veneer that I could neither see nor understand. I rolled down the windows, opened the moonroof, and turned off the AC. The growl from the engine came in through the open windows. It sounded sure. Cocky. Omniscient. The engine purring like a song that never took a breath. I wanted to come back as a V-8 engine. As a straight road. The proud bow of a cruiser.

At fifteen, my self-esteem crumbled under a new and disturbing theory: *I survive by my soaring delusions.*

At sixteen, I felt sorry for myself.

At seventeen, the world could go screw itself.

I also realized that I'd never text Morgan to ask him to give Hadley III some fresh fish. It had been my intention to do so after she had moped away from the rancid trout I had presented to her.

At eighteen, Eve's words played in my head: "Alex Brackett, despite becoming the patriarch of the family, apparently has a strict aversion to family reunions. As far as I, or anyone, knows, he has never again set foot on this property."

At nineteen, I decided to propose to Kathleen the next day. The revelation that had overwhelmed me when we were in the Vinoy had not diminished. I moved it up on the list, above telling Dusty that Beaufort sent his regards. Even above fixing the roof over the screened porch. Also, I needed to come up with a better word than "collide." While at the Vinoy, I'd told Kathleen that she and I had collided. She had claimed the word was too hard and had put me in charge of finding another word, preferably something more "celestial."

At twenty, fences joined me on both sides, like bowling-lane bumpers. Horses and cattle were on the other side of the fences. Like friends observing my journey, their heads turned to follow the truck. I wondered if they were excited for me or observing me as I whistled my way to the gallows.

They're cows, you blithering moron.

At twenty-one and a half miles, an irrigation system kicked in, and the world became green with trimmed grass and bushes. It was like the *Wizard of Oz* going from black and white to color. I flipped open the armrest and took out my Remington 1911 handgun. It was a more serious instrument than the small Beretta that I had sneaked into Carlsberg's place. I placed it under my belt, across my back.

Up ahead, lights beckoned me, and soon an expansive compound appeared. There'd been no reason to set the odometer, for the road ended at the house. A sprawling wood ranch home sat between two barns. The front porch was wider than Daytona Beach. Oak trees hung with Spanish moss domed the ranch like a father's protective arms. The Spanish moss swayed like a woman's long hair being brushed by the breeze. A yellow glow came from the windows of the ranch, as if it were the radioactive center of all that I saw.

David LeClair stood by a dusty black sedan, along with two other men in suits. I didn't expect him, and my nascent hope became stillborn. Dusty was wise to guard her dreams. I should have been more careful.

I got out of the truck. The interior Florida heat bent the air. I missed the road the second my foot hit the ground. I walked up to them. I'd been dancing for my supper ever since Hawkins had washed up with the tide. Why stop now?

"Mr. Travis," LeClair said.

I remained silent.

"We need to search you."

I raised my arms and said, "It's in my back, under the belt."

The two men approached me. One kept his distance, his hand inside his jacket, while the other frisked me. He pulled out my gun and then ran his hands over my arms, torso, and legs.

"Who killed her?" I said, keeping my eyes welded to LeClair.

He seemed amused by my question. "I'm surprised you haven't done the simple math yet."

His answer encouraged me, but I wanted to block hope from commandeering my mind, so I said, "You got another job for me?"

His squinted eyes opened a bit, as if I'd finally said something worth noting. "You performed admirably well. Bernard Carlsberg has agreed to remain silent, although we had to throw a little business his way."

"You lied at the hotel bar. You never had any intention of ruining Omarov."

"Intentions are what one formulates *after* the chips fall. We don't know how the email investigation into the presidential election will play out. What if you failed, and we needed to recultivate the relationship?" He flipped open his hands. "Alas, that won't be happening now. I do hope, as the night's events unfold, that you do not regret your actions. He abducted your sister, abused women his whole life, and routinely used murder to advance his cause."

"I don't need absolution from you. Any other lies you want to come clean on?"

He chuckled. "Lies and truths—they are the same kiss. There was no guarantee that this moment would ever arrive. Going back to what you mentioned earlier, would you be interested in doing some work for us? We know you have ties to your former colonel, but two paychecks beat one, and we were impressed with your play on Omarov's men. It's not easy finding lone rangers. One can't recruit them out of coastal schools."

"Not a chance."

"Worth a try."

"What does Brackett get out of this?" I demanded. The man who took my gun was six feet from his partner. They weren't taking any chances.

LeClair let out another chuckle, as if the whole scene were comical. "That *is* the central question, isn't it? This didn't end how it was scripted. A rose grows best in a pile of manure. Soon, you'll see what he gets."

"You were in on it all along. Weren't you?"

"All along?"

"June 18, '87."

"Afraid I was."

"You never lost a kidney."

"Afraid I did. I had one last righteous conscious thought in Russia and threatened to squeal. That forced Nikolay's hand. It also permanently cured me of the notion of right and wrong. It was all as I told you, except Peter's crime wasn't murder, it was—"

"You're a lying sack of shit. You've fabricated your life to erase your past. To give you an excuse—"

"Jake? Good to see you." The front door opened, and Alex Brackett stepped onto the porch.

Jake? Like I'm his friend. Did the man always sound so damn...pleasant?

I wanted to go into the house. I *had* to go into the house. To know. To settle it. I was prepping myself for disappointment, in the event that my marauding thoughts had misled me and my trundling fantasies were only to be subjugated by the harshness of reality.

"Would you like to come in?" Brackett asked.

All eyes were on me. My surroundings had become a still life. Even the Spanish moss had ceased its swaying and now hung limp and motionless. Part of me didn't want to go in. I wanted to stay outside, where my ephemeral hope still breathed.

"Sure," I said with an air of false indifference. As I walked past LeClair, I stopped and faced him. The man was more questions than answers. "There's a couple in Virginia who deserved better than you."

His expression was blank, as if I had not spoken to him, and then I understood the man. His face, which I'd thought of as soulless when I'd first met him at the hotel bar, was a mask. Whoever he really was, or had become, was buried deep behind his slit eyes. I used to think such masquerade men had great depth. Now I knew they were hollow.

"We'll be outside," LeClair said to Brackett.

"That won't be necessary. Good night, gentlemen."

LeClair paused as if considering a comment and then focused his slit eyes on me. "We'll leave your gun in the front seat of your truck." He turned and gave a curt "Let's roll" to his two men.

"Verby," I called after LeClair. He spun back around.

"Pardon me?" he said.

"What did you call verby when you were a child?"

He looked at me bemusedly, gave an indecipherable nod, and then turned away for the final time. The black sedan kicked up a trail of dust. It was then that I realized the biblical rain I'd passed through hadn't reached the ranch.

"I've been meaning to pave that last hundred yards," Brackett said, reverting my attention back to him. "The dust wreaks havoc when the wind blows from the west. There are things we just never get to. Please...come inside. I'd like you to meet my wife and children."

I wanted to ask him if he could vouch that LeClair was who he said he was, but I was flooded with indifference.

I ground my teeth as I crossed the porch. No lights were on inside, but the setting sun splayed through the windows, rendering an orange glow. A kitchen opened to a great room. The rear wall was solid glass. A solitary figure sat on the patio adjacent to a swimming pool. Beyond her was nothing, for the rest of the world did not exist.

A tattered copy of *Matilda* rested by itself in the middle of a large granite center island. The price tag was still on it. I picked it up. My hand trembled. When I'd confessed to Danny Gilliam that I was coming undone, I'd thought that my center was spinning madly out of control. I had no clue. That was only a precursor—the spark that split the atom.

"Where is she?" I asked.

That was not the question I wanted to ask, for I thought I knew the answer to my true question—a question I didn't have the guts to ask. I could still be wrong. The whole affair had taken on a metaphysical air to it, and two words would break the spell. *She's dead.*

But Alex Brackett did not say that my sister was dead. He said nothing, although his face contorted with emotion. I glanced out toward the figure on the patio. My jolted heart skipped a few beats.

Her back was to me. Her hair hung down straight and a little past her shoulders. She sat erect, her head up, staring across the pool and beyond. There were no books or drinks on the table next to her. Those common distractions held no place in the evening.

"She's fine," he said. "Omarov didn't kill her." Brackett's voice shook as he struggled to control his emotions. He rushed his words out. "I was having sex with a guest... an older woman. We had a...separate room we used for such occasions. LeClair burst through the door shouting that Omarov had gotten into trouble. Done something terrible. We ran back to the room the three of us were sharing and found Omarov on top of her, fighting her. She held her own. He saw me and backed off. She was going to tell your father. He slapped her. I tried to calm everyone down. Pleaded with her to say nothing. But Omarov said we couldn't trust what she would say. He already had complaints against him, and his father had laid down the law. It was my first year in the family business, and I was afraid it would be my last. We panicked. We, the three of us, took her back to my extra room. I don't know why we did that, other than it wasn't registered to anyone. I had a master key, and the room wasn't on housekeeping's list to clean."

"The older woman you'd been having sex with—was she there when you burst through the door?"

"She was. We told her to leave. She—"

"What was her name?"

"Beg your par—"

"*What was her name?*"

"I'm not sure I re—"

"Was her name Eve Davidson?"

Brackett's face tightened. "I believe so. But—"

"Did she see my sister?"

"Does this really matter?"

"*Did she see my sister?*"

"She did," he blurted out, as if I had a gun to his head. "But she was far more concerned about her indiscretion. She pleaded madly with us not to tell, and then she slipped out."

Eve! Eve! Eve! Yours is the greatest sin. I will not carry your weight.

"I told them we had to release her," Brackett said. "Omarov and LeClair argued that doing so would bring charges against Omarov that even diplomatic immunity wouldn't be able to protect him from. Omarov called his father. The decision wasn't ours. She went to Russia with us."

"The Russians smuggled her out of her own country?"

"I'm sorry, Jake. It was your government that came up with that solution. They took her. They killed the investigation."

"My government," I said, but the words held no meaning for me, for I was still struggling to comprehend his last statement. It fit so perfectly. So neat. A thousand years and ten thousand dogs would never have sniffed that trail.

Open your eyes, Jake-o.

He nodded. "Glasnost and all. She was, I'm afraid, too small to get in the way."

"And you?" My eyes kept darting to the solitary figure sitting on the back patio, afraid that if I glanced away for too long, the mirage would be gone.

"And I?" His eyes widened. "I think you know. What did you think when I wished you good luck in Chicago and didn't let go of your hand?"

"That you were a whacko."

He let out a nervous laugh. "Well, then, I failed." His voice was calmer now, as if in some manner we had just successfully completed a turbulent landing. "I had a role to play until certain debts were settled. And the government wouldn't give its blessings until it was certain that Omarov was no longer useful. The government was...fearful, of your reaction once you found out.

"I wasn't sure I was a very good actor, although I was hoping you picked up my drift when I leaned in and told you we were in the final stages of paying off my obligation. I believe I purposely said 'delicate' stages."

"But you blamed LeClair—some stuff about him being on drugs. You gave me no opening for doubt."

"I had no choice. I was not yet free of Omarov. Nor had I received permission—Uncle Sam was still calling the shots."

I picked up the copy of *Matilda*. It had weight. Volume.

"She read it to our children. It's been terrifically hard for her, knowing what happened, both her parents—your parents—gone before she was twenty. You still being out there.

"She went to private school in Russia. Nikolay Omarov treated her like his own daughter. In many ways, she was raised like a Russian princess. I visited there often, and we fell in love. She's wanted for years to get in touch with you, but both governments objected. Kidnapping charges would have ruined Omarov; nor was there any way to implicate him without implicating me, and by then we were married. The situation was beyond repair. It was all we could manage just to get her back in the States.

"Finally, with Peter's ousting, common sense has prevailed. Time marches on. The great issues of yesterday barely warrant a footnote, and then the footnotes themselves get swept into the dustpan of history. Today's comedy was yesterday's tragedy."

"Omarov sent a man to threaten Dusty—if she talked about the money."

His face scrunched in pain. "I didn't know that. I never should have told him. I thought—"

He droned on, but I tuned him out. The details could wait. I put the book down. I moved toward the rear door as if I were observing myself in a dream. I slid it open. Her back stiffened. My heart flopped around in my chest like a drunken butterfly. I took a final step, entered a cathedral of emotions, and planted myself in front of her. I was as confident and sure of myself as I'd ever been.

She stood. She looked like our mother.

"Brit," I said from somewhere.

"Hey, Jake-o," she said with a quivering smile. She took a step toward me. "Look at you. You still need to brush your hair, kiddo."

She reached out and touched my hair, in the exact spot she had in my dream.

Everything you imagine is real.

We had an awkward embrace. I tumbled out, "Is there somewhere we can go? Talk?"

"There's a bar at the corner of the main road," she said, wiping tears from her eyes.

"End of the Road?"

"The choices are limited around here," she said, attempting to sound conversational. "But they've got decent food."

"Any ice cream bars?"

"Shall we eat them from the bottom up?"

I couldn't talk.

Dusty said the longest road leads to the beginning. Brit and I headed down that long road.

ACKNOWLEDGMENTS

I draw inspiration from the places where I write. While I'm often not there long, the momentary stops provide fuel for the long journey. *Naked We Came* gassed up at an old home in Zebulon, Georgia, where, under tall and silent pines, Jake wrestled with his morality, while I scampered out of the way. I got a solid five hundred miles out of a cabin in Townsend, Tennessee, where I returned to make certain that I had it right, only to discover that I had never left. And in Bordeaux, France, where on the deck of a riverboat, patience finally surfaced and I allowed the story to finish itself. As always, I am indebted to the Pink Palace on the fluffy sands of the Gulf of Mexico, where, as F. Scott Fitzgerald said, it surrenders "its shape to the blinding brightness of the gulf."

It is there, like the desk in Mac's study, where I lose all excuses.

Robert Lane
Pass-a-Grille, Florida
February 2017

Be sure to read these previous stand-alone Jake Travis novels:

The Second Letter
Cooler Than Blood
The Cardinal's Sin
The Gail Force

Visit Robert Lane's author page on Amazon.com: http://www.amazon.com/Robert-Lane/e/B00HZ2254A/ref=dp_byline_cont_book_1.

Follow Robert Lane on Facebook: https://www.facebook.com/RobertLaneBooks.

Learn more at http://robertlanebooks.com.